Praise for Patrick Worrall

'Worrall wonderfully conjures the maelstrom of postwar France . . . a dramatic and thoroughly immersive account of loyalty, ideology and betrayal'
Guardian

'In remarkably granular detail, Worrall conjures up a Fifties Paris where historical and fictional characters coexist'
Sunday Times

'A terrific new voice in spy fiction . . . A complex, action packed portrait of a continent in ferment'
Mail on Sunday

'Incredibly impressive, up there with the best in the genre'
Lee Child

'Impressive . . . The scene-setting is finely detailed and evocative, the characters skilfully drawn'
Financial Times

'Fast-paced, intriguing and deeply atmospheric'
Tom Bradby

Also by Patrick Worrall

The Partisan

THE
EXILE

Patrick Worrall

PENGUIN BOOKS

TRANSWORLD PUBLISHERS
Penguin Random House, One Embassy Gardens,
8 Viaduct Gardens, London SW11 7BW
www.penguin.co.uk

Transworld is part of the Penguin Random House group of companies
whose addresses can be found at global.penguinrandomhouse.com

First published in Great Britain in 2024 by Bantam
an imprint of Transworld Publishers
Penguin paperback edition published 2025

A CIP catalogue record for this book
is available from the British Library.

ISBN
9781529176186

Typeset in 9.90/13.25pt Sabon by Falcon Oast Graphic Art Ltd.
Printed and bound in Great Britain by Clays Ltd, Elcograf S.p.A.

The authorized representative in the EEA is Penguin Random House Ireland,
Morrison Chambers, 32 Nassau Street, Dublin D02 YH68.

Penguin Random House is committed to a sustainable
future for our business, our readers and our planet. This book is
made from Forest Stewardship Council® certified paper.

For Simona, my best and bravest

1

Only one partisan does not stand when the sentry leads Greta into the camp. The daughter.

Greta's hair is still wet and limp from the climb up on to the plateau and she blows it away from her forehead. She dumps her pack between her legs and rests the rifle against it so that no metal part touches the forest floor.

A half-circle forms. Expectant faces, trying to read her: a woman of eighteen, always shorter and slighter than people expect, in filthy tennis shoes. The Germans call her The Lady Death.

Only the girl remains seated. She's young, but she has the long legs already.

The general, Laima, strides across the clearing, hauls the girl to her feet, steers her towards Greta. She holds her face with iron hands, forcing her to look at the newcomer.

'Remember this day,' Laima tells her daughter. 'The day a queen came to live among us.'

There is the hint of a lisp when the girl introduces herself. *I am Morta*.

You could slide a five-Reichsmark piece into the gap between her front teeth. When she allows herself a rare smile, the canines are sharp.

She was so happy, Laima tells Greta, as they eat together that evening. Just a grubby, happy pup, tumbling around the campfire with the little ones. The change came overnight, not long after her twelfth birthday.

Greta can see the girl on the far side of the fire, alone at the edge of the circle of light. Morta has a compact mirror and a comb and is scraping at the knots in her fringe with the air of a saint enduring infinite suffering for some higher reward. The fawn's legs under her, at awkward angles. She hasn't worked out how to arrange them gracefully.

'This is the dangerous time,' says Laima, between mouthfuls. 'A bad time to be a beauty.'

August 1944. The turn of the tide. Laima drags a stick through the ash to show borders and battlefronts, pokes at it to mark the towns. The wrecked world that is all around them, and the dead cities: Minsk, Vilnius, Warsaw.

The Germans are retreating to the fatherland. They will abandon western Lithuania soon, but they will try to hold the port of Klaipėda for as long as they can. For the stragglers and refugees, Klaipėda is life.

Three slashes in the white ash: the arrow from the east. The Soviet Army, probing, ravening. Panic precedes them. They are said to spare no one. Soldier, civilian, partisan. Man, woman, beast. They are promiscuous in their fury.

'Drunk on vengeance,' says Laima, with a shiver. She gives Greta a keen look. 'But you of all people must understand. The last of the Three Sisters. Blood cries out for blood.'

'I understand them,' says Greta.

'Do you have any loved ones left?'

Greta frowns, irritated. 'Tell me how many more people are out here,' she says. 'How many woodland camps are there, in all? Who's good? Who is reliable?'

In the night, harsh whispers close by. A boy of perhaps fourteen is backing towards Greta as she lies hidden in a bundle among the leaves.

He is gripping something with both hands. A Walther.

Another lad is stalking towards him, defying the gun. This one might be a year older. He is unarmed but his fists are clenched. She can see his face in the moonlight, the reckless hatred in him.

'I swear I'll do it,' the boy with the pistol hisses. He is retreating from the raised fists, edging towards Greta. When he is one pace from her she snatches at his left ankle with both hands and upends him. She dives on top with a shout, pressing the gun into the soft leaves.

There are curses all around as people snap awake. The sentry, Mindaugas, stamps on the fingers that hold the gun. When they uncurl he kicks it away, then drops his knee on to the boy's belly.

Mindaugas is about to stab a cocked fist into the young face when a word of command stills him instantly. Laima shoves the others out of the way, reaching down for the boy. She pulls him upright and wraps an arm round his shaking shoulders. She leads him away, sobbing, into the trees.

Laima's face is grim. Greta suddenly understands. The boys are fighting over her daughter.

The dangerous time.

Greta leads four men north, towards Tauragė and the main road to Prussia. It is spruce country, the air sultry and alive with biting insects. A green world older than mankind, upon which people have left no mark.

There is the briefest of lulls between the waves – the last of the German occupiers and the first Russian scouts. A free Lithuania, for the life of a horsefly. They call at a farm in search of food and water but no one answers the knocks of the rifle butts. All doors are barred. The country is hunkered down, waiting.

On the third day, a figure in field-grey, sitting straight-backed on a fallen birch.

Observe, don't engage. That was the order. But the men cannot overcome their curiosity, and they do not know Greta well enough yet to heed her advice.

She bites her tongue, seething inwardly, insists on taking the lead while the others fan out. The man is as still as a corpse, his back to her. Greta approaches, walking toe to heel.

The soldier is weaponless. There are no bird calls from the flanks to signal the presence of others. When she places her hand on the epaulette on the man's shoulder, he looks stupidly at the bitten and broken nails, then blinks up at her face. The eyes refocus with great effort.

He hails her in a language she does not recognize, then appears to remember where he is and switches to accented German. He is bleeding heavily from a wound in the lower abdomen. One sleeve has been torn from his jacket and the exposed skin is inhumanly pale. He raises the arm to show her.

'I am a blue man,' he says. It is a joke. He is from the Blue Legion. A Spanish volunteer.

Mindaugas and the youngest fighter have crept close now. They lower their rifles when they see the state of the prisoner. They whisper in Lithuanian as he talks, loudly, to no one: 'I had an idea of what Europe should be.'

'We can't carry him,' says Mindaugas. 'Can he walk?'

'Take him to a farmer,' suggests the youngster. 'Someone who will guard him. I have a medical kit. We can collect him on the way back. Laima will want him questioned properly.'

They both glance at the seated figure as he raises his voice. 'Europe without God. That is what we were fighting.'

'I could make a stretcher,' says Mindaugas doubtfully. He is looking at tree branches and the fallen timber around them.

Carefully, without snatching at the trigger, Greta shoots the Spaniard just behind the left ear.

'I told them to leave him alone,' says Greta.

'And you were right.' Laima brings her food. Mindaugas is checking the guard detail round the perimeter. The other men who returned with Greta will not sit by her side. She is hungry and accepts the morsels gratefully: black bread, ripe cheese and apples. Cold rations tonight. They cannot risk a fire.

When they have both eaten and are patting themselves for cigarettes, Laima says: 'Are you going to fertilize the forest with every enemy soldier you come across? Is this your cunning strategy?'

'If a man is in SS uniform, what am I supposed to do with him?'

'Find out what he knows. Use him. Make a trade.'

'You would exchange a man covered in swastikas?'

'That unarmed man did not kill your Sisters, Greta. Your Jewish girls won't climb back into this world through the hole in his skull.'

She studies Greta's face closely, watches a violent shiver of anger pass over it. The lips are tight and bloodless. Laima nods in approval as the younger woman masters herself slowly, brings her features under control.

'Good. We need restraint, Greta. The Germans are finished, but we have a long war to fight after this one is over. We can't afford to stop thinking. Hatred is not enough.'

Laima raises a finger and makes a circle with it, indicating the camp around them, the men and women lounging in the last of the light. Everyone smokes to keep the insects off.

'There has to be more to us than hatred,' she says.

Laima has sent all the young people away except her daughter.

Greta doesn't see the girl for a week. She is out on reconnaissance at night and the girl is away from camp during the day, scouting, foraging, delivering messages. Morta is expected to do the work of an adult fighter.

A day patrol comes across a staff car abandoned by the road under shellfire. Mindaugas finds the clutch bag under the passenger seat, taps it with a knuckle and sniffs. Black and glossy and strangely hard. Made of that stuff, he thinks. Bakelite.

The bag is fleshy-red on the inside as it yawns open to reveal the ammunition of a German officer's whore: lipstick and L'Oréal eyeliner. Cigarettes, French. No letters or documents. Mindaugas tosses the bag away in disgust.

It lands at the girl's feet, on the pockmarked road, between shell holes filling with rainwater. Only Mindaugas sees the effect the shiny thing has on Morta. He watches it disappear under her rough woollen coat.

When they return that evening, he gives the usual order to pool the day's booty – to surrender all items recovered. The girl hangs back and says nothing.

Mindaugas touches Laima on the arm, an agonized expression on his face. He whispers his tale as the general eyes her daughter through the heat haze of the fire.

Here is the bag now, stowed at the foot of Morta's bed, under blankets. And in Laima's hands, held aloft, as the general calls for the whole camp to assemble.

The girl's fair hair is long and smooth in her mother's grasp. 'Observe,' says Laima. 'The rules are for you, for me, for her. For our Lord and Saviour, should He come back to join us out here.' The first slap echoes around the clearing.

The second and third are done with the open palm. Then Laima switches to the back of her hand, tightening her grip on Morta's hair. *Crack. Crack.* The girl's knees are caving, but she refuses to cry out. The others flinch at the blows.

'For the RISEN,' says Laima. *Crack.* 'CHRIST HIMSELF.'

September passes, and the Soviets reach the border of East Prussia. They have taken everything in Lithuania except Klaipėda and the open country around it.

The woods are alive with evacuees from the eastern cities. Some join the partisans. Others rest for a night, accepting Laima's hospitality before continuing their flight west.

'The best and brightest of us,' says Laima, indicating a surgeon from Kaunas and his wife who are bedding down close to the fire.

'The people who can afford it,' says Greta. 'And the ones who made friends with the Germans.'

'Whoever is left will be at the mercy of the Soviets soon,' says Laima. 'Marshal Cherkezishvili is massing his forces outside Šiauliai. He will drive for the coast within a week. Two at the most. And it turns out . . .' She wipes her mouth with the back of her hand. 'It turns out that I'm a hypocritical sort of old crow. I sent all the other kids to any little farm that would take them. I want something safer for my own daughter. Can you believe it?'

'Of course. Morta is your only child.'

'A miracle! I was forty. There is a place for her at a school in France. Her stepbrother is in Danzig. If I can bring her to Klaipėda, Laisvūnas will take her the rest of the way. I can arrange the papers. But I don't think . . .' She spits. 'Blast this filth. I don't think I can get her through in time.'

Greta swirls the last of her drink. It's the chicory stuff they take from dead Germans. 'Fine,' she says.

'I don't have the legs any more, my girl. Don't have the *sprichst du Deutsch*.'

'I can pass as a native German,' says Greta with a firm nod. 'I'm the only one of us who can do it.'

'You understand that you will have to walk into a city full of them, and smile? Unbutton your blouse? *Jawohl, mein Herr*. No rough stuff. Greta?'

'I'm not suicidal. I'll keep my temper.'

'You get this look in your eye sometimes. There's a vein on your forehead that starts twitching.'

'Tell me the details before I change my mind.'

Greta and Morta follow a green lane at first, hidden from view by steep banks on both sides. Greta forces the pace. They cover seven miles in the first two hours.

Then they cross a place where an ancient people mined, the ground tortured and gashed with deep gullies.

Greta leads them along the river that runs out of the earthworks, flowing south-west in a lazy way. They leap across at points where the banks pinch in close, trying to snip out loops of the river. Greta is thinking about dogs too. They are right on the line of contact.

The girl follows her gamely, girding herself for the jumps, her long legs carrying her across easily. She does everything that is asked of her without a word of complaint. Her wide eyes are on Greta all the time.

'Were they really your sisters?' asks Morta. 'The other two who died?'

'We were very close friends.'

The girl misses the warning note in Greta's voice. 'Everyone says you killed hundreds of Germans in revenge.'

'Nowhere near as many as that.'

'Were you on your own for a long time? Before you came to us?'

'Too long. I was a little crazy. It's not good to be alone out here.'

'You are always looking for a new family,' says the girl.

'Let's save our breath for a while. There's a long uphill section now. We'll rest at the top.'

Greta comes to a halt at the end of an escarpment, looking north-west in the direction of Klaipėda. The city and the sea beyond are under low cloud. The weather is coming in. Morta limps as she crests the ridge behind.

'Blisters? Let me look.'

'It's nothing, Greta.'

She makes the girl sit on a stump and unlaces her boots, kneel-ing. 'You'll live,' she says, at length. 'We won't pierce them. I don't want to waste a field dressing.'

The girl is looking down at the sore, puckered skin doubtfully, blinking away tears. She's red in the face, still breathing heavily from the climb. I'm pushing her too hard, thinks Greta.

'We'll stay here for a while,' she says. 'Long marches and long rests – that's the way. This life isn't easy if you have the dainty feet of a ballerina. You need a pair of hoofs like mine.'

The girl sniffs. 'What are they like?'

'As hard as horn. Covered in fur. And warts.' There it is, at last. A proper smile, like the sun coming out.

'You *could* be pretty if you wanted,' says Morta, and Greta throws her head back. She laughs even harder when the girl's face colours. It wasn't supposed to be an insult.

*

It's not the time or place for a fire, but Greta sets a home-made candle inside a shallow German ration can. Beeswax burns hot, without smoke. The mess tin sits on the stove, the base turning black over the bright flame. The water will be hot enough for tea in twenty minutes.

Morta returns, bearing handfuls of green needles.

'You're still a city girl, aren't you?' Greta asks her.

'I grew up in Klaipėda. Why?'

'These are from a yew tree. You chose the only poisonous evergreen in the woods. Any of the others will do.'

The girl's face is desolate as she heads back down the slope. Be careful, thinks Greta. Or there will be more tears.

When the tea is brewed, the scent is fresh and resinous. Greta can feel it clearing her sinuses. The girl sips quietly, looking into the middle distance.

'You won't get this in France,' says Greta. 'It will be hot coffee and pastries for breakfast. Champagne every night, when you're old enough.' She nudges the girl's arm.

'You're trying to make me feel better,' says Morta.

'It doesn't matter about the tea, darling. We are not all creatures of the forest.'

'Trying to make me feel better about the fact that my mother hates me.'

'You must not say things like that! Everything she does is for you, Morta. Laima is desperate to keep you safe.'

'She can live without me. She isn't sending *you* away.'

The words are quiet but enunciated clearly. The girl scowls at the cup in her hand, looking exactly like her mother for a flash, then empties it on to the soil between her boots.

'I might not know about the types of trees and things like that,' she says. 'But I'm good with people. I know men.'

'Already? That's against the rules.'

It is supposed to be a gentle tease, but out loud the remark has a jeering quality that Greta did not intend. What's the matter with me, she thinks. Why am I getting everything wrong?

'I've seen you sleeping with Mindaugas.' The comeback is as quick and unexpected as a boxer's jab. You hear the sibilance, the whistle through the gap in Morta's teeth, when she is trying to be cruel.

'That's different,' says Greta, aware of the flush spreading across her face. 'We curl up together to stay warm sometimes. We're like . . .'

'Dogs,' lisps the girl.

'Brother and sister,' says Greta.

'They talk about you, you know.'

'The men? How exciting. My life is complete.'

'Not just the men.'

Greta flings the last of her tea away, disliking it suddenly. Thin, greasy stuff. She tries not to let irritation show on her face. The child wears a studied look of polite innocence. Greta frowns past her, looking down the slope into the oak forest beyond. 'All right,' she growls. 'What do the others say about me?'

'They hold strategy meetings when you are away from camp. They argue about you, about what to do next. The Germans have offered us guns.'

'How generous. Mouldy old rifles?'

'And heavier things. The stuff they can't carry away with them. They want the partisans to attack the Russians in their . . . back garden.'

'In their rearguard. The Germans want to use us, in other words. To buy themselves time. What does your mother say about it?'

'That you would never agree to a deal with the Nazis.'

'I'm not in charge. Who cares what I think?'

'Haven't you realized?' The girl cannot contain it. The smile of triumph that has been building for a while.

'Stop playing games, Morta. You are too young.'

'Everyone is *terrified* of you!'

Greta and Morta stay the night at a friendly farm near Judrėnai, two miles south of the Klaipėda road. They make an early start, leaving their rifles and most of the other gear behind.

The going is quicker now, walking due west on macadam with light loads on their backs. But they feel exposed, peering into the low cloud cover and listening for aviation.

The documents supplied by Laima are good enough for the first checkpoint on the road, manned by Slovaks – SS volunteers hardly older than Greta.

The soldiers seem thrown into confusion by the arrival of two pretty blonde girls. Greta stares them down and parries their questions in imperious High German. They are sisters, she tells the men, heading for a reunion with their father. He is posted in the city? *Ja. Ein Offizier.*

She lets the word drop with deliberate subtlety. She wants them to imagine the rank, the power, the consequences of obstruction or delay. The young men wave them through.

It is a different story at the next post, a police station on the eastern outskirts of the city. These guards are older. A greying *Untersturmführer* with a Baltic German accent questions Greta thoroughly and sends their passes into an adjoining room for closer study.

The officer sits and types while Greta and Morta stand waiting in the warmth of a wood-burning stove. There is a map on the wall showing the extent of the Reich before the Russian onslaught. Klaipėda is *Memel*. Lithuania is *Ostland*.

The man at the desk has a pistol in a holster on his belt. A fountain pen with a sharp nib rests on the right side of the typewriter, aligned perfectly with the edge of the machine.

He seems to feel Greta's gaze on him and glances up at her. But his eyes flicker over to Morta, who is resting her head on Greta's arm. A tremor runs through the young girl as she tries to suppress a whimper.

Greta looks down and sees fat tears welling in Morta's eyes. The German's expression softens. He barks a command to his Storm Man in the next room and a voice calls out in answer. The passes are returned, stamped with the eagle.

*

The yellow-brick railway station teems with people.

Some of the refugees are in broad-brimmed hats and sleek coats, sitting on good cases. Many others are peasants in worsted jackets and caps. Some will be deserters, Greta guesses. Men who have done as she has: cast away their weapons and bought themselves counterfeit names.

The windows of the waiting room are broken, the taps in the lavatories disconnected. The hubbub of voices dies as she picks her way back. Far to the east, the faint sound of aircraft engines. People are looking at the sky, shielding their eyes with their hands. Tired, drawn faces.

Morta is sitting with her back to a wall, head bowed.

'Laisvūnas will come,' says Greta, pinching her cheek. 'Your brother will be here. I'm sure of it.'

'He's not my real brother. And you don't know him. You are assuming he's a good person.'

'I'm assuming he won't want to disappoint your mother, my darling. Lest she relieve him of his testicles.'

A smile. The first since yesterday. Greta kneads Morta's temples, watches her eyes close weakly. 'Tell me about France again,' the girl murmurs.

'I've never been, but I've seen it in films. Paris, and the south. It's like heaven down there. The sea as warm as tea. All the smart people go there. The women in their summer dresses. Can you see it in your head?'

'I'm trying. I'm sitting at a café.'

'In a rattan chair. The waiters are in white, gliding around. The sand is yellow.'

'Come with me, Greta.'

'You know I can't, *Schatz*.'

'I did what my mother said. I tried to be as brave as you. But it's no good.'

'This can't be Laisvūnas,' says Greta.

He was a fat slug of a schoolboy the last time they met, shrinking from Laima's unsparing gaze. He must be in his early twenties now but he looks older, in fine navy tweed that drapes well over his long, thin frame.

He is hurrying towards them from the north, almost outpacing the train coming in from the same direction, the first carriages sliding past him. A whistle sounds. All along the platform men are stirring, waiting for the surge towards the doors.

But they make way for the tall young man. All eyes are on him as he passes. Is it the good suit or the actorly way he runs, displaying white teeth?

Performing, thinks Greta. No. Advertising himself, like a salesman. A professional smile.

Laisvūnas comes to a halt in front of Morta. His pocket square is the same shade of gold as his tie. He holds both hands out to the girl, beckoning, inviting. 'Little *sister*,' he says. 'How long has it been?'

Then everything is wrong.

Morta squirming out of his embrace and clutching at her, Greta needing all her strength to prise the girl's fingers from the lapels of her coat. 'I'm sorry, Greta. For all the things I said. Stay with me. Don't leave me. Please.'

Laisvūnas flapping and fussing around them, reassuring Greta, stroking the girl's hair and the girl recoiling from it. The hint of force as he places both hands on her shoulders. His fixed smile.

The only words Greta can find are the wrong words. Her head is a swarm of urgent advice that she cannot articulate.

'Try to write,' says Greta, stiffly. 'Your mother will be worried.' How wretched, she thinks. The voice of a schoolmistress or a maiden aunt, not a friend.

Worst of all, at the end: the girl's face. That last backward look as Laisvūnas shepherds her towards their carriage. The eyes are broad and liquid as they make a final plea. They narrow in accusation as Greta stays rooted to the spot by the yellow wall.

The gap between them widens. Morta's eyes downcast finally, under the long lashes, as she accepts it. Her betrayal.

*

It would be wrong to say that Greta thinks of Morta *often* over the next seven years.

There is little time to wallow in guilt during that perilous spell when the Soviets are tightening their grip on Lithuania. The partisans live like animals, in the burning moment. Another day that ends above the soil, in the glow of the campfire, is a gift beyond hope.

But there are odd occasions when she hears the girl's voice, like a murmur in her ear.

The following August, a commercial traveller with good contacts in the port of Klaipėda drives out to them with a stack of Western newspapers. The guerrillas crowd around, rolling in their mouths the technical terms – radioactive elements, particles, kilotons – along with the strange names of the cities. *Hi-ro-shi-ma*.

Laima is beside herself with glee, pacing up and down a stretch of forest path like a stage actress, clutching Greta's face in her hands and squeezing. 'Don't you see? My little wolf! He will be shitting in his breeches now.'

'Who?'

'Stalin, you fool. The Western Allies will stand up to him at last. They will push him all the way back to Russia with this thing – with the mere threat of it.'

Then they are hugging, Laima's fingertips digging into Greta's shoulders. From nowhere, Morta's words come back to her, quiet but distinct. *Mother can live without me. She isn't sending* you *away*. Greta frees herself gently from the embrace.

The deportations begin in 1946, the year when Greta's last blood relations are shot. She does not quite kill the Russian official who orders their deaths. Still, the reprisals are terrible.

She and others are forced to leave Lithuania, but there are offers from abroad now: bed, board and training. The West has begun to take an interest in the Baltic states at last, and there are opportunities for those who want to take the fight to the Soviets.

What a disappointment it is: Greta's first glimpse of the Free World. London's grey skies and its grey people, with their air of permanent defeat, as though they had just lost the war.

The far north of Britain, the home of Special Operations, is a second Siberia. The trainees drink every evening, in a draughty house called Swordland, to warm themselves and stave off loneliness. Greta shares half a bottle of single malt with one of the directing staff, a handsome older Swedish man, and they collapse on to her bed at the end of the evening.

They lie in a tangle but do not pet each other. At first light she allows him to kiss her neck then puts a stop to it abruptly, sitting up and swinging her legs down from the bed.

Morta again, or words they exchanged once. *No men. Against the rules.*

The Swede rubs her back uncertainly. Greta fits the heels of her hands into her eye sockets and curses, regretting the drink and the broken sleep. A long, cold day lies ahead. Explosives, sabotage, radio communication. The handling of small boats out on Loch Morar, with the wind knifing the recruits and the yells of Royal Marine officers in their ears.

The man withdraws his hand with a sigh. 'Why do you have to be so *hard*, young miss?'

Greta cannot keep away from Lithuania for long, even when ordered to leave for her own safety. The pangs of separation from the others are too much: violent twists in the stomach. The girl's voice once more – as quiet and truthful as ever. *You are always looking for a new family.*

And so the years revolve. Storm clouds over the plain in high summer, in the killing season. Black cars on their sides in green woods. A Party boss and his wife, hanging from the same bough, in curious symmetry: both are missing one shoe.

There are always the safe houses and the cellars under farms and the fishing boats at midnight. Greta is on the run again when she hears the first reliable account of a Soviet nuclear test. She's in Stockholm with her old instructor from Swordland, who now carries the rank of colonel in the Swedish Army. He turns up the wireless and translates the tricky vocabulary for her.

'It's not just the bomb,' he says when the bulletin has finished. 'The Soviets are closing in on all the Baltic networks. I can show you the unedited intelligence if you like. I mean, perhaps Laima will hold out longer than the others. A year or two. Greta? Are you listening?'

She is looking out into the brightness of his garden, at the screen of fir trees at the end. She can smell the needles.

'You can't go back,' he tells her. 'It was a noble cause, but it's all over now.'

The artillery barrage ended more than five minutes ago, according to the cheap wristwatch that Greta no longer trusts. She stays stretched out on the floor of the hushed forest, feeling the damp soaking into her coarse clothes.

The birds begin to sing again, tentatively. She can hear a snipe trilling to its mate with an odd, elegant call. Like ice cubes tinkling into a glass, thinks Greta, aware of a growing thirst.

She pictures a tall, cold drink waiting for her. Bubbles and the scent of orange zest. A round table under a sun umbrella. A café on a broad avenue, with well-dressed people promenading past. Everything is sharp-edged in the pure light of the south.

Stop daydreaming and get up, Greta tells herself. But there is another explosion, some way off, and she stays in position, the knot in her stomach tightening.

With the fantasy – the warm Riviera of her imagination – comes the face of the girl she sent away to France. And a snatch of conversation she has been replaying in her head ever since she crossed into Lithuania.

The Germans offered us guns. That was the secret Morta was bursting to reveal. It might have been yesterday. Greta can see the girl's eyes, shining with excitement. A child who spent too much time around adults with her ears pricking.

Not just rifles. The heavy things they couldn't carry away. You were the problem. You would never agree to a deal with the Nazis.

It's true, thinks Greta. And without those heavy weapons, we never had a real chance. I brought us to this. I doomed us all.

Enough of that! Machine guns crash into life far to the right, and the noise puts up every bird for miles around. You wretched wastrel, she tells herself. Lolling here when the fight is in the east. The main body of the enemy has been crawling down that edge of the forest. The sky heaves with panicked wings.

Greta counts the bodies as she picks her way across the rough ground towards the sound of gunfire – five, six, seven – splayed in the bracken. One is a Red soldier posing as a local peasant in a coarse collarless shirt. His cap has fallen off. She turns him over to look at the face, already discoloured. There was a time many years ago when the sight of a corpse would make her sick. Now she searches his pockets for documents briskly, automatically, finding nothing. She wonders if she is still capable of shedding tears.

Men in uniform, for the first time that day. NKVD – or whatever they are calling themselves now. *Internal Troops*. Filing down from the north-east, creeping towards her across a slight depression through waist-high ferns. They must be one hundred and fifty yards away.

She puts her Mosin to her shoulder and cracks at them from behind a tree stump, watching them hurl themselves down. They are crawling back the way they came. Greta is in a good position. She will be able to hold up another small attack from that direction. For a while at least.

As she is patting her pockets for ammunition, something scythes through the tree canopy above her with monstrous force. She drops and presses her cheek into moss. Everything flashes dark for an instant.

Someone is speaking. 'I'm alive.' It is her own voice, too loud. Her ears are underwater. 'Trench mortar,' she says to herself. The back of her neck is caked with dirt and debris thrown up from the forest floor.

Too punch-drunk to react, she watches them come again. The same patrol of *enkevadisti*, emboldened by the blast. To her right many others, further away but moving quickly in her direction.

The forest shimmers with movement. She shakes her head and her fingers tighten round the rifle.

Greta fires four clips of five rounds, and then there are no more. She moves backwards on knees and elbows until she feels the ground fall away and slides down a steep bank of earth. Her head is above the rim. The Soviets are stealing closer.

She has slipped down a natural embankment, a line where the land has fallen or been eroded away. The sun comes slanting down on her through translucent leaves like a beacon, flashing on and off as the branches of a vast tree sway.

After she has searched every pocket and is sure there are no bullets left, she shuts her eyes briefly and makes a decision. She turns round and shimmies down the wall of earth until she is sitting, facing away from the enemy, head below the parapet. She rests her rifle across her lap and scoops the grenade out of the left pocket of her overcoat.

What better place than this for it to end? Under a spreading oak in the forest that gives us life. She must summon the strength now.

A volley of rifle fire from above and behind, oddly muted. Her head is still ringing from the mortar. Men shout and curse. They are going to swarm her position.

No more of this. It's time.

Time for the last grenade, the one the partisans save for themselves. A final round, or a cyanide tablet sewn into the shirt collar, will not do, because you will still be recognizable, and you can be sure that the servants of Stalin will take pains to identify your body.

Then they will come for everyone you love, to torment and humiliate them. Rip them from their homes and steal their last possessions. Pack them into cattle wagons with nothing to drink for days. The guards hose the trains with dirty water at the stopping places. The children press their mouths to the gaps between the slats.

She cups the grenade in both hands and bites on the pin. She will pull it out and press her mouth against the top so that teeth and facial features and fingerprints disappear in the same bursting ecstasy. She is going to obliterate herself along with whoever is close by.

The gunfire pauses and booted feet drum across the ground, yards from her head. The earth trembles. Come to me, she urges silently. Crowd around. Let one be an officer.

'*Bled.*' The obscenity is Russian in origin but yelled with an unmistakably Lithuanian inflection.

She recognizes his voice as he flies over her head with five more on the far side, all leaping like deer, landing, stumbling, cursing, turning, throwing their upper bodies against the bank of earth at her back, slapping rifles on to the ledge of soil, firing, reloading, cursing again.

He is yelling in her direction: 'Get up and shoot, you daughter of a bitch.' He only sees a huddled female shape, dressed like a partisan and cradling a rifle, cowering with her back to the ditch. It takes a second glance for him to realize that the woman is Greta. He watches her slide the grenade into her pocket.

'I don't believe it,' says Mindaugas. 'You got through their lines. You came back to us.'

Two men carry Laima to the pile of bracken fern while a third puts a sack of buckwheat groats down as a pillow.

'Forever fighting over me,' she says. 'You can all have a dance if you wait your turn.'

They settle her head on the sack gently, as though handling explosives. One unlaces her boots. There is no room for Greta in the wooden hut. The ceiling is so low that you cannot walk upright. Night is falling.

Laima calls out: 'Where is that baggage? Stop groping me and find her.'

'I'm here,' says Greta, from the doorway.

'I thought I could smell you. Have you been rolling around in horseshit? Is that the scent all the girls are wearing this season?'

When the men make room for her, Greta sees that the old woman's left eye is closed from swelling and that she cannot turn her head to look across the room with the right. There is something wrong with her neck. Finger-trails of dried blood run from a gash on the forehead, crossing the many parallel lines on her face. Particles of dirt and small stones are lodged in the grey hair roots round the cut.

'I'll clean you up,' Greta tells her.

'You will do no such thing. Give me your report.'

'I've been with Mindaugas. The bridge was still ours when I left. It's deathly quiet out there.'

'There was talk of aircraft.'

'No. Not a mouse is stirring.'

'They can never do anything at night, can they?'

'No, Laima, they never can. We need to clean that wound.'

'Don't you start pawing me. You are worse than these perverts. Are they still here?'

'Your guard dogs won't leave you.'

'Tell them to clear out and give a poor old woman and a fool of a girl some privacy. They can smoke, but no fires.'

After the men have left, Laima says: 'So you held the bridge. Didn't they try to rush you?'

'They got sick of it.'

Greta can see the wide smile of malice, even in the growing darkness. 'I know you killed more than the typhus. But they could bring up another division tomorrow.' Laima shudders at the thought.

'I've been thinking. There's a way we can blow the bridge without a blasting charge. I can do it just as they are coming across. What did you say?'

'I said we're pulling the shutters down, my best girl. Closing the shop for a while.'

Greta is on one knee. She sweeps her cap off her head and smooths her hair. The men are smoking outside. The smell seeps under the blanket across the doorway.

'You shouldn't be here, Laima. You are supposed to be in the city, deciding our strategy, not out in the trenches. Any of us would have given our lives to keep you safe. Why did you come to the woods?'

'For the same reason you came back, when you heard things were going bad. Because you wanted to be with your loved ones at the end.'

'We need to do something with that cut. One of these boyfriends of yours must have a bandage . . .'

'Stay where you are! Don't you dare touch my head. I need to look as bad as possible.'

'It will become infected.'

'So much the better. A fever buys us all time. The Muscovites will have to go easy on me for a few days.'

She is searching for Greta's face with her good eye, but the young woman's head is bowed. The room smells of cut peat and unwashed bodies and tobacco.

'I have made a decision,' says Laima. 'No one dies tomorrow. A few will remain posted around the bridge – the ones who cannot walk. But the Bolsheviks will not know that. They still fear our rifles and our sharp eyes. Shortly after daybreak someone will walk out waving a white shirt.'

'Jesus and Mary.'

'They will want to take me alive, to extract everything I carry in my head. That means a ceasefire. They know I will fall on a grenade if they do not handle things delicately. While we are wrangling over the details, the young and strong slip through the net. You will be among them.'

'People like me should stay. The unmarried. Orphans. It's not fair on the ones with families.'

'Come. Come to me. Yes. Yes, my child.' Greta's face is pressed into Laima's shoulder as the old woman strokes her hair.

'I know that you came back here to die. I am ordering you to live.' Laima takes Greta's face in both her hands. She has found some strength. 'I have a job for you. You speak French.'

'Only a little.'

'Don't be tiresome. I remember the things people tell me. Your glamorous neighbour spoke to you in German as a child. The fine Viennese lady who treated you like a third daughter. When she

21

hired a French governess for her girls, you joined in those lessons. You were the best pupil.'

'I never said that.'

'You did not need to. I never met your neighbour, your Jewess, but I understand her perfectly. She saw a spark in you.' Laima lets her hands fall from Greta's cheekbones and takes hold of one of the younger woman's wrists. 'I want you to go to Paris.'

Greta repeats the name of the French capital then gives in to a coughing fit, as though all the smoke from the nervous huddle outside has blown into the hut in one great cloud and attacked her lungs.

'You exhaust me,' says Laima. 'I can't spend the whole night hammering things into your thick Samogitian head. Listen carefully. We are finished here. We have been betrayed.'

Greta sinks on to both knees, turning the last word over in her head. She wipes her brow with the dirty sleeve of her coat. 'Moscow knows what we are going to do before we do it,' she says sadly. 'It's the same story in all the Baltic states.'

'It is the fate of every organization that has received help from British intelligence. You are not shocked.'

'You're not the first to say it. Someone in London has sold us to Stalin.'

'I cannot be sure. But I dare not go to St James's Park for help now. Stay away from the British, Greta, until we find out more. Go to France instead. They will uproot us here, and the next few months will be terrible. So, I plant a seed somewhere else. My best, my bravest.'

'That shouldn't be me. I've made so many mistakes.'

'Don't be tiresome. Be quiet and listen. Paris is where all the Lithuanian exiles live. The White Russian émigrés too – the tsar's men, who curse the name Stalin. The French have about a thousand intelligence agencies, who fight each other like cats. A man called Balard stands above them all.'

'Balard?'

'A great hero of the fight against the Germans. They know what it is to resist an occupation in France. You must make alliances with anyone who can help us rebuild our business. It may be that you find help in strange places. Try to keep an open mind. We need friends, money and guns. What is the matter with you?'

'This is all my fault. You wanted to accept help from the Germans, all those years ago. You knew I wouldn't listen. Now we can't defend ourselves.'

'Like all young people, you carry a vastly exaggerated sense of your own importance.'

'I know I have the head of a mule,' says Greta miserably.

'But you are young enough to learn. Whatever has been done can be put right. Now pull yourself together. Eat, then leave before the sun rises. Go to my apartment in Klaipėda first.'

Laima finishes the instructions then makes Greta repeat the whole sequence twice, interrupting to question her on all the details. There is a long pause.

'You are wasting time, Greta.'

'My general. I have never refused a command from you. But I left all my friends behind at the bridge. Mindaugas saved my life.'

No anger shows on the old woman's face, to Greta's surprise. But when she rises to her feet, the grip on her wrist suddenly becomes savagely tight.

'There is something else. Another reason why I cannot die, and why you must do this thing for me. It has been seven years since you placed my daughter on that train.'

'It can't be that long.'

'Count the years on your fingers if you must. It was 1944, a week before the Russians entered Klaipėda. Can you recall her face?'

'Of course.' The girl Greta pictures is unsmiling and defiant. Beautiful, and all too aware of it. The gap between the teeth. 'Morta.'

Laima echoes the name. Her black fingernails uncurl from Greta's wrist and her head subsides on to the rough sackcloth. All the old woman's strength drains out of her in a long sigh.

'The last address she gave was false.' The voice that rises from the green bed is different, weaker now. Both Laima's eyes are closed. Her skin appears translucent in the near-darkness. Greta saw it when the men carried her in and laid her down without effort: there is almost nothing left of her.

'My girl,' says Laima. 'Someone has taken my little girl.'

2

Lucien Fazi, twenty-two but feeling centuries older, does not stand when the guard yells the name *Balard*.

He sits in the room above the hospital wing, hands cuffed in front of his body, as the three visitors from Paris are ushered inside.

The white man who enters first is tall. The Indochinese men are younger and much smaller in stature, but broad-shouldered and powerful. They stare at Lucien boldly, with a restless energy.

One of the native men goes to the window and peers out over the wall of the military prison. You can see one of the lakes of Hanoi from here, and the Red River beyond it. The other Indochinese man plants himself by the door. The tall Frenchman takes the chair on the other side of the table. They all hear the guard turn the key in the lock from the outside. He is supposed to stay in the room at all times, but the regulations do not apply to such callers.

Lucien is in fatigues, the long-sleeved shirt stained and creased but with the collar and cuffs buttoned. He looks at the man sitting opposite through half-closed lids. The residual warmth of last night's smoke is keeping the throbbing discomfort from his eyes and bruised ribs at bay. He is aware of the pain but can still tune it out at will. That will change in a few hours.

'You have been fighting,' says Monsieur Balard. The man is a civilian, with no rank. He has a long jaw like a dog, covered in grey and black bristles.

'So?'

'There are boxing matches in the yard every afternoon.'

Lucien shrugs his shoulders.

'Does one fight for money, or was this a matter of honour?'

'Exercise. Those don't open.' He says these words to the Indochinese man who is standing by the window, fiddling with the bolts. The air in the room is as thick and humid as a glasshouse.

'A Moroccan *caporal-chef*,' says the Frenchman. 'Has been trying to goad you into single combat for some time. As the only white officer in this establishment, you have been rising above these provocations. Yesterday the gentleman went too far. He insulted France, did he not?'

'It was a joke,' says Lucien.

'Several guards saw the incident. This Arab waved a white rag in your face and asked you what it was.'

'A joke,' says Lucien.

'The new flag of France,' says the older man. 'A white flag.' He looks very sombre for a moment, then gives a shout of laughter as he fishes in his jacket pocket. It's a good suit, thinks Lucien, but not too showy. Linen with some silk, he guesses, from the way it catches the light.

'A very old joke,' says Balard. 'But you are sensitive about such jibes. I am the same. Wait.' He is proffering a packet of Caporals. When Lucien's cuffed hands reach out to take one, Balard's long fingers grip the red, distended knuckles of the right hand and squeeze them. Lucien cries out in pain.

'You box each other down in the yard, without gloves,' says Balard. 'Sooner or later the knuckles will split. Or the small bones in the hand break. Then you cannot protect yourself from Moroccan separatists or their friends. Go ahead. Take a few.'

Balard leaves the soft pack on the table between them. There is silence for half an inch of cigarette. Then Lucien says: 'I told them I would admit everything and keep my mouth shut if they let me serve the sentence in Corsica. It will save you trouble. France, I mean. It will save France time and money.'

Monsieur Balard smiles. 'You flatter yourself. Do you suppose I have flown all the way out here to deal with a legal case against a single rogue officer?'

'I wouldn't know. But it has to be Corsica. That's the deal.'

'A tough young man like you, so misty-eyed with homesickness?'

'My mother is dying.'

Balard exchanges a glance with the man at the window, then leans back in his chair and drums his fingers on the tabletop. 'I have many other errands to run in Hanoi, and Mr Trinh here has six children to visit. If you want to see your mother before the end, answer promptly and truthfully. When did you first come to Indochina?'

'1947.'

'And did you follow the events unfolding at home at that time?'

'Only what I happened to read. We get the Paris editions a day late.'

'The truth was worse than anything reported in the newspapers. I believed I was watching the fall of France for a second time.'

'I wouldn't know about any of that,' says Lucien. 'I lost interest in politics when De Gaulle resigned. None of those other characters were fit to clean his boots. I couldn't wait to get away from it all and come out here.'

'My duty lay in Paris. It was like 1940 again. The end of everything. First a Jew in the Élysée! Then Red agitators everywhere. The eyes of Stalin following me from a hundred banners. I scurried through those streets with a pistol in my pocket. The police had surrendered control to the mob. I thought of you, above all else.'

'Me?' Lucien coughs out smoke and raises a damaged fist to his mouth.

'Men like you. The ones out here in Indochina. The best of us. Good soldiers, crushing Communists like cockroaches. I feared you would all return home to find the parasites had taken over France while you were looking the other way. It could still happen. Do you understand? But it will happen over my corpse. I am in the market for men who feel the same way.'

Lucien lays the cigarette in the groove of the metal tray. Mr Trinh has moved to the other side of the window, three steps closer to the handcuffed prisoner. Balard reaches across the table with index finger extended and taps one of Lucien's knuckles, making him wince.

'I need these fists. The Fourth Republic is four years old, and the early years are the most dangerous. The Republic needs protecting from those who would strangle it in its infancy. I need your brain too, and your eyes. I may say that your surname is also useful to me.'

'Fazi,' says Lucien automatically.

'Your cousin's ankles are getting too big for his boots.'

'Paul.'

'Monsieur Paul is not like us. He does not understand loyalty to one's country.'

'He tells me he's a patriot.'

'Ha! Your cousin has begun to work directly for the Americans. He wants to build a personal empire to rival the French Union. What is the meaning of that look on your face?'

'There were times, monsieur, when France needed the *milieu*.'

'Ah. It is true that we had to cut corners in the struggle against Germany. My profession was obliged to do business with the likes of your cousin then. We all had to learn to speak a little Corsican, if you will. Things are different now. Men like Paul Fazi need to be watched.'

'I've fallen out with him,' says Lucien stiffly.

Laughter erupts from Balard. The other men join in. 'You state the obvious, I am afraid. If you were still under your cousin's protection, young man, you would not be rotting in this place. The charges against you would have mysteriously evaporated by now, no doubt.'

Lucien doesn't like the laughter. He frowns as he takes a last drag, then kills the cigarette end. 'Exactly. Paul and I are no longer friends. So I'm no use to you, monsieur.'

'How long does your mother have left, Lucien?'

He swallows, despite himself. It is hard to enunciate the words. 'Weeks. A month.'

'You will be back in Corsica in five days, exonerated by the army. Then you and Paul will patch things up. I do not know what caused you to fall out. Whatever it was, you will just have to eat it for now.'

'For now,' says Lucien, sulkily.

'Do not misunderstand me, young man. If you follow me out of this room, it will be as a guard dog of the Fourth Republic. You bite when I say bite. If I snap my fingers, you lie down.'

Balard has not raised his voice, but Lucien finds that he cannot meet the tall man's gaze. He reaches for the Caporals for something to do with his hands.

'You and Paul will carry your mother's coffin together. Yes, together. Afterwards, you will sit side by side at the feast. You will offer Paul your hand and he will welcome you back into the family. Your cousin will see the same qualities in you that I see. I am not the only one who can make use of a strong pair of hands, Lucien.'

Balard places his fingers on Lucien's knuckles again, but lightly, not with the intention of causing pain. Behind him, the Indochinese man who was hovering at the door has drifted towards the table, as though listening keenly for the prisoner's answer.

'A clean record?' says Lucien.

'All charges dropped.'

'So I can come back here, eventually? When you've finished with me?'

'You could return to Indochina in high style. Choose your own rank. I know you are angry about the way things are being conducted. A man like you could turn this place upside down. Perhaps we might alter the course of the war together. But for now, I need you to focus on the task in hand.'

'You want me to watch Paul.'

'Get close to him. Do what you do best: learn. You will be my eyes and ears inside the *milieu*, Lucien. My fists, later, if that becomes necessary. But I think . . . look at me. Yes. I believe we will need to clean you up first if you are going to survive in that world.'

Balard's fingers seize Lucien's wrists, just below the iron bracelets, with a stronger grip than any man of sixty has a right to exert.

A constrictor takes Lucien's neck at the same instant. He tries to arch his back and force himself to his feet, but Mr Trinh is leaning all his bodyweight on to the seated man as he tightens the stranglehold.

Lucien tries to shout an obscenity, but the sound is choked off. He can feel the trapped blood in his face and neck. Now Balard has both hands round his right wrist. His left is tied up too.

Then he is aware of skilful fingers undoing the buttons of his left shirt cuff. The other Indochinese man is hiking up the sleeve.

The Moor's Head slides into view on the left forearm. A thick-lipped face in boot-polish-black against Lucien's sunburnt skin. A gleam of gold from the hoop in the Moor's ear. It is the old design, the white rag covering the eyes in a blindfold. Clever fingers trace the outline as they make their way up his arm.

Lucien's ears are full of blood. Balard's voice sounds far away. 'No needle marks. Excellent. What about the pupils?'

Then fingers are pulling his eyelids apart and two pairs of brown eyes are boring into the heart of him. They are searching for traces of opium. His mouth is wide open, but no sound emerges.

The three visitors let Lucien go at the same time. He jumps up, turning the chair over, and raises his fists, brandishing the swollen knuckles. Mr Trinh darts away to join the men on the far side of the table. Balard is on his feet, smiling grimly at Lucien, the others flanking him.

'I am still not sure,' Balard says, in answer to a question Lucien does not hear. His ears are roaring and he is panting hard.

Trinh says something in a language Lucien does not recognize.

'I hope so,' replies Balard in French. 'For his sake. A sick dog gets a bullet in the head. There is no such kindness for an addict. Not in their world.'

Lucien is yanking his sleeves back down awkwardly, stretching the chain that links the handcuffs, covering the tattooed arm first.

'Are you listening?' asks Balard. 'If you join the *milieu*, young man, you had better be clean, or they will bury you next to your mother. They may not wait until you are dead.'

3

Friendship, money and guns, thinks Greta. And the first is the most important. The general, thankfully, has many friends.

A farmer drives Greta from the western edge of the forest to the suburbs of Klaipėda, hiding her behind shuddering crates of eggs.

In the tenement flat Laima keeps under a false name, a bundle of letters is waiting for Greta in a hollow Bible.

The old woman who looks after the place leads her to a workers' canteen where the most notorious black marketeer in the city is hunched over a chess opening.

This man walks her through the security post at the entrance to the port for the price of a bottle of home-made, then hands her over to a merchant navy captain with the lilting accent of the Suvalkija region.

She can hear his voice outside the door of her cabin now. '*Friend*,' he says.

All the money she has is on the bed next to her. Two thousand deutschmarks. She will receive eight thousand more when the ship arrives in Germany. She throws the roll of banknotes into her satchel and paces across the cabin.

Three knocks on the door, a pause, then four more, as arranged. Greta opens it a crack, out of instinct, then throws it wide with a little laugh at herself. As if there is anything I could do, she thinks. I'm unarmed. Not even a penknife.

The man from Suvalkija has brought *kefiras* – a last taste of home, sharp and refreshing – and good German Juno cigarettes. His final gift is a cast-off left by the last female passenger to use the clandestine route out of Lithuania: a tube of lipstick the same size and shape as a 7.62mm rifle cartridge.

He holds his cap in both hands, standing before her like a soldier waiting to be dismissed. All the crew are in full uniform because they are approaching the port of Kiel.

'Lübeck is closer,' he tells her. 'But no good for us. Right on the east–west line. Too many checks. Maybe they board and search us. We go all the way up instead.' He whistles and draws the route in the air with a finger. Nice and easy. Friendly people.

When he returns to the wheelhouse, she washes her face in the handbasin in the corner of the cabin and applies lipstick carefully. The floor shudders from the vibration of the engine and the hull flexing against the black Baltic Sea. The lights of Kiel are coming into view through the porthole.

The lipstick forms a red bullseye in the middle of her face as she pouts into the mirror above the basin, her gaze darting and critical. The blonde mop, washed in miserable hand soap, sits on top wrapped in a towel.

The eyes below are an arresting shade of green. Enough men have told her that, over the years. What else do they claim to find in her face, on a good day? Sharp cheekbones. Mischief, and a feline quality.

There is not a lot of evidence of any of that tonight, she reflects. The life of the forest has given her a hunted look.

The captain dismisses the crew soon after they dock. When he knocks at Greta's door again, he has swapped his uniform for a pea coat and black woollen skullcap. The deck is deserted.

The skiff is tied to the stern on the port side so that the body of the ship hides it from eyes on the shore. The shipping lanes are closed now, and the customs officials have shut up shop.

He rows the first part while she squats in the bow, her collar up against the wind that scuds over the water with the promise of winter in it. At the halfway point, he risks some noise. He puts up the oars and yanks the outboard motor into life and they bump over the swell towards the western shore, where tall houses loom out of darkness.

She will walk south from here, keeping the sea on her left. He has told her where to go: a cellar bar that stays open all night. 'A place where a beautiful woman on her own will not be bothered by men,' he says with a wink.

He mutters instructions to himself as the boat nudges the concrete seafront. She might have found his accent comical in happier times. He helps her climb out and throws up her things in a sailor's bag – a parting gift.

When she thanks him, he is suddenly wretched: close to tears. He has taken off the cap and is raking his hair with the fingers of both hands. 'I've done nothing.' There is always this: the guilt, at these moments. It's how the good ones feel.

'You have played your part. And when we look back and write this chapter, as a nation, your name will be in it.'

He looks up at her eagerly. 'I'm getting more out next week.'

'No details. And don't tell them anything about me.' Her coat is heavy, too big for her. She is in tennis shoes that do not match the rest of her clothes. She heaves the kitbag on to her shoulder and looks south along the shoreline towards the lights of the city. When she turns back his eyes are still on her, earnest and probing in the darkness.

'Forget you ever heard the name Greta,' she tells him.

The bar runs down one side of the underground room; and there are four booths along the opposite wall and wooden barrels standing on end in the wide space in between. Men rest their glasses on the barrelheads and prop their elbows on the rims when they want to lean close to one another.

A stout, foul-mouthed woman with strawberry candyfloss hair pours a beer and flicks off the foam with a silver dinner knife. She winks at Greta and smiles at her good German and asks if she is from Austria.

Some of the men are sailors, while others wear civilian clothes. They all seem overdressed for a dark cellar in the early hours of the morning. The captain was right: none of the men drift over to the end booth where she sits alone. Their eyes pass over her quickly.

Greta understands with a jolt: the bar is a venue for homosexuals. She has heard of such places but has no experience of them. She laughs out loud at her own naïvety, and at the absurdity of the situation. That the first place she walks into should be a perfect symbol of the decadence of the West. A bureau of Soviet propagandists could not have arranged it better. Their piety is nonsense, of course. There must be men like this back on the other side – in Klaipėda or Gdańsk or Petersburg. Sailors with a taste for their own kind, looking to slake their thirst.

The pink halo of hair emerges from behind the bar and begins its hunt for empty glasses. The barmaid is accosted by a sailor who wants to waltz with her. She indulges him for a few steps then shoves him away with a volley of obscenities.

The woman is called Heike. She is going to guess again. She is sure that Greta is from Hungary. Really not? Greta is certainly beautiful enough. Heike used to share a room with a girl from Budapest.

If Greta is not meeting anyone, there is a kind of library in the corner. She can stay all night if she buys another beer. It should be more, but Heike will waive the usual spending requirements. She winks again.

The books have been left by other travellers passing through. Greta snatches up a German–French dictionary and sits alone in the last booth, flicking through it, switching from Lithuanian to German to French and filling in the many gaps in her vocabulary.

She is playing out an imaginary conversation in her head when the vastness of the task ahead hits her. Friends, money, guns – and the girl. And the girl.

When the crowd of drinkers has thinned out and she is sure no one will bother her, she takes out the letters and spreads them on the table.

*

It was my idea, thinks Greta. It was the last thing I said to Morta at the railway station: write to your mother. We'll get the letters through, somehow. And the girl listened. Or someone did.

There are thirteen letters in all, pressed together in a fat bundle with a red rubber band round it. Read them in order, Laima told her.

You will understand my fears. I do not believe my daughter is among friends. Morta is lost, as so many children became lost in the world war. How could I have sent her away? I do not deserve to be a mother.

You were forced to become a parent to a whole movement. It was safer for Morta in France. You did what you thought was best for her. I would have done the same.

She was an only child, Greta, like you. She begged God for a sister. But it was too late for me to have another. I can hear her now in a lonely room somewhere, still praying.

But she is not alone. Laisvūnas travelled to France with Morta. Her stepbrother.

Not worth the name! You will meet him in Germany. Be on your guard.

Don't try to sit up, Laima. You must rest now.

Do this thing for me! Be a sister to Morta, as you were to your Jewish girls. The best kind of sister. The one who comes for us, Greta, when we need her the most. The big sister we all pray for.

The most recent letter is the one Greta lingers over longest. It was sent to Laima just over a year ago, on the occasion of Morta's eighteenth birthday. The handwriting is consistent with all the others, but the tone is very different, as florid and dramatic as the earliest ones were simple and heartfelt.

The news related in the letter is too good to be true. Morta is living with a family in the Champagne region. A photograph of a grand house is enclosed, but there are no photographs of the people the girl describes.

They treat her more like an adopted daughter than a lodger, she says. They are politically active, fascinated by the girl's past and sympathetic to the rebels in Lithuania. They have money, she hints.

Morta is embarrassed that she cannot tell these friendly, generous people more about her family's role in the struggle against the Soviets. She is ashamed of herself, too, for not taking up a rifle.

She yearns to return, now that she is of age, and place herself under her mother's command again. But how would a young woman go about smuggling herself back to the east? And where should she go, once inside Lithuania? Can Laima reply with a list of contacts who may be able to help?

The girl can't be that stupid, thinks Greta. Not at eighteen. As if her mother would ever commit such things to writing. The words at the end of the letter are the most overwrought. But the ache that Laima must have felt on reading them!

I long to throw my arms around you, my mother, and kiss your tears away, feeling the bitterness of the years of our parting dissolve in an instant, so that every hard thing we have lived through suddenly seems as unreal as a dream.

Unreal, thinks Greta, turning the pages in her hand. That is the word. The girl who never finished school writes Lithuanian perfectly, with every accent in the right place.

Then there is the handwriting: it does not change. Place the earliest letter next to the most recent and there is no difference. The girl of twelve writes in precisely the same hand as the young adult.

It's wrong, thinks Greta. Every fibre of us changes in the passage of those years. Laima was not fooled either. She sent a contact in France to verify the postal address Morta wrote on the envelope. It did not match the house in the photograph.

This final letter, at least, is the work of a forger readying a trap. You were clever, my little friend – whoever you are. But not careful enough.

Greta reads until her eyes sting from the strain, and she finds herself yawning compulsively and kneading her temples with her fingertips. It is past four.

Heike cranks the handle of the portable gramophone that lives on the corner of the bar opposite Greta's booth. Prehistoric jazz pours out: a fat smear of sound. Greta feels her head nodding. The Hamburg train does not depart until half past six.

Greta waits until eight to telephone his house. She gets the wife: German, still bleary from bed. The voice is bland and incurious, used to strangers calling. Leo will ring back when he returns. *Leo*, thinks Greta. Not Laisvūnas, not any more. What would Laima say about that? Her son. No, she never calls him that. She doesn't even say stepson. *My second husband's boy.*

Greta spends five minutes depositing the sailor's bag in the left luggage office. She keeps the money and the bundle of letters in her satchel along with the dictionary she took from the bar in Kiel. She's leafing through it when the nearest phone in the bank of four next to her shivers into life.

'You're in Hamburg? I'm coming. I have a silver Porsche.' He feels the need to whisper it.

'Congratulations. Do you know the rear entrance to the north railway station? The big black church, almost opposite? Pull up outside. If I don't come in two minutes, drive away.'

'Understood. What's the fallback?' He uses the German word, not the Lithuanian one.

'The what?'

'The, ah, contingency plan, if you can't make the meeting. Is there a protocol?'

'Go home. Make your wife breakfast. Wash your car. Wait for me to call again.'

She hangs up and stands for a moment in the echoing concourse, thinking about the merchant navy captain who delivered her out of the east. A good Lithuanian man is the best kind of man in the world. But when they go bad . . . *You will meet Laisvūnas in Germany*, Laima told her. *Use him. But be on your guard.*

She is just inside the door of the church when the first silver car she has seen since arriving in Germany sails by, slowing but not stopping, turning the corner.

It reappears after a minute, approaching from the same direction, drifting slowly to the kerbside now. It is the same curvaceous sports coupé. There cannot be two of them in that colour in the city of Hamburg. He lost his nerve the first time, she thinks. Had to go round again to compose himself.

Laisvūnas climbs out of the car and spreads his arms wide, his face arranged in a broad grin. His frame has filled out. He might be a prosperous German businessman now, in brown suit and matching silk tie and a full-length ponyskin coat with fur collar that the early autumn weather does not quite justify.

For a moment she thinks he is going to try to embrace her in the middle of the street. She touches his arm quickly and tells him he has a puncture. His face falls.

Greta slides into the passenger seat, her eyes on the driver's mirror. She watches Laisvūnas step off the kerb and squat by the rear wheel on the street side. But a truck carrying beer barrels shudders towards them, and he is obliged to skip back behind the car. Her fingers find the catch under the glove compartment.

The tray drops into her hand, less heavily than she guessed it might. She riffles through documents while the other hand gropes under his seat until it finds what she is looking for: a Baby Browning, loaded. Now Laisvūnas is back on his haunches beside the tyre. She can see the top of his head in the mirror.

In the glove compartment there's a menu from a restaurant in

Geneva, letters and receipts. A handwritten invoice halfway down the pile, from the dealership in Stuttgart that sold him the car. It's a model 356, with a 1,300cc engine. Paid In Full.

He is walking over to the other rear tyre, next to the kerb. Something rolls and rattles on the tray: a diamond tiepin, two or three carats. She pictures him nervously checking his appearance just before their meeting, deciding to remove the jewel at the last second. Too ostentatious.

At last, there at the bottom: his driving licence. The date of birth could be real. It would make him twenty-nine, four years older than her. She pushes the papers back into place and snaps the compartment shut as his torso slides into the frame of the driver's window. He is turning his head both ways, checking for traffic. When he climbs in, the smile restored, she is silently repeating the address on the licence to herself. 'One of the tyres is a little soft,' he says. That's all.

The city centre is a bustling place but when they hit Wagnerstrasse, heading north-east, a desolation of smashed brick stretches out on both sides. The scars the British carved into the city have not healed, six years after the last bombs fell.

They roar out to Ahrensburg, to a shop near the train station where people have photographs developed. Two Czechs run the place – a husband and wife. They are not young.

The woman pulls down a white screen rolled up like a blind and Greta sits on a stool in front of it for the picture of her face.

The couple will need two hours to complete the work of forgery. 'It's the French passport,' the wife hisses to the husband in educated Czech. 'The new book – the one they started yesterday.' She feels the need to remind him of every detail. Perhaps he is becoming vague and forgetful. The words are close to Russian, and Greta can translate most of them, one beat behind the tempo of the conversation.

Greta and Laisvūnas wait in a functional beer garden near the white castle, where an outside bar is still open in early October and a stage is being set up for a dance band. He orders mugs of pilsner and a spread of snacks, making a show of paying for everything in advance, praising German beer but apologizing for the food. Greta does not want to eat anyway.

He prattles about his wife and son. They are a happy unit, although their circumstances are modest. Greta must not be fooled by the extravagant car. The truth is that Laisvūnas can scarcely afford the monthly repayments, but it creates a good image for the business. In his line of work, it is necessary to make a striking first impression on customers.

'And who are they – your clients?' She feels a twinge of emptiness and forces herself to chew a stale pretzel. Direct questions make the corners of his mouth droop. The reply unrolls slowly, pausing and circling back on itself. 'Swiss mercenaries, mostly,' is the answer that emerges at length. 'The Israelis, sometimes.' 'The Yugoslavs,' he says, then regrets it, seeing her eyebrows fly up. 'A totally different kind of Communist,' he insists. 'They hate Stalin more than you do. More than we do.'

From time to time, Laisvūnas gets hold of a special item from the east – a smuggled prototype of a Soviet gun, not yet issued, or a new radio design still being tested in the field – and puts it up for auction among his contacts. The Western intelligence services compete for a sniff of any kind of novelty.

'I'm going to come back and see you,' Greta tells him. 'It won't be next month. In a year, perhaps. When I have serious money. Here's what we're going to need. Tell me how much for everything.'

When she has finished counting off mortars and machine guns and rifles and ammunition, he nods for a long time and runs a finger along his upper lip. Then he takes a small notebook from his inside pocket and writes a figure on a blank page and slides it across the table.

'*Really?* That's the wholesale price?'

'Wholesale. Of course. No margin for me, absolutely. This isn't business. It's a question of patriotic duty.'

'And that's the best deal you can manage?'

'It's where the market is right now, unfortunately. But let's talk in a year. Or whenever you are in a position to put a deposit down.' He is concentrating hard on the plate of fried potatoes in front of him, lest his eyes should stray over to her and alight on the fraying cuffs of her coat, the button missing from her blouse, the dirty elastic band holding the hair out of her face.

'Do you have anything for me now?' Greta asks. 'Another patriotic duty to discharge?'

Laisvūnas glances around at the empty tables and the people setting up the chairs for the musicians on the stage before allowing his features to relax into a smile. 'I thought you would never ask. You have far too much class. Naturally, it is an honour for me to make this contribution to our cause.'

She feels the edge of his wrist brush her bare leg under the table then recoil with a jolt of embarrassed horror. Her fingers find his hand, and the envelope in it. She holds it below the surface of the table and turns in her seat to look down and leaf through the banknotes inside.

'Two thousand five hundred,' says Greta, keeping her voice neutral, 'is a lot less than I was expecting.'

'I'm so sorry?'

'Laima told me that she had left eight thousand marks with you for safe keeping.'

'It was three thousand, Greta. The sum she entrusted to me was three thousand, exactly the notes that you hold in your hand. I was obliged to remove five hundred marks for the French book. Alas, I am not in a position to absorb that cost personally.'

'A good counterfeit book was about two hundred, the last time I bought one.'

'Times change, Greta, I regret to say.'

'The book market has moved too, has it?'

Laisvūnas shrugs. 'You and Laima have been deep in the woods for a long time. Things don't stay still in the outside world. Life is flux.'

'How philosophical.'

He makes a gesture of helplessness with both hands.

Greta sips beer and says: 'I'm looking for Morta. Laima didn't think you would be able to help me find her. Why not? You saw her last.'

Of all the blunt questions she has fired across the table, this is the only one that makes him pause. He takes a drink, buying time. But the answer, when it comes, is smooth and fluent.

'Families. What can one say? They are complicated. I am going to be frank with you now, Greta, and I beg you to try to understand me. I was sixteen when Laima married my father. That is an awkward age to accept a new parent. I think Laima would admit that she never really became a mother to me.'

'Things were difficult between you.'

'I mean, I respect the woman enormously, Greta. Laima is a formidable personality. She fed and clothed me and tried to knock some sense into me, lazy dog that I was. But a young man needs more than a stick and a sharp tongue, Greta. I am being candid now. When you are at that age, what you really need is for people to have a little faith in you.'

'Your stepmother did not believe in your potential. I can see how that must have been painful. How were relations between you and the girl?'

'A little tense, I must say, regretfully. It was my privilege to help arrange Morta's escape to France, as you will remember. I was still young when Laima put that grave burden on my shoulders, but I was blessed with good contacts at a charity for Lithuanian refugees. They found a place for Morta at a convent school outside Paris. The children were all Catholics from the eastern countries – mostly Poland and Lithuania. A few Slovaks. The girl wrote often, and I gather she was happy with those good nuns.'

'You *gather*? Didn't she tell you herself how things were going?'

He shifts in his seat. 'I am afraid that Morta and I were not close.'

'Are you saying that you didn't visit her?'

A tiny crack in the smile. A wince of discomfort. Then he smooths it over. 'Morta was twelve years old when her mother sent her away from Lithuania. I was a decade older. Perhaps that is why we never became friends. The age difference was too great.'

'She was still your stepsister. A young girl alone in a strange country. How did you know she wasn't in trouble?'

'Laima told me she was receiving regular letters. Excellent letters, Greta.'

'Not one visit? You made it out to West Germany just after the end of the war. You couldn't get over to France to check on her once?'

'Those times, Greta! You must remember how things were. The world broken into a million shards. All of us picking through the wreckage, trying to build new lives for ourselves. I was a refugee here too, bear in mind, and still a very young man.'

'You weren't twelve. Have you read any of Morta's letters?'

'Alas, no. I am sure that Laima will have kept them all to treasure. A mother,' he adds, reaching for the glass again and shaking his head pityingly, 'eaten away by worry for her only child.'

Greta looks at him while he drains his beer. Then she stands up. 'It's time.'

His watch is made by the International Watch Company of Schaffhausen. It is thin, light, self-winding. 'I believe we said another half-hour.'

'Those Czechos have had long enough. For five hundred, they can move their arses.'

He likes to drive fast, and he concentrates hard on the road. They exchange perhaps four sentences on the way, until they are in the centre of Hamburg again.

Greta has asked him to drop her back at the Hauptbahnhof Nord, but she makes a sudden exclamation at the last moment and orders him west across the Aussenalster.

Laisvūnas jerks the wheel and snatches at the gearstick, scowling silently at the hoots from other motorists. He is unhappy but does not dare question her.

His eyes are fixed on the traffic ahead until they come to a halt before the junction at Altona and the driver of a big truck next to them motions at him to wind down his window. The plates on the truck are not German. The driver is perched high in his cab and Laisvūnas needs to lean out of the window of the low-slung Porsche to shout up at him: directions to Flensburg, and the Danish border.

Laisvūnas is chuckling to himself as he winds his window back up. A man who has performed his good deed for the day. Greta says: 'I like these little ones too. Nice and quiet. Small entry wound.'

The coat on her lap twitches. The Baby Browning is under it, the end of the barrel showing, pointing at his chest.

It's all about his reaction now, thinks Greta. A man with a clear conscience would be bewildered, angry, indignant. Laisvūnas glances from the pistol to the car in front and nudges them three feet forwards carefully. His left hand is on the steering wheel, and he is rubbing his upper lip with his right forefinger. His eyes are narrow with calculation.

'I'm taking the car,' says Greta, 'unless you can come up with five thousand in cash. I'll let the passport go.'

'Understood,' he says, after a long pause.

'Is your wife really out?'

'*Kaffee und Kuchen*. With the other mothers from the school. She picks the boy up at four and drives home in her car.'

'Let's go to your place. You'll have to change lane then, won't you, for Jork? Left here, and over the bridge.'

He is silent for a while, then he says: 'I don't have anything at home for you.'

'You don't keep cash in the house?'

He wants to reply but he can't perform the mental work quickly enough. His eyes are slits. She knows the Porsche cost him fifteen thousand marks. Surely, he has five thousand stashed away in the family home. In a wall safe, under a false step at the foot of the stairs. She can feel his mind whirring through possibilities and consequences.

'No cash,' he says. 'Take the car.' The last word is a painful croak. He can hardly get it out. He is running through an inventory of whatever else he keeps in that safe or hollowed-out step. Things he does not want Greta to see.

'I'll pull over after the bridge,' he says, swallowing heavily. 'Just drive away. I'll walk back to my place.'

'No. I always like to see a Lithuanian making a go of things. I want to see how you are living, my little friend.'

His home is a half-timbered mansion in the local style on the far side of the village of Jork. The walls are made from thin orange-red bricks slotted together in an elaborate pattern like a parquet floor turned on its side.

Greta walks three paces behind him, the coat draped over her gun arm. He unlocks the door then tosses the keys back to her. She makes him rest his hands at the bottom of his ponyskin pockets and push the door open with his foot. She is thinking about walking sticks that might be hanging close by, or other things he could snatch up and use as a weapon.

Laisvūnas pauses at the far end of the entrance hall, on the threshold of the living room. There is a small table on his left, with framed portraits arranged on it. She can see his reflection in the glass as he looks down at the largest photograph. His face is screwed up with self-loathing. His neck and shoulders stiffen as he tenses himself for something.

'Do it,' Greta tells him. 'Play the tough guy. I'll spray the contents of your skull over those photos. All over that fat slob of a wife. That shitty kid of yours.' She watches his eyes close.

He leads her upstairs, through the master bedroom with the balcony. His study is next door, then the child's room. There are no paintings hanging anywhere that might hide a wall safe. He swears there is no money, Greta. Upon his son's life. He swallows noisily every time he tells a lie.

'I'm reliable,' he gabbles. 'I'm on the side of the angels. A trusted supplier. There are important men who will vouch for me.'

She makes him kneel in front of the family photographs in the entrance hall so that he is looking into their eyes while she touches the pistol to the base of his neck.

'Guns?'

'Downstairs. I only keep one in the house. Greta, I swear to you.' Tears are flowing freely now.

There's a workbench against the far wall of the cellar, with a deep metal drawer built under the surface. The key hangs on a hook in the dark recess below the stairs. He shouts directions to her from the floor. She has made him lie down on the far side of the room, under the single bulb, hands jammed into his coat pockets.

A Sauer automatic is stashed at the back of the drawer wrapped in a fine cloth, the kind you use to buff silverware. It's a model that dates from the war, but it looks unused. There must be twenty metal oblongs lying around it. His collection of knives. He is still a Lithuanian boy, after all. She goes through them, testing the mechanisms.

'Not that one,' says Laisvūnas quickly from the floor. His chest is on the rug, but his face is upraised and his eyes are on her hands, unblinking. 'Please. I just mean . . .' He swallows. 'I'll find you something much better.'

'How generous. But this will do nicely.' The stiletto feels solid, with no play between the frame and the thin blade. She likes the way it licks in and out, as quick as a snake's tongue. There is an etching on the steel that she struggles to make out clearly in the bad light by the edge of the room. A man's head, facing left. He is supposed to be African, she guesses, from the exaggerated features. A blindfold covers the Moor's eyes.

A vibration passes through the prone man with every click of the mechanism.

'Greta. Please listen to me. Ulla will be home soon, with my son. They could walk in at any moment. Whatever you do to me, don't hurt them.'

He's good, thinks Greta. There is a reason why he survived the war and the lean years. A few hours in her company, but he knows which buttons to press. A flash of bravery and selflessness. The last thing I was expecting.

'My boy, Greta. He's only twelve years old. I'm begging you.'

The blade is out and she is tilting the knife so the light shows up the stylized head. *Twelve* is clever, she thinks. A good card to play. The age Morta was when she found herself alone in the world.

And now Greta can't help picturing the girl, along with Laima and the boy in the photograph downstairs. The general's grandson – if that is the word she would use. A child who might walk in at any moment. Assuming any of that is true. She peers down at Laisvūnas, watching for his tell – the gulping noise he makes when he lies.

His face is solemn and still in the half-shadow. He closes his eyes with relief when she retracts the blade with a flick of the thumb. He has played his hand well.

Laisvūnas sags in the grand doorway of his house, no longer tall.

'Every minute,' Greta calls over to him, 'of every day, from now on.' She slams the car door and rattles the window down. 'Is all because of me.'

His head is bowed, and he makes no reply. The tie and collar are askew, and the brown suit is crumpled from the cellar floor.

She pricks the car into life. 'I am the reason you're walking around. Kissing your wife, patting your boy's head. I'm the only reason you're still breathing air. Remember that.'

Laisvūnas mumbles a reply but Greta cannot hear it over the engine and the air that rushes through the open window as she guns the Porsche away from the gaudy red façade.

She will collect her bag from the Hauptbahnhof Nord then tear away south, leaving behind the lies and the bomb damage and the cold and damp of autumn. She will recite the false name and the other details in her new passport over and over in her head as she drives until they are lodged in her memory. She will hit the French border before midnight.

4

Greta is obliged to stop for fuel at an all-night garage outside Metz, ignoring the insolent curiosity of the teenage boys who work the pumps. She does not take a serious break from driving until Reims, after the sun has come up.

None of the cafés around the cathedral are open yet, so she parks on a side street in the shade of a sycamore and tugs her cap down over her eyes. Twenty minutes, she tells herself, just to take the edge off. Or I'll fall asleep at the wheel.

She wakes with a kick of fear and disorientation. It is after eight, according to the watch Laisvūnas handed over, and there is no reason to doubt the craftsmen of the International Watch Company.

Children are filing past on their way to school, talking excitedly. They are fascinated by the car with its long, curving bonnet and they peer in at Greta as she rubs her temples and blinks at them through dirty glass. She feels a stab of shame over her seedy and unwashed appearance.

A young man is setting out tables in the shadow of the cathedral walls. She orders a bowl of *café au lait* and three fat *cannelés* to dip into it. She makes him explain other items on the menu, trying to string the conversation out. It's a chance for her to roll everyday French around her mouth again, rasping the forgotten 'r' against her soft palate. She will practise the sound precisely and relentlessly until it becomes as automatic as it was in her childhood lessons.

The waiter is surly, yawning. It's too early for all these questions, even from an attractive woman.

Then there are the vines on the hillsides, north and south of the ancient road, with the names of the great champagne houses spelled out along the fences. The Marne broadens and the country flattens around it, and she is flying due west in the silver machine, arrow-straight through the loops of the river.

At ten, Paris is there, spread out from one side of the horizon to the other. The dark crossbow bolt of the tower bursts up through the grey plain. It is flatter than London and the buildings are even grimier, on closer inspection. The limestone is almost black at street level. Only Sacré-Coeur shows up pure white, shining from its hilltop.

Greta steers by the tall domes of the basilica on the hill, following the Boulevards of the Marshals anticlockwise round the dial of the city. She is wide awake now, looking intently at the people she passes. The pavements are crowded but there are few cars on the streets. The women are well dressed, the men less so. Parisians have narrow faces, she decides.

It is impossible to drive these streets without projecting the newsreels of childhood on to them. Lines of Mercedes staff cars processing towards the centre. Hitler and his generals, swaggering in their greatcoats like a mob of ravens, the iron tower at their backs. *Deutschland siegt auf allen Fronten!*

Greta takes a room in a humid boarding house in the Batignolles district, paying the bill in advance with a little extra thrown in to waive the rule about surrendering one's passport. The next few days are surreal. She is in France but speaks little French.

Laima has supplied her with many names and a few addresses. They can never be written down, but Greta pictures them as entries on the page of a notebook, all followed by question marks. There are real names and the *noms de guerre* of the exiles – White Russian, Estonian, Czech, Polish and Lithuanian. A rollcall of men and women who have fled the Soviets.

She works her way down the mental list. The first address is the closest: a hotel in a backstreet in Clichy. The White Russian officer is away on business, but a wide-eyed young woman takes down the number of the telephone on the front desk at Greta's boarding house. The major's daughter, thinks Greta, as she pushes her way out of the glass doors. Does she gape at everyone like that, stammering in the Russian of the last century? Or does she know something of who I am?

Greta takes the train along the valley out to Versailles in the afternoon. The antiquarian bookshop near the palace is closed, with steel shutters covering the windows. If she presses herself to them, Greta can make out wondrous things through the gaps, in the dark interior.

In a glass case a huge, illustrated volume, open at the middle pages, glints with gold leaf and red lead. She looks past it, jumps at a black figure watching over the book from the shadows, then curses her jangling nerves. A suit of Japanese armour has been set up on a stand to suggest the form of the wandering knight who once wore it. The stuffed head of a big cat is just visible towards the back of the shop, in an alcove between shelves buckling with books.

There is a gap at the bottom of the metal mesh for letters. She hesitates before writing her first name and the phone number of the boarding house on a slip of paper, then feeding it through the gap. How else to signal her presence in Paris to the man who owns the shop without exposing herself to unfriendly eyes? She feels a constant prickling anxiety about these questions – the subtle arts of operational security. The simple life of the forest has not prepared her for such habits.

Two full days are given up to Poles. Some are recent arrivals who have succeeded in business in Paris. Others are members of the old nobility who fled from Congress Poland in the nineteenth century, when the Romanovs were the enemies of freedom, not the Red tsar who now squats in the Kremlin.

These émigrés listen in silence to her pleas for help, with expressions that hover between the polite and the contemptuous. They have the cold shrewdness of wealthy men hardened to the pitches of supplicants and confidence tricksters.

Greta drags herself back to her room in the evening and collapses on the bed. Has she been saying too little, downplaying her own role in the resistance movement? Worse, is she revealing too many operational details to these strangers?

There is the question of Morta too, the problem of picking up a trail. The French address in the girl's last letter to her mother is known to be false. After a string of laborious phone calls to ancient nuns, Greta establishes that the charity which brought Morta to France and her old convent school have both folded.

A tiny spider is creeping across the ceiling directly overhead, alone in an expanse of dirty white. Greta's body is stiff. The arches of her feet throb. The wallpaper over the headboard is damp against her fingers. She curls a lock of hair under her nostrils and sniffs with displeasure. Only one of the shared bathrooms has running water and it is always occupied. Out in the steamy corridor, cooking smells mingle.

No tears. Just an agony of loneliness and a familiar carping voice in her head. *This is too much for you. You will never pull it off.* Shut your mouth, cretin!

The fourth morning is the worst stretch, punctuated by the slamming of doors and telephone receivers.

But when Greta returns to Batignolles that afternoon, eleven white roses are waiting for her on the front desk, a note resting among the stalks.

A small envelope alongside the bouquet contains a card for a restaurant in Montmartre with lines of elegant handwriting on the back.

The note accompanying the flowers is in the Cyrillic script, the dinner invitation in the heavily accented Latin letters of the Lithuanian language.

'Two gentlemen called,' says the concierge, raising an eyebrow. 'Both a little old for mademoiselle,' he observes after pocketing his tip.

*

From the moment Greta arrives at the restaurant in Montmartre, everything is wrong. The waiters eye her with displeasure as she approaches the door. She sees why as her reflection looms in the glass. The ragged coat, cut for a man, is swallowing her. The cuffs are frayed and dirty.

'My friend is already here,' she tells the waiters.

'*Eh bien* – the gentleman's name?'

She pauses, ridiculously. She does not know it. She cannot call him the Bookseller. They make her wait, shivering, on the pavement while they scan the seating plan. The rain is turning to blobs of sleet.

Very well, says Greta, interrupting the theatre of frowns and shaking heads. If the gentleman is not here yet, she will sit by herself somewhere. But the place she indicates, a secluded table for two with views of all the entrances and exits, is not in the right section.

'One does not sit there if one wishes to dine, mademoiselle.'

She wants to argue but her French is failing her. They are speaking too quickly and idiomatically, forced to repeat themselves. She hears herself making small grammatical errors in reply, feels their contempt growing with every mistake.

Then the Bookseller comes ambling down the steps from the mezzanine floor at the back of the restaurant, waving a hand. He affects a tweed hacking jacket, like an English country squire. A thick skull rising from the collar, bald on top with black wings of hair at the sides that cover the tops of his ears. His eyebrows are extravagant, the smile amused. Has he been sitting and watching the exchange at the door, enjoying her discomfort?

The head waiter throws up his hands in apology. What an unfortunate misunderstanding. Smiles are breaking out among the men. The Bookseller is obviously a regular customer.

Up on the mezzanine a place has been laid for Greta, with more items of cutlery than she has ever seen in her life. 'I ordered for you,' says the Bookseller, as a waitress with dirty-blonde hair pulls the chair out.

He is already in his seat, leaning forwards with hands on thighs. She happens to know that he was born twenty-four years before the

Russian Revolution, but he is still young enough to study her upper body with frank appreciation as she frees herself from the coat.

The waitress takes it with her fingertips, covering her distaste with a false smile. Greta sits with her shoulders hunched, arms crossed in front to hide a stubborn stain on the front of her blouse. Her fingernails need attention, and she feels the urge to keep them below the edge of the table.

'Welcome,' says the Bookseller, raising the small measure of pale white wine that has just been poured for him. 'Welcome to the dustbin of history. It's the other one.' Greta is holding out a tall Cabernet glass for the waitress and the girl is hesitating, biting her lip with embarrassment.

'Your hotel is just down the hill in Batignolles.' He is telling her, not asking her, and putting an ironic emphasis on *hotel*. 'Don't you have friends in Paris you can stay with?'

'We have many, many friends here, monsieur.'

'White Russians?' Greta reaches for her wine and keeps it in front of her face for longer than is necessary. 'I hope not,' says the Bookseller. 'They are all fanatics. And as old as Methuselah now. The civil war was a long time ago. I see them from time to time. I raise a glass. This is Paris, after all. It's better to be on good terms with everyone. How are your many friends treating you? Do you feel safe here?'

'Of course. Why not?'

'A good way of telling me you've just stepped off the boat. Refugees from the east are always a little dazzled when they first arrive. You must keep your wits about you. Such as they are.'

'I'm not a refugee. I'm only staying for a while.'

'Laima wants to play you back in, eh?'

'That's not what I said.'

'I deal in books. Your face is an open book, my girl. You won't go back, by the way. We never do.'

They break it off because the waitress is coming with the shell-fish. He leans back in his chair and Greta can feel his eyes on her torso again, but all his attention is on the faded blouse, not the body below. His gaze catches on every sign of wear, every stitch that has come loose. Greta glares at him across the table as it fills with iced dishes.

He insists on speaking French these days, he tells her, when the waitress has left them alone. 'I was a stateless person, starving and sleeping on floors. The French saw my potential. They gave me a job and a homeland. I'm freelance now, but I never take on clients who pose a threat to the Republic.'

'Was it a Monsieur Balard who gave you that French passport?'

The Bookseller lets out a sibilant laugh. 'It's been a while. I forgot how very direct you people can be.'

He was born a Russian subject. The Germans took him prisoner in the first war. Afterwards he became a citizen of a new country called Estonia, a proud citizen at first, then a disillusioned one. He was a good Bolshevik before he made the mistake of crossing Stalin. He was living in exile in Paris when the Germans marched in. 'I went underground. I wasn't going to let those bastards lock me up a second time. I had developed an instinct for survival. How was your war?'

'We were invaded once by Hitler and twice by Stalin in the space of four years, monsieur. It was difficult to hide. I fought them instead.'

He is pointing to the implement in her hand as if poised to offer advice or criticism, but thinks better of it and chews thoughtfully on a large mouthful of wine instead.

There are wicked little picks of different sizes for the whelks and the lobster claws, pairs of pliers to crack the shells. Greta knows she is making a mess of it all. There is faint amusement on his face as he watches.

'I may not have your courage,' he says, 'little partisan. But at least I'm brave enough to share a table with you, out in the open. A woman of your reputation.'

'What have you heard about me, monsieur?'

'That you almost killed Maxim Karpov in forty-six. He would

pay handsomely for your head on a dinner plate. And yet you come here of all places, to Little Moscow.'

'I hoped to find friends in Paris. Enemies of Stalin.'

'Oh, you'll find plenty of them. This is a watering hole for all the stray sheep of Europe. But who do you suppose is watching the sheep?'

At length she lays down the tiny tools, defeated. 'You know Paris better than anyone, monsieur. Tell me whom I should fear.'

'Karpov collects thugs, the way I collect first editions. Paris is always full of stray dogs with empty bellies. Then there's the other kind. The zealots. Well-intentioned fools. What did the Communists get in the last election here? No? Have you ever thought about picking up a newspaper? Thirty per cent of the popular vote! All those angry trade unionists kicking around the streets. Moscow knows how to find the men it needs. They've been doing it since 1917.'

The girl brings *quenelles à la lyonnaise*. Greta asks her about the ingredients, but she pretends not to understand. The dumplings are made from an unpromising river fish, the Bookseller says, elevated to glory by the genius of the recipe. The other dish is from Lyon too – *choucroute* with champagne.

The wine slips down, but the food is too rich for Greta, and she picks at it out of politeness. He does not appear to care, helping himself generously from the dishes in the centre of the table and eating with silent concentration. It gives her a chance to think. He's a tough, cynical customer. But not immune to flattery.

'The dinner invitation was beautiful,' she tells him. 'Your handwriting is extraordinary. And the Lithuanian was perfect. All those accents in the right place. Better than I can manage myself sometimes. I missed years of school, you see.'

'I consulted a thing called a dictionary. Accuracy is a professional habit.'

'I was told your passports are the best. I might have to trouble you for one.'

'You must have come in on something. Or did you crash the border?'

Greta hesitates. 'I have a French document, but I may need a replacement soon.' He beckons impatiently. She weighs the request, then reaches into her satchel and fishes out a dark-blue booklet with the false name in the little window on the cover.

He wipes his hands carefully before picking it up. 'This is a good piece of work. I know who made it. A Czech gentleman who lives in Germany.' She hides her face with the glass again. He has a habit of chuckling when he makes her cringe. 'The forger left his signature. Three pinpricks in the corner here. See if you can feel them.'

Greta tucks the passport away again, a wave of heat passing across her face. The card he left for her is at the bottom of the satchel and her fingers brush against it. Handwriting, forgery, accented letters. She is suddenly impatient with him, and unexpectedly drunk.

'Now I wonder,' the Bookseller is saying, 'why anyone would want to throw such a good piece of work like that away?'

'We need guns.' She blurts it out, too loud, and his eyes flash in warning. The waitress is coming back to clear the empty dishes away. Will they have dessert? Nothing for Greta. He orders cheese, to soak up the last of the red wine.

When the girl has gone, Greta recites the same shopping list of weaponry she gave Laisvūnas. The Bookseller is shaking his head before she finishes. 'I'm a specialist. I could source a single item for you. Something unusual that musn't be traced. I don't deal in bulk orders like that. Plenty of others do. If you haven't met them already.'

'Well, what the fuck can you do for me?'

He smiles pleasantly. 'Has anyone ever told you that you can be a little *brusque*, Greta? It's not quite right for Paris. It's not how we do things here.'

Her face is burning. It is surely bright red. She brings her voice under control. 'My apologies. I was told that you are a man with many skills and good connections. I am trying to ask for your help, as a fellow Balt.'

'I'm French now. But I like the way you say it. That's much better.'

'Can you put me in touch with Balard?'

'Let me think for a moment.'

And now he is looking at the body beneath the blouse again, eating her with his eyes, following the contours of the neckline, the tops of the breasts, with slow enjoyment. His pleasure is obvious. Her role is to sit and endure it. That is the game.

When he has had enough, he says: 'I can do better than the telephone number of Balard's office. I can introduce you to him personally. Or write a letter of recommendation. Do you want to meet people from London too?'

'What? London? No. *No.*'

His laugh is an unpleasant hiss. 'Are you sure? Do you want to think about it first?'

'What's so funny?'

'A rumour has been circulating about the unreliability of British intelligence. You just confirmed it by turning white at the mention of their name. I don't think you should take up poker, my girl.'

'By God, you're pleased with yourself, aren't you?'

'Don't get upset. If you want to see Balard alone, it's fifty thousand.'

'What?'

'The fee for the introduction is fifty thousand francs. A new passport is another fifty thousand. Yes, I know that's more than the Czech charges. But you can't go back to him now, can you? You obviously burned your bridges there, for some reason. You're in a hurry. You're worried that whoever arranged that first passport in Germany might give the details to the authorities here and put you in a cell. Am I close?'

'Close to making me angry. I'm supposed to be collecting money for the struggle against Stalin, not spending it on men like you. Don't you believe in anything any more?'

'I can't afford to be sentimental. You will learn the same lesson, in time.' He nods at her left wrist. 'Why don't you pawn that beauty if you need cash?'

Her hand flashes across, covering the Swiss watch, too late. His laugh is like the rustle of banknotes.

'It's worth a hundred times the rest of your . . . *ensemble*,' he tells her. 'Whom did you steal it from? I wonder if I can guess. It's too expensive for my old Czech friend. A younger man's timepiece, I would say.'

'Do you know Laisvūnas? Have you worked for him?'

'Who is that?'

'My contact in Germany.'

'My girl, I would never confirm or deny the identity of another client. My customers demand absolute discretion. You would demand it too. But if the name you mentioned is Lithuanian, I can make a general observation.' He leans forwards and lowers his voice, speaking with slow relish. 'A lot of Lithuanians wash up in Paris. I've never met one yet who was not a vicious little lowlife.'

'I have letters in my bag. I need you to tell me—'

'You can put those back. I won't look at them. Client confidentiality is everything in my line of work.'

'I could get it out of you eventually,' says Greta.

The Bookseller sighs with what seems like genuine sadness and holds the last of the wine in his glass up to the light. 'I was hoping things wouldn't become this tedious. You've shown me too many cards. You know I'm close to Balard. You obviously want to endear yourself to him. Hurt me, and Balard will be your enemy for ever.' He says it without pleasure, like an adult reluctantly checkmating a small child.

In the satchel, Greta's hand has released the packet of letters and come to rest on the stiletto she took from Laisvūnas. She rubs the button that releases the blade with her thumb. The scene plays out in her head: the lunge across the table, faster than thought. Broken glass and wine and arterial blood sprayed on the wallpaper. The faces of the waiting staff. They would freeze in disbelief. If one tried to stop her fleeing, she would happily cut them too. There are other diners around, but a blast of horror is a strong solvent, erasing memory. No two witnesses would give the same description.

She blinks, coming out of it. The Bookseller is gesturing to the waitress for the bill, making elegant loops. Even in the air, his hand-writing is pretty.

'I think we'll save the brandy for next time,' he is saying. 'No doubt Paris will knock some of the rough edges off you.'

'I told you I'm not staying for long.'

'Oh, you will still be here a year from now. I'm sure our paths will cross. This is where lost causes come to die. Take my advice and let it go – your lost cause. You will find Paris more pleasant. There: you got something for free. Please excuse me for a moment.'

Only when the waitress presents Greta with an outrageous bill several minutes later does she realize that he walked away from the table with his tweed jacket buttoned up and is not coming back.

She takes out the slab of banknotes from her satchel – all the money she has, newly changed into francs. She counts out the notes, complete with extravagant tip, enjoying the surprise on the wait-ress's face.

When the girl stoops to collect everything, Greta traps her ear-lobe between finger and thumb and pulls her close so that she can whisper.

'Look down your nose at me again. I'll take you outside by the hair and kick you up and down the street until every tooth in your head is gone. Do you understand? Is the grammar good enough?'

'*Ow*. Yes. It's understood.'

'Yes what?'

'Yes, mademoiselle.'

The leaders of the Imperial Officers' Union live on the top floor of a hotel on the Passage Lathuille in Clichy. The narrow street is in permanent shadow and the façade is stained with soot. A dark place for White Russians.

Greta runs into the lobby, out of the rain, at half past ten. Her appointment is at eleven, but she wants to catch her man early, before he has time to prepare his face.

Major Urusbiy is not behind the lobby desk. It's the girl who was there the first time Greta called. She is out of breath, a little flustered. Her father is not ready for Greta yet. A suite is still being prepared upstairs. There is some confusion. Greta has not made a reservation.

Then the lift trundles down in its cage, ten feet to the left, and the girl falls silent. The major smooths his hair as he steps out. He opens both palms, raises them slowly, a priest celebrating Mass.

'You have come to us, at last. If but half the tales are true . . .'

'I too have heard many stories of your courage, my major. And your faith.'

He seems overcome with emotion as he replies in slow, formal Russian. 'It is true that I have fought them all my life. The Red scum who would abolish God.'

Up close, he is the image of Greta's father. A well-kept beard and the same hint of the steppes, of Asian Russia, around the eyes. There is a suspicion of drink on his breath – and she is familiar with that too: the nip of something strong with the morning coffee before a day of hard work. The eternal woodman's right.

He is taking her hand, kissing it, tickling her with his bristles. 'A Russian, a true Russian, proves a steadfast friend at need. Our home is yours, for as long as you need a place to stay. Draw swords with us, daughter, and we answer your call, though the devil himself should bar the way.'

The major was an intelligence officer in the doomed civil war, a former favourite of the imperial family. They can speak French if she prefers, or German, or English, his favourite. He says it without vanity. They are standing close, riding the lift together to the top of the hotel, past the dim landings.

He asks her to wait in darkness in the corridor inside his apartment while he primes the men waiting in the *salon*. When he throws open the door for her, light floods out of the room.

To the left is all glass. Windows from floor to ceiling, a glass door leading on to a narrow balcony. High clouds scudding over and the shower blowing itself out.

The other three walls are covered in hardwood panels. It would be oppressively dark if not for the paintings everywhere. There are warriors in shakos and peasants in tunics gathering the harvest and great vessels of women in whalebone and bustles, sailing through the gardens and arcades of Petersburg. In the centre of the wall facing Greta, two photographic portraits. The tsarina is grim and forbidding, Nicholas weak of frame and watery-eyed but still emperor, as the caption makes clear, 'of *all the Russias*'.

Five men have arranged their chairs in a semicircle, below the portraits, looking in at Greta. The major is the youngest man in the room, and he must be sixty. The man at the centre of the half-circle is closer to ninety, she judges, his scalp a Metro map of dark veins and liver spots. Greta insists that he does not try to stand.

The exiles are wearing medals the tsar once pinned to their chests, over civilian clothes. There is a flurry of introductions, with very precise ranks: major-general, lieutenant-general, general of the infantry.

The officers Greta sees before her, says the major, are men who live *on their suitcases*. They sleep with uniforms packed under their beds, ready for the day when the fat Red Spider falls from his web and they are free to return. They pray to Holy Mother Church that they all live to see his downfall.

The daughter arrives, toting a bottle of Eristow and white wine for Greta, which she refuses. She will have vodka, like the men, and a man's measure at that. The major chuckles with delight.

Warmth from the spirit steals over her. She feels the tension drain from her face and neck for the first time in days. Good Russians. She has forgotten what it feels like to be among them. Their kindness has an intensity that overpowers all resistance.

He takes her on to the balcony to smoke. Gusts blow the last of the rain sideways into her face and she closes her eyes, hearing church bells and the black-headed gulls of Paris. The vodka is kneading her shoulders and she feels the sudden urge to shout or laugh or embrace the major. She is listening to him, but the words do not sink in.

He has plans for Greta. The White Russians do not possess great riches, neither is youth on their side. She can see that. Their wealth lies in useful friends. Contacts cultivated over many years. Greta's reputation has preceded her, and there are men of influence in Paris who are eager to know her. The major's first task will be to arrange a summit. A great conference of the powers of light.

Inside the *salon* the daughter is stumping around moodily, offering more vodka, tea from a samovar. She appears to hold everyone in the room in contempt except their visitor.

Greta kneels next to the oldest man, the highest in rank and the leader of the group, for ceremonial purposes at least.

'Your name rings out, sir, among all the peoples who still cherish their freedom. I am told that you commanded partisans like me on the Northern Front.'

The ancient general does not answer for a long time. His yellowing eyes are on one of the paintings – a blade of a man in Caucasian dress – and he appears to be lost in memory.

'The baron,' he says eventually, with the loud voice of the hard of hearing. 'Did you know him? The greatest of us. The only man who saw the whole thing clearly. *We shall save Russia, even if we have to burn half the land, and kill three-quarters . . .*'

A loud cough drowns out the final words. The major is touching Greta's elbow, helping her rise, steering her away from the old man with an anxious expression. Your rooms are ready. My Annichka will show you the way.

Upstairs, Greta lies back on the bed and exhales as the girl fusses around her, stowing away towels and bedding.

'I couldn't wait to get out of there,' says Annichka, confidingly. 'It's like God's waiting room.'

Greta laughs happily. The suite is small and bare but even lighter than the *salon*, with windows on two sides in the bedroom. What a place it could be, with some love. A little sanctuary.

'Are you tired?' the major's daughter asks.

'More than I realized. Things have not been going my way.'

'You are among friends now.' Annichka is hovering, biting her lip. 'There is something I have always wanted to ask you, Greta. But father would kill me if he found out.'

'Ask me anything you like, *dorogaya*.'

'Are you really the one who slit Maxim Karpov's throat?'

The name is like the trill of an alarm clock, cutting through a pleasant dream. A frisson of memory: dandruff and sweat in a man's hair. Blood and fear and a new razor blade. Karpov. A name to spoil any good mood.

Greta sits up, feeling a queasy mixture of emotions. Pleasure, despite herself, at the admiration that is all over the Russian girl's face. And unease. People here know too much about her. She rubs her temples. That was a lot of vodka. She lost focus. There was something else earlier, on the balcony. Another ringing bell, which she ignored.

'Oh God,' says the girl. 'I've upset you.'

'No. No. Sit next to me, darling, and I will tell you all about Maxim Karpov. But answer me this first: who are the influential friends your father wants me to meet?'

The girl beams. She likes being pulled into the intrigue. She is sick of the men ignoring her. 'Father is close to the British embassy. They rely on our networks in Russia for reports on conditions there.'

'Of course. Of course, they would. And do these gentlemen know that I am in Paris?'

'An Englishman is on his way here now – a surprise for you! What is wrong?'

As Greta darts back down to the *salon* to retrieve her coat, the oldest member of the company is holding forth to the others in the stage whisper of the terminally deaf.

'My greatest regret,' she hears the general hiss, beating the air with a crooked finger, 'is that we did not take a stronger line with the Jew-Bolsheviks.'

There is nothing for it but to fabricate a forgotten appointment, ignoring the embarrassment and the cries of surprise, the troubled face of the daughter and the creaking and shuffling of ancient soldiers rising from their chairs.

The cage is approaching as Greta clatters down the staircase that wraps itself round the lift shaft. A man from the British embassy.

He will not harm her, of course. That's not the British way. She knows the type well, from London and Scotland. He will be a member of the officer class, descended from one of the noble families – or the rich *kulaks* who copy their manners. The most charming men in the world. But when they go bad . . .

Stay away from the British, Greta.

The dark shape in the lift is faceless under a hat with a narrow brim. She hides her own face with the lapel of her coat as the lift rises past, close enough to touch.

Perhaps the man inside is a blameless functionary. But he will draft a report, as soon as he returns to the embassy, in a room with high ceilings and a portrait of King George. For general circulation among the relevant departments. Subject: Workname Greta.

Someone in London has sold us to Stalin.

When she gets out on to the narrow street, she breaks into a run. A sanctuary, she thinks bitterly. So stupid.

There will be no rest for me. It's like I've been cursed. Everything I touch goes to hell.

5

Each Sunday evening, Lucien Fazi buys half an ounce of morphine base from an old Dao man at an Indochinese restaurant in the thirteenth *arrondissement* of Paris.

He is happy to pay over the odds for the quality of the product and for discretion, although there is no need to bribe or threaten the Dao kitchen hand into silence. He knows Lucien's reputation from the old days, from the jungle.

Lucien divides the lump of modelling clay into seven grey pellets, scraping a millimetre off here and there with his stiletto. He is always trying to reduce the daily dose. He smokes last thing at night, so that no one from the family will see him intoxicated.

The mornings are hazy. He shaves carefully and keeps his hair neat, trying to avoid eye contact when he looks in the mirror.

The Hexagon. It was Lucien's nickname as a schoolboy, a reference to the sharp geometry of his strong chin, jaw, cheekbones. Above them, a plump Medici mouth, then the deep-set hooded eyes that distinguish the men of the Fazi clan.

There are bags under the eyes. The skin below is pale. He forces himself to visit a health club three times a week, but it is becoming harder to swing the iron weights around or push them overhead. He knows the poppy is bleeding him, sapping his strength.

When Ange Suzzarini calls for Lucien, he tamps it all down – the fear of physical weakness and the self-hatred and the raw, whining nerves. He controls the involuntary movements of his body and makes his face impassive. Then he takes it all out on the men Ange pushes into his path.

It doesn't matter what kind the pair happen to be visiting. A bookmaker neglecting to pay his taxes to the House of Fazi. A housebreaker or pimp who has been passing names to the Paris Prefecture of Police to save his own skin.

Lucien chases them all down. Drops a knee on to their bellies to pin them to the pavement, or props them in the doorways of shops, eyeing their bodies the way a butcher looks at a hanging carcass, dividing it into sections.

Fat Ange puffs up behind, dragging him off. Enough! Lulu, *putain*. It's enough. Sometimes Ange arrives a little late and looks down at the men and says: my God, my God.

The only time Lucien feels sorry for any of them, these dregs of the *milieu*, is when Ange Suzzarini bends over them to spit the final insult or warning into the bee-stung eyes. That sandpaper voice in their ringing ears. All that cracked leather, up close. The face of a gargoyle.

On the Thursday, Ange drives him to a corner café up in the twentieth, the base for a gang of Tunisians who are selling hashish without permission. There they are, outside on rattan chairs, playing cards: four thin young men with high, haughty cheekbones.

Lucien is out of the car and barrelling into them before Ange has switched off the engine. He is aware of the older man standing to the side, watching him work. He sees Ange plant a foot inside the door of the café and flash two inches of pistol at a drinker standing at the bar, someone who had been thinking about coming outside to help.

At the end there is only one Tunisian left on his feet. Lucien has the man's head on the table, the point of his elbow against the temple. All his weight is pinning the squirming figure against the metal tabletop among scattered banknotes, a queen of spades, broken crockery, slopped coffee.

Lucien has his belt in his right fist, but before he can commence the punishment Ange's scraping voice calls from the doorway in disapproval. 'Come on, Lulu. We're not talking about pocket money.'

He means that the offence is a serious one, the balance of unpaid taxes substantial. Lucien understands, smiles grimly. Loosens his grip, lets the belt run through his palm, tightens the fingers round the end of the strap where the holes are. This is a job for the buckle, not the leather.

When it's over, Ange says: 'Now the mother.'

'What the fuck are you talking about?'

'The guy's mother is in charge of the whole operation. She's hiding in there, behind the bar. Drag her out by the hair and give her the belt too.'

Lucien pauses, looking into the dark interior of the café. All the customers have run out of the back door except one, a toothless old man who refuses to abandon his wine.

The excitement in Lucien's system is subsiding and he can feel the delayed pain from slaps and blows now. He raises a hand to his cheek, hesitating. Something in his expression makes Ange double up with mirth. 'The guy's mother! My God. I nearly had you!'

Ange is still chuckling as they drive south into the city. 'His old ma. The look on your face. We're going to have to toughen your hide. Wait for me next time, though, Lulu. Don't barge in on your own like that before we know how many there are. Do you want to kill yourself?'

'Sometimes.' But Lucien is sucking his knuckles and Ange doesn't hear the reply over his own wheezing laugh.

Lucien is muscle. That's all he is for the first two months in Paris.

He writes a report for Monsieur Balard once a week, leaving it in an envelope with the concierge at the Travellers' Club on the Champs.

His cousin never grants him an audience, but that's how Paul warned him it would be when they spoke at his mother's funeral. 'You don't ride around like a lord straight away, Lulu. It's not like being back at school. First you muck out the stables for a while.

It's the same for everyone. All of us had to take a turn shovelling the shit.'

'There weren't any stables at the school, Paul.'

On the Saturday after the Tunisians, Ange leaves him to his own devices. By nine he is in the bathroom of his smart flat, dodging his reflection.

He is thinking about Indochina, the unprocessed opium with the raw green smell and the finesse of the Dao men who used to prepare it for him, cooking it first over a lamp on one iron wire, then drawing another – red-hot – across it to make the smoke bloom. No pipe for you, the men would cackle. White soldiers are too clumsy, wasting the smoke, clogging the mouthpiece with their drool.

Lucien heats his stiletto with a lighter, watching the carbon steel change colour. He is tense with anticipation. The morphine that rests on the blade is beginning to catch and smoulder. He hunches over it, a metal tube between his teeth.

Next door, in the bedroom, the telephone explodes.

Ange drives them across the centre of Paris to the Paname. It's a private party tonight. The doormen have waved on the usual customers: the American negroes enjoying the freedom of dancing with white women; the tourists looking for a naked cabaret; the business travellers released from their wives and hunting for *poules*.

Ange leads Lucien to the side door of the club and warns him to guard it against all comers. Then Ange leaves him alone for a while, thank God, to sweat and pace the alcove, shifting his weight endlessly from one foot to the other, scowling at the stabs of discomfort from his stomach.

Someone with a notepad asks Lucien's name. A young reporter who has wandered around from the front entrance where a pack of them are gathered. Before Lucien can reply, a flashbulb pops on the other side of the street.

The photographer has the camera under his raincoat. The man retreats until his back hits the glass of the shopfront opposite. He tells Lucien that Lucien cannot touch him.

Lucien takes the camera from round the man's neck, not gently, and raises it above his head for a second before dashing it on the cobbles between them. He squats to pick the spool of film from out of the wreckage and straightens up, holding it between his thumb and two fingers.

'That's my property,' says the photographer. His voice is a strangled, high-pitched thing.

'Isn't this what you wanted?' Lucien asks him. 'To see the *milieu*? Well, this is what it looks like. Next time you fucking eat the film.'

'Crazy!' The door of the nightclub has swung open behind him. There are two figures silhouetted in it. The man on the threshold is rangy, with a Picasso face half in shadow. Behind him on the first step of the carpeted staircase stands an older, stockier man, red-haired and smiling.

Lucien crosses the street, the whining voice of the photographer receding. He embraces and kisses the ugly man, then extends a hand past him. *Ça va*, Dodo? *Ça va*, Dutchman? *Ça va bien*.

Dodo is flying, slapping his face in disbelief. Cocaine has numbed the nerve endings. 'Want some?' he asks, catching Lucien's glance.

'No thanks.'

'What are you, a grandfather? Have a sniff.' Dodo bumps his chest with a fist as they walk. There will be something clenched in it – a pillbox or an envelope packed with powder.

'Not for me.'

The red-haired man is ahead of them, turning to watch the exchange, smiling with satisfaction. 'He's a good soldier, Dodo. He respects the rules.'

'Who asked you, you big orange bastard?' Dodo is still feeling round his cheeks, the jawline. Well, that was a test, thinks Lucien, if ever I saw one. A trap set by Paul, I suppose. You don't get me that easily, cousin.

The three men are approaching the double doors of the *grand salon* and Lucien can hear the music swelling. He knows he must control his body language and facial muscles now. Pain and discomfort must not be allowed to show.

There is an atmosphere of hilarity all around the cavernous room. The band is smooth and well drilled, the dancefloor half full. The big brothers and little brothers started drinking early this evening, helping themselves to the champagne bottles bobbing in iced water on every surface. They are birthday gifts to Paul Fazi from politicians, high officials and industrialists of the Fourth Republic, the marque and vintage identifying the rank of the benefactor. There are no cards. No written evidence.

Ange Suzzarini is seated at the top table, his deeply wrinkled face beaming around at the younger men. Paul's mother, Maman Fazi, is next to Ange, staring out through enormous lenses that magnify her eyes alarmingly. A girl Lucien doesn't know is sitting on the other side of Maman.

He finds that the girl is looking straight at him, curled over a sickly green *diabolo*, her lips round the straw. The soft drink makes her younger. Could be seventeen, thinks Lucien, or twenty-four, older than me. It's hard to tell with young women.

She wears a frock with a floral pattern and a sweater over her slight shoulders. The buttons are all done up over her *décolleté*. Her straw-coloured hair is braided in a single thick cable, weaving in and out of itself like Jewish bread.

When Paul Fazi walks in from the door behind the bar, everyone stands. The smiles stiffen. The brothers run their hands over the buttons of their suit jackets and the knots of their ties while Paul takes his place at the top table to cheers and applause.

Lucien cannot bear to sit again. He needs to move his feet, do something with his hands. This restlessness comes just before the real sickness. He walks over to the bar and calls for a double Ricard, drains the glass.

Paul is leaning over to talk to Ange. He is touching the blonde girl at the same time, lightly, absently. Lucien can see his cousin's fingertips on her arm, then the upper thigh, just below the hem.

There is a circular table next to the dancefloor with twelve or thirteen more girls round it, of a lower grade. The dresses have a boxy outline that year, the shoulders thickly padded. The shoes are heavy. All these young women have the same regulation shoulder-length hair, set into a wave, parted at the side and pinned down.

From time to time some ripe observation or dirty joke passes round the table and there is a ripple of laughter. The girls tip their heads back, showing white necks and good teeth. Maman throws a sharp glance at them, and they become silent and vacant again.

Then Lucien is aware that people are looking at him. Someone is calling his name. Paul Fazi is on his feet, waving him over.

Lucien mops his brow with a napkin from a pile on the bar then strides across the dancefloor, holding his jacket closed with one hand, feeling the alcohol beginning its work. He is forced to stop when dancing couples glide across his path. The girl holds his gaze as he approaches the top table.

His cousin's fingers find his face and they are thinner than Lucien remembers. 'Crazy Horse! It's good to see you looking smart. You're a soldier again. Look, Maman, who has come back to us.' Paul switches to the Corsican language for the last part, and his mother purrs her approval. 'He was like a wandering prophet,' says Paul, indicating with a hand the length of the beard Lucien grew.

Lucien leans across Paul to kiss Maman on both cheeks. The old woman is speaking quickly in Corsican just as the band lurches into 'La Mer' and Lucien strains to hear her. He is pale, she tells him. Losing weight. He needs a wife to cook for him. The old woman's huge eyes search his, looking for something.

Paul is speaking too, struggling to compete with kettledrums and slithering strings. His voice is weaker than it used to be. 'I said we're going to Marseille.'

'We?' Lucien is leaning in close so his ear hovers next to Paul's mouth.

'I need a driver for a few days next month. Don't look at me like a schoolgirl. You've earned it. I know you're doing well.' Ange growls in agreement and bangs his hand on the back of the bench seat. 'You're starting to make money for yourself,' says Paul. 'But there is more to learn.'

'Marseille,' says Lucien. He knows what *driver* means. He

pictures himself following his cousin around like a shadow, on duty at all hours. The two of them sharing the same hotel room. No private time, for days on end.

Lucien sways, slightly off-balance. He touches the blonde girl's elbow to steady himself then apologizes. She looks up at him curiously, blinking. Her skin is flawless. Lucien tries not to stare back. He turns to Paul and forces out words of gratitude. His stomach aches. His heart is beating fast. He can feel sweat soaking into his shirt, up and down the spine.

6

Greta spurs the car across the river, seized by a sudden compulsion to get away from British diplomats, émigré districts, the boarding house where her presence is no longer a secret and all the Paris of Haussmann, with its broad avenues that offer no cover from pursuers.

She follows the orbital road clockwise. At Porte de la Chapelle she tears north-east, pushing the silver car to its straining limit. Escape velocity. She does not allow her shoulders to relax until the spires of Senlis drift past on her left and she is among trees again.

It is the forest where the French surrendered to Hitler in 1940, but she cannot retrieve the name from memory until a sign flashes up: Compiègne. The name of the town still eludes her, but she knows that it sits at the feet of a famous château. Someone will give her directions.

She has seen images of the castle on postcards smuggled to Lithuania via the same sea route she used to escape, but she is not prepared for the real thing.

The town grovels before it. Its vastness is dizzying, creating a kind of pressure in the head as you mentally heft the weight of the stone. The round turrets soar up out of delicate woodland as incongruously as the Egyptian pyramids erupt from the bare sand.

A man is on the wooden jetty next to the lake that once supplied the lords of the castle with fish, crouching to catch a rope thrown from a drifting pleasure craft. She is not sure if it's really him until he straightens up to his full height. Then there can be no doubt.

Greta watches the young man hand the three women out of the pedalboat. A mother and her daughters. She can hear his lowing voice, and their compulsive laughter. His French must be good by now, to joke so easily. The women are walking past Greta, away from the lake, unsteady after an hour on the water. The youngest cannot help turning back to look at him but he doesn't appear to notice. He is tying the boat to a metal post, looping a knot round it expertly. A man in a striped mariner's jersey and trousers cropped short to spare the hems. His feet must be in and out of water all day.

At five paces Greta stops and waits shyly. Her hands cup her elbows. She can feel the jetty swaying beneath her. He looks at her at last, sweeping the hair out of his eyes. It is bleached the colour of straw, the same way it always looked at the end of the long summer holidays.

Greta hears him mutter a mild Lithuanian oath, under his breath. '*Perkūnas!*' By thunder! She has forgotten that his eyes are the same green as hers. People used to say she could be his sister. He is six feet six inches tall. Her cheek thumps against the bottom of his chest. His arms envelop her.

'Your brother's all right,' says Greta quickly, reaching up to touch his frowning face. 'Mindaugas is alive. That's not why I'm here.' She watches him exhale slowly and pass a hand over his eyes. 'The last time I saw your brother, he was tearing through Russians like a fox in a hen coop.'

'Every time I write, I tell him to get the hell out of there and come and join me here.'

'I know. I saw one of the postcards you sent to Lithuania. With the lake on the front.'

'I suppose that wasn't too smart.'

'I always remembered the castle. It's how I knew where to find you, Robertas.'

The tall man's frown turns to a smile. 'Been a long time since anyone called me that. I say it the French way now.'

The boathouse is an ugly shoe box in a town of mansions. The boats are kept in a storeroom on the ground floor, and he lives above them. The man who owns the business lets him stay for free because he is renovating the upper storey. The biggest room has windows on three sides, a mattress on the floor in the corner, a tiny kitchenette and dining table. The office next door is home to the cracked leather sofa on which Robert will sleep while Greta is his guest.

She watches him change the mattress cover, listens as he begins an account of himself and the intervening years. Slow everything down now, she tells herself. You're on leave from the front and taking a trip. It's what normal people do. Keep it light until we know what he's made of. Robert is not the same man as his brother. He is a civilian.

'Now!' he announces, pushing open the third door off the passageway and yanking the cord, a little nervously. He smiles when it comes on. A bathroom, newly tiled and gleaming. Only the electrics on the far side are unfinished – trailing wires poking out of holes. 'One day,' he says, 'a woman is going to look at me the way you look at that tub, and I will know it's true love.'

Greta can't remember her last hot bath. After an hour drifting in a strange place between sleep and waking, she hears a polite knock and lurches up out of scummy water that has become cool, gasping and rubbing her eyes.

He has been to the pharmacy for her, left the things she wanted in a bag outside the door: barber's scissors and a bottle of L'Oréal dye. The woman behind the counter gave him something else for free, a product Greta has never seen before: an aerosol can of Spray Net, which she fingers suspiciously, then almost blinds herself with. There are clothes too – jerseys and trousers from his working wardrobe, shrunk in an accident at the *laverie* but still clownishly big for her.

When she walks into the largest room in a Breton jersey as long as a tunic dress, the cuffs rolled back four inches at the wrists, Robert groans piteously. 'What have you done to yourself, *Gretute*?'

'A girl gets bored.'

'I loved those golden tresses!'

'It was time for a change. How is it at the back?'

'You're a mess,' he grumbles. 'I need to fix you. Give me the scissors.' He levels the hair at the base of her neck with great care, taking pains not to let the blades tug at the soft down above the collar of the jersey.

He cooks for them that night, whistling to himself, while she sips red wine. She is at the table, her newly black, cropped hair still wet. The alcohol is warming her empty stomach and she feels honest hunger for the first time in many days.

She gives herself silent directions all the time, like an actress. *Smile*. *Relax*. After a while, the subconscious mind obeys and the tightly wound mechanism in her head begins to uncoil as she watches him work. His shoulders and upper back are broad, but not overburdened with muscle. A long, lean torso. A rower's body, Greta decides.

Robert mixes four eggs in a bowl with ferocious thoroughness, then tips them into the pan and agitates them briskly with the fork. Neither butter nor eggs are allowed to brown. He folds the omelette in on itself from both sides before sliding it on to a plate for her.

The eggs are kept in a biscuit tin with chunks of black truffle filched from the restaurant where he works in the evenings. They take on the hum of the truffle through their shells. Greta does not have the vocabulary, in French or Lithuanian, to describe how delicious it is.

Mindaugas put Robert on a boat to France when he was eighteen and Robert has never seen his big brother or returned to Lithuania since.

He speaks their native language in a halting way at first, breaking off frequently and snapping his fingers in frustration. By the time they are halfway through the bottle of wine his fluency has returned and they have lapsed into the deep Samogitian dialect of early child-hood, when war and exile were disasters beyond all imagining.

'You see how I am living, *Gretute*. I'm a dogsbody, understand? Fixing up this place for him, cooking in his restaurant, always the worst shifts. When I should be head chef at the Coq d'Or by now! I don't know why he doesn't stick a broom up my arse so I can sweep the floor at the same time. You must take me for a village idiot.'

No, she thinks. A real Lithuanian man, that's all. Good with the hands, industrious and honest to a fault.

'Will he mind me staying for a few nights,' she asks. 'Your landlord?'

'Is there any reason why he should mind? It's just a holiday, isn't it?'

Greta smiles brightly. 'That's right. I always wanted to see Paris.'

'My boss is a tricky one to figure out. Hot and cold. Sometimes we're best friends. Other nights he'll bring . . . someone back here and expect me to shove off and loaf around the town like a tramp. But, I mean, when he sets eyes on you . . .' Robert looks her up and down and inclines his head slightly. He doesn't want to say it: she is no longer the pretty adolescent he used to walk home from school across the fields. She is a beautiful woman now.

'You don't like paying a girl a compliment, do you?'

'Don't want you to get too big for your boots.'

'That's very Samogitian.'

He shakes his head. 'I'm French now. Passport and everything.'

'Do you know any Lithuanians in the city?'

'I avoid them, if you want to know the truth. I'm not going to be one of those émigrés always pining for the old country. Singing "Ant Kalno Mūrai" and getting weepy. Jesus and Mary, you've turned pale!'

She forces another smile. 'I thought you might be able to intro-duce me to a few people in Paris.'

'Greta. I'm sorry. I'm not my brother. I don't take an interest in politics.'

It might be a dead end and it might not, she tells herself, fighting disappointment. Ordinary civilians sometimes have a part to play. If he's no good for anything, I'll stay for a night or two then move on. She takes another sip and holds on to it, feeling the alcohol heating her mouth and the tannins drying it. Three, at most.

She's out in the middle of the lake with the first light on the ripples and the dragonflies skimming and diving around her when she hears him calling. The water is very cold, with a rainbow film of oil on the surface.

'It's not safe,' he is saying, hands on hips on the edge of the jetty as she takes the last, lazy strokes. 'This isn't Lithuania. There are rocks from the castle and all sorts of old junk on the bottom. Your feet could get snagged.'

'You would dive in and rescue me.'

He smiles ruefully. 'You won't believe it, but I'm not a strong swimmer.'

Robert squats to help her, but she plants the heels of her hands on the jetty and boosts herself up out of the water and on to her feet in one movement.

'Couldn't you sleep?' he asks, shaking out a towel and holding it at arm's length. She's in her underwear, the skin pink and raw from the cold.

'I woke up before dawn. I think I had too much wine.'

'I see. And you're one of those people who needs to punish themselves whenever they have a good time, is that it?'

'It's an excuse for another bath, that's all.'

She is wallowing in the luxury of the tub again when she hears raised voices at the front door.

'Knickers on the washing line? What am I interrupting, *m'petit Robert*?'

Feet thump angrily past the bathroom door. She can hear voices in the room where she slept – one shrill and angry, one deep and soothing. I left the satchel in there, she thinks. Stupid girl. Money, guns, passport. She pulls on her clothes and opens the door a crack.

'*Une salope*,' cries the Frenchman. 'A tart, in my bathroom.'

'Isn't that who it's for?'

The landlord's eyes widen as Greta walks in, rubbing her hair with a clean towel. Ah, she thinks, studying him. Big bark, small dog.

The landlord is a little Renaissance courtier, with a beard styled fussily into a sharp point and a moustache, not quite waxed at the ends. He goggles at her: the cheekbones, the figure, the borrowed clothes hanging from it. He has the eyes of a small boy, though he could be thirty-five. If he shaved his face a barman would refuse him a drink.

'I beg your pardon?' he says, in answer to Greta's question.

'Why build a new bathroom, if it's not for the girls you bring back here?'

'I am a married man, mademoiselle.'

'But you are a Frenchman.'

She doesn't see where they go to talk, but she can hear raised voices somewhere in the yard, through the open window over the stove.

Robert's tone is placatory at first, almost wheedling. His voice grows louder as he loses his temper, and she can make out the words: 'Call her a whore again. Her name is Greta. She is a class-mate of mine. From the same town.' If there is a reply, she does not hear it.

The Frenchman emerges into view below her, heading for a toy-like English two-seater which he has parked in an arrogant diag-onal slash across the entrance of the boatyard. Then he spots the second car.

Robert has hidden Greta's Porsche in the far corner, behind a stack of boats and covered in a tarpaulin.

The landlord strides across the concrete square and lifts the plastic sheet, exposing the number plate. He stays crouched next to the front wheel for a moment, then replaces the sheet carefully and walks back to his own car, fingers stroking his chin.

She watches his car cruise along the sloping road that leads up to the town. She can follow its progress around the streets from here, a red-orange dot against the honey stone. The car stops in the square and does not move for a full minute. What is the landlord doing? Dashing into the café there, she guesses. Why? An urgent phone call, while the registration number of the Porsche is still fresh in his memory?

Robert's face is clouded as she belts past him down the stairs. 'That's my boss. You didn't have to insult him.' Then he sees her expression, the way she is groping inside the satchel as she runs, checking the contents. She is angrier than him.

'And *you* did not have to tell a stranger my fucking name.'

It takes Greta exactly three minutes to cover the half-mile that leads to the town square. When she pulls up, panting, the sports car is nowhere to be seen. There are no other vehicles on the square yet.

She leans against the war memorial in the centre, catching her breath and calming herself, looking along each road that leads away from the square. Of course, the café with the telephone is not open, this early on a Sunday. The landlord could not have alerted anyone to her presence.

Relax, Greta tells herself. The flowers are bright outside the town hall and the tricolour is flying from its balcony. A few shop-keepers are beginning to unbolt their doors.

She buys a can of engine oil from the garage on the Paris road, a bottle of wine to replace the one they finished last night and today's bread, still warm, from the boulangerie that never closes. Bread is important here, Robert says. They ran out of it once and they had a revolution.

The news kiosk in the centre of the square is open and the words of the Bookseller return to her, from nowhere: *ever thought about picking up a newspaper?* The question stung her at the time. Her ignorance of politics must have been obvious. She selects a *Life* magazine in English and all the French dailies: *World, Figaro, Combat, Cross, Humanity.*

'You are struggling to decide who to vote for, mademoiselle,' says the man behind the hatch, amused. All the political views are there, he explains, from left to right. Greta smiles but does not reply. She does not want to be remembered.

Coffee is bubbling on the stove when she returns to the boat-house. Two cups are waiting on the side.

'Thank you,' she says. 'I'll go afterwards.'

'What are you talking about? Go where?'

'Back to the city. It's where I need to be.'

'You're staying,' says Robert. 'I told him to go and hang himself. I can't let him walk all over me for ever.'

'There's no point in both of us ending up with nowhere to sleep.'

'What would my brother say if I threw you out?' He brushes the side of the hot coffee pot with a fingertip and swears. He picks it up by the handle and fills the cups. 'You're obviously here on business.'

He wants to do things for her. Check the tyres on the Porsche, top up the oil and water. Greta resists, then gives in. It's his way of apologizing for blurting out her name.

She sits cross-legged on the mattress and spreads the newspapers over the floorboards. There are technical words she does not have time to look up in her dictionary, but the general sense of each article is clear.

Industrial stories dominate all the front pages. Production targets, the need for modernization. Whole sectors of the French economy are clearly still on their knees, six years after the war. They took a beating in there, she thinks.

American money is the great hope, but the domestic political scene is bewilderingly fractured, the shifting alliances impossible to penetrate at a glance.

When Robert returns, she fires questions at him about the parties and the personalities mentioned in the articles, but he raises a hand to fend them off, grimacing over the lukewarm coffee he left by the sink.

'Why are you asking me? I'm a farmer's boy from Mažeikiai. I don't read that stuff. *That's* the Communist Party paper though. Even I know that.'

She is flicking through *Humanity*, shaking her head. He didn't need to tell her the political affiliation. It's astonishing, she thinks.

The authentic Soviet style, on every page – that violent declamatory voice that has been thundering in my ears for half a lifetime.

The French and West German governments have been drifting closer, it seems, agreeing to pool their coal and steel. It is glaringly obvious how the Kremlin feels about this display of European unity.

There is a French byline underneath the piece, but she pictures the author taking dictation down a crackling telephone line from Moscow. And people here pay fifteen francs to read it.

The picture magazine is a relief, although the life of an American housewife is as incomprehensible to Greta as the mindset of a French Communist. The editors of *Life* place the hard politics stories towards the back. The first one follows a full-plate advertisement for a film about the life of Rudolph Valentino.

When her eyes leave the great actor and alight on the faces of the five men on the opposite page, she kicks over the cup by her knee and jumps up, cursing. Robert mops the inky coffee from the wooden boards with a cloth while she rinses the cup in the sink.

'I'll do it,' says Robert, spreading broad palms over her shoulders.

Greta walks slowly and purposefully back to the magazine and arranges herself in front of it again with an effort of self-control. The face of the man who ordered the deaths of her mother and grandmother glowers from the bottom corner of the right-hand page.

This is the photograph of Maxim Georgevich Karpov that always appears in the Western press. His face is last in a gallery of four. Malenkov comes first – fat-faced, with the single unruly black curl. Molotov is next, with his moustache and strong features that recall Lenin. Bald, doughy Mykolan is the only member of the quartet who looks cheerful.

The disembodied head of Stalin floats above them all, with the hint of a sneering smile. The Boss is supposed to be dying. The article speculates about who will succeed him, citing unnamed sources close to the different factions in Moscow. Robert watches her from the sink, drying the glasses they drank from the night before with a clean cloth.

*

Outside, he sweeps the tarpaulin off the car and stands forlornly holding it until she nods at him sharply and he climbs in the passenger side with a grin.

She is glad of the company. The face of Maxim Karpov has disturbed and dislodged things.

There are secret places deep inside Greta where her war dead live on: parents, grandmother, best friends. She can feel the ghosts moving around in the locked and barred rooms – the chambers of the heart. She cannot afford the indulgence of reminiscence yet.

I'm a bag of nerves, she thinks. Last night helped, though. Wine and laughter. Robert helped. Let's see if he's good for anything else.

She busies him with road maps, then calls out questions while his finger is tracing the route east towards Reims. When the mind is engaged with practical things, it's harder to lie without pausing to think.

'Does the name Laima mean anything to you, Robert? Did Mindaugas ever mention her? The general?'

The answer comes without hesitation. 'My brother never talked about the people he was working with, if that's what you mean.'

'What about a man called Laisvūnas? A few years older than us. He went to the other school – the Gymnasium.'

Robert shakes his head firmly. 'I'm sorry, Greta. It's been a long time.'

Vineyards slope away to the north-west. They are approaching the village Morta mentioned in her last letter to her mother.

The grand home of the kind French family who are supposed to have taken her in ought to be here. But when Laima asked a contact passing through Paris last year to investigate, the man found no trace of the house. Greta wants to see the village for herself anyway.

The address is on the main street. The house they find there bears no resemblance to the photograph tucked into the envelope. That was an imposing mansion with nine shuttered windows and a bristling beard of greenery climbing round them and a broad driveway in the foreground.

This is a slim, damp townhouse, the windows blacked out with old newspapers. Greta runs a hand over the iron number hanging on the door, then lets her fingers fall to the slit for letters. It has been blocked from the inside.

A stocky woman is slouching in her doorway on the other side of the high street, watching Greta indifferently. When Robert gets out of the car to stretch himself, the woman's expression changes. 'Long gone,' she calls out.

'I beg your pardon, madame?' He speaks without any trace of a foreign accent. The voice is deep and strong. He has a kind, open face. The woman's eyes expand as he strolls across the street towards her door.

'Empty for years, my dear. They were Jews.' She says it without emotion. 'The mail is redirected to the post office.'

'And where is that, please, madame?'

'Épernay. Shut today. And the next two days. Strike.' The woman is automatically fussing with her hair.

'To be sure,' says Robert. 'The unions are protesting about Indochina, I think? Or is it Algeria?'

'Always something, dear. Wish I could go on strike.' She tosses her head and Greta is aware, as she listens to them talk, of piping voices inside the door behind the woman. She could be the children's mother or their grandmother. The life of the countryside ages women brutally here. The lines on her face are deep as she smiles eagerly up at Robert – a rare gentleman caller. She is taking obvious pleasure in the conversation, moistening her lips with her tongue.

Greta crosses the street towards the woman, pulling the letter and photograph out of her coat pocket.

'I think we may have the wrong address. We were looking for this place.'

'Oh! Someone's playing a joke on you.'

'What makes you say it, madame?'

'If you lived around here during the war, you would know that house. The other side of Épernay, going towards Reims.' The woman grins at the print, showing bad teeth. 'Gestapo! It's where they had the headquarters for the whole of Champagne.'

'Who lives there now?'

The woman shakes her head derisively. 'They don't know what to do with it. A place full of terrible stories. They're talking about knocking it down.'

'Then my friends can't be living there. It must be a mistake.'

Greta takes Robert by the arm and steers him back to the car. She can feel the Frenchwoman's eyes on him as they leave.

'I don't know what I was expecting,' she says as they pass the sign that tells motorists they are leaving the village. 'We knew the address was an invention.'

Something makes her gnaw her knuckles. A physical pang of hopelessness at the scale of the task. A young girl, alone in a country as vast as this.

If Morta is out there somewhere, she is a grain of sand among the dunes. Or perhaps the girl is really gone, gone for ever, and her handwriting is the only memory of her, preserved by the forger's skill to bait a trap. Dead or alive, someone is using her.

'I get it,' says Robert when they are back on the main road. 'You're looking for someone. You don't want to say who. You can't go to the police because you're here illegally. I know I'm a giraffe, but I figured that much out.'

She can't help laughing at the expression. It's a private joke from the schoolyard they once shared. It means he's not only tall, but slow-witted. It takes a while for thoughts to travel up his long neck to the brain.

'I could do it for you,' he says. 'I'm a French citizen. I can open a missing person's case at the police station if you give me the details.'

'Where do you think a young girl would end up,' Greta asks, 'if she found herself in Paris with no money or friends?'

'You could try the Saint-Denis.' He says it with a laugh then shows a palm. 'I'm sorry. That's not funny.'

'What does it mean? What's Saint-Denis?'

'A street, Greta. I shouldn't have said it. It's *the* street, understand, in Paris, where the women stand in the doorways. There's one in every city.'

'And all the girls are young there? In their teens?'

'Greta, it's not somewhere I spend a lot of time. I've walked up it a few times. I've never stopped to strike a bargain, before you ask. There are all kinds of girls. Young, old. But, you know . . .'

'What? Spit it out.'

'A place like that, understand. If you close your eyes and throw a stone, you're going to hit a young girl who's in some sort of trouble.'

Robert begins the evening meal as soon as they get back. He piles flour on the work surface and makes a well for the last of the truffled eggs. There is no pasta machine, only a rolling pin. He works quickly and expertly. Eggs and flour and salt. 'No water,' he shouts, although she hasn't suggested it. 'Not even a drop!'

Neighbours with relatives on local farms have donated fresh cream and smoked pork. People are generous here, he says. Everyone in the town is kind to him. I can imagine, says Greta, picturing a procession of housewives and widows leaving offerings by his door.

He snatches the glass of white wine from her hand, ignoring the shout of complaint, and dashes some of it into the pan to complete the sauce.

She is mopping her plate with a hunk of bread when a horn sounds in the yard outside and they both bristle.

It's Robert's landlord. His sports car's bright paint is dim in the fading light. He trots towards them up the outside staircase, a bottle of champagne in each hand. And many apologies.

The landlord is mortified. They got off to a bad start. She caught him at a difficult moment, and he was unforgivably rude.

The champagne is from the refrigerator in his restaurant, still cold. Three glasses, the correct shape. He hopes she will have time to visit his place. Unless her stay in Paris is coming to an end already? His eyes never leave her face.

The restaurant is in *the first*, he says, as though no further explanation is needed. As if Greta is an old Paris hand and has committed the snail-shell layout of the *arrondissements* to memory.

What are their plans for the rest of the week? Everything will be closed tomorrow because there is a strike and a demonstration against the government. But they should not allow the leftist rabble to prevent them from enjoying a stroll through Paris.

When he refills their glasses, he is struck by an idea. An actorly finger jabs the air. He will be forced to close the restaurant to patrons tomorrow night. But why don't Greta and Robert eat there? He will leave the key with the big brute. Then Robert can help himself to the best of everything from the refrigerator and show her what he can do in a real kitchen.

The landlord knows a great deal about the route of the demonstration. He will tell them how to avoid the crowds. It will be quite an experience for her – a French restaurant all to herself, complete with private chef.

Tomorrow night then. It's decided. He must go now, alas. He will leave the second bottle for them. To their health!

'What in God's name was all that?' asks Greta, squinting at the bubbles streaming up from the bottom of her tall tulip glass.

'I told you he was hot and cold. A blazing row, then all smiles. It's not the first time.'

And Robert tells her about his early months in Paris, as a teenager, penniless and friendless. Begging for any kind of work and reduced, he admits for the first time, to sleeping in the tunnels under the city for a while, until he heard about a charity for refugees.

'Run by the Catholic Church?' Greta interrupts.

'No. It might have been one of the unions. They were interested in people from the east. They found us work in restaurants, in factories. My boss had a thing for Lithuanian boys, Poles. I thought he was queer at the beginning. But that wasn't it.' He chuckles at a private joke. 'That one is definitely not queer.'

'Why did he do it then? Politics?'

'I didn't ask too many questions, Greta. I was offered a job and a bed, rent-free. I took them.'

They talk long into the night while they drain the second bottle, and he shows her his treasures from childhood. There is a deck of playing cards that belonged to his father, where the aces are national monuments of Lithuania and the kings are Grand Dukes from the Middle Ages: Mindaugas, Traidenis, Gediminas, Vytautas the Great.

His mother gave him a book of Lithuanian folk tales when he came to the West, and he has kept it safe through many hardships so he can read the stories to his children one day.

Robert turns out to be an impressionist, like all the best people. He takes off the schoolteachers she remembers and other characters from their little town. They play *Trinka* – a painful game where the winner raps the loser's knuckles with the deck. He always seems to come off worst, flinching from her blows with feigned agony. He has the mobile features of a comic actor. It has been a long time since she laughed so hard.

It's still dark when she wakes, to the echoes of a telephone. Dream or memory?

She rolled off the mattress in the night and slept on the hard wooden floor instead, head resting on the satchel. She is not hung-over but she can feel the alcohol, a heaviness that slows all movement.

Greta pads into the bathroom to splash cold water on her face, then dresses quickly. Robert is stretched out on the sofa, head and feet spilling over the ends. He yawns extravagantly as she tiptoes past.

'I want to check out this Saint-Denis,' she says, by way of explanation. 'I'm driving into Paris early, before the crowds gather for the demonstration.'

'Wait for me. You need a bodyguard.' He looks more like a lazy house cat stretching its back, the hair not yet licked down. She suppresses a smile. But she lets him come.

'The truth,' says Greta as they head south on a straight road through deep forest in the half-light, 'is that I need your help today.'

'It's easier for a man to approach this kind of woman. Is that what you mean?'

'I need you for other things too. Your French is better. You are good with people.'

'You're going to have to trust me and tell me who we're looking for, *Gretute*.'

When she doesn't answer, he looks at her and sees that her eyes are on the driver's mirror. 'What is it?'

'That big black thing. Two cars behind. What do you call those?'

'I think that's a *Traction Avant*, but it's too dark to say.'

'Could it be the local *gendarmerie*?'

'I don't think so. Too expensive.'

'That's what I thought.' The car reminds her irresistibly of the limousines of the Soviet *nomenklatura* class. It's a long, black Citroën, a handsome pre-war shape, low-slung and lithe. There is something sinuous about the way it pours itself round the corners.

'What about it?' asks Robert, gripping the handle that winds the window. They are accelerating steadily.

'It's been with us over the last four turns. Always two cars back.'

'You're breaking the speed limit now, Greta.'

'And he wants to stay with me. Look at him sticking his nose out. He's thinking about overtaking. Gestapo headquarters. It wasn't a fucking joke!'

'What are you talking about?'

'It was an insult, not a joke. The standard Soviet insult.' She's spitting the words, angry with herself. But smiling oddly too. Alive, and wide awake.

'You're going too fast,' says Robert, gripping the handle tight. 'There's a sharp bend coming up.'

Greta brakes, eyes flashing between the mirror and the road. The Peugeot immediately behind them grows larger as she kills their speed.

'Whoever forged that letter could have slipped a photograph of any house in the world into the envelope. They put in a picture of a place the Gestapo used in the war. They can't help themselves.'

'What do you mean?'

'They love calling anyone who stands up to them a Nazi. And by the time someone travels here and finds out what that photograph is, it's too late. Here he comes. He's overtaking. He's just behind the Peugeot now.'

'Who is he?'

'One of the thugs that Karpov collects. Or . . . what was it? A *zealot*. We think this is the West, but they know better. It's theirs. They can swagger around here all they like. They've been kidnapping and garrotting their way around France since the Bolshevik Revolution. I'm going to speed up, then stop. Brace yourself.'

There is no time for Robert to argue. One last glance in the mirror, a wolf's grin, then she shifts down into third and rips away from the car behind into the belly of a curve in the road ahead. The Peugeot at their back recedes. The car behind it reacts quickly, swinging out to overtake again.

She waits until the long black Citroën is entirely on the wrong side of the road, abreast of the Peugeot, then swerves into the left-hand lane too and stamps on the brake pedal.

Driver and passenger are flung forwards. Robert presses both palms against the dashboard. Greta wrestles against the shoving force of deceleration with stiff arms, but her forehead bumps the top of the steering wheel. The car screams in indignation.

The Peugeot's horn blasts as it flashes up on their right. Greta is suddenly level with the outraged face of the driver. She can see his mouth moving as he passes them, yelling obscenities.

Her Porsche is shuddering to a complete stop in the wrong lane. She locates the pistol in her satchel with one hand but does not take it out.

The driver of the black Citroën has not sounded his horn, even though he was forced to brake sharply too and throw his car to the right, slotting in behind the Peugeot to avoid smashing into Greta.

They hear the Citroën's engine roar as the driver speeds up again. He has decided to pass them quickly.

Let's have a look at you now, little friend, thinks Greta. You should be even more angry and confused than the first driver. He wouldn't have hit me, but I could have killed you. You really ought to pull up and give me a piece of your mind.

But the Citroën accelerates past, the driver's eyes fixed on the road ahead. He's alone, she sees. He won't want to shoot it out, against two. As he draws level with Greta, he throws up his left arm to obscure his face. All she gets is a flash frame. The smooth white dome of a shaved head, a gruff staff sergeant's moustache bristling underneath and a mass of flesh below that.

Walrus. Big old walrus. Grossly corpulent but still dangerous, if you make him angry. Well, my big beast, she thinks, as the Citroën's rear end disappears, I would pick you out of a crowd again from a mile away. But you didn't get a proper look at my face, did you?

'You're not even going to explain—'

'Shut up.' One hand is raised, quivering. She is wheeling them through Versigny, Baron, Rosières. An illogical, circular route. Only one car is visible behind them, a quarter of a mile back.

'Kidneys,' says Greta.

'What?'

'Kidneys for breakfast. Every morning. They only told us why at the end of the course. So that we would remember the rule. You always have two of everything, in case one fails. Can you see what that car is?'

'I think it's multicoloured. There might be a sign on the roof.'

A long bend puts the car behind out of sight, and Greta throws the Porsche left so violently that it makes Robert exclaim. They carve across the opposite lane on two wheels and crash through a break in the trees. It's the start of a rough track for farm vehicles, with deep ruts carved into hard-baked mud. It has not rained out here for a long time.

They bump along the track for thirty yards. The way is narrow, and the side mirror brushes the leaves of young oaks on Greta's side. After seventy yards the single lane swerves left, almost at a right angle. The hedges on both sides are thick and tall, shutting out the early sun. Just after the bend has straightened out, Greta brakes and kills the engine and the lights, leaving the car in the middle of the track. She tells Robert to get out.

They can hear the other car trundling towards the bend as they settle on their haunches in the thick branches of the hedge that screens both sides of the track. When the nose of the car appears, Greta braces for impact. The grey light is very dim. Their pursuer will only have seconds to react before ploughing into the blacked-out Porsche.

But the car creeps round the sharp curve slowly and cautiously. It's a boxy Simca, black with a red roof and a sign perched on top: *Taxi Parisien*. The light is on in the cabin and Greta sees that the driver is a woman in mannish clothes, biting her lower lip from nerves. A woman on her own, who has decided to show her face to anyone waiting for her.

They watch the driver's mouth fall open and hear the brakes yammer as the taxi slides to a halt, inches from the Porsche's rear bumper. Before it has stopped completely, Robert is at the driver's window, tapping the glass with the barrel of the Browning. The woman has not had time to take in what is happening before Greta is in the seat behind her and the cold metal of the Sauer is against the nape of her neck.

'*Hostia*,' says the woman, breathing slowly and deeply and studying Greta in the mirror with great interest. 'Your hair. But I like.'

7

'Kill the engine,' says Greta. 'Are you the reinforcements? Are there more?'

There is a moment of incomprehension, then the Spanish woman shakes her head and wags her finger. 'No, no, no. They don't have enough people for this. Only one man today. Two altogether, working in shifts. They pick you up since you cross into France, more or less. We have been follow them.'

'And who is *we*?'

The next words the woman speaks are her most grammatical because she has rehearsed them. 'I represent an agency providing professional services to overseas nationals in Paris. We understand our clients' needs perfectly because we were all immigrants ourselves.'

'I don't have money for you.'

'Not necessary. We offer you information. It is, ah, *goodwill*. They don't just watch you. There is operation plan.'

'I knew it.'

The woman looks hurt. 'You have some information about this already.'

'No. Just a feeling.'

'Ah. *Sí.*' She nods sympathetically. 'This kind of feeling is important, no? We don't survive without it.'

The woman pauses because Robert is bristling impatiently at her window. Her eyes follow the small movements he makes with the gun in his hand. Greta tells her to wind down the window, then leans across and asks Robert to go back to the Porsche and wait for her, please, but if this daughter of a bitch tries anything, kindly empty his pistol into her until she stops moving.

'Crazy language! What did you say to him?'

'That you like my haircut.'

The woman grins. 'Do you want to search me?'

'No. But keep your hands on the wheel.'

'You want to drive around? Your friend can follow.'

'I'm not going anywhere with you, darling. We never let anyone take us to a different place, do we?'

'Ah. No. It's a good rule. You are right. Always better to fight where we are, no?'

They nod at each other for a little while. Then the woman clicks her tongue. 'We worry about you. White Russians! Bad security. And then this man.'

'Him?' Greta nods at the Porsche. Robert has dimmed the head-lamps and is looking towards them with a surly expression, arms crossed behind the steering wheel.

'Tall? No, no, no. About him, I have no information. This man you will have to read yourself. I am absolutely sure that you are capable. Is the little one who owns the house for boats.'

'He seemed harmless.'

'Sorry – my French.'

'The landlord did not appear to be a dangerous man.'

'His friends who are dangerous. I have something for you.'

The woman produces a stiff white card envelope from under her seat. There are shots of three men inside. A great blob with a walrus moustache and a skeletal man in spectacles, photographed separately and together. Greta has already met the third subject. Robert's landlord is clean-shaven in these pictures and looks much younger.

When Greta has studied the prints and asked a great many questions, she puts them back in the envelope and grips it in both hands. 'How did you know I was coming to Paris?'

'We hear from your woman. Sorry. Your lady general.' The taxi driver bites off the next word and squeaks with discomfort because the tip of the pistol barrel is jammed into her left ear.

'Be careful what you say next,' says Greta.

'I cannot lose this ear. Is my good ear. You never think why?'

'Why what?'

'Why someone helps you get out of Lithuania. No *tropas internas* guarding the port. No one searching the merchant ships.'

There is nothing but the sound of the two women breathing for a little while. Then Greta says: 'Yes. It occurred to me at the time that it was too easy. Where is Laima? Is she still alive?'

'They are all in the same penal colony in the east of Russia.'

'Your professional services agency has contacts there?'

'We do what we can for your prisoners.'

'Let me talk to the general.'

'No. Ow! We have some communications, but I cannot send a message to her at this time. I am sorry.'

The woman closes her eyes, steeling herself for whatever is to come. Now, thinks Greta, a lot of people in her shoes would have told me anything I wanted to hear. Just to wriggle out from under a loaded gun. Most of us would lie, play for time, promise the earth, to get themselves out of a hole like this.

'Last question,' says Greta. 'Make this answer an honest one too. Why are you helping me?'

'Because we do not like these men and we hope that you will kill them for us.' The woman is gesturing towards where she imagines the envelope to be, but her eyes are shut tight.

They will not make it into Paris before the crowds of marchers gather now. She is silent on the way back to the boathouse, refusing all questions. She sits at the dining table and takes the photographs out of the envelope, keeping them close to her body like a card player. Her face is a sheer crag. Robert slumps in the chair opposite, watching meekly, a six-foot-six man made small. Then she turns the prints round for him to look at.

'They can fake photographs nowadays, can't they?' he says. 'Who was that woman, anyway?'

Greta shakes her head. She is asking the questions.

'But you weren't surprised when she showed up.'

Greta does not answer. She is thinking about Laima, wounded and hoarse, on a bed of rushes in a hut in the deep forest of western Lithuania, with the men smoking outside.

You may find help in strange places. It wasn't the words, it was the brutal pinch that accompanied them, the old woman's thumb and forefinger catching the skin on Greta's forearm and twisting it with all her fading strength.

There was something else: the eyes flickering towards the doorway of the hut, the voice dropping. Fear, Greta would have said, if it were anyone else but Laima.

Greta says nothing, holding up the photographs in turn and watching Robert's eyes play across them. This is how they do it in Moscow, she thinks. It's how Maxim Karpov interrogates his captives. A desk with an envelope on it. The file, and the silence.

'I suppose that's my boss,' he says, at length. 'He didn't have the beard then. When was this taken?'

'At a street protest in September 1939. The Communist Party of France was demonstrating against the coming war with Germany.'

'*Against* it?'

'How quickly we forget. Stalin was in bed with Hitler then. He had all his servants agitate against the war. He reversed the policy instantly when the Germans invaded Russia.'

'My landlord was a Communist.'

'And still is. A leading member of Cominform. A Marxist who inherited three businesses from his mother and drives a British sports car and has a great dislike of paying his workers an honest wage. At the same time, he is capable of great generosity, isn't he?'

'He has never asked me for a centime in rent.'

'And he lets young men stay above his restaurant for free too, doesn't he? Always Poles, or Czechs, or Balts like us.'

'I told you. It was a charity that helped refugees. They put me on to him.' Robert is holding his head in both hands and can barely force the words out.

'The headquarters of this particular charitable organization are on Lubyanka Square in Moscow. The founder lives on Red Square. He takes a passionate interest in émigrés who flee from the east. He believes they are all plotting to kill him.'

'Oh God. Dear God.'

'Don't worry about your Frenchman. He is reimbursed for the lost rent.'

'It's not him I'm worried about.'

'We don't shoot people for stupidity. But it's very important that you tell me everything quickly.'

Soon after Robert moved into the boathouse, he had a furious row with the landlord. The Frenchman insulted him, and he lost his temper. If you only knew, Robert told him, what kind of man my brother is. What Mindaugas and his friends in Lithuania are capable of.

That was all it was – an ominous hint. The landlord turned on a sixpence. He was back the next day with a bottle. He wanted to know more. Robert gives a shout of desperate laughter. 'I couldn't tell him anything else because I didn't know anything. He became frustrated with me. Threatened to throw me out on the street. Then he changed his mind yet again.'

'He's lousy at this kind of work. But he reports to others who have more brains. They were curious about you and told him to play nice. They will be curious about me now. You gave him my name to pass on to them.'

Robert's head has sunk close to the table, still propped on two hands with the elbows on the edge. He is clearing his throat, trying to speak.

'Spit it out,' she tells him.

'My boss telephoned early this morning. You were still asleep. He is desperate for us to go to the restaurant this evening, at six precisely. He says we'll have to come on foot because the strike will snarl up the whole of the centre of Paris. He told me exactly which way to walk.'

'I see. How did he sound?'

'Friendly, like yesterday. Too friendly. What have I got you into?'

Greta stops listening to his apologies after a while. She busies herself taking the Browning apart, cleaning and checking the mechanism, laying the pieces on pages torn from *Life* magazine. She breaks down the smaller pistol first and snaps it back together and has it ready and loaded before she starts on the Sauer. Robert watches with an expression of acute discomfort.

'You have to let me come with you tonight,' he says.

'Not this time.'

'Mindaugas will never forgive me if I let you walk in there on your own.'

'It's my affair. Not his. Not yours.'

'I've been a fool. Let me make up for it. I'll do anything you want.'

She is finishing up with the larger pistol, wiping it with a cotton handkerchief. Performing a practical task with her hands has improved her mood. 'Anything?'

He misses the playful note. 'It's a matter of honour.' He's frowning hard. His face looks hot.

'And you'll really do anything I say?'

'Greta?'

'There's only one thing I need, before I go out to meet God knows what. It might be the last time. But you're no good for that now, are you? Look at you. Like a schoolboy caught scrumping apples. It's a shame it makes you so irresistible.'

'Greta, I don't understand what you're saying.'

'You're pretty enough when you're smiling. But like this? All clenched and determined. You're the most beautiful boy in the world. And you're no bloody good for it.'

'What language is that?'

'English. Did you catch any of it?'

'Not a word.'

*

They start hunting for a girl at the bottom of the Rue Saint-Denis, but it's no good. The *poules* there work out of the hotels, and there are always men watching over them.

Robert was right about the variety of women on display. Greta realizes that she is assessing them like a buyer as she passes by. Bad skin on this one, but good teeth. A slender waist over there, in the alleyway. It's so easy to fall into. She feels a shudder of disgust.

A café south of Les Halles is better. Greta stands in a doorway opposite and watches him sitting alone, smoothing back hair that is still tawny after the long summer.

Three women approach him in twenty minutes, but they all have long hair and the wrong silhouette. A better kind than in Saint-Denis, though. The type who will go around with a man for a while and sit through dinner with him first, especially if she gets to choose the restaurant.

Then he is craning his head. He has spotted a woman by herself, six tables along the pavement. Only a little older than Greta, with dark hair cut almost as short.

Robert gets up and ambles over to her with a boldness that surprises Greta. She watches the woman's expression change from surprise to amused irony. Eventually, a slow smile of real pleasure. God knows what he is saying, but it comes fluently and naturally. He doesn't need any coaching. Greta's stomach is twisted up and she cannot watch any more.

She runs to join the marchers heading west along Rivoli. She will blend in with the crowd for the length of the Tuileries then turn north towards Vendôme, approaching the restaurant from the south. Robert and the dark-haired *poule* they hope will pass for Greta from a distance will take the exact route suggested by his boss on the telephone. It's half past five. They are thirty minutes early.

Among the demonstrators, Greta is suddenly disorientated, looking around in bewilderment. It feels like another country, where the banners and flags of parties and trade unions are written in a different language – or a code to be fed into a machine: *CGT. SKF. CPDE.*

Rivoli heaves with bodies moving in currents. There are surges, when people press Greta from all around, and she feels the beginnings of panic. But what better way to move through the streets without being seen? She hides in knots of marchers, peering over their shoulders.

The procession is divided into platoons and battalions of workers with their own uniforms and liveries. Ranks of men in cloth caps march with flags held in their armpits. *Gendarmes* have been bussed in from the countryside to bolster the police presence.

Opposite the Rue de Castiglione, the *gendarmes* are chivvying along a group of students and the young people are sitting down all along the pavement in protest. The gesture seems to enrage the police more than an offer of violence.

It's ugly, suddenly. They are taking girls by the hair, pulling them to their feet. When boys intervene, they are met with spectacular flurries of blows. The *gendarmes* are as petulant as children. They slap and curse and spit and kick out at anything within range of their feet. They don't appear to want to arrest anyone.

A phalanx of miners, five abreast and ten deep, arrives at the junction. The policemen part to let them through. These men are older, grim-faced under heavy helmets. They stare down the young *gendarmes*.

Greta hangs back as the men march past, then merges with a gaggle of women behind the main body. A handwritten sign proclaims that they are miners' wives. One of them takes Greta's arm with a smile.

Rue Cambon on the right. A thrill of dread. The way is shut, blocked by metal barricades. What if all the remaining side streets have been closed off on the north side of Rivoli? She will never get to the restaurant for six o'clock.

The women around her are singing the 'Internationale'. Greta knows the tune but not the words, not in French. Her mouth forms meaningless syllables as she looks left. She can breathe again. The Rue de Mondovi is open to pedestrians.

Then she sees the Walrus on the corner of the street.

She is twenty yards from him, with the singing miners' wives between them. He is scanning the passing crowd, talking to another man. They might have been posted here for hours. She sees all seven decades etched on his face, the nicks from a cheap razor all over his pale skull, the permanent sunburn of the lunchtime drinker.

He is spilling out of a bad brown suit. Every few seconds, he tugs the trousers up. Suit and owner are alike, she thinks. Both abandoned in the back of a wardrobe and forgotten for many years before being unexpectedly pressed back into service.

Now she can see the fellow next to him properly. Laurel and Hardy, she thinks, but it's not quite right. Everything about the Walrus's comrade is thin – body and hair and the frames of the spectacles and the face, whose sharp bones threaten to poke through the papery skin stretched over them. Both men are bareheaded.

The woman beside Greta smiles, showing gold teeth. 'Sing up!' she says, beating time in the air like a conductor.

The man next to the Walrus must be sixty as well. His checked suit is slightly better. Greta can see the freckles that cover his forehead and his pale pig's eyebrows. He was a gingery sort of thing once, she guesses. Another face that is red and very lined from a life of philosophizing in cafés. As she draws nearer, she sees that the thin man's mouth and eyes are alive with involuntary tics and twitches.

'Why don't you sing, my sister?' The woman is squeezing her arm.

'*Pas bien*,' Greta croaks, indicating her throat with her free hand. '*J'vais pas bien aujourd'hui.*'

Both men are showing her their backs now, looking north along Mondovi. The restaurant is a sprint away from their position. Up to the end of the quiet side street, then a sharp right.

Was there a signal from that direction? A two-fingered whistle? It's hard to be sure from here, with the rumour of the crowd all around her. The Walrus grabs his comrade's arm, tugging at him.

Now they are striding away from Greta, away from the noise and pressing bodies, leaving Rivoli and heading north up the narrow street. Greta shakes her arm out of the grip of the miner's wife.

Mondovi is deserted. Shadow covers the left-hand pavement and the surface of the road. The men walk down the middle, throwing the occasional glance behind them. But Greta has ducked out of sight, running bent over, scurrying between the parked cars.

You can only turn right at the end. Robert and the woman he picked up in the café in Les Halles sail round the corner just before the Walrus and his friend reach it. Robert's landlord is in the middle, his hands on the others' shoulders. He is smiling and talking fast, hustling them along.

Greta runs, stooping, across a gap between a Citroën and something older and more handsome – a Delage. She squats behind a back wheel, feeling the flowing line of the running board with her hand.

The Walrus spreads his arms as Robert and the landlord and the girl from Les Halles pull up in front of him. He repeats the same syllable: the squashed Parisian *yes*, brayed with the insuperable confidence of officialdom: *way, way, way, way*.

Greta hears the woman's sharp voice for the first time. *Qu'est-ce que tu veux?* The Walrus is producing a rectangle from his jacket. A leather pocketbook? Passport holder? No. She sees the game: it will be a police identification card. Greta curses under her breath. Robert is a good French citizen now. A realistic police pass is sure to stop him in his tracks.

The *poule* launches into a fierce defence of her rights, stabbing a finger in the air. Every third word is shit, whore, brothel. The Walrus is telling her to be quiet. Robert's low voice underneath, trying to calm everyone.

Robert's landlord joins in, his voice rising in pitch. 'It's not her,' he is saying, over and over. The smile is sliding from his face. He looks wretched. 'It's the wrong girl.'

The thin man is drifting south towards the protestors, troubled by the noise. He wanders past the spot where Greta is crouched low, the tops of her thighs feeling the strain. He does not see her. His eyes are scanning the throng of people shuffling along Rivoli, checking to see whether anyone is looking in their direction.

'They are both coming with us,' says the Walrus, and he grips the girl by the arm. Robert turns to square up to him, a gentle soul finding his fists at last. 'Good boy,' says Greta under her breath. 'We never let them take us anywhere. We fight where we stand.'

The *poule* tries to wrench herself away from the fat man, shouting. A hand is clapped over her mouth. Robert snarls and takes the Walrus by the shirt collar. With a yelp of protest, the landlord tries to wedge himself between the two men.

The skeleton hears their raised voices and his head snaps back to the north. He starts to run back towards the others where Greta is squatting. She darts out from behind the parked car in a low crouch and takes him like a rugby player tackling an onrushing opponent.

Greta butts her shoulder against his hip and wraps both arms round his legs and hangs her weight from him. The stiletto is in her right hand. He looks down, staggering, then tries to grab at her, but he is too stiff to bend at the waist properly. Old dog, she thinks. Too old for this line of work. She cuts him carefully behind the ankle.

His back slaps the ground hard and she sprawls on top, smearing herself across him diagonally, her chest against his. He draws his good leg up and plants the foot close to his body to try to lever himself up and push her off him.

She grabs hold of the ankle and makes another deep, sawing cut. Now both his feet are flopping unnaturally. A marionette with the strings snapped. He raises his head and looks down at the angles made by his shoes hopelessly.

Greta takes a breath and glances at the others. They are shuffling themselves around, a quartet exchanging partners in a strange dance. The landlord has the girl from behind, arms pinned to her sides. She is spitting like a cat, trying to stamp on his feet.

The Walrus has Robert against a wall, arms wrapped round him with a wrestler's instinct. He is trying to crush the taller man into the stone and lean all his bulk against him.

From below, a hand finds Greta's face. Fingers are groping for her mouth, her eyes. She is aware of the cool touch of a wedding ring. She cuts the thin man across the face out of sheer temper and the strength in the hand dies.

She nicks the man again twice, more thoughtfully. His mouth is wide, but his throttled screams do not escape over the threshold. His tonsils are showing to the sky. The eyes protrude like a man on the point of death. She shifts her weight and reaches behind his knees.

There is a thump from nearby, disturbingly loud but not sharp enough for a gunshot. Greta scrambles to her feet, reaching in the bag round her neck for her own pistol.

'Fascist,' shouts the Walrus.

'If you like. Let her go though.'

The Walrus has the *poule* up on her tiptoes. The forearm barring her throat is as thick as a young tree. Robert's form is stretched out lifelessly on the macadam in front of them, impossibly long. The little landlord is looking at the automatic pistol in the Walrus's hand and trying to sidle away.

'Nazi assassin,' snarls the Walrus. '*Cagoulard.*'

'Call me what you want,' says Greta, 'but the girl is a civilian. You are a professional, like me.'

'Professional!' he cries. He is gripping the Frenchwoman more tightly than he realizes, threatening to choke off the blood supply to her brain. Both her hands are worrying at his wrist, uselessly. Her eyelids are fluttering. When he shoves her forwards, she drops straight on to her knees.

He fires twice, directly over the falling woman. The shots must pass inches above her head. For a second the three of them are aligned perfectly, the kneeling woman between Greta and the Walrus, eclipsing the lower half of him. All three mouths are open. The noise from the gun has stunned them, as though their ears have been cuffed.

There is no pain, but Greta knows she has been hit. Her finger snags on the trigger. She can't shoot straight back, with the woman in the line of fire. When the Walrus breaks into a run, dashing east towards the Rue de Mont Thabor with an astonishing burst of speed, Greta cracks off a shot, but everything is wrong. Her arm will not assume the correct angle. The signals from the brain are distorted.

Then she is on her hands and knees, looking intently at the grimy surface of the street, watching it swim in and out of focus. She can see every detail of the patina that covers the stone. Cracks filled with black bitumen. It's bad, she thinks. You know it's bad when it doesn't hurt.

When Greta raises her head, the *poule* is crouching next to Robert, feeling for a pulse. The woman looks over at Greta and says: 'That fat swine hit him on the back of the head with the gun.'

The meaning dawns on her with stupid slowness. Greta sees a pair of men's shoes in fine-grain leather and remembers that they belong to a vain little Frenchman who once gave Robert a place to live. The landlord is staring down at Robert's prone body now, wringing his hands piteously and shifting from one foot to the other like someone trying to hold on to their bladder.

There are shouts at her back, from the direction of Rivoli. The sudden fear of pursuit and capture drives Greta to her feet. She points the pistol straight up and fires again. A chorus of screams, in answer, from the crowd.

Then she is holding the landlord by the collar at the back of his neck. It is not clear which one is keeping the other upright. The Frenchwoman is kneeling by Robert's head. She looks up at them questioningly.

'Take your jacket off and put it under his head,' Greta tells her. 'See that he doesn't swallow his tongue. When we are out of sight, shout for help. Make them call an ambulance.'

The woman nods vigorously. She is older than Greta realized, and there is a toughness in her. The face of someone who survived a long war. A flash of silent understanding passes between them. 'You need to go now,' the woman tells her.

The landlord's restaurant is one block to the east on the corner of Mont Thabor and Cambon. God knows what the landlord told them, to steer Robert past it and into the arms of the men waiting for him.

All the landlord's showman's patter has dried up now. He is not capable of speech as he fiddles with the heavy door that will get them off the street. It opens on to an alley that runs south along the side of his restaurant. Greta can smell cat's piss and discarded cooking oil and the remains of vegetables.

The door clangs shut behind them and the Frenchman sags against the brick wall. There are no sirens yet. More clumsiness, with the key to the side door of the restaurant. He stops at one point and raises a hand for patience, like someone about to be ostentatiously sick. Greta presses the barrel of the gun deep into the flesh of his lower back.

'Were the comrades going to bring me back here?'

He hesitates until she points the gun at his heart. 'I think so. Yes.'

'Then what? Slow boat to Petersburg?'

'I don't know. It's the truth.'

'Were they going to sedate me? Did they leave drugs?'

'There is a medical bag.'

'What about a clean blouse for a waitress?'

'I can give you a man's shirt.'

They are in the kitchen. She must sit now or fall. All the world is pulsing, in and out.

She makes him open the first aid kit and lay the contents on the smooth metal work surface. The sight makes her laugh out loud. Ampules of morphine and antibiotics with Russian military markings on them.

'What a clown show,' she says bitterly. 'A pair of geriatrics like that. Can you imagine: *me*, getting tagged by a fucking pensioner? It was a lucky shot.'

'I'm sorry. I can't understand you.'

She switches back to French with an effort of concentration. 'Get the penicillin ready. The little bottle with the needle. Take the bandage out of the wrapper. Then light a gas ring.' Everything takes twice as long as it should because of his shivering hands. Fine movements are hard for him.

He turns away when Greta injects herself in the arm through a tear in the sleeve of her blouse, an inch above the livid wound.

'Stop being so pathetic,' she spits. 'Come here and take the knife out of my bag. Press the button to open it. Put the blade in the fire until it changes colour.'

Everything surges and she needs to close her eyes. A knocking sound brings her out of the swoon. It's the gun barrel tapping the concrete floor next to her chair. The fingers that hold it have lost almost all feeling. When she can focus again, she sees that the landlord has moved a yard closer to her chair. He is hesitating, gripping the stiletto with both hands. She smiles weakly.

'Do something if you're going to do it. Make a decision. Be a man.' The landlord shakes his head abjectly. He backs away from her and dips the knife into the swaying blue flame on the stovetop. 'I didn't think so. Now listen carefully. When I'm gone, the first thing you do is find Robert and make sure he is taken care of. If there are medical bills, you pay them. If the police are hassling him about this, you hire a lawyer. Robert never met me, he doesn't know anything, he's an innocent bystander. Do you understand?'

'Yes, Greta.'

'When he's out of hospital, you sign ownership of the boathouse over to him. You'll have to find somewhere else to take girls you want to fuck. The only reason I am letting you live is so that you can do these things for me. If you screw any of them up, I will find you.' He winces in sudden pain. 'Well for God's sake use your common sense! If it's getting too hot, hold it with a cloth.'

He gives a long moan as she slips out of her white blouse. One arm is saturated with blood.

'Look right into the wound,' she says. 'I can't see bullet fragments, can you? I think it bounced off and took some meat with it. The arm still flexes, so the muscle is working. Look.'

'Please.'

'I'll open it up for you. Look inside.'

'Please don't make me.'

'You pathetic baby. Can you see any pieces of shell?'

'No.'

'Give me the knife now. Observe. I need to cauterize the wound.

If there's an internal bleed this won't do much good, but we will have to take the chance. Do you think there is a haemorrhage in there?'

He cannot form words now. A dry, animal noise comes from the back of the throat. He is weeping like a beaten child.

'Open your eyes, or I'll kill you now. Keep watching, curse you. This is what I do *to myself*. Do you understand?'

'Name of God.'

'Do I need to spell out what will happen to you if you disobey my orders?'

'No. Please. My God.'

'Don't you dare look away. THIS IS WHAT I DO TO MYSELF.'

A rainbow has spread across the carbon-steel blade. When it touches flesh, it makes a noise like paper catching fire. Another sound builds in her, but she refuses to let it erupt into the room. There is a fight to hold it in. After a little while, she is able to put the knife down, but it rattles against the metal work surface.

The sound of her panting breath fills the room. He has slid out of view, but she can hear him sobbing somewhere, cowering in a heap. She can't look at her arm yet – at what she has done to it. She takes the cloth that held the stiletto, still hot from contact with it, and mops the sweat running down her forehead.

'If this is what I do to myself, imagine what I will do to you.'

8

Lucien doesn't recognize the girl at first.

Too early on the Sunday after Paul Fazi's birthday, he finds himself parked outside a big grey house in Billancourt, inspecting his pupils in the driver's mirror. He is still soaked in last night's smoke, the bones soft and the limbs hanging loose. He is floating outside himself.

He should not be driving, but Ange called in the small hours to ask for a favour. The telephone rang many times before Lucien answered.

A fucking taxi job, he croaked. Why can't Dodo do it? An unamused silence from the other end of the line. It's a bitter kind of joke. Everyone in their circle knows that Dodo cannot be left alone with women.

The house is where they hold the most notorious *partouze* in Paris, every Saturday.

There are many such gatherings across the city, but this is the one that excites the real connoisseurs. It is the party with the highest ratio of beautiful young *poules* to powerful old men.

The girl called Marie has kept him waiting for half an hour.

Lucien gives the horn a blast, imagining the scene behind the shuttered windows: a Versailles floor covered in bottles, discarded clothes from the Paris collections and the bodies of the exhausted nubiles. It's probably nothing like that, he thinks sourly. Orgies must get boring after a while, like everything else.

The girl was not supposed to stay for the whole night, but Ange Suzzarini is reluctant to punish the regular who reserved her.

'Just check the cash,' Ange told Lucien. 'There should be more than usual. We respect him, but he can't take liberties with our princess.'

A pair of long, thin legs in a wrap dress descends the steps to the waiting car. She has a winter scarf doubled round her neck. Her hair is piled up on top and stuck with long wooden pins like a Hanoi bar girl.

When she opens the back door, the low sun forms a halo behind her head, and he doesn't see that it's the same young blonde girl who was sitting next to Paul in the Paname until she climbs in.

Her make-up is smudged, and she looks older in the unsparing light of early morning. The features change curiously when she turns her face or tilts her head slightly. His eyes are drawn to the mirror constantly as he drives east.

'I'm supposed to make sure our friend gave you enough,' says Lucien.

'You must be new. No one cheats me.'

'I'll be in trouble with Ange if you don't show me the money.'

'Tell him to take it up with me. I answer for myself. And keep your eyes on the road, soldier.' There is a little smile of quiet triumph on her lips. Lucien turns on the radio.

The girl is silent as they cross the Pont Mirabeau. She lifts the armrest that divides the back seats and lounges across both, almost horizontal. The blue scarf looks like cashmere. She lights a cigarette without asking permission.

On the radio, a segment on Korea is coming to an end. A French battalion is supposed to be in the thick of the fighting there. They no longer mention Indochina in the news programmes.

When the bulletin is over, the girl says: 'It's a nice car.'

'Straight from the showroom.'

'You play cards.' It's a statement, not a question. 'So you drive a good car this week. Next week you have to pawn it. That's cards.'

'Not the way I play.'

'I know who you are. An up-and-coming thug. Paul is taking you to Marseille with him.'

'That part is true.'

Her eyes flash in the mirror. Another victory. 'I've heard all the stories. They call you Crazy Horse. But Ange told me I would be safe with you.'

'Oh? I'm chivalrous?'

She snorts with amusement. 'You only like oriental women. Do you want to know what else the men say about Crazy Horse?'

'Not especially.'

'No?'

'I'm not interested.'

'Liar. Your knuckles have turned white. We all want to know what other people think of us. You must have heard things about me.'

'My cousin has so many girls.'

'But only one princess.' She is winding the window down to flick away her cigarette end.

'Never once,' says Lucien, 'has Paul mentioned your name.'

'Liar!' The tone is different this time. She is upright suddenly, the boredom and sophistication slipping. He has wounded her.

Lucien takes one hand off the wheel and turns the radio up. The girl doesn't speak again until they are approaching the eastern loop of the river, on the other side of the thirteenth.

'What *shit*,' she says, as if to herself.

'Me?'

'This report. It's rubbish. The Third Force are finished. The MRP will stay in government.'

'The Republican Movement? I thought they were finished too.'

'They lost half their vote but they hold on to foreign territories and colonies. That's the deal. What are you grinning at?'

'How old are you, Marie? Seventeen?'

'I'm *nineteen*. I'm going to get out here in the middle of the traffic if you don't stop laughing.'

'I can't help it. It's too much. Do you throw in the politics lessons for free or do the men pay extra?'

When he pulls up at her hotel near the Paris Zoo, she slams the door behind her. Ange will collect her later. She can be left alone for a few hours. Marie is their best girl.

The afternoons are endless. Lucien's headaches begin at midday. Adrenalin is the only thing that can shift the tension. But Ange is resting him, leaving him to curdle. There is nothing to write in the weekly report for Monsieur Balard. Lucien stalks the streets, his eyes flashing a challenge at every man he passes.

On the Thursday he is walking past a newsstand when he sees that the MRP, the *Mouvement Républicain Populaire*, has indeed reached an agreement with the other parties of the coalition government. The ministers of the foreign and colonial departments will be selected from the ranks of that party, exactly as the girl predicted.

Lucien's Italian woman, Romana, is supposed to call at his apartment on the Friday evening. She has promised to cook for him. He smokes a small pellet of morphine in the early evening, before she is due to arrive. It disappears in three long draws.

He paces the bathroom, waiting for the glow to build inside him. All the tension in his body ought to drain away any second now. It is the sensation of sliding into a hot bath.

Lucien feels nothing. He kneads his face. A desperate feeling of being cheated. He is close to tears.

The remaining speck of clay in the tobacco tin is harder and darker. The smoke is thicker this time, almost blue in colour.

He wakes up in last night's clothes with a naked woman smoking beside him on the bed.

'Did I hear the phone?' he moans.

'Your cousin is on his way over,' says the woman. 'I think that's his car now.'

It takes Lucien a geological age to lever himself up on his elbows, his brain arranging fragments of information.

'My cousin Paul,' he says weakly.

'That will be him outside. You'd better clean up that mess before they come in.'

A beat of time. Then terror propels Lucien out of the bed. The bathroom door is jammed shut. He shoulders it open, but his feet slip on the tiles, and he sprawls on the floor next to the washbasin.

Charred fragments of morphine base are scattered all around. On the side of the bath: the stiletto, still open, with the dross burnt into the blade. The cheap lighter next to it. The fumes. My God. The air is still heavy with the tarry smell.

Lucien tries to stand and cracks his skull on the edge of the basin and howls. He subsides back on to the floor, holding his head with both hands.

'*Fada*,' shouts the woman from the doorway. She is drawing a gown round herself. 'No one is coming here.'

'Jesus,' says Lucien. 'Oh Jesus.'

'I wanted you to see what you have become. Get up and look in the mirror, *fada*.' She bends down to snap her fingers in front of his face, but he is covering his eyes with his hands now. Blood is trickling from the cut on his head. He draws his knees towards his chest and rocks backwards and forwards. His suit is as violently crumpled as a loser's betting slip.

'Don't call me crazy,' he whispers, but she has swept out of the bathroom already and his hands muffle his voice.

When they are back in bed, Romana lights a cigarette for him and ruffles his hair the way a child pets a dog.

'I don't know why you're wasting your time hanging around with me,' Lucien tells her.

'Don't you recognize a friend when you see one?' They're sitting up, side by side, and she gives him a look of mock innocence. There is nothing under the gown. Both her nipples are showing. He has never met anyone so indifferent to nakedness. He laughs, despite himself. Then he says: 'I'm sinking like a stone, Romana. I can't go on like this. What do I do?'

'I've already told you, Lulu.'

'Not that. Not him.'

'*Allora*. If you are ill, you see a doctor. If you need a good doctor, you find a Jew. Who else?'

'Lellouche is the last person in the world I would go to. If he breathed a word of this to anyone, I would be dead before the sun went down.'

'You fool. Jacky is petrified of you. Do you think that little rabbit would ever cross a man like Lucien Fazi? He's the perfect choice. Now take that suit off. I'll try to do something with it while you're out.'

'Where am I going?'

'That was Ange on the phone. He wants you to pick up some girl at ten. From a house in Billancourt.'

It's the same townhouse in the deserted street near the tennis stadium. His throat swells when he sees Marie again, slathered in white powder and paint like a Pierrot. She has another scarf round her neck, silk this time, the colour of a blood orange.

She bangs the car door shut behind her. 'You again. The same old *fucking* faces.'

'Exactly what I was thinking.'

Then the idea hits him like a slap. It's no accident. The best girl, the prettiest on the books. A good talker too. The kind who dangles knowledge, who pulls you in. Ange feigning engine trouble, two weeks in a row.

They are pushing her into his path. It's another test. Paul, you clever bastard. Lucien's lip curls into a sneer.

'We'll have to sit here for a moment,' the girl is saying from behind her hand. 'He's gone to fetch the money from his safe. He will come to the gate to pay you.'

'What do you propose we talk about while we're waiting, Marie?'

She's still yawning, missing the edge in his voice. 'I don't know. Tell me something, and don't be boring. How is the thuggery business?'

'You people must think I came down in the last shower.'

'What?'

'Ange said you would be safe with me. Because I only like Indochinese girls.'

'Yes. So what?'

'I was a last-minute replacement for him. When did he say those things to you?'

She shrugs. A little puff of annoyance. 'He rang the house early that morning to warn me someone else was coming. Do you think I'm some kind of spy?'

'It's a hell of a coincidence. Ange's car happening to play up every Sunday.'

'So he's lying. He's lazy and hungover. He wants you to do the job instead of him.'

'And a girl with a face like this just happens to be waiting for me.'

'You have a high opinion of yourself. Why would anyone bother spying on Crazy Horse? Another thug from the thug factory?'

Lucien laughs viciously. 'Let's leave it alone. I'll put the radio on.'

'I don't want to know any of the secrets of the thugs. Don't say a word if you don't want to. I'll tell you about my business instead. Last night wasn't so bad. Do you know what we call it? A mannequin job.'

'No thanks. Not interested.'

'We make ourselves stiff, like this. We become dolls. They manipulate us, move the arms and legs around, then we stay in position, completely still. The eyes are the main thing, though.'

'Enough.'

'You need to make your eyes go dead. Look.'

'Stop it, Marie.'

The girl comes to life again with a burst of laughter. 'Give me a cigarette then.'

Lucien holds out a Caporal. She rests her hands in her lap and leans forwards and opens her mouth for him to place it between the lips. She waits expectantly until he produces a lighter with an ironic flourish, like a waiter in a café.

As she is sucking the tobacco into life, he takes hold of the scarf and tugs the folds away from her neck. Her spread fingers cannot cover what is below the silk: a constellation of red points like a bad rash that runs from below the jaw down to the collarbone. There are bruises where fingertips have dug into her neck.

'It's what he pays for,' says the girl carefully as she watches the expression on Lucien's face change.

'Is that him? Coming out of the door?'

'Don't you understand? He pays extra for it. It's what he likes. You can't . . .'

This guy ought to be worn out, thinks Lucien as he crosses the pavement to the iron gates. Drinking all night, pounding the mattress and throttling girls half his age. But look at the swagger on him. He's as fresh as a newly caught roach. The man's curly hair is a little too long. He wears a resort shirt with a wide collar. The door of the house is open, fifteen yards behind him.

'The usual,' says the man. 'Plus a little extra.' It's not a question. There is no fear in him as he reaches the inside of the gate, touches the iron lightly with a finger. He has a fat pocketbook in his left hand.

Lucien ignores the proffered banknotes and takes the man's wrist instead. He grasps one of the bars with his other hand and rattles it, checking the lock. 'How much do you have on you?' he snarls.

The man stiffens, tries to pull his hand back, then watches the grin spread over Lucien's face. He answers it with a mirthless, patient smile. 'Plenty,' he says. 'Business is good. No more for you guys, though.'

His face hits the thick bar with a smack. Lucien has yanked the man forwards with brutal force, pulling himself close to the ironwork in the same motion. They could kiss each other's cheeks, except the upright bar is between them. The man cries out.

Somewhere behind Lucien, the girl is shouting the word *no*. Lucien has driven his left arm through the gap beside the man's head and is gripping the back of his skull, keeping the face squashed tight against the metal.

Then he lets go of the wrist and feeds his right hand through the gap on the other side of the head so he can interlace his fingers in the shaggy hair at the back.

All the muscles of Lucien's upper body contract as he squeezes the braying face into the iron bar of the gate. It runs down across the man's eye and cheek and the corner of his mouth. It is creasing and distorting the soft tissue so much that he is already unrecognizable.

Lucien hugs the man into the metal, so hard that he begins to feel the smaller bones of the face – then the structure of the skull itself – flexing under the pressure. The girl is thumping his back and clawing at him.

Lucien lets go when he senses the man is about to pass out. He falls to his knees and grips the bars with both hands. His pocket-book has fallen on the street side of the gate. A few thousand francs. Lucien takes the cash and drops the wallet back on the pavement in front of the kneeling man.

The girl has climbed back into the car and is holding her face in both hands when he guns the engine. 'Not for me,' she is saying. 'You can't do things like that for me.'

'Calm down. We're leaving.'

'Another thug,' the girl says.

'That's right.'

'A violent piece of shit like all the others.'

'Exactly right. Calm yourself. Breathe deeply.'

'You have no idea who he is, do you?'

'Your friend there? I know him very well. I have spent half my life around men like that.'

'He is the next interior minister of France,' says the girl, with cruel relish.

Lucien has a cigarette case full of morphine in his left breast pocket and six handwritten pages for Balard in the right and it's all he can do to stop his hands flying up guiltily when Ange hails him from the other side of the Avenue Montaigne.

Ange is driving a German car. Dutchman and Dodo are in the

back. It will be hard to fight three, although only Dutchman is really tough. But when Lucien settles himself in the passenger seat, he knows he doesn't have it in him. I've never been so tired, he thinks. So weighed by disgust. I've been like a rock, ever since Indochina, falling into a bottomless pool. He closes his eyes.

'You don't look too good,' Ange is saying.

'The flu.'

'We called at your place. You don't answer the phone.'

'I know I fucked up with that politician.'

Dodo laughs with delight. 'You had a banana.'

'We all get one, sooner or later,' says Dutchman soothingly. 'We all slip up.'

This is how it was always going to end, thinks Lucien. There will be kindness now, some laughs. We're all friends, going for a drive. If they don't kill him now, they will take him to Paul, to the White House, where the guards will search his pockets.

He says all the things he has rehearsed. He acted in good faith in Billancourt, for the honour of the family. The man damaged the girl's throat. That means a loss of earnings. If a punter doesn't respect the rules, he needs to take his medicine. He trails off when he realizes that none of the men are interested.

Dutchman wants to talk about the fights at the Palais des Sports, the horses. The others join in, but Lucien is drifting out of himself. His eyes close, sunlight and shadow playing on the lids. The noise of the Paris traffic. His head falls on to his shoulder. Where will they bury him? It will be a relief. His mother's face appears, unexpectedly. When she was young and strong. He can't hear what she is saying. I'm so tired.

The bang wakes him. His shoulders spasm, and he gasps loudly. Ange is looking at him from the side, chuckling. They are outside Lucien's apartment block. Dutchman has jumped out and is running across the four lanes of the avenue to a *tabac*. The explosion was the door slamming behind him.

'You're not in trouble.' Ange is repeating the words. 'Your cousin appreciates your commitment to the cause. You went too far with the politician, but there's nothing to fear from that guy. We'll have our hooks in there, very soon.'

'You mean the teeth,' says Dodo, with a sneering laugh.

'Ah, it's true. We're sinking our teeth into his backside.' Ange's hissing laugh, as he joins in the private joke.

Lucien is rubbing his eyes. Ange is holding something out for him. A business card.

'Go and see this prick, if you've got the flu. He's the family doctor. You call on him day or night. You don't pay anything. The pervert belongs to us. Take next week off if you need it. Paul wants you on good form.'

'Paul? For what?'

'He's taking you to Marseille on the third. You're flying first-class, kid. Pay attention, you're going to learn from the master down there. Why doesn't he smile any more?' Ange is slapping Lucien's face now, playfully. 'Don't you think Lulu should cheer up, Dodo?'

'Lulu gets away with fucking murder,' says Dodo from the back seat.

Everyone wants Lucien to see a doctor, but he can't go to a real physician, especially one who belongs to the House of Fazi.

When he comes out of his bathroom the following evening after washing his face and neck, Jacky Lellouche has been and gone.

'He's scared of you,' says Romana. 'I told you. He didn't want to hang around. I put everything in the bathroom.'

Lellouche has left strict instructions. The correct sequence must be observed. First comes pure Hmong opium, two days' worth. Then Lucien must switch to the Turkish strain, which contains less morphine and more thebaine. After that comes a bottle of codeine tablets, to stave off the sickness for a little while.

'And then?' says Lucien.

'He says it's like a bad cold for a week.'

'It's much worse than that. What are the other bottles?'

'Aspirin and sleeping pills. He said it wouldn't be too bad for you because you have already been cutting the dose. And don't forget that you have a beautiful Genoese nurse to mop your fevered brow.'

'You can't sleep with me when I'm in the tunnel, Romana. It's disgusting. I've watched men go through it. Better to leave me alone.'

'Who is going to listen to your stories, *fada*?'

'What do you mean?'

'You *talk*, after you smoke opium. More than I've ever heard you talk before. Don't you remember afterwards?'

'No,' says Lucien. 'What do I talk about?'

'Your childhood. Indochina. A girl who isn't me. You talk so beautifully. Jacky says it's normal.'

'You told Lellouche? What did he say?'

'That the poppy is . . . wait. The greatest truth serum ever devised by nature.'

'Go on.'

'And that Monsieur Lucien would not be the first man to reveal all his heart when he is under her spell.'

9

The fever begins in earnest when Greta is passing Orléans. It soars as she approaches Châteauroux. The air rushing past the open window of the Porsche is cold, but her blouse clings to her as though she has been drenched in a storm.

She does not enter the towns or cities. She has been banished from the ordinary human world. At the quietest roadside stopping places she pushes the door ajar and vomits weakly, shivering and hugging herself.

Greta injects the second vial of penicillin just after crossing the River Creuse, glancing nervously at the passing traffic. The scar on her arm is turning yellow. She presses a finger to it and imagines she can see the microbes swimming below the surface. A gust of nausea passes through her. The closed wound is painful to the touch. She knows it is time for morphine now. The drug is in a Red Army syrette, a copy of an American design. The Russian word for *poison* is on the side.

Then there is a half-hour of great lucidity, when she believes she is rallying, followed by a period of faintness when she swerves on to the verge and sinks back in her seat, head nodding on the edge of sleep. She slaps her face and forces herself on.

There is woodland on both sides and Greta finds that her eyes are drawn to it for increasingly long spells. She believes she can see things moving in the greenery – small animals swimming through dense undergrowth. She swears and pulls the car back on to a straight bearing. Concentrate, stupid.

A sign for the turn-off to a town looms up and she stares at the letters in disbelief. It cannot be real. La Souterraine? The underworld? The name rings with the power of a supernatural warning. Whatever force is dogging her every step and cursing her to failure has surely placed the sign here in her path.

The tyres have drifted over the line that runs along the side of the road. She snaps to attention and jerks the wheel back to the centre. The car is travelling at one hundred and thirty kilometres per hour. Her head flops again, and she forces it upright. Is the end approaching? Or is this the afterlife?

Greta takes the next turn that leads away from La Souterraine and tears through villages, dangerously fast, waves of heat emanating from her forehead. She is mumbling to herself.

After Chamboret Greta has become possessed by the idea that she is already dead. She slows at the outskirts of the next village and is unable to prevent the car from shuddering and stalling. Her hands and feet no longer obey simple commands. She abandons the Porsche on the edge of the settlement, seeing dark, irregular shapes ahead. Walk, she tells herself. Stay awake.

The first shape is the skeleton of a house. A timber frame faces the sky like a ribcage. The façade of the next building is intact, but grey light shows through every window. No, says Greta, out loud. A rough wooden sign planted in the dirt rebukes her: SILENCE.

All that remains of the house on the corner of the square is the central mass of its chimney. Iron pots are arranged round the hearth. Pans hang on hooks on a fragment of stone wall. 'Please,' she whispers. 'I know this place. I came from here. Don't send me back.'

The rest of the village obeys the order for quiet. Greta is the only moving thing. No birds sing here now. But the streets echoed once, with unendurable anger. Her memory supplies the soundtrack: the Stukas climbing, black crucifixes strung out against the sky, tipping over at the top of the arc, beginning their whining stoop. The prey chokes the roads below.

She is outside her body, seeing the lines of refugees from above. Bent old women who have shambled along through an endless night. They all have the face of her grandmother. The sun has come up, but the sun is black. Along the dim horizon, all the little towns are on fire.

Greta sways at the centre of the village square, leaning heavily on something made of iron. Words are etched into the metal, out of focus. It is inscribed with names. A rollcall of villagers, with their dates beside each name. The date at the end is the same for everyone: 10 June 1944.

'*Brûlés*,' she says aloud, disturbing the quiet. 'All the people were burnt. *Brûlés par les Allemands.*' The village has been preserved exactly as the Germans left it that night. She unpeels her hands from the plaque and tries to stand properly.

It's just the morphine, she tells herself. That was a dose for a burly Russian soldier, not a slip of a girl. It nearly knocked me on my back. The feeling will pass.

The sun is emerging from the edge of the clouds, weakly. She is suddenly very cold. This is the overworld, still. She is coming back to reality.

The farmhouse commands the high ground, warm yellow against the grey bared teeth of the Corbières Massif which soar up on the far side of the valley. There are vines in stepped fields on either side of the dirt track that leads along the hog's back to the farm.

The new metal gate is padlocked shut and Greta rests her forearms on the top bar, letting it take her weight as she looks over the buildings. They match the description she has carried in her head for years. The walls are local stone. The biggest blocks come from an abbey in the valley that was destroyed in an ancient war. Climbing plants obscure the drainpipes that cling to the front of the house. The shutters are a pale mint-green.

A woman in her middle fifties is striding towards the gate in rubber boots, taking long steps over the puddles in the track. A naturally kind face, restrained by wariness. A look of concern comes over the woman as she approaches Greta.

'Mademoiselle? Are you unwell? Do you need help? You have broken down?'

'Madame Clothilde?'

'Yes?'

'Friends. Told me to come here. If I found myself in a tight corner. I hate to show up like this. Without warning.' Greta has to pause for breath after every few words. Her legs feel oddly light. There was another phrase you were supposed to say. Not exactly a password. 'You and I have never met,' Greta tells the older woman. 'But we have old friends in common.'

'Is that right? *Old friends in common*. And yet you are so young. I cannot believe you were involved in the war.'

'It was afterwards. I worked with people who remembered your kindness. British officers. They told me about this place.'

'Who told you, mademoiselle?'

'Mr Teale. Mr Haglund. Colonel Rattray. They were my instructors in Scotland.' Greta is gripping the metal bar with white knuckles. The wound on her arm throbs angrily. She grits her teeth.

'Those are good names, miss. Names with many tales attached to them. But you could have overheard them in a café . . .'

'Whatever it is, we're not buying!' A cheerful man in filthy work clothes is puffing towards them. His hair and beard are white. The face is red, but not from drink. From the life of the fields and woods. When he sees Greta properly, he makes a show of snapping his fingers. 'It's one of my mistresses. The ballerina. She's tracked me down. I'm so sorry, darling.'

'Comedian,' says his wife. 'We need to take her to Jacky. She has a story. I want Jacky to hear it.'

'That loafer can get up and walk out here. But for pity's sake, Clo. Look at her.'

Greta's eyes are shut, and she is swaying perilously. I have reached the end, she thinks. We all reach the end, sooner or later.

Madame Clothilde takes Greta's face in her hands and presses her lips against the brow the way a mother takes a child's temperature.

'She's on fire. Jump over and catch her, before she falls. Quickly, Jeannot. She's going. I can't hold her!'

They give Greta an upstairs room in the main house. On the second night she lurches out of bed roaring, and when they run into the room she is shadow-boxing an imaginary intruder in the corner. She has knocked over all the framed photographs that were arranged on a table there, below an oil painting of General de Gaulle in jodhpurs.

Madame takes Greta by the shoulders and leads her back to bed. Her soothing words of reassurance are mixed with gentle questions. Before she leaves, Clothilde sets the photographs straight. They all feature the same young woman.

On the fourth morning the feeling of cold deep in her bones has departed, but Greta is pitifully weak. She is thinking about calling out for water when there is a knock on the door and a small, neat man in a chalk-stripe suit cut with pre-war generosity enters.

'So,' the man says, puffing out the legs of the trousers with fingers and thumbs, 'here is Chaplin.'

'It's not that bad. But you need a shave, monsieur.'

'I have been on my back for a while, like you. A bad chest. Today is my first day out of pyjamas. Yes, Jacky Lellouche, who wouldn't go out for cigarettes unless it was in a suit made by Waltener. It's a scandal. Now tell me what you need.'

'Just water. No, wait.' She licks her dry lips. 'English tea.'

'*English* tea. Grown in the tea plantations of Kent.'

'I mean black tea, with cold milk.'

'You have come to the only place in the south-west of France where such a request has a chance of being granted. I will make enquiries.'

'Also, I had a chocolate bar in my coat pocket.'

'It is on a shelf in the pantry. I know this because my hand crept towards it and was knocked away by a rolling pin. I will fetch your chocolate. Just describe Lewis Teale and Colin Rattray to me first.'

The request is slipped in so easily, while Greta is still laughing, that it catches her by surprise. Then she begins to mimic one of Teale's rambling lectures. She barks orders like Colonel Colin striding along the side of the assault course, and describes the layout of Swordland, as well as things no aerial photograph would reveal: the brown tea left to stew all day in vast urns. Porridge and jam and devilled kidneys after the morning run. At length the Frenchman throws up his hands in surrender.

'You pass the test. I cannot smoke any more, and you should not, as it ages the skin, but will you walk with me?'

They follow the ridge down to the gate she collapsed against, then turn and plod back up slowly, both becoming so puffed that they are unable to talk. Greta is shocked at her feebleness. The great massif hovers in the west through a curtain of hazy air.

There are four other guests at the farm, all dishevelled men in their thirties or early forties, a little younger than Jacky. They are ripping a line of rotten fenceposts out of the ground on the edge of a field of vines in the north-west corner. As one man they all turn to study Greta.

'I want to work too,' she says. 'I know that's the arrangement. It's the only reason I came here.'

'In truth, there is little to do for the rest of the year now, after they have finished with the grapes. It's a polite fiction that you work for your bed and board. I am sure monsieur and madame can find a task to occupy your hands if it makes you feel better.'

They will not hear of her performing strenuous labour, but Clothilde consults Greta closely on her plans to redecorate the bedrooms upstairs. Greta plays along, a blanket over her shoulders. They build the fire so tall that they need to leave the front door ajar, in November. Madame lays out a colour chart on the kitchen table. 'God has sent me a woman, at last,' she tells Greta. 'I am going to make use of you.'

The fever returns that night, on the Sunday. A doctor calls before dawn, a younger and more handsome man than she is expecting. Greta glimpses Jacky pacing in the corridor outside, fingers in his mouth, as the doctor prods at the wound on her arm. When he leaves she hears them talking in the corridor. The doctor is spelling out a word: *sul-fa-nil-a-mide*. 'I can't get it now,' he says. 'All the stocks are being sent to Indochina.'

Very late on Monday night, Clothilde appears at Greta's bedside with a packet of powder taken from a cardboard box with US Army markings. 'A present from Monsieur Jacques,' she tells Greta, before winking happily. 'It's better not to ask.'

The young doctor returns two days later. Jacky sits on the end of Greta's bed and jokes about the three of them going into business together. 'You write the prescriptions. I take care of the supply chain.' Jacky has shaved, leaving a thin moustache. He has a sprite's face, the nose and ears a little too big. His eyes are lively.

'What does she do?' asks the doctor, playing along.

'Advertising. We'll put her in a swimsuit.' Jacky touches his hand to the back of his head and blows a kiss. A flash of camp. It's the first time she has noticed it in him. The men are flirting with each other, she realizes.

Eventually the doctor throws Jacky out of the room and packs his instruments away in a leather roll. 'I'm no expert in bullet wounds, but I think you did have an internal bleed. Sometimes they heal themselves if they are very small and you are very lucky. That other matter you asked me about.'

'Yes please.'

'I can't see any sign of infection. And there is no physical abnormality. Not that I specialize in the female anatomy.' He raises an eyebrow archly, a cue for her to giggle.

'I have been doing some reading. It's not uncommon for a woman's monthly cycle to stop completely if she is placed under extreme physical stress. Apparently, it's well known among dancers and athletes, if the levels of fat become very low. We saw it in women who were imprisoned in the war.'

'I haven't been in prison.'

'But you have led a taxing life. You don't want to tell me about it, and I don't think I want to know. Whatever it was has taken a toll. You are strong, mademoiselle, but underweight. I don't have my callipers with me, but the eye tells me there is nothing under here but muscle and sinew.'

'I need feeding up. Please don't tell Clothilde.'

'Ah. She is trying to stuff you already.'

He stows the roll away in his bag and straightens his tie, waiting patiently for the question he knows is coming.

'Do you think things might return to normal if I put on some weight?'

'We shall see. Rest and relaxation for now. Good food. Try not to worry about anything. Wait a month or two. If nothing happens, you will need a specialist. I'm afraid you won't be able to pay that kind of doctor in eggs and milk.' He is getting up to leave. She is still light-headed, tired from the effort of concentration. The urge to sleep washes over her.

'You give me hope, monsieur.' She yawns wide as she watches him head to the door. 'I thought something was wrong with me, on the inside. I was convinced I would never have children. As a punishment for my many sins.'

The doctor pauses on the threshold and watches her eyes close. He does not reply. She is mumbling to herself in Lithuanian.

As soon as her temperature dips below thirty-eight, Greta insists they lend her a bicycle to fetch the bread from the village each morning. On the first day the round trip takes forty minutes, measured on the Swiss watch she took from Laisvūnas. She improves on the time every day. After a fortnight, she has turned the long uphill ride from the gate to the farmhouse into a furious sprint.

Clothilde and Jeannot stop trying to prevent Greta from doing physical work. She joins the four other men who are staying on the farm, climbing ladders on to the roofs of the buildings that need to be patched up and waterproofed before the real winter sets in.

One evening, after the day's tasks have been completed, Greta plays cards with the men, getting used to their southern accents and the wartime slang they use. She asks them if they can teach her poker, but they are only interested in *manille* and piquet, played with thirty-two cards. They were *résistants* together. All their talk is of the past.

They insist on pouring a glass of wine for Greta, her first since she left Paris. Monsieur Jeannot smuggled it out to them earlier, against all the house rules, with strict instructions not to tell his wife. They are sitting around on the floor of the outhouse where the four men sleep on camp beds.

The youngest was in Spain until recently. For work, he says, not for politics. He is a pilot by training. There was some kind of trouble. He doesn't want to talk about the details.

Later they wind a horn gramophone. Greta is obliged to dance with all the men in turn. She likes the oldest one the best. He is the gentlest and the saddest too, with a beard that is turning grey. Then Madame Clothilde sneaks into the outhouse, bearing a bottle of wine from the year before last. They are not to tell Monsieur Jeannot about it.

The man with the beard takes madame by the hand with a cry of delight. 'I want the cat, not the kitten.' Greta is left waltzing with the youngest Frenchman. His fingers are splayed across the middle of her back, and she can feel his fingertips pressing into her, one after the other, as though playing an instrument.

She doesn't realize how drunk she is until she walks across the yard to the farmhouse and climbs the creaking stairs. She gropes her way to bed. The room is not spinning but it is not quite still. She will take her clothes off in a while, after she has rested her eyes.

When she wakes, it's hard to say how much time has elapsed. The tip of a tongue is searching her ear. The pilot is beside her, facing in the same direction, his unwashed body fitted close into the curve of her back. She can feel his prick.

Greta rolls away from him but he levers himself on top of her, propped on his hands. He is moving his groin against hers. He tries to press his lips to her mouth. She turns her head to the side, but he settles his weight on her and guides her face back into position with one hand tight round the jaw. She knows she must allow him to kiss her.

Greta is trying to say something gently, and he pulls his tongue out of her mouth.

'What, my darling?'

'Do you have anything?'

It takes him a second to understand, and then he says: 'There is no need for any of that, angel.'

'I have a *préservatif*. In my bag.' His fingers grip her face again, not gently. A hint of the force he could employ, if he chose to. Her eyes are liquid in the darkness, clouded by wine. 'Let me put it on you,' she says. 'Then you can do whatever you want.'

He plants the hand on the mattress beside her and holds himself in the push-up position while she reaches out to the side table for her satchel. She is rummaging in the bag with one hand and feeling for his prick with the other. His body goes rigid as he holds his breath. It's too dark for him to see what is in her other hand. He is aware, too late, that the object is bigger than a tin for contraceptives. The wrong shape.

She blasts his eyes with the hairspray. As he rears up, she grabs the back of his head and looses off another long spray into his open mouth, just as he is gasping with surprise. He rolls off the bed with a thump. She is still wearing her shoes. The heel catches him on the side of the head.

Greta can hear voices outside the room. She springs off the mattress and turns on the main light. The man is on all fours, making a noise like a cat coughing up fur.

She thinks about the stiletto but clubs him over the head with the spray can instead. It is light but the metal is stiff and forms a sharp edge at the bottom.

Greta has hammered the young man three times round the head and neck when Monsieur Jeannot charges in and catches her arm at the top of the next swing.

10

Greta finds herself dancing again, the following evening, with Monsieur Jacques. Clothilde and Jeannot watch from the kitchen table. They have cleared the chairs away to make room. There is a jazz programme on the radio.

'I threw them all out on their ears,' madame is saying. 'The others complained that it wasn't their fault. I don't care. We'll have a quiet Christmas now. Just the four of us.'

'I was a fool,' Greta tells her. 'I forgot what men are like. I suppose I spent too long out in the forest.'

'We always apologize for them, my dear. Why should we make excuses for those rogues?'

'You say it like we're all the same,' says her husband. 'Some of us are perfect gentlemen, isn't that right, Jacky?'

'Well, none of the ladies are in any danger from me.' When they have stopped laughing, Jacky says: 'Sometimes it's the ladies who are dangerous. Can you remember what to do with a German officer when you're dancing with him, *chérie*?'

'Oh. The right hand round the neck, like this. Pull him close, so he can't see what your hands are doing. Don't panic, I'm not really going to kiss you, monsieur. Then stab with the left, diagonally, up into the heart! Always upwards, so the blade goes under the ribs.'

Clothilde applauds. 'Colonel Colin could not have done it better. Don't try any nonsense with her, Monsieur Jacques.'

When Greta cries out in her sleep that night, it's Jacky who comes and kneels by the bed. He tells her stories of his childhood in Algeria.

The week before Christmas, Greta drives Jacky into Carcassonne. There is snow on the highest hills, but he never looks at the landscape. His eyes and hands are on the Porsche's upholstery, the dials on the dashboard, the chromium sill on the vent window.

They walk a section of the walls, but it is too cold to enjoy. There is an old haunt he wants to visit again, a café with a billiard hall upstairs that used to be popular with American servicemen.

Jacky is the oldest man in the upper room by twenty years, and the only customer in a suit. When he swaggers to the bar for the drinks, he pulls out a fat sheaf of notes and leafs through them. All around, eyes are on him.

He beats Greta at American pool, taking three turns at the table to clear the balls. He is giving her advice all the time. 'Move your hands further down, so the cue is balanced. Now put your head right next to it.'

After he has dispatched the black with a loud whoop of triumph they sit over their drinks, until a short, round man waddles across from the bar and respectfully asks if he can play them for the table. 'It's the house rule,' he says.

Jacky takes on the man alone, shouting like a matador every time he pots a ball. His opponent doesn't like the noise. As the man falls behind, he starts to argue about points of law.

'If you take a free shot,' he says, 'you must nominate the ball you are aiming at.'

'But we are not in America,' says Jacky.

He has two balls left against five and now he's grandstanding. The eight-ball is a long pot into the left corner which he rifles home with his eyes fixed on his tubby little opponent. Jacky throws the cue on to the purple baize and shakes both his fists in the air. Then he walks over to Greta and drains his mug of beer, stroking her face. 'What are you doing?' she asks.

A cash bet is proposed and accepted. The short man's luck improves instantly. Whenever Jacky comes to the table, he finds that the white has wound its way into a difficult position, blocked by his opponent's balls, or resting tight against a cushion so that the cueing is cramped and awkward. Soon, Jacky is a ball behind and no longer showboating. He misses his last pot from a rebound. A thousand francs.

Now it's Jacky who is grumbling. 'How about a frame on the carom billiards table? A gentleman's game.'

'No,' says Greta, 'I'm bored of this now.'

Jacky strolls to the next table – light blue, with no pockets. He sets up three balls and calls out to her, stabbing down on the white to demonstrate the art of advanced cue ball control. She does not go to him. He swears when the ball doesn't end up in the place he is indicating with the tip of the cue. He sounds drunk. Greta tells him she wants to leave.

'Ten thousand,' says the little man.

Jacky's eyes flash, big and white.

'Don't tell me you're scared now,' laughs the man. 'You're the one who wanted the rematch.'

'Twenty,' says Jacky, swallowing hard. 'Twenty thousand.'

And now the balls always go where he wants them to go.

No one follows when they leave, but two boys in their late teens are waiting by the Porsche, fiddling with cigarettes. One is tall, one stocky. Jacky is swaying slightly and singing to himself. Greta is five paces behind, scowling.

Jacky starts when the rangy boy asks him for a light. His hands drop to his trouser pockets. The tall boy spins him round and pulls his jacket down from his shoulders to tie up the arms. 'What happened to her?' says the other boy. 'Where is she, *putain*?'

Greta clubs him round the side of his face with the grip of the Sauer. Everyone hears the eye socket break.

That evening, Jacky sits on her bed while she paces. 'All I am saying is that if you are going to do anything here, Greta, you need to be in Paris or Marseille. Both will be dangerous for you unless someone smooths the way.'

'I'm not wandering around France hurting people while you stand and watch.'

He shrugs. 'I'm not a fighter. I've made my peace with it. It's why I need you.'

'A bodyguard.'

'Not just that. I need a woman, for other things.'

'Is this a seduction now?'

'You're not funny. Don't try to be. I have some projects in mind. I need a woman to pull them off properly. We split everything we make in half, like today.'

'Oh, I see. You're one of those honest thieves.'

He shrugs again, jutting his chin forwards.

'Talk to me like this again,' says Greta, 'like we are the same. As though I am a common criminal. See what happens, little man.'

Relations have improved by Christmas Day, and Jacky insists on spending his share of the winnings from the billiard table on the lunch: two Bresse chickens, cakes for dessert, Tribaut champagne.

Clothilde works fine slices of black truffle under the skin of the chickens then rubs them with olive oil that has been flavoured with the truffle. The twang, sour and earthy at the same time, which permeates the kitchen reminds Greta of the meals Robert cooked for her. She puts the tall shape of him out of her mind with an effort and pours wine for everyone, smiling brightly.

'It's perfect,' says Jacky. 'You can't really taste the truffle after it's cooked. But it gives a depth to everything.'

He never cooks but he knows good food. He has worked in hotels and restaurants in half a dozen countries, although he is reluctant to share the details. He does not like talking about periods of his life in which he was compelled to seek an honest living. Greta forms the impression that these were temporary interludes.

By the time they are picking at the cakes the talk has turned to politics, despite madame's best efforts.

'The French Empire,' says Monsieur Jeannot, 'is dying. And a dying animal is a dangerous thing. It thrashes around in the last throes. It does not care who it injures.'

Greta lapses into silence as the names of men and the acronyms of political parties and coalitions swirl round the table, along with many words she does not recognize.

'I don't know how a foreigner is supposed to keep up with any of this,' says Jacky with a sympathetic glance in her direction. 'What a country. The right-wingers call themselves leftists. The Catholic party calls itself Republican. The Communists want the liberation of all workers – unless they happen to be Algerian.'

'Be positive,' says Clothilde with a smile. 'Even with all this chaos, we have to remember that things are better now than they were a few years ago.'

Jacky's mouth is full, but it doesn't stop him scoffing. 'So the Germans are gone. What about their friends? How many *collabos* in Paris?'

'We can't lock up half of France,' madame tells him gently. 'We have to forgive people eventually.'

'I can't forgive! Do you blame me? When I'm forced to walk past them in the street and look at their faces.'

There is an intensity in him Greta hasn't seen before. The others are giving way before his anger, looking down at the tablecloth.

'What was the word you used a moment ago?' Greta asks. 'When you were talking about the man none of you like.'

'Ah. A *Cagoulard*.'

'What does it mean?'

'A man in a hood. Like those fellows in America. We had them here too.'

'You're talking about the Ku Klux Klan? But in France?'

'Of course. Before the war.' Jacky spears a cube of *clafoutis* with his fork.

'Don't exaggerate,' says Monsieur Jeannot. 'They were not the same, Greta. They did not murder negroes.'

'Mmm. Only Communists,' says Jacky. 'The same philosophy as her.' He indicates Greta with the fork.

'That's enough politics,' says Clothilde.

'Let him talk if he wants to,' says Greta. 'He's a big, tough boy.'

An unpleasant leer has spread over Jacky's face. 'I wonder who killed more Reds – the *Cagoulards*, or you and your rebels?'

'If someone tries to take over my country and hurt my family, I'm going to stand up to them. It doesn't matter if they're Communists or not. What would you do?'

'I wouldn't creep around cutting people's throats. I've seen enough blood for a lifetime.'

'And I have had a bellyful of this kind of talk,' says madame, rapping her knuckles on the table.

'There's no fight left in you,' says Greta. 'That's it, isn't it, little friend?'

Jacky looks at the other three slowly and the sneer fades. Then he snatches up the bottle and refills everyone's glass.

'Clo is right,' says Jeannot, putting an arm round his wife's shoulders. 'No more politics tonight.'

'That's it,' says Jacky quietly as he tops up Clothilde's glass. 'That's it exactly.'

Out of nowhere, the fever makes a comeback. Greta returns to bed for two days, in the dead time between Christmas and New Year. On the third morning her body throbs as if from great exertion, but she bathes and dresses and, looking in the mirror, feels in her marrow that the illness has truly passed at last. No more of this lazing around now, she tells herself severely. There is work to do.

When she walks into the kitchen, Clothilde and Jeannot rise from their chairs at the same time and stand in silence. 'Who has died?' asks Greta.

She knows there can be no mistake about what has happened, but she runs to the barn anyway, in shirtsleeves despite the cutting frost, and stares at the empty space where the Porsche stood. He has even taken the tarpaulin that covered it.

Then Greta is seized with another awful thought and sprints back to the house. The money that was in her satchel is missing too. Jacky has left something on Greta's bedside table next to the bag – a card for a café in Montmartre.

Madame is close to tears. Jeannot tries to press banknotes into Greta's hands, all the cash they keep in the house. He is beside himself. 'That's the last time,' he says to his wife through clenched teeth. 'After this – no more Jacky.' Clothilde cannot form a reply.

Greta accepts two hundred francs – a loan, not a gift. It's enough for the journey to Paris.

There are still tourists willing to sit outside the Café Tabac in Montmartre in the depths of winter. Greta passes them, swaddled in their coats and hats. A middle-aged man, English and wealthy, judging from his brogues and silk scarf, and the silver cigarette case next to the carafe in front of him, is eating with a much younger woman. She is dark, Balkan, undernourished.

A couple blink across a table at two children who are miniatures of themselves. All four wear thick spectacles. They are obviously cold. The woman is unhappy. They all look up when the sash window grinds open above their heads.

'Is that a new suit?' Greta asks him.

'One of three.' Jacky grins down at her, taking in the people dining close by. He is freshly barbered, and the shorter hair and glowing face make him look even more elfin.

When he opens the door on to the street he glances left and right and does not see the pistol until it is almost touching the bridge of his nose.

A gasp ripples around the diners at the nearby tables and some-one swears loudly in English.

'All is well!' laughs Jacky. 'We are old friends. It's a toy gun. She is joking around.'

'There is no joke,' says Greta, calmly and clearly. 'I am going to kill this man.'

The family with the weak eyes have stopped eating to stare at her as one. One of the waiters is on the pavement, arms loaded with plates, looking at Greta open-mouthed.

Jacky pulls her through the door quickly then releases her arm and backs away from her up the stairs, gabbling. He makes it to the third step before she is on top of him, smashing his back on to the sharp edges of the staircase. It knocks the wind out of him, but he manages to talk between gasps. 'Upstairs. I have it all waiting for you.'

It's a handsome place but almost bare of furniture. The leather soles of his new shoes squeak on the wood as he waddles painfully to the table by the biggest window, the one he opened to hail her. There is a pile of cash in the centre, weighed down by a set of car keys.

'You staked my Porsche on a football match.'

'It's not a normal bet. Please don't shoot! So, I put a lot of money on Olympique last month when they were the favourite. But I know they have two of their best players injured. No one else knows it yet. The newspapers haven't heard, okay? When the bookmakers find out the odds change quickly, but it swings too far the other way, when it's a shock. Now Saint-Étienne are a slight favourite, for a while. You have to know when the news is going to come out. I know in advance, and I bet on Green. Now I can't lose either way. It's a small margin so I wager everything I can scrape together. So . . .' She is letting him stand up, finally. 'It's a five per cent profit.' He scratches the back of his head. 'It's your money back, plus twenty-six thousand.'

'And my car is safe somewhere.'

'Wrapped up like a baby. I can explain everything more easily if you put the gun away.' He watches Greta run her thumb down the edge of the pile of thousand-franc notes. 'Give me a week and we double that for you. We split everything down the middle from now on.'

'I can't be in Paris. There are people hunting for me.'

'I have a friend who can fix that. If you're worried about that man from the march in Rivoli, the one you butchered with a knife – wait!'

'How do you know about that? Quickly.'

'You talked about it when you had a fever! You told me many things. I sat up with you every night. I fed you English tea, one sip at a time. Put cold flannels on your head. Don't you remember?'

'I know what you're trying to do, you little reptile.'

'Please put that away. The girl you lack—'

'What?'

'My friend can find people too. The same one who will fix things in Paris for you. He can help with your missing girl.'

The owner of the apartment is away for a month. A childhood friend from Oran, says Jacky. A very dear friend. But on the day they are due to leave, he gets up before dawn and removes all traces of their presence, cleaning and polishing every surface with gloved hands, paying special attention to the door handles.

They stay in a hotel in Sèvres until 30 December, leaving without settling the bill. It's too close to Paris for Greta's liking.

Jacky tells her she is being irrational. 'Every last thing went wrong for me in that city,' she snaps. 'I nearly got two civilians killed. You try it and tell me how you feel afterwards.' She has been making Jacky telephone the hospitals across the city to try to trace Robert. There is no word of a tall Lithuanian man with a head injury.

Monsieur Jacques installs Greta, under protest, in a third-floor apartment in Versailles on New Year's Eve 1951. He leaves her alone all day to pace the empty rooms.

It's late when Jacky returns, bearing bottles and a bag of ice, which he dumps into the kitchen sink. He lines up five glasses on the side while the wine is cooling. The odd firecracker can already be heard, ahead of midnight. You can almost see the courtyard in front of the Palace of Versailles from in here, but Greta stays away from the windows.

'What's wrong with you? You are like a bag of cats. So look – these are all sparkling whites.'

'I told you I don't like Versailles. There's a man I don't want to bump into. He runs a bookshop here.'

Jacky laughs so hard that he is obliged to stop pouring. 'The book guy, of all people. I don't know how you survived here without me.'

'I made a lot of mistakes when I crossed over. I wasn't thinking clearly.'

'*Voilà*. I mix them up and you don't see the labels. First you put them in order, from sweet to dry. Then you tell me what flavours you detect. Fruit, biscuits, *brioche*?'

'I was hoping you were out tracking down Monsieur Balard for me, not buying champagne. Forgive me. Not *stealing* champagne.'

Jacky grins. 'Only one is champagne! That's the game. The others are similar but a quarter of the price. Two Crémants and a Vouvray. You must tell me which one is the real thing.'

Greta passes the glass under her nose as she talks. 'I made the same mistake twice when I first came across. I met two men, one in Germany and one here. I wanted information. Both knew more than they let on. I threatened them but let them go in the end. That's the worst of all worlds. Do you see? To make an enemy and then let them live.'

He is swirling and slurping, making a fish mouth to swallow air along with the wine. But his eyes are on her, unblinking.

'I'm not going to make the same error again,' she goes on. 'If you can't find Balard, I'll go back to both those men and finish those conversations. I'll finish the men if I have to.'

'Greta. You don't understand France yet. You're not going to find any civil servant in their office in Paris at this time of year. I promise you that we will catch up with Balard after the holidays. Now at least try one for me.'

'It's not pretty,' says Greta, holding up her glass to the light. 'But my group has a kind of signature. If a man betrays us, we make two cuts. Here and here.'

'You . . . remove the eyelids?'

'So everyone will know the traitor for what he is. And to remind him too, of course. Every time he feels the urge to blink. It's easily done with a razor, but you need a second man to hold the head still. You are that second man, if we are partners.'

He watches her empty her glass and refills it hastily. Then he raises his own flute and says: 'To us, to Monsieur Balard, and a better year. To 1952.'

Greta swallows the pale-golden wine in one gulp and dashes the empty glass on the floor next to his expensive shoes, making him dance away with a yelp of alarm.

11

'Our scholar,' says Paul Fazi with the puddle in the back of his throat. 'Always hungry for knowledge, isn't it?'

'Ravenous.' Lucien is drumming his fingers on the wheel and willing the lights to change. He has driven them into the centre of Marseille from the north to avoid the Arab neighbourhoods, but they are close to the Porte d'Aix and top of Noailles here.

Two hundred thousand North Africans, he thinks, since the end of the war. The statistic is in all the newspapers. South of this intersection is the biggest immigrant community in France.

'Welcome to hell,' growls Paul, looking in the same direction.

Lucien's eyes rest on a group of men loitering outside a *tabac*. He knows they are Algerian, even from a distance. All bones, with the jackets hanging off them. It's not the hair or the complexion. It's the cut of their suits that gives them away – that baggy, pre-war shape. They wear second-hand clothes and send everything they make back to the old country. They are always in gangs, always men. You never see the women on the street.

'How are you feeling these days, Lulu?'

'Better,' says Lucien. And it's true, he thinks. But that doesn't begin to cover it. How is he feeling, really? *Newborn* is the word that comes to mind. Naked, raw, tender. Thrown into a world of deafening noise and blinding colour, where every surface leaves a bruise.

'You left your gun at the hotel like I told you?'

'Yes, Paul.'

'Too many police around these days. The Arabs make a lot of trouble. Go straight.' He's making the wet sound again. 'This is still ours, between here and the water. This is still France.' He means that the district ahead of them, sloping steeply towards the Old Port of Marseille, remains Corsican in character.

Above the car, struts of wood are jammed between the leaning walls of the tenements. Rotting ship's timbers, propping the whole city up. The streets are narrow. People step aside for the car with an ill grace. Every so often, someone peering in recognizes Paul and shouts a wild greeting.

'I thought you would be angry with me,' says Lucien. 'About the politician in Billancourt.'

'A year ago, I would have been. Lucky for you, your timing is good. We're just about to get him on the hook, and he is never going to wriggle off. You can rough that guy up to your heart's content soon.'

'You're getting your teeth into him.'

'What's that, Crazy?'

'Ange said something about teeth. A joke I didn't get.'

'Sure. The missing teeth. He was talking about an old trick. How do you catch a slippery fish like a crooked politician? The old routines are the best. People don't change, you know, Lulu. It's something you realize as you get older.'

'What are you going to do to that guy?'

'I'm going to put him in my debt. I'll tell you the whole thing another day. One lesson at a time. Answer me this. I'm holding up how many fingers?'

'Jesus. Five.'

'If you can count from one to five,' says Paul, 'you can understand the *milieu*. Say a guy comes to you for wheat. You charge him how much?'

'Five. Five per cent a week. As all the world knows.'

'But let's say you don't have the money to lend. You go to one of your big brothers. You reach out to Ange. He charges you what?'

'All right.' Lucien has to pause. 'Three.'

'So you're borrowing at three per cent and lending it out at five. You're making something. You preserve a small edge. Now think. Ange borrows from who?'

'No one. It's Ange. He's got more wheat than a baker.'

'The big brothers get short, like everyone else, from time to time. And when they run out, they come to the *Caïd*.'

'You?'

'Me. Now what do I charge them – my captains?'

'I have no idea, Paul.'

'Think. Five down to three down to one. It's one per cent a week. Ange doesn't have to Jew me down. It's all I ask. So that he retains a margin too. How could it be otherwise? Everyone needs an edge, or the machine stops spinning. Now think it through. What does it all mean?'

'That the boss can't be greedy.'

'*Voilà*. All that education wasn't wasted. Everything depends on the generosity of the boss. If the *Caïd* becomes greedy, the machine breaks down. Haven't you ever wondered why I'm still at the top of the pile, after all this time?'

'Because everyone is afraid of you, Paul.'

'Stupidity. They're only scared when you are by my side. The people love me. They need my capital and they respect my generosity. Here endeth the first lesson.'

Lucien pulls up opposite a tired bar just off the Place Sadi-Carnot, but Paul waves him on after a minute. 'I don't like it. Too many civilians, and his girl isn't there. We'll come back. Let's eat now.'

There is no need for him to name the venue. They always go to the same place down on the waterfront. The food is indifferent, but the kitchen is fastidiously clean. Paul no longer drinks at lunchtime. He eats like a child instead, wolfing the main meal so they get to the dessert quicker. It's all ice cream, *tatins*, *brûlées* these days. His weight is dropping, despite all the sugar.

'What else?' gabbles Paul beneath mouthfuls. 'Come on. Mmm. It's logic. If everyone is lending and borrowing at the same time, what happens?'

They're in a booth at the back, in shadow. Lucien is on the end of the bench seat so that he can see whoever comes through the entrance.

'It keeps everyone on their toes. Is that what you mean? If I have to pay Ange every week, I can't go easy on any of my debtors. I need to come down hard on them, or it's my neck instead.'

'Sure. That's part of it. Keep going. What kind of cat do you want to lend to, at five per cent a week, if it's your neck on the block?'

Lucien shrugs. 'Guys who can't go to a bank.'

'Surely. There will always be people like that. Our friend round the corner has a police record, owns a bar under a false name. He can't get a bank loan, so he comes to us. Is he a good prospect, though?'

'Vincent? Christ, no. He's a gambler. A real gambler, I mean. He loses.'

'The worst kind of prospect, isn't it? A rat who can't control himself. Who puts his own family in danger. And there will be a hundred rats like this, queuing outside your door, holding their paws out, every week, when you are a man of respect. Are you going to break a thousand fingers a week?'

'If I have to.'

'There he is! My Crazy Horse! It gets boring, though. It gets messy. What do you have to show for it, at the end? You take over a lousy bar that doesn't make money.' He has finished eating at last. He hunches over his coffee, blowing it. A finger quivers in the air. 'Much better to lend money to the kind of man who will pay you back quickly, with interest.'

'And how many of those are out there?'

'Very, very few.' Paul leans forwards and lowers his voice. 'Ask me what it is that I do for a living, Lulu. Really.'

'What do you really do for a living, Paul?'

'I am a *talent scout*.' He slurps at the coffee for effect. 'I spend my life scanning the horizon for people with a talent for earning money. A couple came to see me last month. They work for an

Italian industrialist. He drives the boss around and she takes care of the twins. Beautiful blonde babies. My man has the whole thing worked out. But they need another car, a house to hide out in, where no one can hear the kids crying.'

'Babies,' says Lucien.

'Not literally. I mean, the kids are four or five. Who wants to wipe arses all day? Anyway, you get the idea. These are the kind of people I'm looking for. Ideas, drive. Haven't you ever wondered why we tolerate a man like Jacques Lellouche?'

'The little guy?'

Paul laughs. 'Don't pretend you don't know Jacky.'

'I play cards with him now and again. He knows every way to cheat that has ever been invented. It's an education.'

'But you don't like to shout about it. Because he's a Jew, and a *maricón*, and a crook who can't piss straight. Listen. I had to break his ribs last week. We laid him out on the railway tracks. Jacky Lellouche doesn't respect the rules. You shake hands with him, you check you've still got your watch, isn't it? Why don't I put a bullet through this guy's cheek? Little Jacky?'

'Because he's also an earner.'

'Hallelujah! We put up with all kinds of stupidity. Because they bring in the wheat.'

They sit in the car across the street from Vincent's bar for an hour while it thins out. The crowd is very young: students grabbing a cheap *apéro* before heading off to their parties or rallies or debates. The barman shouts farewells. He is the same age as the customers, dressed in the same American style: checked shirt with the sleeves rolled up, long hair combed back. The son of the owner.

Lucien can see him polishing glasses behind the bar, wiping it down with a cloth. The place is chronically neglected, but the boy is trying to keep everything clean.

There are fresh flowers on the wicker tables along the pavement outside. A woman's touch. Lucien can see her too, sitting at the end of the bar, or the shape of her. A good shape. The son's girl, in a slip dress. She comes every evening, to keep him company while he works. The neon tube in the window that forms the name *Vincent* hides her face. But Lucien can see the effect the girl has on the kid every time he looks over at her.

There are only three customers left when Lucien and Paul walk in. They might be schoolboys, all clustered round the pinball machine.

The Corsican men are like visitors from another world. Older, both dressed in shimmering suits made of mohair and silk. Paul wears a camel overcoat. Lucien's is black, pure cashmere. They are as solemn as undertakers.

The boy behind the bar takes a breath and plants both hands on the polished wood in front as if to steady himself. Lucien has his card out in its leather holder. It identifies him as an employee of the City of Marseille.

'Do you know who I am?' asks Paul, taking the stool next to the girl.

'Yes.'

'My colleague here is head of the department that investigates unlicensed gaming machines.'

The boy looks from one man to the other in honest confusion. 'The *flipper*? But my father paid for the licence.'

'You don't buy a licence and forget about it. You pay a percentage of the takings every week. Your papa let a lot of things slide before he left, Bobby.'

The girl perched on the bar stool next to Paul gives a little hiss when he uses her boyfriend's name. Paul reaches out and touches her affectionately, next to the strap of her dress, and she stiffens. The hand lingers on her bare upper arm.

Lucien has taken up a position by the pinball table, looking over the shoulder of the blond boy who is playing. The lad is a true *flipper* addict, one who saves up the right coins and pays for all the games in advance so that he gets seven for the price of five. That's enough for hours of play for an expert. The two friends bring him drinks so that he does not have to turn away from the flashing lights for an instant.

The machine is decorated with quintessentially American motifs: helmeted football players and a cheerleader brandishing pom-poms, her tight dress made of stars and stripes.

The boy doesn't notice Lucien until he walks round to the side of the pinball table and squats close to it, his fingers gripping the underside. His trousers ride up and show his sock garters. The machine must weigh a hundred pounds. It flies straight up, turns over in the air and crashes down on its side.

Lucien hears a scream from the girl, cut off by Paul's hand. The boy who was playing is still standing in the same spot, looking at Lucien with an odd, troubled expression. The glass tabletop is lying all round his feet in shards. The plug is still in the wall and the flippers are moving. All the signs are in English: One Thousand Points When Lit. The boy's friends are backing towards the front door of the café, but the pinball player holds his ground.

'We are closing early today,' Lucien tells him.

The boy considers this and says: 'But I still have money inside. For three games. No – two.'

'For God's sake, come on.' His friends are edging across the threshold of the café now. They can see what the boy cannot: the distilled murder in the eyes of the man with the geometric face.

Lucien reaches inside his coat carefully and finds his pocketbook. The boy looks at the note Lucien holds out, folded in half. 'It's too much,' the boy says. 'I don't have the right change.'

'What the fuck, Lulu?'

'All right,' Lucien calls to Paul. 'It's all right. I understand him. He is one of those. Everything must be done according to the rules.' Lucien turns to grin at Paul and sees a shape in the door behind the bar, the one that leads to the kitchen. An ugly face pressed against the glass.

Both the men who barge through are North African, in chef's whites. Lucien knows he must not let them out into the broad room, where they will be able to circle round him and attack from both sides. Where the man in front will have the space to swing with the meat cleaver that is in his hand.

The gap in the bar is on the right, at the other end from where Paul is now on his feet, arms round the struggling, whimpering girl.

Lucien hits the first man with a wooden chair before he can get through the gap. It's a chair at first, anyway, until it breaks apart in his hands, and then he uses the leg as a spear, stabbing at the North African man's eyes and windpipe with the splintered end. Then his spear hand is empty, and he grabs the arm wielding the cleaver with it. He throws clubbing punches with his free hand.

The second chef is trapped behind his friend. He climbs on to the bar and is about to leap down when Lucien grabs his trouser turn-up and yanks the leg out from under him. The man catches the edge of the bar as he falls and cries out.

Lucien was obliged to let go of the one with the cleaver and now he must retreat, allowing the man to come out from behind the bar into the empty room.

The Arab slashes the air with his weapon. His feet crunch through the broken glass. There is the beginning of a smile on his face. Now he has the space to hack properly.

Lucien takes out his stiletto and lets the man see the Moor's Head. He holds it with the blade pointing out of the bottom of his fist, so he can still punch with the knife hand. The heels of his shoes grate against the floorboards as he widens his stance and rotates his feet. It's as though he is screwing himself into the floor. Whatever happens now, he will not take another backward step.

The man with the cleaver looks into Lucien's eyes, searching for fear, finding none. He turns to look at his companion, who has one hand on the central section of the bar and is trying to pull himself up from the floor. Paul is on the far left, gripping the girl's shaking shoulders with both hands. The young bartender is crouching, peering over the bar at the man with the meat cleaver. He shouts a word in Arabic. The chef makes a dash for the front door. Lucien lets him go.

The other man in whites has made it on to one knee now. Both hands are reaching up to grip the edge of the bar. Lucien walks over and sets himself in a leisurely way, then kicks the man in the side of the head. The others turn away instinctively at the sound of the impact.

'Don't trouble yourself,' says Lucien, between gasps. He bends over, his head almost touching the glass shards on the floorboards. His heart is drumming against his chest. 'You just leave it all to me.'

'I knew you could handle them. Come. Our young friend will pour us all a drink. Perrier for me, brandy for everyone else.'

It takes a while because the bartender's hands are trembling. Paul kneads the girl's shoulders while he watches him perform the operation.

Paul checks the rim of the glass for cleanliness then raises it to Lucien, and they drink at the same time, eyes locked. The boy hesitates but follows suit when Paul motions at him. Only the girl refuses the glass offered to her.

'Listen and attend,' Paul tells the boy. 'Your father cannot pay his debts, so you are on the hook. It's how much, Crazy?'

'Five per cent a week. Arrears are added on to the initial sum.'

'You are already a long way behind, Bobby. We're getting into what kind of territory, Lulu?'

'Finger.'

'The tip of a finger, let's say. We are not greedy. You can lay your hand out on the bar now and close your eyes. Alternatively . . .' He squeezes the girl's shoulder blades with his fingers so hard that she grimaces with discomfort. 'You give me exactly one minute with . . .'

'*Ow*. Monique.'

'With Monique.'

A car is pulling up to the pavement outside. Lucien strides to the window and glowers at the two police constables in their 4CV. He stands under the neon sign so they can see his face. Two young men with moustaches in stiff caps. The driver recognizes him and raises a hand quickly in acknowledgement. The tyres squeak as the car pulls away.

Lucien goes back to the bar and reaches for the brandy bottle. Both Paul and the girl are looking at the bartender, waiting for a decision. The boy's eyes are on his shoes.

'You have to say it out loud,' says Paul. 'So that everyone knows you are in agreement. A minute of Monique. It's got a nice ring to it. You can time it on your watch. Or you spread your hand on that bar.'

The boy mumbles something.

'I can't hear you, Bobby.'

'All right. One minute.'

'Start counting.'

Paul slides off the stool and tears at the buttons that run down the back of Monique's dress. The girl tries to pull away and he clamps a hand over her mouth from behind, trapping the beginning of a high, keening wail. No one was expecting him to be this rough with her.

'*Voilà.*' He rips the buttons off and jams the girl against the bar, using his body to pin her in position so he can claw at her bra strap. She doesn't make it easy for him. She has some spirit, thinks Lucien.

Paul drags the girl away from the bar with an effort, so the boyfriend can see her chest is bare under the dress. He is staring at Paul's hands as they reach under the loose fabric and scoop up the girl's breasts greedily. Paul's face is pressed hard against her neck. He whispers to her constantly. She closes her eyes.

'That's it,' says Lucien. 'That's your minute.'

'Is he watching?' Paul can hardly talk through the sound of spittle that has collected in the back of his throat. 'Is he getting it?'

'I said that's enough,' says Lucien, louder. Paul is lost in the girl, squeezing and kneading her, snuffing up her scent. Lucien slaps his empty glass on the surface of the bar so hard that it shatters under his hand. '*Putain.* It's enough.'

'*Eh bien.*' Paul is panting, showing his tongue. He lets the girl tear herself free of him. She turns and shrieks at all the men, a string of meaningless syllables. She tugs the straps of the dress back up over her shoulders. Then she breaks and scampers through the gap in the bar. Lucien is expecting her to slap the boyfriend's face on her way, but she pushes past him towards the kitchen door without acknowledging him in any way. Bobby's eyes have returned to the floor.

'That buys you a month,' Paul tells him, behind a trembling forefinger. 'Then the repayments start. Unless you deliver your father. Give him to me and I wipe out your debt. Have a think about that.'

Lucien is wrapping his hand with a paper towel from the bar as they leave. There's a deep cut across the knuckles.

'What were you looking at outside, Lulu? Police?'

'Ours.'

'This town! There is nowhere on earth like it.' Paul pauses to take an extravagant sniff of the air of Marseille before he climbs into the passenger seat. 'What did you make of the lesson?'

'Fucking wonderful.' Lucien is feeling around the knuckles gingerly, checking for breaks in the small bones.

'You weren't paying attention. You didn't look at the son's face. You can beat a guy like plaster, and he forgets all about it in a couple of weeks. Or maybe he comes back at you. But *that*' – he gestures at the bar with a hooked thumb – 'is how you take a guy's manhood away for ever. From now on, that boy will pay up as regularly as a government bond. Always learning, isn't it? Aren't you happy?'

'Ecstatic.'

Paul's fingers are round Lucien's jaw and he is looking into his cousin's angry red face, checking the swelling. 'You were always like this, after a rugby game.' He slaps Lucien gently. 'I don't get my fingernails dirty often these days, Crazy Horse. I show you how it's done this time, but you do the next one. How is the hand?'

'Nothing. A cut.'

'Look at me. You do the next one yourself. I need to know you're not soft with women. We can't afford it, Lulu. We can't be weak with half the human race. Understand? Here endeth the last lesson of the day. You can thank your professor later. We'll eat someplace different tonight.'

12

'I can dress her up like a beautiful woman,' says Romana, 'but will she ever *feel* like one?'

'She must learn to pretend.' Jacky is padding around the big room in a slow circle. 'Like the rest of us.'

'For God's sake, get on with it,' says Greta, snapping her fingers for the next dress. She is in practical underwear in the middle of an unheated workshop on the edge of Nanterre, under the steel rafters of a high ceiling. Her teeth are beginning to chatter.

She slips fifteen garments over her head in quick succession, none of them warm. Slim sheath dresses with high necklines and gowns that leave the shoulders exposed and thin cotton pieces with bold checked patterns. Christian Dior is the only name she recognizes from the labels.

'That one is for summer,' says Romana, 'but you are going to the south. Anyway, I make everything now, for the whole year. It doesn't matter about fashion. I need to see the different shapes. What suits you, what doesn't.'

They nag Greta into parading in front of a mirror that covers a full third of the longest wall, between expanses of bare white brick. There are high windows on the opposite side of the room and a bank of sewing machines under hanging ceiling lights, where Romana will sit after the others leave.

She will stay all weekend, copying the pieces selected for Greta. She will go back to Paris and return the original garments to their hangers in the shop on the Rue du Faubourg Saint-Honoré before it opens on Monday morning. The kind of handbag Greta likes is trickier to copy, and Romana does not work with leather. They will have to wait for the bag.

Romana's face creases into a sympathetic smile as she follows Greta's progress in front of the glass.

Jacky whistles with derision. 'Like a boxer striding to the ring.'

'Well how the fuck am I supposed to walk?'

'Look at your elbows. They stick out at the sides. That's how a man carries himself. Now point the elbows backwards. Keep them tucked into your body. See how it makes you stand up straight and stick your chest out? Not too much, you don't need to put our eyes out with those. Keep walking, slowly. Relax. Elbows back, let the arms hang. Now. You're a woman.'

'I never noticed the elbow thing before,' says Romana.

'If you want to know how a racehorse runs, you don't ask the horse. Not too much, Greta, we're not on the Place Blanche!'

'What does he mean?'

'It's where you find the most beautiful *poules*,' smiles Romana. 'But they didn't start out as girls. They exaggerate everything.'

Jacky claps his hands. 'Better. Now walk like a cat. Put one foot where the last one was. Imagine a single line of prints in the snow.'

'What is he talking about now?'

'He means swivel your hips. That's it!'

Jacky has lapsed into silence, watching keenly with his chin resting on his fist. 'Can you do something with the rest of it, Romana? I can't see past the hair. She's like an Orthodox housewife in a bad wig. The kind of woman my mother wanted for me.'

He skips down the fire escape to the *tabac* to see if the man they have been trying to meet since the New Year has returned any of their calls. When he comes back Romana has applied make-up to Greta's face and is painting her fingernails, murmuring instructions. Leave a gap on each side of the nail and it appears longer. Romana stands back and runs her fingers through the dyed black roots, picking up handfuls of hair and letting them fall again.

'Who is she, Jacky?'

'If you knew her real name, darling, she would have to kill you.'

'I mean who is she when you go away tomorrow? Who is she going to be?'

'Ah.' He is standing off Greta's shoulder so he can see her face in the mirror. He props his jaw on his knuckles again. 'So, she is going to be an actress for me.'

Greta is a star of the Swedish stage, no less, recently recruited by one of the Hollywood studios and in need of suitable accommodation for the summer. It's another patriotic war film, set during the German occupation of Greece, with Provence standing in for Crete.

You don't flirt with the man who owns the villa, says Jacky. You are a higher order of being. The role of everyone around you is to try to please you in all things. Keep that at the front of your mind and they will fall into that role.

The owner invites her to begin her tour on the ground floor. 'No,' she tells him, unsmiling. 'The view first. If the view is bad, the rest doesn't matter.' The owner indicates a flight of marble stairs and he and Jacky hurry after Greta, watching her legs and hips rotate in the tight sheath dress as she mounts the marble stairs.

She sits on the sun terrace and glares at the owner expectantly until he snaps to attention and offers her a drink. 'A Perrier,' she purrs, rewarding him with the first smile of the day. Then, to Jacky: 'My cigarettes.' She doesn't quite click her fingers.

Jacky is dismayed, patting himself down. He has left them in the car. He will run to fetch them for madame. He will let himself back in if it is convenient? The owner blinks at him, bewildered by the sudden flurry of demands. He is in his sixties, sleek and tanned, a little slow. 'The front door key,' asks Jacky, 'if I may.'

The owner fetches water and then it is a business of questions, an infinity of them. Who are the neighbours? Will they respect her privacy? Where does one bathe?

They climb the last staircase to the roof garden: bushes of lavender, alive with bees, and palms in vast pots. Could the lease be extended for a whole year? Could a swimming pool be installed, temporarily? Questions of money never arise.

Jacky finds them eventually, breathless and full of apology, jingling the house keys on their ring. He could not see them up on the roof. She tells him the desire to smoke has passed now. They have another appointment, but she is content to linger for a while, shading her eyes and taking in the view.

When they leave, Jacky opens the passenger door of the Porsche for her and says: 'Well done. That was outstanding.'

'How did you get on?'

'It was exactly where I thought it would be. A safe from the last century. You can hear the wheels clicking like this.' He snaps his fingers loudly. It takes him a while to locate first gear and then he pulls away, not too fast.

'How much?'

'Ah. Not too much cash. But some valuable items. We'll have to see what it comes to.' They are at the next junction before he realizes her eyes are still boring into the side of his head. 'What? I said we'll see. Whatever we make, we split down the middle. You don't trust me?'

'No. Stop grinding the gears.'

'Exceptional! Don't trust anyone. You are learning fast.'

They stay in the far south for a week, in a tiny flat in Hyères. The beaches and promenades are empty in January, and Jacky tells her it's safe to walk the streets openly. 'This is where Krivitsky hid from the Russians, after he changed sides. You know Krivitsky?'

'I know of him. Why did he come here?'

'No Communist can operate this far down. The *milieu* is too strong, in Toulon, in Marseille. The Corsicans don't suffer any rivals. I wonder what it is about islands. The Sicilians in America, the Corsicans here. Who do they have in London? In that district that is like Pigalle?'

Greta has to think. It's been a while. 'The place is called Soho. I think the gangsters are Maltese.'

'There you go. It's always the islands.'

Then Jacky tells her incredible stories of the Corsican *parrains*. How the men of respect helped the Allies roll on to the beaches of the Côte d'Azur in 1944. How they broke the strikes around the docks in forty-seven, when Washington feared France would become the first country in Western Europe to fall to the Reds. The Americans have protected the lords of the southern underworld ever since.

'They sound like useful men to know,' says Greta.

His smile is thin-lipped, that of a tolerant parent correcting a child. A palm steals towards the middle of his chest but does not touch it. 'My dear. They are killers.'

Romana's dresses have suddenly made all Greta's other garments look stained and faded and ragged beyond endurance. She is seeing the squalor of her former self for the first time. She isn't ready for a busy town yet, so she gives Jacky money. He returns with cotton blouses, black plimsolls, white canvas shoes, a pea coat in blue melton and a pair of thick cashmere sweaters.

She runs barefoot in the morning, when the beaches are empty, in the Breton sweater and cropped trousers she borrowed from Robert. The girls setting out the tables outside a seafront café look at her curiously as she sprints up and down the same stretch of sand, six times, seven, eight. Her lung capacity has not returned to normal after the illness.

When she returns to the flat with the bread and newspapers, Jacky takes her head and kisses her brow, before recoiling in disgust.

'You are like a carthorse, covered in foam.'

'Women don't sweat. We perspire. No, wait. What is it? We glow.'

'Well, you are glowing like a whore in the front row of the church. So, I have news.'

'He called?'

'Monsieur Balard left a message for me this morning.' He can't help seizing her shoulders. 'He has agreed to a meeting, at last. We are going back to Paris!'

*

They take the mountain road through Gap. The car devours the sharp corners, relishing the challenge. Greta insists on stopping at Verdon to look down into the gorges while Jacky sulks in the passenger seat.

'We have to get to the shop before they take their lunch break,' he grumbles.

'This country means nothing to you, does it? I've never seen you glance out of the window once.'

'I am a son of the desert. That is my idea of beauty. I'll go back to the desert when all this is over.'

Old Benoit does not let anyone into the shop unless his son is with him. One waits behind the glass counter while the other unlocks the heavy door, taking a good look at the customers in the process. No more than two are allowed in the shop at once.

There are few browsers on the streets of Grenoble today. The east wind has a knife in its hand. The handful of pedestrians who pass the front window, with its serried ranks of necklaces and Swiss watches, are frowning above raised collars.

So it is that Benoit and Son are pleased to see Jacques Lellouche in a good suit, hopping from one foot to another and rubbing his hands, but braving the cold to take an apparently urgent interest in the tray of diamond rings on the right side of the display.

When Jacky knocks at the door, the son is already waiting to slide back the bolts. Greta, slumped in the passenger seat of the Porsche on the other side of the square, can just about see Jacky's shape as he stands in front of the counter.

She's fussy, he will be saying. It must be a princess cut, nothing round or oval. After all, the girl is a princess herself. Behind the counter, father and son will smile sympathetically. Men who have been in love themselves. She has an eye for diamonds, says Jacky. There must not be even a trace of yellow. He does not glance at the prices on the white labels.

With a wink, Benoit *père* produces something from under the counter – a leather box with more rings inside, sitting on a silk cushion. These are the best we have, he says. The best you will find anywhere in the east of France. The stones begin at a clean carat and go up to five. Jacky handles the biggest diamonds respectfully. Now he checks the price tags but does not react to them.

He will fetch the girl, he says, and return immediately. It would be nice to surprise her, but one does not make a mistake with a thing like this. She will wear it for the rest of her life – with a bit of luck! Everyone laughs as Jacky dashes out.

The son waits by the door for twenty minutes before putting on his hat and a heavy tweed coat. They can't hear him, but they know what he will be saying. Another window shopper. Full of talk. He is going for lunch.

When Jacky knocks on the glass panel in the front door five minutes later, with Greta in his wake, the sign says the shop is closed. They watch the old man emerge from the back room.

Benoit comes to the door but shakes his head and taps his watch. He cannot let them in until his son returns, he says loudly. He raises a hand in the air to illustrate the younger man's height.

Jacky is nodding sympathetically. He understands the old man's predicament. He glances at his own watch and runs a palm over his face in agitation. They do not have much time.

Wait! A finger in the air: a flash of inspiration. Mademoiselle can look on her own. He pats the young woman's shoulders, grinning, emphasizing her slightness.

Then he mimes a twist of the steering wheel. He will leave his betrothed here while he goes to fetch their car. Greta smiles demurely at the old man through the thick glass. Jacky is already backing away from them, ignoring the jeweller's protests. They both watch him run across the square, waving a hand.

The fiancée stands before Benoit, biting her lip. The old man's face relaxes. A good sort of girl, he will be thinking. She is clutching a small satchel in her gloved hands. She seems nervous. Doesn't like being left alone with a stranger. The old man sighs and reaches up to unbolt the door.

Standing in front of the counter, Greta is careful to keep her body between the pistol in her hand and the shop window.

Benoit disclaims all knowledge of a special stash of rings until she touches his Adam's apple with the tip of the barrel and begins to count.

'You are very striking,' the old man tells her, watching her pluck the rings from the silk backing. He has recovered himself quickly. The voice is steady. 'How long do you suppose it will be before the police catch up with you?'

'*La Cagoule*,' says Greta. It takes a few seconds to hit home. Then his eyes flare and he breathes in sharply. 'The *Cagoule* in thirty-seven,' she tells him. 'The *Milice* in forty-three. You were up to your neck in both. We have documentary evidence. That is why I can afford to be so striking, monsieur. Because you are not in a position to call the police.'

She walks across the square, not too quickly. Everything is as calm as Jacky promised it would be. There are no alarm bells at her back. He is in the Porsche with the engine running and the heater on.

'It's like I told you. There's no hurry. We could stay and have lunch.'

'Let's get out of here, for God's sake. Did I say everything right? *Cagoule*? *Milice*?'

'Perfect.' She hands the satchel to him while she starts the engine and he peeks inside, groaning with pleasure at the sight of the rings. He kisses her cheek impulsively. 'Like always.'

The Paris landmarks do not open to visitors until half past nine. Greta arrives at the Arch before eight and a pair of oriental men are waiting for her with arms crossed at the top of the stairs that lead down to the tunnel. One man stays in position while the other opens the metal concertina door and leads her down the steps. Rows of electric lights are burning all along the tunnel, just for her.

She struggles to keep up with the guard as he bounds up the spiral staircase that winds up to the terrace on top of the Arch. The heels of his shoes have been repaired with metal wedges and they clang and spark against the steel plates on the steps.

And then she is on the roof of the city, far above the grime. The sun is stronger up here. The grey-bearded man waiting for her has his hands in his pockets, facing the Avenue de Wagram. He looks like an English gentleman in a covert coat and bright paisley silk scarf.

'Jacky told me you could be theatrical,' she shouts above the breeze. Balard raises an eyebrow. A curious, amused face, long and dog-like. He is bareheaded. He was handsome once.

'I hope you appreciate the symbolism. We are at the gateway to Paris. And here is another barbarian, banging on the door and asking to be let in.' He says it with a twinkle as he looks her up and down. She is in one of Romana's dresses, a light tweed, closely tailored. His pleasure in her appearance is obvious, but he is not the kind of man who allows his eyes to linger provocatively on a woman's chest or hips. 'We had the Vikings, then the Protestants, then the Germans. Now come the Lithuanians. Do we let you pass?'

'I was hoping you might.'

'The consequences of disappointing you terrify me, young lady. What else did Jacky say about me?'

'That you two met in the Resistance.'

'And can you understand what that signifies? The kind of bond that we share?'

'I am a *résistante* too. I would die for my comrades at home.'

'And yet you left them behind. Here you are in Paris, in the sunshine.' He turns from the railing to face her and pulls his coat open with a gloved hand, allowing it to rest on his hip in a lordly sort of gesture, like an English barrister pomping in front of a jury. Greta tries to meet his piercing, unsettling gaze. She watches his features soften into a smile. 'What else does Jacky say about me? Does he call me a zealot?'

'No, Monsieur Balard.'

'People sometimes accuse me of being a fanatic. A kind of crusader. It is unjust. I happened to have a ringside seat during the drama of 1947, that is all. Does the year mean anything to you?'

'No. I'm sorry.'

'Picture it: France ablaze with strikes and demonstrations.' His eyes sparkle again, and he chuckles. 'I am making a joke. It is always like that here. But you must imagine it ten times worse than usual. I sat in my office for a week, waiting for another government to collapse. There was a loaded pistol in my desk drawer. On the Friday, my colleagues in domestic intelligence stopped answering the telephone. I shoved my way through crowds of men flying the hammer and sickle. It took an hour to reach the Rue Nélaton.'

He flashes his eyebrows to see if she understands and Greta shakes her head. 'Pardon my ignorance.'

'The headquarters of the service that busies itself with the internal security of Metropolitan France. That is the DST. Not my SDECE. Not the *Sûreté Générale*, nor yet the intelligence directorates of the national police, nor the Paris police. And definitely not to be confused with either of the agencies that carry out surveillance on behalf of our minister for the colonies. Will you remember all of that?' They both laugh.

'I found the DST building entirely undefended. I strolled in without challenge and went up to the sixth floor and found my opposite number throwing all the files in his office out of the window. They were making a bonfire down in the yard. They believed it was the end – the new Fourth Republic would fall to Communism that very evening. The men who were supposed to be guarding the doors had left their posts to join the protestors.'

'I had no idea.'

'Very few people understand how close we came to another revolution here. That is why I take a strong line on the Reds. I make no apology for it. Now, leaving out details of serious crimes, tell me about yourself.'

'What can I say?' Greta begins. 'I too am an enemy of Stalin.'

He has a talent for quiet. She knows the ploy, but its power is irresistible. You talk to fill the silence of the interrogator.

'The Lithuanians are a brave people,' she tells him. 'But we need guns. There will always be willing hands. It's a question of filling them with steel.'

'Logistics,' says Balard.

'I knew the men they sent after me were no good. They looked like pensioners. They did not have time to make a proper plan and get the right resources in place.'

'Indeed.'

Greta drops the names of Soviet officials known to be running the counter-insurgency effort in Lithuania. She hints that Laima could provide an ally with a list of all such names and a detailed biography on each if her release from prison could be contrived.

She does not mention her conviction that someone in the British Secret Intelligence Service has betrayed the Baltic resistance networks. This is a gem that must not be yielded up cheaply.

'I'm talking too much,' she says. 'And it's your fault, monsieur. An old trick.'

Balard is at his most canine when he grins. He is still smiling when he says: 'Tell me why I should not have you arrested and thrown in prison.'

Greta swallows. 'I didn't kill anyone on that day. It was a deliberate decision. I held back, out of respect for you. For the French authorities, I mean.'

'You severed a man's hamstrings,' says Balard, 'along with both his Achilles tendons. Very deliberately. Then you carved a curious design on his cheek. He was a retired policeman who had spent the best years of his life serving as a guardian of the peace in Paris. So. Now. I see you have mislaid your tongue.'

After a long pause, Greta says: 'It never occurred to me for a moment that they would be real police officers.'

For a while, the face of Balard is that of a hanging judge. Then all the gravity dissolves, and he gives a bellowing laugh. 'Why on earth would it occur to you? Or to anyone who comes from a place where sanity holds sway? How can you be expected to understand France? Where a young immigrant from Russia can carve out an exemplary career with the Paris Prefecture of Police while remaining a lifelong agent of the Soviet Union. I am not altogether sure that he bothered to keep it a secret. He was involved in at least two kidnappings of White Russian émigrés before the war, to my certain knowledge. What a country!'

'Where is he now?'

'In a convalescent home for policemen on the Opal Coast. He is confined to a wheelchair. I do not know if he will walk again. What was that mark you scratched on his face, out of interest?'

'The Double Cross. The symbol of Lithuania. I was hoping it would get back to Moscow. A message for Maxim Karpov.'

'Telling him to back off and leave you alone?'

'Warning him not to send a pair of fucking pensioners next time.'

The laughter of Balard is so loud that the ants below them, scurrying to their jobs in the shops and hotels of the Champs, can surely hear the sound spiralling down from the top of the triumphal Arch. 'And do you know where the Walrus is, monsieur? The second man escaped uninjured, despite my best efforts.'

'A walrus! Very good. Your Walrus has taken to the sea. Fled the jurisdiction. He is also a former policeman, and well known to me. His description has been circulated widely and if he returns to France he will be arrested immediately. You need have no fear on that account.'

'What will you do with him if he turns up?'

Balard pouts. 'Drop him down a mineshaft. Hand him over to you.'

'You would do that?'

'If I am feeling generous. If we become friends.'

His eyes sweep Greta again, and she has the uncomfortable feeling of being subject to a cold, scientific scrutiny. There is nothing prurient in his gaze. He might be guessing her height and weight and measurements with a view to filing them away in an official record later.

'The first case I handled was that of a Baltic woman,' he says. 'A pretty Estonian. Perhaps not *quite* in your league. She was seducing our air force officers on behalf of the Abwehr. It turned out that Stalin had his claws in her too, as so often. I am afraid I alerted her German masters to the duplicity. She lost her head at Plötzensee.'

'Lost her head?'

'To a Prussian axeman, in February 1935. I suppose they use the guillotine now. Some things change. Some things do not. I have never forgotten that young Estonian. Pretty women from the east still make me uneasy.'

He turns away from Greta and rests his forearms on the iron railing, looking out. 'This is a clock face. Do you follow? We are in the middle. Twelve streets branch off from the Arch. Wagram is at one o'clock. This is not really one of the gates. The closest is over there: the Porte Maillot. You have already passed the ancient boundary of the city.'

He waits to see if she catches the meaning, then they both smile at the same time. 'Feel free to enjoy Paris again. Perhaps we will be friends later. There is plenty of work here if you want it. But all in good time.'

'I need friends, monsieur. And money, and guns. I want to go back to Lithuania and continue the fight.'

'Then you should meet some of the other barbarians who have made their homes here.' He smiles at her confusion. 'One or two of the Americans who infest Paris specialize in that kind of adventure. Oh, I am not the jealous type! I will introduce you.'

'Thank you. That is more than I hoped for.'

'You are surprised? I am a realist. This is the American century. Do you know who prevented the Communists from taking over in 1947? Mr Caffery, the US ambassador, with one sentence. *No Reds in the cabinet, or no more Marshall Plan.* The coalition government suddenly found some courage. Money talks, and on that occasion it spoke decisively, with a pronounced southern American twang.'

'I do not know what to say, monsieur.' Greta can feel herself blushing. He extends a hand and she takes it, feeling cold leather. Before she releases her grip, she says: 'I need to ask one more thing of you. There is a girl.'

13

Monsieur Balard has started to make those sighing, wincing noises when he settles himself into low seats. Getting old, thinks Lucien. A grey wolf now. Still a wolf.

His master asks the Indochinese driver to get out and leave them alone in the back for a moment. 'If you would be so kind, Monsieur Trinh. Stay close by, please. Thank you so much.'

The older man wrings his hands. It was supposed to be fifteen degrees today. It is cold at the top.

'Well, it was her all right. There cannot be two of them, with those green eyes. She is smaller than I expected. Have you seen her close up?'

'Not yet,' says Lucien.

'I wonder why she is in France at all. Trained by Special Operations Executive, but she does not go back to Britain for help. There is more to the story than she wanted to reveal.'

'Sir,' says Lucien.

'The British again. May God protect us from our allies. I wonder how much you have heard about their antics in the Levant? Or in Madagascar?'

'Nothing, sir.'

'Ha! You will, in due course. It is in the interests of both sides to keep it out of the newspapers. France does not wish to appear weak. The gentlemen do not want their low cunning exposed to the world. A thieves' agreement. Talking of which, our woman has fallen in with Jacques Lellouche, of all people. I do not know if that helps us or not. I suppose it means you can get him to introduce you to her. Or is Jacky out of favour?'

'No more than usual. Lellouche is always trouble. They give him a beating now and again. But he earns money. If you earn money, all is forgiven.'

'So that is the rule,' says Balard, grinning. He finds it exciting to talk about the *milieu*. His personal life is famously dull. Like De Gaulle, he has never taken a mistress.

'Keep an eye on her, will you? It may be that she has fallen out with the British. I might throw her something small if the right job comes up. She will want to impress me. She needs money and she is desperate to meet the *Amerloques*.'

'I can imagine, sir.'

'She says she is looking for a missing girl. Another Lithuanian. I did not get the whole story. Make of it what you will. It could be nonsense.'

'A girl. I'll remember that, sir.'

'All off the books, Lucien. You understand?'

He clears his throat. 'Am I on the books yet, sir?'

'My dear young man! You will receive a special military pension from the twenty-eighth of this month. I dictated the letter myself this morning. I trust you were not expecting an identity card and a gun in a ceremonial holster.'

'It's becoming harder to stay out of trouble,' says Lucien. 'Paul is expecting ever more of me. The talk is of serious crime.'

'Armed robberies and the like?'

'That kind of thing, sir. If you read my last report—'

'As impressive as ever, Lucien. You are compiling quite an encyclopaedia of the underworld. The location of the heroin factories is certainly valuable information.'

'What about the women, sir?'

Balard smiles indulgently. 'If you are talking about building a criminal case against your cousin, it would be better to stick to narcotics. It is hard to interest our prosecuting judges in prostitution.'

'Paul buys and sells these girls like livestock.'

'I am sympathetic, Lucien, but you must remember that brothels were legal here but five years ago. Judges are old men, like me. We find it hard to adjust to a changing world. Narcotics and banditry, I think, will prove more fruitful avenues for investigation.'

'What happens if they ask me to take part in a robbery, sir?'

'One needs to earn money in that world. Isn't that what you said? Your task is to penetrate the organization as deeply as possible, Lucien. Do whatever is necessary to maintain your cover. If you can keep these escapades outside Paris, so much the better.'

'What if I'm arrested?'

'Do not get arrested. If someone hinders you while you are on official business, you ring a telephone number which the gentleman waiting outside will dictate to you before you go. Memorize it. Do not write it down. You say nothing about me to the police or any other employee of the French state. Call that number and everything will be taken care of, from an official perspective.'

And then you drop me, thinks Lucien. Is that it? You drop me like a coffin in the fucking ocean. A military pension, so that there is no paper trail linking you to me. If I screw up, we never met.

'But you do not need any advice from me about keeping your mouth shut,' Balard is saying, with a grin.

'No, sir. I'm Corsican. Not Sicilian. We don't talk.'

'Ha! No need for a service pistol either then. Or I hope not. If you are the kind of man who has difficulty sourcing firearms, I have made a serious error of professional judgement.'

'There's no difficulty,' says Lucien. 'There's no error.'

'Shake my hand then. It is all I have to offer. Welcome to *Service Action*. There are no rituals. What is it again, a picture of your patron saint? And you set fire to it, do you not?'

'That's the Sicilians, sir.' Lucien is opening the door to get out. The Indochinese man is ten yards away from the car with his back to them, his hands linked behind him, slowly turning his head from one side to the other as the ordinary people pass by on the pavement.

*

The next time Lucien picks the girl up from the party house, she's still drunk or drugged from the night before. When he arranges her gently across the back seat she lunges up for a kiss, but he dodges it. He isn't sure Marie remembers who he is, until he asks about the recent ministerial appointments and she laughs and says, 'I told you so.'

'I have a television set in my room.' She is slurring her words but talking in complete sentences. 'I watch all the politics programmes. Don't you have one?'

'No. Only the radio. They were talking about Hannachi this morning, Marie.'

'That television was a present. I keep all the gifts now. I'm the only girl with that privilege. It's a special term I negotiated. I have a Hermès scarf for every day of the week.'

'Djamel Hannachi,' says Lucien, 'the Algerian leader. They were talking about whether the authorities will put him under house arrest.'

'They won't. They'll detain him then let him go quickly. They want him out and about, so the thugs can get at him. Didn't you know that?'

He thinks she's going to try to kiss him again when they reach the end of the journey, but she spits in his face suddenly, then laughs uproariously. He raises her dark glasses carefully and the eyes are rolling behind them.

What am I doing, thinks Lucien. What am I doing with her?

The trouble is that whatever the girl says always comes true.

She doesn't attend the next *partouze* because the following day is the third Sunday of the month, when she has her medical checks. Paul sends another inmate from the house instead, a young Eurasian girl.

Lucien is parked on the other side of the street, one hand dangling from the window, when Marie comes out of the residential building with the brass plate.

'I go back on my own on the train, after the doctor,' she tells him, standing in the road and leaning down. She looks very pure and sober.

'I'm not a thug,' says Lucien. 'I'm not who you think I am.' He realizes he is trembling.

He has taken a suite in a tourist hotel in the fifteenth. They send up two plates under cloches and half a litre of pinot noir. 'I am only allowed salad at lunchtime,' the girl says in a tiny voice. She suddenly seems unbearably young.

'Who is going to find out, Marie?'

She doesn't know what to do with the hamburger. She is about to cut it in two with her knife and fork until she sees him pick his up with his hands. The meat is rare in the middle. Unctuous, bloody pools form on their plates.

'Tell me about Algeria,' says Lucien.

She is licking her fingertips. 'It's the next thing. Indochina finishes soon. Then it's Algeria.'

'There are two hundred thousand French Union soldiers in Indochina, Marie.'

'It won't end this year. It will be nineteen fifty-three or fifty-four. Everyone knows that Algeria is coming. They need to save their strength for that.'

'Then why not pull out of Indochina now?'

Her deep laugh. 'American money. They want to squeeze every last dollar out of Truman before they admit it's a lost cause. The money trickles down and everyone holds a bucket out to catch some for themselves. Paul, the generals, everyone.'

'Tens of thousands,' says Lucien. 'Tens of thousands of men have died out there. We are not going to give up just like that.' His face is becoming hot. 'How are you so sure about all these things anyway?' He says it angrily, without thinking. He knows the answer. The men tell her.

When he takes his hands away from his face, she is very close and her eyes are enormous.

'If you really want to kiss,' says Lucien, 'I won't be able to say no. I'm not that strong. But I won't be able to trust you either.'

'You still think I'm spying on you!'

'Paul does nothing but test me. He threw me into a bar fight in Marseille. He made sure I didn't have a gun when I went in there.'

'You're paranoid. How can I be a spy when it's me that does all the talking? When do I ask you for anything in return?'

'I've already told you my secret, Marie. I'm not like the others.'

'That's what every man has said to every woman since the beginning of time. Shall I tell you something crazy, Crazy?'

'All right.'

'Marie is not my real name.'

Lucien drives for her after that, every time they allow her to come to the city alone. He waits like a dog outside the house in Billancourt and all the other private houses and all the hotels. He gets twenty stolen minutes with her, an hour if the traffic is bad – the same length of time she would plausibly spend in a Paris taxi. She pockets the money they give her for the fares.

It's the day after the Communist demonstration against Ridgway and the streets are scattered with the detritus the marchers have left behind. Paris is becoming hot, this spring.

Marie does not know Ridgway, but other NATO generals have passed through the White House in recent weeks. It's where they come for French hospitality: the military chiefs, the foreign ministers. Italian and German men, the occasional *Amerloque* from Washington or Virginia.

'All the guests whisper about Stay Behind.' She can't resist pausing, smirking with amusement.

'Well,' says Lucien.

'You really don't know what it means?'

'Don't play games, Marie. What is Stay Behind?'

'Weapons stashed all over Europe!' She drops her voice. Her eyes are alive with excitement. 'Networks of partisans are being trained across the continent. A secret army waiting for the day the Soviet tanks come rolling in. They operate behind the lines, attacking the rearguard.'

'Who is in charge?'

A man she doesn't know. A Colonel Howell. He writes the cheques, puts the right people in post. He is said to favour West Germans, preferably former Nazis. They have a natural obsession with secrecy.

They are driving along the left bank of the river. The police are everywhere. Dozens of them are supposed to be in hospital after yesterday.

'Did they really shoot a protestor?' the girl asks, with a shiver.

'Two,' says Lucien. 'This is a dangerous town at the moment. Tell me about the trick with the teeth.'

'With the what?'

'The missing teeth. Ange keeps making jokes about it. I think they're going to do something to your politician.'

'He's not mine. He likes the new girl more than me. The half-Chinese.'

She falls silent until they swing north on the Pont de l'Alma. Then she says: 'The only thing I can think of is a story about a woman who worked at the house before I arrived. She had her teeth taken out.'

'She was connected to the politician?'

'No! This was a long time ago. She was an African girl, a favourite of one of the Paris magistrates. He was a thumper. He liked her because she took it without complaint.'

'How rough are we talking?' Lucien is suddenly gripping the wheel hard.

'He liked to slap her face. Paul indulged him. Didn't put a stop to it. So the judge got worse and worse. One day he punched the woman in the mouth, and she ran from the bedroom screaming.'

'He knocked her teeth out?'

'Well,' says the girl, 'there are different versions of the story. But the next day the woman showed up at the judge's chambers, demanding to see him. Shouting at the police guarding the entrance. She was a real sight. Everyone could see a gaping hole where the front teeth used to be.'

'What did the judge do?'

'Paid up, of course. The whole world could see what he had done. There was a lot of gossip about it.'

'He had to pay for a dentist?'

'Much more than that. Money every month, for years, to shut her up. Paul bled him out. And the judge was on the hook forever after, of course. He threw out every case they tried to bring against the *milieu*.'

'They talk about it like it's a trick,' says Lucien. '*The old ones are the best*.'

The girl shrugs. She is becoming uncomfortable. 'There are different versions. I don't know. It's possible that Paul set the whole thing up. I mean, the man hit her, but there was nothing wrong with her teeth really. Paul paid a dentist to remove them.'

'A dentist took the teeth out? And the woman let it happen? Did Paul force her?'

The girl is hugging herself. She wants to change the subject. 'How should I know? It's just a story. The bitch probably agreed to it, for the money. Perhaps the teeth were black anyway and it was an improvement.'

'Perhaps. Marie? Do you ever think about running away?'

'You're not allowed to ask me that. I told you.'

'You're going to have to get out of there sooner or later. Wait!'

'When I say it's a rule, I mean it. There are some things we don't talk about. Or I jump out here and you never see me again.'

'I'm sorry,' Lucien says. He has never seen her so angry. Her hand is on the door handle, and he places his own over it. 'I'm sorry. Please don't get out here. It's too dangerous.' He touches her face. 'I'll take you wherever you want to go.'

'Does she have a name?' Romana asks Lucien.

'Who?'

'The reason you don't want to fuck me any more.'

'I'm sorry. I was tired.'

It makes a change, she says, sliding out of the bedcovers and hunting for cigarettes, rifling through his sports coat. On her hands and knees on the mattress, and showing him everything.

Her first drags on a cigarette are always long and extravagant, then she gets sick of it. Lucien slips out of bed and goes to the chair and takes his pocketbook from the trousers of the suit and offers it to her, but she holds it closed with long, strong fingers. Her grip is formidable. She does all kinds of physical work: waitressing, cutting hair, sewing clothes for the fashion houses. Anything that does not involve reading or writing. She only sees two or three other men in the evenings now. They are like Lucien. Almost lovers.

'Tell me about Paul's people,' he says, trying to prise the pocketbook open again. She holds it shut fast.

'You don't pay for that either.'

'Who are those Italians that are always hanging around? Are they brothers?'

'Not really. That's a thing they like to say. They were all in Toulon together, then they came up here. Dodo got into trouble with them.'

'Woman trouble?'

'How did you guess? Dodo took a girl that belonged to the leader. He kept her locked up in a house for a week. She had to go to the hospital. The Neapolitans were going to kill Dodo, until Paul paid them a lot of money.'

'To settle the matter.'

'To wipe out the dishonour. The vendetta was cancelled and now they are all best friends. They understand each other. Paul uses them for small things.'

'What about the young blonde girl from the White House? The one they call the princess?' Lucien tries to make it sound offhand.

Romana stubs out the cigarette half unsmoked. She pads into the bathroom to wash in the tub, standing up. She does not care that the door is wide open.

'Just a girl,' she calls out. 'Paul bought her from someone when she was a kid.'

'Doesn't it bother anyone?' He shouts questions while her mind is engaged with other tasks, so it is hard for her to lie without stopping to think. 'What do people say about her?'

'That your cousin picked her up when she was a starving little waif and he treated her well. She lives in the White House in a special room. No one saw her until a year ago. Now she's allowed to work outside the house. But only the top clients.'

'And does Paul still sleep with her?' Lucien's eyes are closed. The effort of making his voice sound nonchalant is strenuous.

There's a pause, but not to buy time for a lie. A clatter of something falling into the bath, glancing off the enamel. Romana swears and grunts as she stoops for it. 'He doesn't touch the princess any more. He lost interest in her when she turned sixteen. That's how it is with men like that. *Madonna*. I can't talk about it. What horror.'

The taps are off. Lucien hears two dull impacts as Romana steps out heavily on to the waiting towel. When she comes out of the bathroom her wet hair hangs straight down between the shoulder blades, long, black and liquid.

'Venus,' says Lucien, 'emerging from the scallop shell.'

'Shut up. You know I don't get those jokes.'

'Diana sporting among her nymphs.'

'Don't tease me. We didn't all go to boarding school.' She sits on the end of the bed and throws one leg over the other, painted toes feeling out the end of a tightly rolled stocking. She unrolls it with the same slow skill she used to employ when she adorned him with contraceptives.

Lucien climbs out of bed and goes to the wardrobe. He feels along the line of jackets, dipping into all the inside pockets, until he finds the film. He almost takes it out instinctively to study, then stops himself in time. Exposing negatives to the sunlight of his bedroom.

'What are you looking for, Lulu?'

'A film I took from a photographer outside a nightclub. I'm going to get the shots developed.'

'A likely story. Dirty pictures of your new sweetheart, more like.'

'Romana.'

'I know you better than anyone, Lulu. And she's one of them, isn't she?'

'One of whom?'

'Those girls from the east of Europe. They're all like dolls.' Romana says it simply. There is no jealousy left in her, not really. All of that was scrubbed away in early life.

She has pulled a dress over her head and is smoothing the material over her belly, studying her figure in the bedside mirror. 'All the world can see I'm not one of the top girls, like the ones at the White House. But who would want to be? Living with Monsieur Paul. Maman screeching at you. Do you know what those girls do at the end of the shift? Clean the place, like skivvies. Go down to the kitchen and chop vegetables for the old hag. Whatever those chickens are making, it's not enough.'

'Can you do something for me?'

'As well as cooking for you and mopping your face when you get sick and listening to your problems like your damn mother?'

'Romana?'

'What do you need?'

'Lellouche. I need Jacky Lellouche again.'

14

The restaurant is Greta's idea. It takes Jacky a while to open the lock. He doesn't want her to see what he is doing with the little tools in their suede roll, streaked with oil. His trade secrets. The back door of the restaurant yields more easily.

The kitchen looks much the same as on the day she left it, although the landlord obviously cleaned up hastily before he fled Paris. There is no sign of her bloodstained blouse.

Robert's old boss has left the refrigerator plugged in and switched on, but most of the fresh produce has spoiled by now. Jacky goes through it all, picking out cured meat and cheese and sniffing suspiciously. They will have to use what they can, he says. They can't afford to waste anything. The first few months are never easy. He is cheered by the contents of the wine cellar.

The bills that have piled up by the bolted front door are all in the landlord's name. 'They will change it,' says Jacky. 'They will do everything we ask if we pay the arrears. Plus a little extra in the right pocket. What shall we call this place? *La Greta*? Or *Chez Jacky*?'

The three single rooms upstairs are clean but spartan, almost cells. The landlord never stayed there himself, Greta remembers. Those beds were for refugees from the east, trusting young men who did not realize they were supposed to pay back their benefactors in useful intelligence.

The image of Robert is before her as she scrubs the windows

with a fistful of newspaper. Not his face – his torso. She glimpsed it one evening when he pulled off his soiled work clothes at the bottom of the stairs that led to the flat over the boathouse. Those muscles that reach round the abdomen under the ribs. The godlike line of the iliac crest, at the sides of the pelvis.

Greta throws the windows open to disperse the smell of white vinegar. Jacky calls out cheerily, from below. There are footsteps on the stairs. Too heavy for Jacky. She lets it happen. As she is looking out into the tiny yard behind the restaurant, hands gently obscure her eyes. The size tells her everything. She has dreamed of this moment and rehearsed a long speech of apology and remorse in preparation for it. All that dissolves in the sudden intimacy. She can feel his chest at her back.

He takes his hands away from her face and shrinks from her, regretting his boldness. Greta turns and looks up at him. 'I tried to find you.'

'You did, eventually. Jacky tracked me down. He tells me you are looking for a chef.'

She stands on tiptoes to find his mouth with hers. His hair is much darker now, she thinks. Then she closes her eyes for a long time.

Robert is a master of meat and sauces: calf's liver with *persillade*, chicken ballotine, *choucroute* with sausage. He hires a wiry half-Algerian kid to take care of the fish and seafood. Marcel is hardly out of school but has completed an apprenticeship at a grand hotel in Deauville, filleting sole and dressing crab for fourteen hours a day. His knife skills are excellent, but he is a bundle of nerves at first, terrified of making mistakes. They squeeze the truth out of him late one evening, over a bottle. He was sacked from the hotel for stealing food from the cupboards. They paid him so little that he lost a fifth of his bodyweight over the year of the apprenticeship.

'It's good that you came clean about it,' says Greta, pounding his shoulder. 'From now on, you eat with us.' And whenever she is at the restaurant at the end of the service, she sits down and dines with Marcel to make sure he is keeping his strength up.

The business barely survives for the first six weeks. Then they trial a *menu express* from noon and it takes off with the office workers around Vendôme. In the evenings Jacky fills the tables outside with drinkers. He is on his toes, cracking jokes, flirting with men and women. He boasts about selling champagne by the glass cheaper than any other restaurant in the first, and the word spreads. At quiet times he paces up and down the pavement, hailing in English and German the tourists who wander up from Rivoli.

On Mondays they draw the curtains and the restaurant becomes an academy of gambling, with Jacky as headmaster. Greta has been demanding poker lessons. He insists that she begins with something robotic: memorizing a grid showing the best choices a player can make at every stage of the simpler game of twenty-one. A French-Canadian man who teaches mathematics at the Lycée Louis-le-Grand drew up the chart after years of experimentation.

'It cuts the house edge to around two per cent,' says the Canadian. 'You still lose in the long run, but there will be times when you hit a winning streak. Of course, the difficult part is walking away from the table while you are ahead.'

The chatter distracts Greta. She dithers over a decision. Jacky barks at her. 'Always split aces and eights. *Merde*.'

'I'm sorry, curse you.'

'Do you want to get to the Americans or not?'

'Yes.'

'This is the way in. More practice.'

Robert has gone to the boathouse to make sure everything is in order. Jacky has finally given Greta a seat at the poker table. Romana, who has started waitressing at the restaurant at weekends, makes up the four. 'There isn't enough time to really teach the women anything,' Jacky says. 'Just try to pick up the rules and play along.' He talks to the Canadian in numbers: odds and fractions and percentages.

Sometimes the men replay interesting hands, showing the cards that were hidden and lapsing into the dense language of mathematical probability, while Romana yawns and flashes her eyes at Greta.

'You had about a one-third chance of making the flush with two cards to come,' the Canadian is telling Jacky. 'With one card to come the likelihood goes down to a fifth.' Jacky is nodding, scribbling notes with a pencil.

'Too boring,' says Romana. 'It's like school.'

'And I have real school first thing in the morning,' says the Canadian.

'There's time for one more hand,' says Jacky.

Greta beats his ace-high with a pair of tens. Romana guffaws and bangs her ringed hands on the table. 'I'm ready for a real game,' says Greta. He is dealing again quickly, before the others can protest.

'Don't be ridiculous. You got lucky. Tell me how many starting hands I have played out of the last twenty.'

'I don't know.'

'Then you have no idea what kind of player I am. Were you paying attention earlier when we talked about making a flush? What are the odds, precisely, of me picking up another heart now, to go with my ace and king of hearts?'

'Not a clue. But I know you're lying through your teeth about the cards in your hand.'

And she calls every bet he makes until he has shoved all his chips sourly into the middle. Greta has two fives in her hand and one on the board. Jacky does not have a single heart. The look on his face leaves Greta and Romana helpless with hilarity. The amiable Canadian is laughing too as he stands up to cast about for his hat, but Jacky yells at them all to be quiet.

'Wait. How did you know I was bluffing?'

'Instinct.'

'Not good enough! Tell me what you saw. Tell me exactly.' Jacky is gripping Greta's arm. The Canadian is looking at him curiously, hat in hand.

'You looked at your cards for too long at the beginning,' says Greta. 'You were trying to sell the idea that they were valuable.'

'What else?'

She needs to think about it. 'You stared at me when I was deciding whether to call your last bet. You stopped blinking. That's nerves.'

'Outstanding. I had no idea. Now tell me what the *professeur* does.'

'He mutters to himself if his starting hand is weak.'

'Yes. Yes! I saw that too. What else?'

'When the cards are good, he glances at them and lays them down very quickly and then takes a quick sip and looks again.'

'Just wonderful!'

'Good heavens,' says the Canadian. 'Well, we have all learned something today.' And he takes the slim bottle of cognac that Jacky produces from nowhere, like a magician, as payment for his time. Everyone kisses and embraces.

There are no casinos in Paris, Jacky informs her. The place on Wagram may look exactly like a casino and offer the same diversions, but that word must never be used. They are in a *cercle* tonight.

Paul Fazi does not own it, officially. The deeds are lodged in the unblemished name of a man who helped run a wartime Resistance network known as the Brotherhood of Our Lady.

Even if there were no need for subterfuge, Paul would not attend the tournament this evening. The *Caïd* cannot speak a word of English. It is a failing that eats at him. It means that he must rely on his younger cousin to act for him in all the family's dealings with representatives of the United States.

The American Club of Paris has taken over the whole venue. The new ambassador, Mr Dunn, has just been presented at the Élysée.

There are eight tables of eight players. The last three to survive at the final table receive a cash prize. Everything else raised tonight goes to Franco-American war veterans. If Jacky wins money, he will make a show of donating it to the cause. The tournament is nothing. The cash game that will follow later at an upstairs table, with no limits on the betting, is everything.

Greta is there to mingle and observe, wandering between the tables. Who is easy to read? Who plays the most starting hands? It is the first time in her life that she has been exposed to Americans in large numbers. She is not prepared for them.

Older women shower her with compliments, then drag her over to their husbands to have her prettiness confirmed. Single men ravish her with their eyes but are incapable of flirting. They outdo each other with tedious, drawling small talk. She is obliged to make her excuses.

It has come at last – her first period in more than a year. What a stupid thing to have to deal with, she thinks. And I imagined I would welcome it when it returned. Weep with joy at a sign of health restored, and the promise of a new kind of life after this one. I had forgotten the ridiculous inconvenience of it all. And always at the worst possible time.

In the ladies' powder room, stunning indiscretion is the order of the day. Five minutes in a toilet cubicle is enough for Greta to establish that a Colonel Howell is the best American player in attendance this evening. He heads the Office of Policy Coordination and is resisting Washington's efforts to bring his people under the full control of the Central Intelligence Agency.

I could sit here all evening, she thinks, and just listen to them come and go, shouting state secrets at each other across the basins. When she leaves, two young diplomatic wives are taking it in turns to spritz clouds of cologne into the air for the other to walk through.

Jacky is sitting on the far side of the circular bar. There are four players left at his table. People are already going bust, returning to their hovering partners with looks of sheepish helplessness.

His opponents are playing cautiously, folding most starting hands with little frowns. He is taking advantage of their timidity, playing almost every hand when he is in an early position in the betting, trying to steal small pots with stakes that look bigger than they are. He throws his chips on to the baize with dramatic exclamations, trying to give the impression of recklessness.

In fact, his bets are carefully calibrated. If cautious players raise back at him, he generally folds quickly without too much damage done. He is only half bluffing most of the time.

The strategy pays off just before the next gong. Jacky has stolen two pots in a row and the American on his left is becoming tired of his antics. He clearly suspects that Jacky has been betting on nothing all night. He calls the Frenchman's bet and an aristocratic woman in a magnificent ballgown stays with them both. Greta can see she is the kind of player who is incapable of bluffing. The woman smiles when her pair of aces matches a third ace in the middle of the table, beating the Frenchman's two pairs. Then Jacky lays two fours against the two others on the board with a modest shrug. Four of a kind. He pauses politely before reaching out for the chips.

Jacky has just taken his seat on the final table and is talking animatedly with the player on his immediate left when a thin-lipped man in a double-breasted dinner suit walks over and grips his arm firmly. A doorman almost as tall as Robert is in his wake. The smile that flashes between Jacky and the floor manager is vicious and knowing.

They hiss at each other in French, glancing around at the well-fed men, the women smoking cigarettes in holders. Greta catches the words 'nerve' and 'banned'. '*À vie*,' emphasizes the manager. 'For life.'

'*Mesdames et messieurs*,' gushes Jacky, turning to the other players settling themselves into their high-backed chairs. 'So, I am called away on urgent business. I hope you will permit my fiancée to take my place at the table.' There is a ripple of consent. All the remaining players are men.

Jacky has his hand on Greta's back and leans in close, wriggling out of the manager's grip. 'Add up the starting cards, like I showed you. If it's less than twenty-four you fold. If it's more, you raise.'

Then he is dragged towards the exit, unyielding hands gripping his elbows. Greta sits.

The player on her left is peering at her with deep-set eyes, folded over what looks like a very large scotch.

The action goes round to a man in his sixties who has selected his clothes with less care than any other American in the room.

He wears a faded, open-necked shirt in a Hawaiian print under a camel sports coat with soft shoulders. His face is creased with lines that suggest work and wisdom rather than dissipation. The player at his left elbow could be his grandson: pink-cheeked and immaculate in pressed sack jacket, striped Ivy League tie, spectacles in heavy frames.

Greta tries to remember Jacky's instructions. The idea is that you combine the face values of the two starting cards. A ten is worth ten points, a jack is eleven and so on. An ace is fourteen. There's more to it, but she can't remember the details. You add points for a pair or suited cards. How many?

The player closest to her is sipping from his whisky glass, still watching her from the corners of his eyes. His face is sharply defined, like the lower half of a hexagon. The young man in the striped tie is whispering to the grandfather of the table.

'Gentlemen,' says Greta, nodding around at them. But the deal begins, and the men enter the tunnel of intense concentration. No one acknowledges her presence.

Greta folds the first few hands. There are a fourth and fifth man at the table, but they have so few chips left that they cannot survive for more than a single hand. The square-jawed fellow next to Greta finishes them both off with a pair of kings and they bow out, to polite applause.

Now there are four left in the game. Greta tries to concentrate on the faces of her opponents. It is like finding a handhold on sheer rock. The telltale flickers round the eyes, the moistening of the lips with the tongue, tiny disturbances in the rhythm of the breath – all the usual clues are absent. The betting is bold and decisive.

You are not supposed to drink alcohol when you are playing seriously. Not even one glass, Jacky says. Greta hails the waiter. *Une coupe de champagne.* She is the only player who has spoken aloud so far. The only other audible voice is that of the chief croupier of the *cercle*, murmuring a running commentary in English. 'Colonel Howell raises to ten thousand. Monsieur? Monsieur Fazi folds. Thank you very much.'

The champagne arrives and Greta drinks half of it. She is obliged to throw in chips to start the next pot, even if she does not play the hand. The croupier sends a king and an eight flying to her and she tosses them straight back. The forced bets will rise soon. She will bleed out if she does not take a stand. A crowd has gathered round the table. Women are looking at Greta, smiling encouragement.

As the croupier is skimming the first cards off the top of the deck for the next hand, Greta stands up abruptly and says: 'I'm all in, blind.'

Now she has their attention.

'Madame?' says the croupier.

'All in,' she repeats. 'Without looking at my cards. Who's with me?'

'This is a pot limit game,' says the croupier. 'You cannot bet all your chips yet, madame.'

'The gentlemen can agree to a rule change,' says Greta, looking at the other players in turn. 'If they are feeling brave?'

The man on her left with the square-cut jaw looks at her curiously but without emotion. The old American in the Hawaiian shirt is chuckling.

'All right,' says Lucien Fazi. 'I'm all in too.'

'Well, I'll be damned,' exclaims Howell. 'Are we playing poker or Russian roulette over here? All in before the flop?' He says it loudly, for the sake of the audience. Affectionate laughter.

Then he switches to exquisite French. 'I regret, mademoiselle, that I already took a glance at my cards. They are not strong, but I would not be truly blind, as you are. I was too hasty. I cannot come with you on this ride.'

'That is very honourable,' says Greta.

The young man in the striped tie rests his hands on the table. He is wavering, for the first time.

'Did I see you take a peek there too, champ?' drawls the older man quietly.

'No sir.' The young man's face colours. He slides both hands off the baize tabletop and drops them in his lap.

'You sure about that, Brooks Brothers?' Howell breathes it so the spectators cannot hear.

'Guess I'm out too,' the young man announces, after a moment. His tie is suddenly too tight. He takes a swig from the highball next to him.

'Ace-ten,' says the croupier, indicating the cards Lucien has spread on the table. 'Against a pair of sixes.'

'That's about even money,' says Greta. 'Do you want to run the board twice? We split the pot if it's a draw.'

'I think you are ahead. Slightly ahead. You are throwing me a lifeline.'

'A professional courtesy,' says Greta.

'Let's not prolong the agony.'

The flop comes queen three seven. The fourth card is another three and there are shouts of glee from some of the female spectators. Their champion's pair of sixes is the racing favourite. Then a groan of horror. The final card is an ace. A gift for Lucien, out of the heavens.

As he is raking in the chips, with the sound of clapping all around them, Greta plucks up his empty scotch glass and sniffs. There is no hum of alcohol.

'Apple juice,' she says.

Lucien smiles. 'Whisper it.'

'I heard there was a game upstairs later. Give me a chance to win my money back.' She knows it sounds clumsy and grasping before she has finished saying it.

The young American cuts in sharply. 'That's a private table, ma'am.' The older men stare at him in an amused way. His superior is about to reply to Greta, but the youngster leans in for a frantic whisper, reminding him of something. Lucien raises his eyes at Greta in sympathy while the two Americans confer.

'I regret that we have no empty place for you upstairs this evening,' Howell tells her reluctantly, in French. His face is more mobile now he has finished with the game. His white eyebrows need a trim. 'And the talk would bore a young woman, I fear. A lot of private jokes that only old comrades would find funny.'

'I understand,' says Greta. 'Forgive me for being so forward. I am a newcomer in Paris, looking for work here. One tries to make friends quickly.'

'Another time.' When Howell gets to his feet the other players rise too. He offers his palm to Greta as he walks behind her seat, the broad room echoing with applause again. For a second she thinks he is going to kiss her hand, but he shakes it for a long time, with surprising strength. The unkempt eyebrows bob with amused interest.

15

When Greta returns to the restaurant, the light is on in Robert's room. Every time they drink they end up locked together, mouth on mouth, but they have not taken it further yet. They tremble on the edge of it. It is torture. It is heaven.

She patrols her cold room for several minutes, feeling the champagne. When she steps out on to the landing he is opening his door at the same time. Kissing, standing up against the wall, is uncomfortable.

'Giraffe,' Greta scolds. She walks him back across the threshold and pushes him on to the bed.

There are no more jokes. His hand slides down the front of her skirt and finds the right place, instantly. He settles himself in the space next to her on the mattress. There is no clumsiness when they are lying down. Their bodies dovetail. He kisses her face from the side, lightly, devoutly, as his hand works at her.

There is a sensation in her, mobile like a living thing. It grows and recedes and shifts around, and nothing exists but the need to chase that feeling down and kill it. She squirms against his hand to direct him to the centre of it.

'Deeper,' she tells him. 'You're not going to hurt me.'

Time passes. Everything is pure instinct now. He reacts to the subtle prompts in her breath, her voice, the motion of her hips. When the final movement swells, she knows she is no longer in control of her body. There is a look of outrage on her face as it builds. Every nerve is stretched as taut as piano wire for three racking seconds. Then she swears in Lithuanian and her head bobs, over and over. Warmth floods through her. She is under morphine again.

They fuck clumsily, the first time. In the morning, with the early light coming round the curtains, it is less urgent. Robert wears the sober expression of a man performing important work with great care. She senses his concentration as he addresses himself to technical questions of rhythm and variation. Angles of incidence.

He restrains himself until the momentum they have built together cannot be stopped. Curses and blasphemies erupt from them, almost simultaneously.

She does not realize she has fallen asleep again until she hears Robert jumping out of bed. Someone is banging on the bolted and shuttered door of the restaurant. It is ten in the morning and Marcel, Robert's young assistant in the kitchen, has arrived for his shift.

The two chefs are busy with their preparations for the lunchtime service when she comes down to make coffee. Marcel hands her the envelope that was lying on the doormat when he arrived.

It was delivered by hand. There is a single word on the outside: *Greta*, with double quotation marks inked round the name. It's so knowing, so heavy with meaning, that she thinks immediately of the people in Paris who are aware of her past.

Did you see anyone, she asks the boy. Was there a G7 cab waiting on the street when you arrived? What about an official car, with an Indochinese driver? She realizes she is holding his arm too tightly. Marcel was always a little scared of her. He's all legs and big shoes, one of those boys who got stretched out by a growth spurt in his teens. He walks on the balls of his feet.

Greta mutters an apology and lets him go. Jacky walks into the dining room as she opens the envelope. He is tight-lipped, trailing a cloud of cologne. The sheet of paper inside has a motif at the top – the crossed flags of the French Republic and the United States of America.

'A shooting party,' says Greta, answering Jacky's raised eyebrows. 'I'm going to need a nice gun.'

'I can't watch Europeans haggle,' says Jacky as they follow the valley out to Versailles. 'It makes me want to die.'

'You are French, not Algerian.'

'You know exactly what I mean. I want you to stay in the car and let me handle him. We are talking about a tricky sort of animal here.'

'He will want to see me. He will be curious. Come and wave if he asks for me.'

It takes Jacky twenty minutes to appear in the front window of the shop. The Samurai armour glowers at him from the shadows behind. The Bookseller comes to the front door and opens it for Greta, then locks it behind her. He is in shirtsleeves, his reading glasses hanging on a cord. He walks three paces behind her as they pass the groaning shelves. She knows he will be looking at her hips shifting in the tight dress. It's one of Romana's best creations.

Greta is about to take a seat at the table at the back of the shop where the men have been negotiating, but the Bookseller stops her with a raised hand and she complies, pausing with her weight on one foot and a hand on her hip. She looks past him into the middle distance, cool and detached.

'Truly remarkable,' he says. 'The effect Paris has on the roughest piece of flotsam. Like the sea working on a jagged piece of glass. Turn round for me, my girl.'

Greta revolves slowly on the spot then sits, kicking one leg over the other and smoothing the fabric over her thigh.

'I believe the criminal life is good for the female complexion,' says the Bookseller. 'There is colour in your cheeks. And you have obviously been learning things. Why keep a dog and bark yourself? You send a Jew to do your bargaining for you. Excellent. Lellouche and I have agreed a fair price.'

'Thank you, monsieur.'

'Very meek these days, eh? What do you have there?'

'I thought we would drink that brandy we didn't have last time. It's a good cognac. Or that's what they told me in the shop.' A little laugh at herself as he studies the label. There is an iron staircase at the back that leads up to a heavy door set in the wall. There must be an annexe through there. He wants to keep it private. There is a combination lock which he shields from them with his body. The door is ajar for a brief moment. Greta senses Jacky's intense interest.

The Bookseller has two shot glasses in his hand when he saunters back down the stairs. 'You will be driving, Lellouche,' he says. Greta fills the glasses to the brim and giggles again. 'I am not French yet. I can't get used to sipping. I still drink like a Balt.' And she tosses it back, looking the Bookseller in the eyes. He hesitates for a moment, then follows suit. Neither allows any discomfort to show on their faces as the liquid goes down.

'I was rude last time,' says Greta, refilling his glass first.

'I am steeling myself to forgive you, my beauty. When I first heard that you and Lellouche had found each other, I did not believe it. But seeing you together, there is an inevitability about it. The dregs of the same barrel. It's good to become what you are.'

'To your health,' says Greta.

He shows her the shotgun. It's handmade in Italy, the action beautifully engraved. He has shortened the barrels himself. His voice is becoming deeper, with the hint of a slur. She splashes brandy into his glass while he is running his fingers over the metalwork above the trigger.

Half the bottle is gone. Greta toasts the Bookseller again then produces a slip of paper from her pocket and slides it across the table to him. He balances the reading glasses on the end of his nose. Sweat has formed on the bald dome of his head.

'More guns,' he says.

'It's a shopping list. I know you won't want to fulfil an order of this size. I am trying to reach the man I mentioned last time we met. Laisvūnas. A Lithuanian dealer who lives in Germany. Don't worry, monsieur! I haven't forgotten what you said about confidentiality.

I am not asking you to say a word. But if you could pass this on to him . . .'

'You are still trying to fight your lost war,' says the Bookseller, reading the items on the handwritten list.

'This is a different project, monsieur. I am hoping to set up a deal with some French customers. No one who would embarrass yourself or Monsieur Balard. Men who are on the side of the angels.'

He smiles with great satisfaction. 'Excellent. The *milieu* need firearms too, eh? And you fancy yourselves as brokers? No? What's in it for me?'

'A percentage of the entire deal, monsieur. We are open to negotiation. I was . . . brusque with Laisvūnas the last time we spoke. I need someone to intercede on my behalf.'

The Bookseller studies the list for a while in silence, performing calculations. The drink has slowed his brain. Then he smiles and pushes the slip of paper back to Greta.

'I am still a Balt too, it seems. I can still hold my drink, in any event. I do not confirm anyone's identity, drunk or sober. If your Leo in Germany exists, you will have to go back to him and grovel yourself. Lellouche? I think it's time you two fucked off out of my shop.'

'The bastard is actually right,' says Jacky as he drives them back towards the city. 'I have never seen you looking better. I prefer your hair really short like this. Better than those rat's tails. Did Romana do it?'

'What? No. Not any more. I go to a salon.'

'What are you smirking about, Greta? After all that. I was worried that you were going to shoot that bald swine with his own gun.'

'Certainly not. He isn't as clever as he thinks he is. *Leo in Germany*.' She nearly shouts it, then breaks out into laughter, banging the windowsill with her palm on the passenger side.

'Who is Leo?'

'A man our friend obviously knows. A Lithuanian who goes

by many different names. But I have never used that one in the Bookseller's presence before. *Leo!* Don't mangle the gears.'

Robert drives Greta to the address printed on the invitation in the late morning. It's the first time she has seen him in a suit.

'I feel naked without the hat,' he complains.

'You're not a chauffeur, you're my bodyguard. Big and strong.'

'I think Jacky is annoyed with you.'

'I can't bring him here. Every American in Paris saw him getting thrown out of the *cercle* like a beggar.'

'He was lamenting about how different his life would have been if he had been tall, and a Gentile.'

'Don't forget handsome.' She kisses him quickly and kneads his thigh as he parks the Porsche at the end of a line of impressive cars near the coach house. 'I'll be a couple of hours. I'm sorry.'

'Don't worry, *Gretute*. You'll find me loafing around here with the other servants.'

There are no drinks on arrival. Later, Colonel Howell will serve wine made from grapes grown and pressed on the estate. But alcohol and firearms do not mix, ladies and gentlemen. The duck season is a week away and Howell is rigid about that too. The party will shoot at targets on the lawn that slopes gently down to the river, a safe distance from the house the people of Reims gave him as a present in 1945.

The first guests to arrive are treated to a tour of the downstairs rooms and the grounds. 'Liberation,' says Howell, summing up his talk, and the people nod solemnly as though there is nothing that can be added to the poetry of the word.

The party breaks up into small groups and Greta stands alone on the chessboard tiles of the grand entrance hall until the young bespectacled American who sat to Howell's left at the poker tournament touches her arm.

'Buckland.' She never finds out if it is his surname or his given name. 'You're first up,' the boy whispers to her. His eyes shine with excitement. He guides her to the door that leads to the basement where the master of the house keeps his workshop.

Howell has thrown his jacket on to a sofa down there. He takes Greta's shotgun and wedges it into a vice to remove the short barrels. 'I don't intend to ask why you need those,' he says, raising his eyebrows. The longest sporting barrel will be too much for her, he decides after watching her pose with it. They agree on twenty-eight inches.

Squares of red rosewood are set in the parquet floor. 'I'm not allowed to wear anything but slippers in here,' he says, glancing at her. 'I guess stockings will do just fine.'

Howell speaks simply and directly in English. The whole of world affairs is in his grasp. He carves brilliant sketches with a few sharp strokes. They circle the globe, from South America to Africa to Europe, then Korea and Indochina. Billions are fighting another world war, whether they know it or not. Howell has the gift of objectivity. How do his masters see the situation? How do the Reds see it?

When they switch to French, he becomes more philosophical. 'You must understand, mademoiselle, that Algeria is not just a colony, like Indochina. It is a *département* of France itself. Losing Algeria would be a dismemberment and those who support it will not be forgiven.'

'Thank you for explaining everything. There is still a lot I don't know about this country.'

'You are a fast learner. But I wish I knew why you keep laughing at me.'

'It's just that everyone addressed me as mademoiselle when I first arrived here. Then suddenly I became a madame, overnight. It's nice to feel young again.'

'I am getting to that age when every woman I meet feels like a mademoiselle.'

She waits until they are speaking English again before she brings up Stay Behind.

'Worst damn secret in Europe,' Howell says. 'And you're late to the party. Everyone else dipped their glass in that punchbowl already.' He is finishing up with the barrels.

'I have German and Russian. A lot of practical skills. There must be something I can do.'

'I don't doubt that you could run the whole goddamn show, miss. You're starting late, is all.'

She is checking to see that the gun snaps shut properly when Buckland knocks loudly. 'The next petitioner,' she says, and Howell smiles.

When Greta reaches the door at the head of the stairs, the American boy is hovering outside. The man waiting with him has his head bowed, hands held behind his back. When the head snaps up she sees that it is Monsieur Balard. He is wearing the same coat he wore on top of the Arch. The grey beard is freshly trimmed.

Balard takes in the flushed smile on Greta's face and the broken shotgun in her arms. They both know that she has taken precedence over him.

'You are not angry, monsieur?'

'We are all on the same side, young lady. I was slow to introduce you to our friends here. You used your initiative. But please do not leave without speaking to me. I have some light work for you. A matter of surveillance. I may be downstairs for a while.' She hears his voice drifting up as he descends. 'If I have to wait, so do you. Princess or peasant, everyone must wait in line at the bank.'

They use solid rounds, not buckshot, against targets set up on the lawn. She shoots badly before she adjusts to the long barrels. By the end, she is firing with the accuracy of an automaton.

Monsieur Balard does not shoot but stands off her shoulder, watching. When she breaks the gun for the last time, he comes close as if to congratulate her. He cups both hands round her ear, ringing from the noise, and utters a single name: *Hannachi*.

After the lunch, Colonel Howell leads a few selected guests on a circuit of the ancient orchard to the north of the house. The apples are all Calvilles. It's too early in the year for them, and they are not sweet even when they are ready to fall. But they retain their shape well in the oven.

Greta breathes deeply. She has felt it ever since they established themselves in the restaurant: the steady energy of a growing optimism, a feeling of being equal to the tasks set for her.

'Keep your chin up,' Howell tells her when they are out of earshot from the others. 'Said you were late to the party. Party isn't over yet.'

He cuts into an apple with a pocketknife to show the texture. The blade is stamped with the Moor's head – thick-lipped, earringed and blindfolded. Greta looks at it all the time he is working at the apple.

Robert is standing outside the Porsche facing off with a much shorter man in a striped waistcoat and tie. The body language is tense. The man's face is clouded with dislike as he peers up at Robert, squinting from the afternoon sun.

They are speaking Lithuanian, she realizes as she draws closer. The short fellow has seen her and tosses his head at her contemptuously. 'Nothing changes,' he snorts. But the men separate slowly and climb into their cars. They are not going to come to blows.

'Who was that?'

'A scumbag. A guy I knew when I first came to France.'

'He looks rough. Were you on the street together?'

'I don't want to talk about it.' Greta ruffles his hair. He is irresistible when he scowls like that.

The evening service has not yet begun when they return to the restaurant. She can see Jacky pacing in the empty dining room.

'Tell me again,' he says. 'Guns, money and friends. That was it, wasn't it? Those were your orders? Plus the girl?'

'Plus the girl.'

'And what if you can't do everything, Greta?'

She reaches out to take his face in her hands, a face drained of all its mischief and humour. 'What has happened, Jacky?'

'I have something for you. But answer the question first. What if you can't do it all? If you find the girl first, you're out. Isn't that it? You drop the rest of us and get out of France with her. How could it be otherwise?'

'Stop babbling and tell me what you have for me.'

A single monochrome print, four by five inches. The girl is walking away from the photographer, framed by the square shoulders of the burly men on either side of her. It was taken at night. Most of the face is lit by a flashbulb. Around a third is in shadow. The girl has been caught in the act of turning to look at the camera, as if in answer to a shout. The movement of her head blurs her features slightly. A busy Paris street with the start of a neon sign on the edge of the shot.

Her eye is drawn to the girl's hair. Blonde and woven into a single cable. You don't see that style in France. It's very Slavic. It might be Baltic.

Curse me, thinks Greta, biting her knuckles. Why am I not sure? Whenever I imagined this moment, I thought there would be less than this to go on. And that would be enough. Recognition would hit me like a thunderbolt. But when someone gives me a photograph to study, I can't be sure.

There is a French address, handwritten, on the back of the print. Greta does not recognize the place but Jacky nods in answer. His expression is grave.

She turns the photograph over and holds it by the sharp edges. Her nose is almost against the silver paper. A child pressed against a window, looking in. She mouths the name silently. Morta. Morta.

16

'There are conditions,' says Jacky. 'We don't need to be there until nightfall. Please slow down.'

Greta is pushing the Porsche past ninety, past a hundred. They are on Autoroute 13, heading north-west in the direction of Rouen. She curses as she slows for a farm vehicle. 'Who gave you the photograph?'

'A friend. I can't say who. It's one of the conditions.'

'I could get it out of you eventually.'

They both look straight ahead in silence as Greta swerves in and out of the opposite lane, looking for a chance to overtake.

He has a map on his lap, tracing their progress along the valley of the Seine with a finger. They will follow the loops of the river until they arrive at a straight section with a strip of dark-green ink along the north bank to signify a forest.

Greta exhales slowly and brakes, sliding back in behind the farmer. 'I'm sorry. You did a good thing. This could be a breakthrough.'

'Or it could be nothing, Greta, as you said yourself. That's why this is a reconnaissance patrol and nothing more. Please tell me you are unarmed. It is a strict condition. Otherwise I don't help you.'

'I'm not carrying a gun. Just the opera glasses.'

'There are guards in the grounds, so we wait until dark. Then we get close to the treeline and observe from there. The girl has a habit of standing in her window in the evenings with the curtains open. All the guards know it. They all like to ogle her while she's brushing her hair. You will be able to see her clearly through the glasses. But whatever happens . . .'

'We don't rush in.'

'We don't rush in there. *Bien*, Greta.'

The White House is truly a castle, he says, in a country where every man who has more than four bedrooms calls his home a château. There is no difficulty in finding it, as long as you leave the autoroute at the right place and follow the ancient road that clings to the south bank of the river. The house was built to command it.

The old road is empty of traffic. They look left as they pass the entrance to a long drive that leads uphill to the front of the house, arrow-straight. The black iron gates halfway up are open. A single car is parked just inside them. The drive is lined with a coarse gravel that will announce any approaching feet or tyres.

Jacky has been told that regular visitors like to use a narrower track that winds through the wooded grounds to the rear gate. There is a low wing that used to be a stables behind the main house. The guests appreciate the privacy back there. But all the entrances will still be guarded day and night.

They see the north-west corner of the house first, the late-afternoon sun making the white stone blaze against the soft-green background. The land all around is sleek and curvaceous, rich with forest. It's hunting country, a paradise for a medieval king.

They leave the riverside road and swing round the house on the narrow back way, thickly wooded on both sides. She pulls on to the verge and switches off the engine but they both stay seated, looking due east towards the château with the last of the sun low behind them.

Ahead, above the trees that surround the house, the sky is growing dark. Only the roof is visible. The cylindrical towers at either end of the main façade are topped with tall cones of black slate. A sliver of white stone below, peeping over the screen of oaks. All the colours are unusually rich in the late sun.

'Where is her window?' asks Greta.

'So, in one of the witches' hats. It's like an attic room.'

'Can you get to it through the main part of the house?'

'It doesn't matter. You are not going inside. Greta. *Greta*. You gave me your word.'

'Reconnaissance,' she says. 'I promise. Sit tight and don't move unless you hear shooting.'

'But you need to wait until nightfall. It won't be dark for an hour.'

'Bring some knitting next time.'

The forest is another world. The shadows enfold her like a familiar embrace. They calm and reassure her. The kind of clumsy men who guard these grounds will never be able to match her speed over heavily wooded terrain like this, if it comes to a foot race.

She is aware of many things, below the threshold of conscious thought. The best path to the house would be invisible to a city dweller but it is as obvious to Greta, even in the low light, as a street marked with paint. A line of soft ground with fresh grass to swallow the noise of footsteps.

Navigating her way to the north-west corner of the house is as effortless as breathing. The stars in the clear sky, the alignment of the leaves of plants, the pattern of growth of the ivy round the trunks of trees, all point to the north as one. She picks her way round a patch of thick ivy whose fallen wood will make the going noisier, then reorientates herself without effort.

The edge of the woods is an iron fence of four parallel bars. She stays in the shadow of a beech for a long time, looking both ways along the treeline. She smells tobacco before she sees the sentry. Then there is the rhythmical noise of fluid sloshing in a container: a hip flask or water bottle. An amateur mistake, she thinks with satisfaction. He's sniper fodder.

The man passes her quickly, the end of the cigarette lighting his craggy features as he takes a draw. Walking briskly to stay warm, in that cold spell around dusk. A side-by-side shotgun is broken over the crook of his arm. He does not even glance towards the trees.

When the guard is out of sight, Greta vaults over the fence and darts to an old stone well halfway between the woodland and the walls of the house. She crouches behind it, becoming tiny. The well would reach her waist if she stood next to it. It is three feet in diameter. A steel grid is bolted over the opening.

Two squares high up on the side wall of the house are brightly lit. Greta will be able to see anyone who comes to the glass, but they will struggle to make her out in this gloom. There will be no need for the opera glasses in her pocket. But no human shapes are visible in the windows.

How long will it take the sentry to complete a circle round the house? He must be right at the back now. She follows in the same direction, anticlockwise, picking her way from well to fountain to summer house to wood store.

The stable block that juts from the rear of the house is grander than the name suggests. The gravel is deeper here, combed in waves. Evergreen bushes are trimmed into perfect spheres and plumes. Crouching by the edge of the store, she counts five doors in a row, smartly painted. Miniature trees have been placed next to each entrance, aluminium champagne buckets standing in for plant pots. The apartments promise luxury and seclusion, for the most honoured guests. One light is on, in the room furthest from the main mass of the house.

Another ember, a pinprick of orange in the night, over to her right. The smoker coughs into his fist. She has to wait for him to pace away from the stable wall to make out his shape against the landscape beyond. It's a different man – in a uniform, steel-grey, she thinks. He is playing with a dark shape, revolving it in his free hand: a peaked cap. He's a chauffeur.

The sentry with the shotgun hails him. If it is a French word, she cannot make it out. It is more like the bark of an animal. Their conversation is impossible to catch. Are they local peasants? Corsicans? Men from the south, speaking Provençal?

A broad wooden door opens at the back of the main house with a sharp creak and a female shape is silhouetted in the rectangle of light. A small, stout woman with her hands pressed against her hips, elbows out. It is too dark to see her face, but Greta can feel the waves of malice radiating from the woman as she stares towards the two chattering men, her body stiff. A flash of moonlight is reflected in the woman's spectacles.

The murmur of the men's voices is stilled immediately, and the sentry turns on his heels in the gravel and walks away. The chauffeur raises a hand towards the open door in what might be a signal of apology.

The back door of the château smacks shut, and within a minute the door of the last room in the stables opens and a shock of thin silver hair appears. Its owner looks both ways, glancing at the loitering chauffeur without offering a greeting.

When the man crunches out on to the gravel, Greta can see his features in the light from the doorway. A scrawny old fellow with a weak chin. He is sliding a suit jacket on, shooting the cuffs. He puts on a pair of spectacles, the kind without rims. The head is too big for the neck that supports it.

Without a word, the chauffeur jams his hat on and trots away. To prepare the chariot, thinks Greta. The emperor does not speak to the slave. They both understand the routine perfectly. The last thing the customer wants is to have to talk to another man.

She looks through the door he has left ajar, seeing no signs of life inside. There must be a young woman in there, thinks Greta. Washing herself, consoling herself. I wonder who this prized customer is?

An old man, she thinks as he walks gingerly away over the shifting stones. That's all he is. Stiff and frail. She could take him down now, in the dark. Pull him to the ground and claw out his eyes. But there will be an endless queue of others.

Greta can see his face very clearly now. She can guess why he comes here. Not for the pleasure of the sexual act, but rejuvenation. It must be like a drug, she thinks. A kind of alchemy, a magical gift of temporary youthfulness that only a young woman can bestow.

Then she notices the bench against the wall of the stable block.

Wooden slats over a wrought-iron frame. The block is low and flat. If she stood on the back of the bench, her hands would reach the lip of the roof. One hundred feet to her left there is a window just above the line where the roof connects to the rear wall of the château.

A reconnaissance patrol and nothing more. She imagines Jacky sitting and fretting in the car. *What if you can't do everything, Greta?*

Something rebels in her. Who says? Who says I can't do it all?

The full moon of the spring equinox is a disc of beaten silver. The curved edge is just visible in the gap – about the span of a man's hand – which the girl has left between her curtains.

The room is cool, but she has thrown the covers off. You imagine her thrashing on the edge of sleep, troubled. Was a customer with her, earlier this evening? Greta cannot smell men's cologne – or anything seamier.

The girl is in blue, a silk nightdress that gives off a faint shimmer. The sleeping face is proud, the features set hard. The gap between the front teeth is smaller. Age, thinks Greta. No – expensive dentistry. Look how perfectly aligned they are. This close, there can be no more doubts about the girl's identity.

Hope begins to drain from Greta. She feels the weight of the eight years that have passed since they last met. It's too long, she thinks. Too much has happened to her.

Too many fading men have been drawn here, to this luminescence. Greta can feel their presence imprinted on the room. The bated breath as they enter, hushed and timid as pilgrims. She pictures them dressing afterwards, repairing their dignity with slow movements, pot-bellied and preposterous in socks and garters.

The nightdress has ridden up, exposing the girl's long legs. Greta does not notice her wake. The eyes were shut, and now they are open. The rest of the girl's body is still.

'I know you remember me, Morta. I have come for you.'

There is no response. Greta sinks to her knees beside the bed.

She has rehearsed the things she is going to say next. As she says them out loud, she realizes they are all untrue.

'Everything that has been taken from us can be restored,' she lies. 'Every bad thing can be made good again, in time.'

The girl is stirring, sitting up in the bed, shifting slowly away from Greta. She bends forwards to pull the sheet and blanket up over her knees, then draws them towards her chest.

'You are still young,' says Greta. A terrible lie that makes the girl screw up her face with discomfort. 'We live many lives. It doesn't matter what happens to us in childhood. We can always start again.'

'*Tu*,' says the girl. You. It is the same word in French and Lithuanian. She pats the empty space next to her on the king-sized bed, twice. *Come*.

And Greta goes to her, the way the men do, the other supplicants: across the bed, slowly, on hands and knees. 'Do you have clothes?' she hisses. 'Good shoes?'

The girl is reaching out to touch her face. A finger traces a semi-circle under Greta's left eye. It is wet with tears.

'You,' the girl says again. There is a small table on her side of the bed. Her other hand stretches towards it, the fingers extended. Searching for an object she left on there. Spectacles? No, the hand is feeling *underneath* the wooden surface. A switch, Greta realizes, too late. A silent alarm.

The next words the girl says are in French: 'You patronizing little bitch.'

17

Greta flies from the bedroom and dashes to the left, back towards the window she climbed through to get into the house.

A man is lumbering along the corridor towards her. He is heavy but unarmed. At fifteen paces she can see that he has a baby face and is not much older than her. The bulk is fat, not muscle. He moves slowly, uncertainly.

When she is ten paces from him, he spreads his empty arms wide as if to block the passageway. There is an expression of reluctance on his face. Greta goes into a sprint when the man draws level with the half-open window – her escape hatch. She flings herself into the air like a hurdler at the last moment. Her knee hits him in the flabby chest with all her bodyweight behind it.

She ducks out of the window and drops on to the roof of the stable block. The far end is closest to the perimeter fence and the woods beyond. It will be a leap into the dark, off the edge, then a short, desperate dash across open ground. She is playing it out in her head when, halfway along the roof, electric torches flash into life on both sides of the block.

Huntsmen are stalking towards the stables in pairs. Greta sees fat barrels, foreshortened, and flattens herself on to the pitch. Dogs are barking. She turns and crawls back towards the window in desperation, moving fast on knees and elbows. Has the man inside recovered? She will have to take her chances.

A shape appears in the window frame ahead of her. Another heavy-set guard, but not the one she knocked over. He leans out and she can see him clearly in the moonlight. He has the most wrinkled and tanned face she has ever seen, deep lines carved into caramelized meat. She can hear the dogs close by on both sides. The spray of gravel that covers the surface of the roof is biting into her forearms. The man is smiling down at her. He holds a MAC police pistol in his hand.

Inside, Ange Suzzarini hits her twice. The first blow is a sharp poke in the belly with the gun barrel, enough to break the tension in her abdominal muscles. He wants Greta to stop lifting her feet and kicking out at him while the baby-faced man holds her from behind. Ange transfers the gun to his left hand and steps into the second punch.

It's enough. She is aware of her knees dragging on the thick carpet as they carry her along the passageway with the crooks of their elbows under her armpits. The men bump her down a flight of stairs, cursing in Provençal.

Greta is on a bed. She must have passed out for a while. There is a surge of horror at the thought of having lost consciousness while in the hands of men like these. Adrenalin sets her body quivering and snaps her eyes open. She is facing the cold outside wall of a small, whitewashed room.

Over her shoulder she hears the word 'handcuffs'. A door opens and slams shut again.

A voice says: 'Gentlemen. I really think this could all be solved very easily with one telephone call.' There is a snarl, and Greta turns over just in time to see the wrinkled man smashing Jacques Lellouche against the wall on the far side of the room. Ange's fingers are round his windpipe. The gun is tucked in Ange's waistband, at the back. He spits a single word in Jacky's ear: '*Maricón.*'

The man Greta knocked on his back in the corridor saunters into the room. He walks over to the bed warily and takes hold of her left wrist. He has a pair of heavy iron cuffs for her. They might be police-issue, like the pistol. She sees that Jacky's hands are already in bracelets, hanging in front of his body. Ange has let him go, and Jacky is groping under his chin with the linked hands. His suit is creased, his hair wild.

When the fat, nervous man follows Ange out of the room, Jacky hisses at him: 'Momo! One phone call: *Lucien Fazi*.'

'Oh, we'll make some calls. Don't worry about that.' The man rubs his chest and glares at Greta. The door slams behind him, the lock clicks and his heavy footsteps recede.

'Will they ring your friend?' asks Greta, when she has swung her legs on to the carpet. Jacky raises a finger to his lips. His ear is pressed to the door.

She sits for a while, bent over from the pain in her stomach. Then she rises with a grimace. The window above the bed is locked too. She looks around the white room, from the single bed to the writing desk and the upright piano in the corner. It's a spare, unloved space reserved, she guesses, for captives. Or employees in need of correction.

The only painting in the room is over the piano. A beach somewhere, with cliffs, crudely rendered in oil. She walks over to the picture, limping slightly, thinking about the wire it must hang from.

'What are you doing, you ridiculous woman?'

'Picking the lock on my cuffs. You know about things like that. Help me.'

'It won't work with these,' Jacky says bitterly, looking at his hands. 'Save your energy for the firing squad.' He is pacing next to the piano. 'You promised me you wouldn't break in.'

'And you swore you'd get the hell out if there was any sign of trouble. Couldn't you find first gear?'

There is no answer. He dumps himself on the piano stool and allows his shoulders to sag. His head droops.

They hear hysterical laughter from below. Their jailers are celebrating, or letting the nerves slacken, one floor down. There is a sharp sound that might be a bottle or glass scraping on a tabletop. Jacky lifts the lid of the piano and taps a single note lightly with his right forefinger.

The keys are yellowed like bad teeth, but the timbre is pleasing. He forms a minor seventh chord with four stretched fingers and plays it as a soft arpeggio. The instrument is in tune. Another peal of high-pitched merriment from downstairs. That baby-faced hero, thinks Greta.

She takes down the painting and tears the thin wire from the back of the frame while Jacky plays what sounds like Debussy: extended chords, rippling and overlapping. He can only play the right-hand part, the left resting on top. He holds the right hand-cuff as far away from his fingers as it will slide to prevent it from clacking against the piano.

Jacky switches to the treble half of a ragtime arrangement while Greta is trying to fit the sharp end of the wire from the picture into the lock of her cuffs. It's an awkward, fumbling business, the flimsy wire snapping eventually. There is a pained expression on Jacky's face as he watches. Then he hisses a warning and lifts his hand from the keyboard. Floorboards creak outside the room. A thirteenth chord hangs in the air.

A meaty fist pounds the door. 'Not long. They're on their way.' Dark laughter. 'Hey, Jacky: *chouffe!* Heat it up. Play something we can sing along to.' The footsteps disappear into the distance again. They can hear taps, a toilet flushing somewhere.

Greta throws the painting and the length of wire on to the floor by the bed and walks over to the piano. Jacky's eyes are on her as she stares at the battered lid, the gold letters of the maker's name, the sheet music he is ignoring.

As he launches into the lead melody of 'La Mer', she releases the toggles that hold the main wooden panel in place above the keyboard and slides it up, revealing the guts of the machine.

She has never seen the strings of a piano exposed before, upright like a harp. The first impression is of deadly sharpness and frightening tension. You imagine the strings snapping under pressure and the stinging ends whiplashing around.

The treble wires are so intensely stiff that no amount of effort can loosen the pins that fix them in place. Greta runs her hand over to the left side, feeling how the strings become thicker and looser as they descend in pitch. At the very bottom of the scale, the single bass strings can be thrummed with a finger.

Jacky is watching her, unblinking, playing as loud as he can. Her thumbnail fits exactly into the groove of the pin that holds the second-thickest string under tension. Either the pin will turn or she will rip the painted nail away from her flesh.

The next time they hear footsteps, Jacky starts 'La Mer' again from the beginning, singing along now: 'The sea in the summer sky . . .' A boyish voice, deepened and loosened by alcohol, joins in from the corridor: '. . . infinite blue . . .' They hear the key turn in the lock. Greta shoves the painting out of sight under the bed with her foot and settles herself on the mattress.

When the young man with the baby face enters, she is curled on the bed as though unconscious or paralysed by fear, her knees up to her chest and her back to the room.

The piano is opposite the door. Jacky turns away from the keyboard and smiles up at Momo, anxiously, ingratiatingly. Jacky shifts along the piano stool to make room for him, indicating the bass end of the keyboard with a bob of the head. 'I can't play this on my own,' he says.

'But I don't know the chords,' says Momo, reaching out and letting his fingers fall on the ivories at random. He is still looking carefully at the woman folded on the bed. There is no sign of life. The space where the painting hung is right in front of him.

'So, we can change key,' Jacky is gabbling. 'Look, Go to G there. One lower. Then down to E minor. Here.' Jacky stands deferentially, the cuffs jingling, and the fat man takes the empty stool. He studies the keys.

On the bed Greta turns over, an inch at a time. How much did Babyface drink, downstairs? A man recovering from an ordeal, settling his nerves. Too much? She watches his lips move now as he mutters the names of the notes, dredging up memories from childhood.

When he strikes the second key from the bottom the hammer clicks mutely, and he frowns. She reads his thoughts, as her stockinged feet pad across the carpet. That's strange, he will be thinking, piecing together the structure of the instrument in his mind. Well, it's an old thing. One of the strings must have come loose. The strings.

Perhaps he hears the handcuffs clank behind him, or a floorboard, despite Greta's efforts. Whatever the reason, his hand flies up and he jams one finger between the thick bass string and his bulging neck before she can pull the loop tight.

That fat finger saves his life. It isn't a clean strangle. A little blood continues to reach his brain. A bull's instinct propels the man to his feet and he staggers backwards, smashing Greta into the wall next to the door behind him.

He claws at the coil of steel round his neck. She clamps her teeth round his ear. He lurches forwards one step then throws himself backwards again. Her spine hits the wall hard and it knocks the breath out of her. He leans back, settling all his bulk on her, and begins to stamp his feet desperately – once, twice. She jumps her legs up, ignoring the scream of outrage from the muscles in her stomach.

Greta crosses her ankles in front of him, feeling the heels digging into his gut. All the weight of her body is hanging round his hips. She can feel the string pressing against the carotid artery. He is subsiding on to the floor when two other men crash into the room.

A clang of discord, as Jacky is shoved into the piano. Ange Suzzarini's ravaged face is suddenly close to Greta's and she smells the strong drink on his breath. She is on her back on the carpet with Babyface on top of her, his bulging eyes staring at the ceiling. His bulk obscures most of her body.

Ange reaches for Greta's eyes, and she lets go of the fat man's ear and bites at Ange's fingers instead. He recoils from the snapping mouth, straightens up and aims a kick at the only vulnerable part of her that is visible – the left side of the ribcage.

When her vision clears, Ange is being pushed aside. Someone is saying her name, repeating it. A second man bends over her. A strong, geometric face that is impossible to read. There is no trace of emotion in it. He holds the gun sideways so she can see the safety is off. Then he touches the barrel to the centre of her forehead.

It takes Momo a long time to roll off Greta, even after she has let go of the piano wire and put her hands above her head. The sound of painful breathing fills the room for a while.

Jacky has pressed himself against the wall next to the piano. Ange is standing close by, massaging his fingers. He grimaces as he watches Greta spit out blood, a gobbet of meat from the earlobe.

'Well,' Ange growls. 'You obviously know her. Who the fuck is she?'

'Talent,' says Lucien Fazi.

He brings them into a room with a telephone and gives them a drink. A better room. Greta and Jacky sit together on the sofa while Lucien paces with the receiver. The conversation is slow and full of repetition. Monsieur Paul is in Beirut and the line is bad.

'It's my fault, if you like,' says Lucien. 'I met her at the *cercle*. She said she was looking for work and I challenged her to impress me. To *impress* me. She thought I would be on duty at the house tonight. I don't know. To prove herself. Creep up on me, stick a gun in my mouth, then ask me for a job. The princess heard her creeping down the corridor past her bedroom and pressed the button.'

There's a pause for a string of questions from the other end. Lucien says: 'One of those White Russians. She says she hates the Reds. I don't know.' Another long silence. 'What? I happened to be out west. No, it's a coincidence. She climbed in through a window that some fool left unlocked. It turned out to be near Marie's room.'

Lucien looks hard at Greta during the next pause. Then he says: 'If that's what you want, Paul. I ought to tell you that she claims a connection with a government man. Something like *Balard*. Does it mean anything to you?'

They can all hear Paul's reply: a curse, screamed into the receiver so that the signal distorts.

More questions. Greta thinks she can make out the last one, repeated twice. 'What are you doing, Lulu?'

Lucien's voice is very level as he answers: 'Exactly what you taught me to do. Talent-spotting. Looking out for people with drive. I have something for her, Paul. Give her to me for a month.'

He hangs up and splashes more brandy around. No one is in the mood to raise their glass.

Jacky says: 'You got to the girl in time?'

'She'll keep her mouth shut if you do,' answers Lucien, nodding at Greta. 'You never heard of Marie. You didn't know she was here. It's all a coincidence. Remember that you're Russian, not Lithuanian. Oh – one more thing: you belong to the *milieu* now.'

Greta swallows a mouthful. 'Will you talk to the girl when she calms down? I need to see her.'

'You've got spirit. But don't push your luck. Paul just instructed me to drive you up to a disused mine on the Belgian border and drop you down the East Shaft. I thought you were making it up, but the name of your contact in the French state appears to have saved your life.'

Greta looks up at him. The glass in her hand is heavy as she revolves it in her fingers. The pain in her mid-section is making her lean forwards.

'I'll do what I can,' says Lucien. 'But you're in a lot of trouble. Paul will collect on the debt.'

Greta places her glass on the carpet next to the corner of the sofa and stands up. 'What do you want me to do?'

'We'll be in touch.' He glances at the door. 'Ange is coming. I can't let you waltz out of here with a smile on your face. You're going to have to take a shot of medicine. Do you understand?'

'Yes.' She closes her eyes and tries to tighten the muscles of the abdominal wall. She can hear voices outside the room. 'Do it then,' she says, 'if you're going to do it. Quickly.'

Jacky's cry of alarm is the last thing she hears for a while. Blood surges in her ears. She tastes carpet and tries to turn her head to the side. Men's shoes. Hands are reaching under her armpits, scooping her from the floor. A tanned claw slaps her face, then holds her jaw.

She cannot even lift a hand in response. Her vision clears slowly. Ange's face is so doughy that she wants to sink her nails into it and squeeze the flesh like putty.

'Still with us?' he asks, with a chuckle. 'Just about, eh? No one cracks like Lucien, do they, sweetheart? It's like a car hit you. Hey – *maricón*. Go ahead of us and hold the door open.'

The pain is bearable when Greta can ride in the passenger seat with her knees pulled up. But when she is obliged to climb out of the Porsche and straighten up, she groans. The two remaining customers sitting outside the restaurant break off their conversation to look at her.

Romana runs to Greta and supports her on one side. Jacky ducks under her other arm and they all hobble to the entrance together. When they are sitting down inside with the doors bolted and more brandy sloshed into glasses, Greta says: 'Who is he? Who is this Lucien?'

Jacky looks at Romana and they both chew their lips.

18

Lucien Fazi turned seventeen on the day the Germans surrendered at Reims in May 1945.

The other boys crowded round the wireless. They cheered when the news was announced. Relief filled the room. A classmate pounded him between the shoulder blades. It's all over!

Lucien's face burned with shame and disappointment. He was clinging on to his place at the boarding school despite many infractions and many warnings. The Japanese were clinging on to Indochina.

When they surrendered in August, France began to claw back control of its colony. The war never ended out there. The fighting did not pause for a moment in the east. Lucien knew his place was where the action was.

It was two years before he made it out to Hanoi. Cousin Paul arranged the house for him in a Chinese neighbourhood where the same merchant families had lived since the reign of Louis *Seize*.

The exchange rate was favourable, and his cousin liked to boast that he could source any luxury. There was a brand-new Sibir waiting in the kitchen, unplugged. Lucien never met another soldier or official in the city who owned such a thing.

He stuck photographs to the side of the refrigerator. Pictures of his mother and sister and a girl he had been sleeping with in Paris. Most were of the officer cadets he trained alongside.

The best shot was of Lucien and the three other Corsicans in his year group. They were in uniform, sitting round a table outside a café near the Gare de Lyon, kitbags scattered about them. The waiter operated the camera. They smoked insolently. They thought they were men.

The air was close in Hanoi. You felt the humidity grow through the afternoon until the pressure behind the temples became unbearable. The storm broke at four exactly.

It was cool for an hour afterwards and Lucien liked to walk the streets then, watching the housewives in trouser suits haggling bitterly with the peasant women who squatted by their piles of sour mango and *gắc* fruit. The wares were heaped on bamboo trays, broad and shallow like bigger versions of the hats the women used to fan away the insects. They could rest like that for hours, on their haunches.

Everything in Hanoi gave the impression of slimness and elegance. Lucien liked the tall, narrow houses of the Old Quarter. Willowy girls in *áo dài* dresses cycled past his window or strolled in groups of two or three. He could not remember who arranged his girl, although it became an important question later.

Her French was passable. She was supposed to prepare meals and keep house. They did not discuss other duties until, one Sunday afternoon before the storm, she parted the net round the bed and joined him on it. Her skin against his. It soothed him. He understood now what the older men said about the local girls. *Commes des glaces*. They are like ice creams. They cool you down.

A man sold fruit on the pavement outside in the mornings: lime, papaya, rose apples, mangosteen when it was in season. Lucien kept the windows shut at the front of the house because of the high smell of the fruit in the sun.

One day, the stall was gone. The girl had ordered the fruiterer to move his pitch. The young master could not stand the smell any more. But wait, Lucien said. He had never mentioned it to her. She could read his thoughts now, she told him.

*

Lucien was on the intelligence staff at the new headquarters near the Sword Lake. He read all the dispatches from the forward bases in the north.

He could see his side was not winning, but did not include this assessment in his summaries. The style was terse and factual, and a report ran to a maximum of six pages.

The Communists, the *Việt Minh*, were abandoning weapons in great quantities, but the guerrillas always slipped between the arms of the French advances. They had a talent for avoiding capture.

He saw Hanoi as a circle of light cast by a street lamp. All around was the night of the tropics, quick to fall and absolutely dark. The Communists waited out there, as patient as huntsman spiders.

The Corsican boy sitting on Lucien's left in the photograph was the first in his class to die, bombed by his own side while leading a platoon of Algerian infantry. It was napalm, according to the paperwork. A single shell the size and shape of a rugby ball.

Dark rumours persisted about the *Việt Minh*. They castrated prisoners. They cut away their captives' scalps to wear as trophies, like American Indians. When Lucien asked his contact in the SDECE about these stories, the old spy laughed in his face.

The youngest and best-looking and bravest of the four cadets was next to appear in the casualty lists. Missing, presumed killed or captured. His reconnaissance patrol ran into trouble in the mountains north of the city, less than thirty miles from the office in which Lucien sat perspiring in starched uniform, shuffling through the dispatches while an antique fan revolved above his head. He still took great pride in his appearance at that time. The girl ran a cool bath twice a day, for both of them.

The prints on the refrigerator became shadowy, then black spots of mildew appeared round the edges of the gelatin silver paper. Lucien took them down and stowed them away with his mail in the top drawer of the dressing table in the bedroom – the one the Indochinese girl had taken for her own, sitting before the mirror to brush her long black hair.

*

In December 1948, Lucien went to Lieutenant-Colonel Weber to request a transfer to the front near Thái Nguyên. You had to go to the compound early because the senior officers rarely returned to their posts after lunch. The sentry was already asleep in his box at the entrance.

Lucien asked how you went about marrying a native girl who was not a Catholic and how you made a will. Weber raised his *képi* and dragged the sweat away with the back of his hand and grimaced. We are running out of imagination, he said. Among many other things. Did Lucien suppose he was the first? The first this month, even?

'I can shoot,' Lucien told him.

'The girls here, my God. They know how to use that thing the Lord has given them. They really put the hex on a man. You know what the Americans call it? The yellow fever. *La fièvre jaune!* Does Lucien want to fill all France with yellow whores and their brats? *Avec les yeux?'*

I know how to shoot straight, *mon Colonel.'*

Lucien's tone made Weber withdraw the tips of his index fingers from the corners of his eyes. He had completed the training? In Mont-Louis? He had the certificate?

'This,' said Lucien, 'is my certificate.' He loosened his tie carefully and undid the top buttons of the grey-green shirt. It would leave fewer creases than rolling up the sleeve. He slipped the shirt over one shoulder, drawing it down to show the tattoo on the upper arm.

The Moor, coal-black. The glint of gold from the hoop in the Moor's ear. The white blindfold.

Weber stuck out his lower jaw and groped the stubble round it. *'Tu est de Corse,'* he said, swallowing the 'de'. You are Corsican. A hunter. He repeated Lucien's surname thoughtfully: Fazi, Fazi.

For a month, the humidity built and broke in the late afternoon and the schoolgirls in their *áo dàis* shrieked and splashed through the water on the street outside his house and the pressure built again and the thrumming fans moved the heat around.

Lucien played cards until he had beaten everyone he knew, and they no longer invited him to the games. He drank a great deal. The old hands claimed it was a necessity for Europeans in such a climate. Alcohol helped regulate the body temperature.

A week before the lunar New Year, he became angry with the girl. She had been asking too many questions about his work, the thing he wanted to forget. He threw the bottle he was swigging from across the bedroom. It hit the opposite wall but did not break.

She ran from the room, but when he woke in the night with a snap, lifting his pounding head and staring around in confusion, she was curled up beside him. In the morning he wept and kissed her hands, her belly, her feet. It was supposed to be a time of holiday when she went to her parents in the south of the city. He begged her to leave him, but she refused.

They remained on the mattress together all that day. In the evening the yellow lantern on the bedside table threw their silhouettes across the wall, the edges blurred by the nets. In the early hours, Lucien padded out to the front room for water and found a letter lying on the bamboo mat by the door that opened on to the street. Delivered by hand. The writing was familiar.

Two men were sitting at a corner table in the bar of the Intercontinental when Lucien walked in, against a background of duck-egg blue. Swallows in gold leaf flitted round their ears.

The Asiatic man wore linen, off-white. The European next to him was in pale-grey sharkskin. The Shark's eyes were already fixed on Lucien while he was still glancing around the crowded room, blinking from the change in light, sweeping off his red beret.

When the oriental man rose, Lucien saw that he was too big for an Indochinese. He might have been Manchurian from the beard, and the bulk that a good tailor had used all his skill to try to conceal.

The man nodded at Lucien in greeting and fluttered a hand, palm down, to summon a waitress. Whisky – no water, no ice. He was not the kind of man who said please, not to serving staff. Lucien would like a large beer, thank you very much, whichever kind was coldest, with a dash of Picon.

'A bath of sulphur,' said Paul Fazi, staring up at the girl, unsmiling. She leaned in close and made him repeat the phrase several times before shaking her head in apology.

'He is making a joke,' Lucien told her. 'He means a Pernod. A glass of Pernod. Thank you so much.'

'They don't speak French up here?' his cousin asked, before the girl was out of earshot. 'Every tart in Saigon knows what a bath of sulphur is.'

Paul did not rise to kiss Lucien. The younger man made no objection. His cousin's cheeks were so sickly white that you feared a brush with one of them might leave a streak of greasepaint behind.

'*Voilà*,' said Paul, from the bench, flicking a limp white hand towards Lucien. 'Mr Li? My nephew: Crazy Horse.'

'All right,' said Lucien. 'All right.'

'My ten-million-franc horse that fell at the first fence.'

'Come on,' said Lucien.

Mr Li was enchanted to make his acquaintance. The Chinese man did not understand this talk of horses and millions, but he heard the edge in it and wanted to move on quickly. 'Your uncle has told me about your exploits on the rugby pitch.'

'Enchanted. I'm afraid Paul stretches the truth. I was a keen player as a schoolboy, but not exceptional. And he is my first cousin, not my uncle.'

'I have the same habit of exaggeration, also born of affection. I tell everyone this wonderful man is my brother. It is a metaphor. I do not suppose anyone believes we really share the same mother.'

'Lucien's school,' said Paul, ignoring the pause for laughter, 'cost me ten million bullets. He doesn't like it when I talk about it. He hates it when I call him crazy too. Isn't it, Crazy Horse?'

There was no reply. Lucien's beer was ice-cold, darkened and strengthened by the bitters. He drank more than half the glass in one pull.

'I sent him away from Corsica when he was small,' said Paul. 'I wanted to spare him from the malaria, and a lot of other things. He paid me back how?'

The Chinese man did not answer. He was taking a great interest in the mirror polish on his shoes.

'Come on now,' said Lucien. 'We are not going to go through all that again. Do you want the poor man to die of boredom?'

'The best *lycée* in France,' said Paul. 'Pretending to be an English boarding school. Nearly a million a term. Who knows what those guys did all day? Played rugby. Played with each other in the showers afterwards. No war for them. No food shortages, no deals to make. They stayed at each other's castles in the holidays.'

'It was nothing like that,' snapped Lucien. His face was becoming hot.

'A young man,' said his cousin, 'who could have been an advocate for us. A deputy of the Fourth Republic. He does what? Beats a teacher half to death just before the final exams.'

'Ah,' said Mr Li. Perhaps he can see his face in the patent leather.

'Lucien was gone by the time I heard about it. Jumped out of the hot soup and disappeared. He was thumbing a ride down to Castelnaudary when my people found him. That's a place you go, Mr Li, if you hate your family. The Legion will give you a new surname.'

'Youth,' said Mr Li, nodding solemnly.

'Me.' Paul jabbed a finger towards the diamond stud in his tie. 'Only the first cousin, not the uncle. I was the idiot who scooped this one up from the side of the road. Sent him to Canada. Then, since it had to be the army or nothing, I put him through officer training. Arranged a commission out here. An intelligence posting at headquarters. Opportunities, for all of us. Naturally, he is determined to throw it away and get himself killed.'

'Now I understand,' said Lucien, 'what happened to my transfer application.'

They were still glaring at each other when the tray arrived. Mr Li was grateful for the interruption. He nodded his approval at the waitress's neat movements. The whisky disappeared in one gulp. It coloured his broad face almost instantly and he flapped out his pocket square to dab at himself.

'I regret that I must abandon you, my friends. I have another appointment.' Mr Li looked from Paul to Lucien with great compassion. 'Life is kinder than we suppose. There are always second chances. And experience forgives youth.'

When the two cousins were seated again, Paul ran a hand down his tie and over the buttons of his suit jacket. He tugged at his trousers so the fabric would not become stretched over the knees and sag there. Black garters held his socks up.

'You came to Hanoi to see him?' asked Lucien.

'You give a fuck about our business since when?' Paul was pouring the water into the Pernod, watching the roiling clouds form. He held the glass close to his unblinking eyes, looking for fingerprints or traces of lipstick or some other pollution. 'I've been in Saigon for a month. I'm here for the rest of the week, then it's a plane to Cairo.'

'It's not the worst kind of life.'

'I'm getting too old for it. You would know all my movements if you had read my last telegram. You obviously wiped your arse with it.'

'I'm sorry I didn't reply. There's a war on. I want to go to it, Paul. I'm losing my mind in Hanoi.'

'You want to die for France.' The contempt in his cousin's voice was immeasurable.

'I want to fight for her, like you all did. You had your chance, with the Germans. I want mine.'

'As if you have any idea what the French Union really is,' said Paul, setting his glass down carefully and studying Lucien for some moments. 'I am one of ten guys in the world who can explain how this machine of ours works. But you're too pure to take an interest in our business, isn't it? As if you would listen to a thug like me. A *malfrat*.'

'Never once,' said Lucien, 'have you asked me what that schoolteacher did to deserve a beating. Aren't you even curious?'

Paul glanced at the same waitress as she swayed past on her way to another table, his gaze locked on to her tiny middle. In a country where women covered themselves from neck to ankle, men's eyes gravitated to the waist.

'Reservoirs of bacteria,' Paul said, not quietly enough. 'Hanoi is a perilous town for a young man. The local fauna is dangerous.'

'You've been spying on me.'

'No need. People talk. I introduce you to the best girls in Hanoi. Fathers in the colonial government, on the general staff. In the fucking *deuxième*! You turn your nose up at all the French girls. For a *citron*.'

'Let's not talk about her.'

'Listen, Lulu.' Paul leaned in conspiratorially. 'We all like tarts. We're men. It's logical. But you don't marry them.'

'Better not talk about that girl.'

'You are taking some leave next week,' said Paul. 'I have arranged everything with your boss. An envelope is sitting on your doormat right now with a plane ticket inside. First class to Macau.'

'No thanks. There's a war on. My friends are dying out in that jungle.'

'Mr Li has the New Moon over there. Not like this place.' His voice shrank to a whisper. 'It's where they invented the *helicopter*. Heard of it?'

'No, Paul.'

'You choose a girl from a line-up. Any kind you like. Mr Li buys them in from all over the world. Indochinese, if that's what you want. She hangs upside down from a trapeze. Like a circus performer. With the rope wound up. It unwinds as they lower her from the ceiling.'

Paul spread his legs slightly, speaking in a sharp whisper and glancing around at the nearby tables to see if anyone was watching. He traced a circle in the air with a fingertip to show the head of the spinning girl, the suspended girl, her mouth pointing straight down as it descended towards the crotch of his trousers. '*Voilà*,' he said with satisfaction. 'The helicopter. The head spins round while she sucks. You can't imagine.'

Lucien drained the last third of his glass. 'You blocked my transfer to the front. Weber belongs to you.'

'I promised your mother you wouldn't get hurt. Think, Lulu. You're the only boy in the family. And I'm getting old.'

'You have a son, Paul!'

'I can't do anything with him. You're the only one who is worth something.'

'You and your friends fought the Communists for years. Then you smashed up the Germans. I've done nothing with my life. Can't you understand? I'm supposed to be a paratrooper. Do you know how many jumps I've done?'

'Two, in training. And you're a fool for risking your neck.'

'What choice did I have?'

'So naïve. What do you think every other officer does? You find a poor kid who needs a few francs. You give a few more to the *sergent-chef* and he changes the names on the jump list. There's no need to give me the famous stare of doom. You're like a baby. If you had asked me, I would have explained how it works. How many jumps do you think Weber has ever done?' Lucien did not reply. He had not blinked for a long time.

'I get it,' said his cousin. 'You're bored in that office. I don't blame you. Listen, okay? You're out of there. Tomorrow. We transfer you. But not to the front line. That I can't allow.'

'You can't allow it?'

'It's like the rugby, Lulu. We all have to negotiate. Let's say you play out on the wing, but not in the scrum. I don't pay all that money so you break your neck. You have to meet me halfway.'

'I have to? I *have to*?'

Lucien's knees jolted the table edge. Paul could still move nimbly when the need arose. He folded sideways, his cheek sinking into the velvet that covered the bench. The base of Lucien's beer glass thumped against the wallpaper where his cousin's head had been a second earlier. It hit a golden swallow in the eye and fell. The rim rolled around on the dark wooden floorboards, making a noise like a snare drum.

Lucien loomed over his cousin and swore at him savagely as Paul cowered on the bench. Everyone around them was staring.

There was a craven, canine quality in Paul's eyes now which Lucien knew well. He had seen it many times in taller, broader men on the rugby field. It was the expression that replaced the smirk on their faces when he swept their legs away and smashed them into the mud for the first time.

It was the look the schoolmaster who taught him English wore at the end, a man who was neither tall nor broad but still a smirker, in his own way. A dandy too, like Paul. A man who could not keep his hands out of the waistbands of the youngest boys, until one of them came to Lucien in anguished tears.

'It can all be taken away,' said Paul. 'That aeroplane ticket lying on your bamboo doormat. The beautiful refrigerator. That sweet yellow ice cream.'

Lucien called his cousin the filthiest word he could summon. An Indochinese matron at the next table gasped and spread a hand over her heart and looked at him as he stalked past her towards the door. She wore a long white scarf and a string of huge pearls round the collar of her *áo dài*. The glass was still rolling on the floor.

Lucien prowled the hills between Thái Nguyên and Tuyên Quang for less than five months. He was alone for much of the time, bivouacked in the jungle with a standard MAS-36 for company. He stayed with Dao families when the hunger and isolation became too much.

There were days of apocalyptic rain in the highlands, when the air grew so thick with falling water that you felt you would struggle to breathe. No one could move around in that kind of weather. The war paused and you rested. You took up your rifle again when the skies cleared. You were an animal: sleeping in the day, predating at night. You established a territory.

Lucien emerged from the forest into a Dao village while it was preparing the festivities that marked the first day of the seventh lunar month. There was an open wound on his calf and he was running a fever. He had a few grains of gold left. They placed him on a stretcher in the square so he could watch the women wrapping rice cakes in banana leaves and stacking them in piles. The head-man's son went to the French fort by motorcycle to fetch a dressing and a bottle of iodine. Lucien refused many offers of opium. When the young man returned on his motorbike, he brought with him a rumour about a girl from Hanoi.

An enemy agent of some importance, or her death would not have been remarked upon. The circumstances were unusual too, and a single word of army slang caught Lucien's attention as he lounged, drained and restless and shivering in the mountain mist: *ventilateur*. Helicopter.

There were no French officers at the fort when he arrived, only native soldiers. Lucien was unkempt and wide-eyed. The men sneered until he barked at them in perfect Dao and they came to attention. Three of them drove him to the Lo River in a Coventry vehicle.

He had been using a false identity document and he knew his luck would run out soon. They would hit a military police check-point before long and his subterfuge would be discovered. Weber had surely reported him missing without leave.

It was only a few miles west of the northernmost spur of the hills, but the going was slow. The jungle did not fade entirely until they reached the edge of the wide ribbon of brown water.

A well-spoken Parisian eyed Lucien with displeasure and told him he must go to the town if he needed treatment for a fever.

'I'm all right, doctor. Are these the bodies?'

The young man made a gesture suggestive of helplessness. 'Not a real doctor. Just the company medic. And you are not supposed to come from that side. They want all the certificates done today. I told them I can't do anything until we establish a proper perimeter. All the land around here is contested.'

'Are these the bodies you dragged out of the water?'

'Wait. You can't . . . No, I won't allow it.'

The girl's face had been smeared into something unrecognizable. A cheap bracelet Lucien won in a card game formed a tight pink circle above her left hand. Very small, rough Burmese pearls bit into a bulging discoloured wrist that had once been brown and slender.

He thought about trying to remove it, then dropped the limp arm and covered the body carefully. He walked through sucking mud to the edge of the river and squatted to wash his hands in the water, very thoroughly.

When he came back to the medic's side, his voice was quiet and controlled. 'How long have we been doing this?'

The Parisian was muttering in disapproval and glancing anxiously along the horizon on the far side of the river, shielding his eyes with his hand. He was tall and lean, his stick legs exposed between shorts and heavy boots.

'Doing what? Oh no. Oh no you don't.'

'Shoving people out of helicopters, five thousand feet up.'

'No. I won't have that kind of talk. There is no evidence of anything like that. We don't know what happened but I have a theory, okay? Some of the prisoners were *Việt Minh*, and the others were mountain tribesmen. They hate each other so they start fighting, in the back of the helicopter.'

'And they all push each other out at the same time? And there are no guards to stop them?'

'I am not in charge of this investigation. I don't interview the pilots. I assess the injuries. It's not a difficult job. It's obvious what killed them. Get away from there!' A band of naked boys were creeping close to the four bodies where they lay side by side in the mud, six feet from the lapping water, covered in tarpaulins. The children scattered with shrieks of laughter when the Parisian shouted at them.

'And you've never seen this before?' asked Lucien.

'Not once. I can guarantee this is not something French Union forces indulge in. We simply cannot have that kind of talk. I forbid it.'

'A girl captured. Is that unusual?'

'In this district, I can say it's uncommon. My men whisper about her. I gather there are a few stories. I mean, I can't speak their language!' He snorted with laughter.

'Well, of course not! What an idea!' Lucien was fishing in his breast pocket for cigarettes. His face was hot in the full sun. He wiped his hands on his trousers and placed two Caporals in his mouth and lit them both and handed one over. The men smoked hungrily.

Eventually, Lucien said: 'What kind of things do your men say, out of interest?'

'That she was a high-value Communist cadre. Too good for this area. The prettiest girls are all sent to Hanoi, apparently. I gather they are supposed to seduce the Frenchmen and screw secrets out of us. I can't say I would mind, personally.' He laughs and coughs out smoke at the same time. 'I mean, who can say if this one was pretty before, you know, before . . .'

'Before the accident.'

'Who can say now? Damn these children. Get out of there. *Dégage!*'

'You have no idea,' said Lucien.

'These brats. Always barefoot. It's crawling with parasites out here. We did a campaign, but how can you teach anything to people like this? They can't be bothered to wipe their children's snotty noses.'

'You have no idea how beautiful,' said Lucien, but his voice was a husk, and the Parisian was striding away from him towards the bodies and the giggling boys, yelling and flapping his hands at the children like an enormous wading bird, to their boundless amusement.

19

It's Romana who finds Greta eventually, wandering the streets of Montmartre in the early hours. She was in one the cabarets – Heaven or Hell, she can't remember which – drinking alone and telling the men who approached her to buzz off.

'Can't get drunk,' she tells Romana. 'No matter how hard I try.'

'We need to get you something to eat.'

There is a basement place Romana knows where they stay open all night and serve desserts along with the drinks. The champagne comes in coupe glasses.

'To Marie Antoinette,' says Romana. 'And her tiny little tits. And to you, Greta. The strongest, the bravest.'

'That's not me. But you're being very kind.'

'I know you will come back from this. You are carved out of granite. But tell me. How did you get that way?'

Greta tells Romana about the Lithuanians, in between mouthfuls. Their strange language, unlike anything to the east or west, and the pagan gods they once worshipped, and the glories of past centuries when the Grand Dukes drove their ponies from the Baltic to the Black Sea. How the Nazis had invaded once and the Soviets twice, by the time the war was over. Fire and death.

Her own story. The Jewish friends, as precious as sisters, gunned down by the Germans. An entire family smudged out by the thumb of Stalin. How the faces of the dictator and his hangman, Maxim

Karpov, stare out of the pages of magazines, rebuking her. Haunting her dreams.

'How old were you when the soldiers came?' asks Romana.

'Fourteen.'

'I was the same age when my father died. I was living here by then. They take your childhood, don't they? And when it's gone, no one can give it back to you.' Romana reaches for Greta's glass. 'You've had enough. Let's go home.'

'Jesus and Mary. You telephoned him?'

Jacky is leaning against the wall outside the club, hands in pockets. He takes them out and clasps them in entreaty. 'I know you're angry, Greta. But be reasonable. I told you not to go charging in there.'

'I'm not angry with you, you fool. I'm furious with myself.'

Jacky says he wants to show Greta something. Romana bids them goodnight. She will be up again at sunrise, to dress and feed the child she leaves with a neighbour in the evenings. She has half a dozen jobs and refuses to share her earnings with any man. She made that mistake too many times in the past.

Jacky leads Greta downhill towards the river, slowly walking it off. 'Robert has been prowling the streets all night,' he tells her. 'Looking for you. As have I.'

'I don't know why he bothered. We're fucking, that's all. And what would you care if I got hit by a tram?'

'I don't think you know what you're saying,' says Jacky.

'Why were you out here really, monsieur? On the hunt for Arab boys? We've got one in the kitchen now. Why don't you pull his trousers down one night, if you can pluck up the courage?'

Jacky's smile is tight and restrained. A parent attempting to keep his temper. 'So that is really what you think of me?'

'I've seen you embracing that boy. Getting him drunk after the end of the service.'

'Marcel is half my age, Greta. He is the age I was when . . .' She slows down and his arm slides out of hers. 'He is at the age when you need advice from someone older.'

Greta runs to catch up with him. 'I'm still drunk,' she says. 'Forgive me.'

'Actually very hurtful, darling.'

'I'm sorry, Jacky.'

'I am human, you know. And in any event . . .' His pious expression cracks into a grin. He can't keep it up. 'Marcel is more French than North African. Not at all my type.'

He won't tell her where he is leading her, but they cross the river and sit in the gardens at Invalides as the sky lightens by degrees.

She leans over and rests her head on his lap. He says: 'You need coffee, not sleep. We've got to come up with a plan. You and I are in a lot of trouble, darling.'

'I can't go back today. Robert won't want to look at me. I'm black and blue from the neck down.'

'I think you misjudge him. He is beside himself with worry. I wonder if it will be easy for you to walk away when the time comes.'

'From a man?' she scoffs.

'From all of it. Paris gets into our blood. But it is very difficult to operate here. The true performer knows when it is time to leave the stage. The best way is with . . . *voilà*. The puff of smoke. Not here, Greta.' Her head is nodding. Sleep is coming for her. 'We'll be arrested for vagrancy. Let's go. I want to show you something.'

When they arrive at the Tower, she closes her eyes for an hour despite Jacky's protests, propped against him on a bench in the gardens around the vast iron legs of the Tower with the last of the magnolias falling around them. When she shakes herself out of it a crowd of sightseers is gathering near the turnstiles.

'Come on,' says Jacky, patting her thigh. 'My old friends are starting early.'

The young man with the flimsy trestle table is called Marius. 'A Romanian,' says Jacky. 'I know them well, but they won't acknowledge me in any way.' Greta doesn't understand at first. It looks like a one-man operation.

A young man with an old face, hair cropped like a soldier, long fingers agitating the three cards laid out on the table: flipping, sifting, caressing. He wears an Eisenhower jacket. She can hear his accent when he calls out: 'Find the lady, find the lady.' They are close enough to see the fine movements of his hands, through a circle of curious faces. The queen of spades is in the middle, the red aces on either side.

Someone is yelling: a coarse fellow with a belly, in a billowing suit. He knows the trick. 'I'll prove it,' he sneers. A hundred francs on the first card. There is applause and laughter as the card is turned over. It's her: the frowning queen.

'You sniffed me out, sir,' groans Marius, counting notes from a wad and thrusting them at the man in the suit, who is crowing loudly. 'He's in on it,' Greta whispers to Jacky. 'He is here to drum up trade.'

'Very good. What else?'

'Oh!' She sees them now: a wizened old woman and an under-nourished boy of about fifteen who might be the son of the man in the baggy suit. They have the same good teeth and strong, black hair.

'Two dippers,' hisses Greta, squeezing Jacky's arm. They've taken a wallet each already.

'Outstanding. That's the real game. Distraction. Make the marks all look in the same direction. There might be fifty people in the crowd later. You could take every wedding ring while they are craning their necks, looking for that queen.'

'What's your record?' she asks, pinching him hard.

'Wait. Keep watching. I think . . . yes.'

A sudden ripple of action. There is a commotion on the far side of the knot of people clustered round the cards. Greta cannot see what is causing it. Then she hears a whistle blowing. A chorus of shouts answers it. Marius is stuffing banknotes into his pockets. Someone else snatches up the table and hares away towards the north entrance of the gardens without bothering to fold it.

When she looks back, Marius has vanished. Others are shouting. Police! Run! Everyone for himself! The constable is a big, huffing, red-faced brute. The audience scatters as he shoves his way through. They hurry away from the spot where the table was set up, instinctively, even the well-dressed tourists who have lost the bets they slapped down before the cards were turned. She can see the furtive looks they cast at the policeman's broad back. They have somehow been drawn into the crime, made complicit.

'So?' asks Jacky.

'The gang are clever. They think quickly when the police arrive. They use the panic to grab all the money. The marks aren't going to complain that they have been robbed in case they themselves are accused of illegal gambling. Most of them aren't French. They won't know the law.'

'Excellent,' smiles Jacky. 'There's one more angle. Did you spot it?'

'I don't know.' Greta is rubbing her temples with her knuckles.

'You're exhausted. We'll leave it for next time. Let's get you back before the boys start preparing for lunch.'

And Greta sees that she really has underestimated Robert. He slips into bed beside her and rubs her back and shoulders while they listen to Marcel crashing around in the kitchen downstairs. Robert goes to check on him and returns with a tube of Rhône aspirin, black tea with milk. He drops the tablets into a glass of water and stirs it for her. The last thing Greta sees before sleep takes her is Robert putting on his chef's whites, swaggering a little as he punches his long arms through the sleeves, like a samurai dressing for battle.

He is reluctant that night, afraid to touch her, as she feared. She has stretched a nightdress over the livid bruises on her ribs and lower abdomen. She summons him to her, whispering meaningless things, priming him with her hands, trying not to make a face as he manoeuvres himself into position.

The idea of not fucking is intolerable. They both understand that it needs to be done. It is a thing outside them, a fire that must be tended. He looks around the room with satisfaction afterwards, arms folded behind his head. She has moved her small things – lipstick, nail polish, hairspray – into his room and arranged them on the dressing table. There are no perfume bottles.

*

Labour Day dawns bright with a strong breeze. The mood is peaceful at first. General de Gaulle is in full uniform. He removes his *képi* to address the crowd in front of a wall of flapping tricolours. He is still outside the government of the Fourth Republic, a looming, thwarted presence. He cannot pull off the great comeback that his supporters want.

They discuss closing the restaurant in the evening. Everyone knows that the mood on the streets of Paris can change in an instant. It is the great time of demonstrations. It seems there are deaths every week.

It is hard to keep up with the news. Protestors block the Champs-Élysées, shouting for freedom for Morocco. Or are they against it? Someone tosses a hand grenade into the press of people, right there on the Champs. What *horror*. The talk in the cafés is dark. Leftists, rightists, terrorists. The hidden hand behind the hand that throws the bomb.

You hear the word 'Algeria' constantly, and the names of the men agitating for independence there, the same ones appearing on walls all around Paris: Messali Hadj, Ben Bella. One name above all: Hannachi. Everyone avoids the topic of Indochina now. Even the radio bulletins have tired of the endless wars. Or perhaps it is all one war.

Greta emerges uncertainly into the late-morning sun. The tables outside need to be set for the lunchtime service.

A young woman with blonde hair is sitting at one of them. Her handbag is on top of the table, an elbow planted next to it, the hand cupping the woman's jaw. She is dressed for the catwalk.

'You asked me if I had any clothes,' says Morta. 'The last time we met. Does this answer your question? It's a Pierre Cardin. A real one, not a cheap copy.'

She stands to show off the sharp lines of the fawn pencil skirt, the close-fitting blazer made of the same luxurious yarn, buttoned up to the neck. She wears a pearl bracelet, a fascinator, elegant shoes a world away from the blocky style of the working women.

'There is a wardrobe full of pieces like this in my room. I would have showed you if you hadn't taken me by surprise. Then you would have understood my value.'

'Let's go inside,' says Greta hoarsely, 'off the street.' She can feel the moving parts of her heart hammering like the components of an engine.

'There's no danger,' smiles Morta. 'You are so naïve. Do you think they keep me locked up in that house? I have been able to leave for a long time now, to move around the city. It took me years to earn that privilege. And you blunder in and want to smash up everything I have been working for.'

'I don't want to smash anything, I want to take you away from all of it, Morta. We can start again. It hurts now, but one day it will seem like a dream.'

'My name is Marie.' She clicks across the gap between them. Her eyes sweep Greta. She is three or four inches taller in the heels.

'The dress suits you,' she says. 'But it's a copy. I've heard about the Italian tart who runs them up for you. It looks good now, but it won't last. The material is cheap.'

'You can teach me about clothes, darling. We can shop together. Won't you come inside?' There is a weakness in Greta's voice that she despises.

'I'm worth millions of francs,' says Morta. 'Do you understand? This is just one outfit. Cardin, Chanel. All real. I keep every gift they leave for me. I worked for that. Think about the scarves and jewellery alone. Imagine how much I'm worth.'

'And what did you have to do to earn those things?'

'The same things you do for free! Who is the idiot?'

'Morta.'

'It's fucking Marie! Don't you try to make me feel ashamed. I like men. I'm not embarrassed about it.'

'I've seen the creatures who come to the house. Senile fools.'

'You are talking about the most powerful men in Europe! And they eat from my hand.'

Both women have raised their voices now, and people passing by are glancing over: a mother pushing a pram along Mont Thabor, a man loafing with a newspaper.

Greta says: 'You are a fool. They will use you and discard you. They are killers.'

'Lies! There are rules. Loyalty is rewarded. I am the most loyal.'

'Your mother,' Greta begins.

'Don't you dare mention that woman. Say her name again and this is the last time you will ever see me.'

'Do you really think I'm going to let you walk away from me after everything I have been through?'

Greta doesn't realize that she has grabbed Morta's wrist until someone shouts from behind. 'Greta. No. You're hurting her.' Romana has come out of the restaurant and is looking on with alarm.

'You can't afford me,' Morta is hissing, 'in your cheap imitations. You'll be old and ugly soon. You're more like a soldier than a woman. You can't stand it when you see the men going mad over a younger—'

The slap makes Romana shriek, but the girl does not cry out. The flat noise of it reverberates around the street. The bystander with the newspaper is folding it, beginning to walk towards them slowly. Greta can hear Jacky's voice from the entrance of the restaurant.

Morta is on her knees on the pavement, gasping for air. The little hat has fallen off and Greta takes her by the hair.

'Not another word. We are leaving now.'

'You daughter of a bitch,' says the girl.

Greta pulls her stiletto out but does not open the blade. Romana is wailing at her. Jacky is trying to keep his voice steady. 'Greta. Stop. Think. She's a kid. Are you going to tie her up?'

'She is coming with me and that's the end of it.'

'In the boot of a car?' asks Jacky. 'At knifepoint? Think, for God's sake.'

'You're going to help me,' Greta tells him.

'Not this time.'

'Pederast,' growls the girl, and Greta lets go of the blonde hair and steps back.

Romana and Jacky have taken her by the upper arms. He tries to prise the knife out of her hand. She lets him do it.

Morta pushes herself to her feet and staggers away from them, still spitting curses: hag, slattern, streetwalker. It is these words, not the hands gripping her shoulders, that keep Greta fixed to the spot as she watches the girl retreat. A final insult, as Morta turns to run: *nevala!*

It's not the meaning of the words but the language they are uttered in. There is a deep place of memory inside the girl which all the men and the life of the White House have not erased. When she is pushed to the edge, Morta swears in the dialect of lowland Lithuania.

20

The driver isn't right for this, thinks Greta. An actor who has wandered on to the wrong set on the film lot.

She's in Marseille, four days after the night at the White House, paying back the debt. Her stomach still hurts from the punch.

'Boys,' said the voice on the telephone. A voice she didn't recognize. A man who answered her question with a sneering laugh. 'No, I'm not Lucien. You don't belong to him alone. He has to share you. Go to the Gare de Lyon. Take the first train south. Yes, right now: you can sleep on the way. Three boys will be waiting for you in Marseille. Do whatever the oldest one says.'

The young man who greets her sweeps his long hair out of his eyes and offers a hand. 'Bobby,' he says. He asks her permission before he takes the wheel.

The four of them are squashed together in the little Peugeot. The lads in the back are even younger than Bobby. Their long coats are weighed by heavy objects in the pockets.

The C3 is in a green army rucksack. She fiddles with straps and buckles as they drift downhill towards the docks. The car must stay out of sight, but someone needs to watch for Greta's signal. Bobby is the best dressed. The boys must help them with the guard. The dead weight of a body is heavier than you realize, says the youngest boy sagely.

'I just told you that,' says Greta. 'Am I speaking fucking Swahili or something? Wait. Where are the detonators?'

'That's all there is,' says Bobby from the seat next to her. He's a nervous driver, fixated on the road.

'There should be wires with metal caps on the end. Otherwise we can't blow it.'

One of the boys pipes up from behind. 'That stuff is high-explosive. The highest there is.'

'That doesn't mean it goes off on its own, genius. You need a charge to trigger it. Or it just burns.' Their faces are blank. 'It doesn't go bang. I don't know how else I can say it.'

'It's all I was given,' says Bobby. 'Several kilos. Enough for the whole warehouse.'

'Not if we can't detonate it. Jesus and Mary.'

Bobby parks before the wire fence begins after the second dock and gets out. Greta slams her door. The boys stay in the back of the car. They're still on high ground – the shoulder of land before the steep run down to the water. She can see slow ships queuing to the north and the coastline behind, the grey fortresses strung out along it.

'We have to do it tonight,' says Bobby. 'If you know where to place the charges, I'll stay behind to make sure they blow.'

'Shut up and let me think.'

'I know this won't mean anything to you, madame, but if I don't get this done tonight, my father is a dead man. I'll stay behind to set it off. Up close, with a pistol.'

'That won't work.' She looks at him. 'What did those other boys do to anger Monsieur Paul?'

'Stole a car from the wrong man.'

'Jesus. This is a penal battalion, isn't it?' She uses the Soviet term: *shtrafbat*. Bobby blinks at her. 'We're the lowest of the low,' she says. 'Fine. Tell me the names again.'

There's a thing she has seen the best streetwalkers do, as they pad the pavements of Saint-Denis. They allow their heads to bob, to wobble with every step. It's as if they are sprung, not equipped with a spine. The constant motion gives the women an irresistible air of looseness. I can hardly hold myself upright, it says to the men who are passing. I belong on my back, with someone stretched out beside me. You?

Head wobbling, hips rotating, Greta approaches the sentry hut that guards the service road leading to the last warehouse on the northernmost quayside in the port of Marseille. The basket in her hands is covered with a white dishcloth.

'With the compliments of your friends!' she announces, as a man in a dark-brown boilersuit steps out of the hut and scratches the back of his head. 'Courtesy of Tommy and François. Many happy returns.'

It takes him a while to get the idea. He roots around in the basket without meeting her eye. Pastries wrapped in paper. A bottle and two glasses. The smile comes slowly.

'We're breaking all kinds of rules,' he tells her.

'You finish your shift in an hour. François is taking over. He'll bring another bottle.'

'They really paid you for all this?'

'François Droz and Thomas Bauer.'

'And you are going to keep me company for an hour.'

'If you want me to stay?' Her green eyes have never been so wide and round.

'What about afterwards?' he asks, his voice suddenly low and serious.

'We can talk about that, you bad man. You are all the same, aren't you? For now, it's a drink and maybe a birthday kiss, if you are very lucky and very well behaved.'

'Come inside,' he says. 'Let's sit down. If anyone drives up, they won't see you from the road. Give me that bottle.'

'Let me do it.'

He is not just a lowly watchman. There are many other responsibilities. He lists them for her proudly. His job is more difficult and dangerous than it appears.

'You're making me nervous,' says Greta, refilling his glass. His chair is in the corner of the cabin, and he leans a shoulder against the unfinished concrete wall.

'No need to be nervous,' he says. 'Things are quiet now, but it is important to be vigilant. Forty-seven. That was when things were hot around the docks. The local villains tried to move in and take over when the workers went on strike. They didn't succeed everywhere. This warehouse is the last place where all the staff are union members, Party men. Either the criminals have forgotten us,' he says, yawning, 'or they are using us.'

'Using you, monsieur?'

'People say the Americans pay the *milieu* to keep the Reds out of the docks. Now imagine you are a cat, madame.'

'How lovely! Here.' She tops up his glass again. Her own is still untouched.

'You're a cat, and the king pays you to catch the mice in his palace. What happens if you eat them all?'

'Why, then I would be out of a job, I suppose.'

The guard covers his gaping mouth with the back of his hand.

'Excuse me. Out of a job, precisely. No more cream for you. It's better to leave one or two mice alive.'

'Yes. I can see that.' She is watching him closely as his head comes to rest against the wall. She pries the glass from his fingers.

'It doesn't need to look like an accident,' says Bobby. 'This is a declaration of war. They're sending a message to the Communists. Give some of that to me.'

'You can't touch this stuff without gloves. It's poisonous. Take these instead.' She drops shotgun cartridges into his palms. 'Get all the black powder out. Pile it up on a piece of cardboard for me.' His hands are shaking. She pinches his cheek and twists her fingers nastily to snap him out of it. 'Get yourself under control. Think about your worthless father.'

She is still working away by the time he has finished, moulding lumps of putty round the steel pillars that hold the roof up. 'Plastic explosive will slice straight through metal,' she says, 'if the charges are shaped correctly.' God knows if they have enough powder to set it off.

The other boys have steel *boules* in their coat pockets. They go to the administrative building behind the warehouse and blast the windows out. It's the calling card of the *milieu*, a reminder of the vicious street fighting of forty-seven. One boy sluices petrol from a jerrycan into the window while the other fingers a thing she has not seen for a long time: a green army grenade that looks enormous in his grubby little hand. 'Idiot,' says Greta. 'You need a spark to start a fire. All that will do is spray the glass over us. Give it to me. Now get back to the car.'

When she is certain that the youngsters are out of danger, she lights the end of the powder trail, perilously short, then runs for the door she has left ajar. There is a moment of strange uncertainty as she stops and looks over her shoulder through the gap into the warehouse, hands over her ears. When the blast comes it's a strong hand in the middle of her back, throwing her on to her knees. The noise of the fireball is like ripping fabric. It drowns her shout of pain.

Bobby pulls over by the side of the coast road that hangs over the Plage de la Lave and they all spill out. They are like boxers, bouncing on their toes and shaking the tension out of their arms. Greta is trembling from head to toe from the after-effects of adrenalin.

They look south towards the waterfront and the city behind it. The glare from the burning warehouse has swollen into an orange dome that mirrors the sun setting over the sea in the west. The consequences of what Greta has done are suddenly dizzying. What chain of action and reaction has she set in motion, with one flick of a match?

'It went bang after all,' says one of the boys, snaking an arm round Greta's waist. She elbows him away and he and his friend both laugh. To her surprise, Greta hears herself laughing too.

Bobby does not join in. When Greta has released everything that was bottled up inside her, she goes to him and touches his arm. 'I can't see any fire engines down there. No sirens. Won't they call the *pompiers*?'

He snarls at the boys suddenly. 'You two shut up. They will call,' he says, turning back to Greta and shielding his eyes from the low sun. 'The *pompiers*, the police. They will call everyone. But this is Marseille. And we are in the summer of the *milieu* now. No one will help them.'

All the long day's drive back to Paris, Greta thinks about Robert, needing him and hating herself for it. It is very late as she parks the Porsche on the street behind the restaurant, but she will elbow him awake when she gets inside.

As she turns the corner from Castiglione into Mont Thabor, she sees four men sitting outside the restaurant with their legs spread wide. Their table commands a view of all the converging streets. There are no other customers, and the lights are off inside.

All the men are dressed in the Neapolitan style: sports coats over open-necked shirts with wide lapels. Everything is new, neatly pressed, thin, disposable. The shoes are cheap shiny leather, highly polished. The men clap their hands as she approaches, but the applause dies when they see her expression. There is more on their faces than just Italian arrogance: a tension round the eyes. Their hilarity is forced. Greta thinks about the shotgun stashed in her room upstairs.

'This is my place,' Greta tells them. 'And we're closed.'

'*Principessa*,' says the man on the far right.

'No.'

'You could be. There's a room waiting for you at my place if you want it. But we haven't been introduced. I'm your new boss.'

The other three laugh at everything he says. They are sitting in order of age, she guesses, from left to right. The man who spoke to her is the oldest, or the most weather-beaten. His black hair is piled up in a high pompadour, backcombed and puffed with a dryer, shining with spray or pomade. He fusses with his hair to make up for the face, thinks Greta.

'Paul Fazi is the boss,' says Greta. 'Tell him I want to see him.'

That gets another laugh. 'You don't make demands,' says the

oldest man. 'You shovel the shit until the debt is paid. You work for us now. Remember these faces.'

'They are unforgettable.'

'Do you think we are all brothers?'

'You could be their father.'

There is a collective sharp intake of breath. Someone hisses a question, with his name at the end: Fabio. He shakes his head in answer. The others wait to see if he is going to laugh, then they join in.

'It's a tragic story,' he tells her. 'I was poisoned, as a young man. It altered the way I look.'

'Poisoned.'

'By a neighbour. It's not something you hear about in this country. The place where we grew up is a little bit more . . .'

'Primitive.'

He smiles, but all the humour has gone. He is getting tired of her mouth. His right hand is resting on a folded copy of *Corriere della Sera* and he taps it with his knuckles. 'Have a read when we leave. The details of your next job.'

There's a sudden noise from the entrance of the restaurant and everyone turns to look. Fabio calls out. '*Ciao, nenella*': hello, sweetheart.

Jacky closes the door behind him but does not lock it. He keeps the keys in his hand. '*Messieurs*,' he says, nodding at each man in turn. 'There is the small matter of the bill.'

'Ah. You have been patient.' The man with the quiff stands and the others rise hastily. He reaches for his pocketbook. He is tall for a southern Italian. 'Jacky is always very accommodating. Even when he is waiting to get his ribs smashed with a sledgehammer. Just lies there and takes it without a word of protest. What kind of man does that?'

'A patient one,' says Jacky, inclining his head politely.

The Neapolitan chuckles and indicates the newspaper before flicking banknotes on to the table next to it. 'Look underneath,' he tells Greta. 'There's a tip for you.'

'Take it with you. I don't read Italian. Tell Monsieur Paul to come and speak to me himself next time. You can keep the money too, pig. Buy yourself some new clothes.'

They both stand their ground, Greta with her fists on her hips, Jacky jangling the keys, in his good suit, while the men leave.

It happens two nights in a row, while Greta is out on business commissioned by Monsieur Balard.

The first time isn't serious enough for Romana to mention. A couple of men order shots of grappa and walk off without paying. They don't scurry away, they leave slowly and deliberately, with many a backward look. Romana is alone. She can't run down the street after them.

'You know these men,' says Greta, and Romana raises her knuckles to her mouth.

'Idiots,' Romana says. 'Small-timers from the margins of the *milieu*. Neapolitans.'

'Fabio?' asks Greta.

'Not him. Two of the others. But they brought a Frenchman with them when they came back tonight. Not so small-time.' Does Greta know Dodo?

'I've heard the name.'

'They ate a big meal, complaining about everything but ordering more and more. Almost shouting. Frightening away the other customers. *Zoticoni!* Louts. They stayed late, then Dodo went into the kitchen and started talking to Marcel. You know, like this.' She tweaks her own cheek roughly. 'The poor boy was terrified. I tried to go in, but Dodo shut the door in my face. He said the men had important business to discuss.'

'Where was Robert when all this was happening?'

'I think he went out to smoke. It was just after the end of the service.'

'Typical. Where is he now?'

'He walked home with Marcel in case anyone was waiting for the boy.'

'Good. What did Dodo want Marcel to do?'

'Take care of a package for him.'

'And where is this item now?'

There is a look of desolation on Romana's face. 'In the wine cellar, behind the brick that comes out.'

Greta looks up at Robert for a long time when he comes back. She can't decide if she is angry with him or not.

He thinks he was followed by a lean young man in a golfer's jacket.

Romana's daughter is with her grandmother tonight. 'You'd better stay here,' Greta tells her. 'Take my bed if you want to sleep. Make the coffee if you don't.'

'What is it?' asks Robert, prodding the fat envelope on the table with a finger.

'Heroin or cornflour, I suppose,' says Greta. 'Depending on what they are trying to pull. We'll find out soon enough.'

'Where's Jacky?'

'Upstairs, fetching my shotgun.'

She jumps from her seat when a cry of shock comes from the kitchen. Romana has burned her wrist on the coffee pot, that's all. 'I've got two left hands tonight,' she says miserably. 'Why can't I be brave like you?' Greta looks around the kitchen, eyeing the ingredients on the shelves, while Romana runs the burn under the cold tap.

Greta bolts the front entrance but leaves the side door on the latch for the men who will surely come for the package.

It's an easy pick for a professional, but they make a meal of it, rattling the lock for minutes on end before it pops open. It is just after two in the morning and the street looks very bright.

The boy who followed Robert has a carpentry tool in his hand instead of a gun or knife. He wears a short beige windcheater and his eyes are very wide. The one creeping in behind him is the youngest of the four Neapolitans, in a shirt with short sleeves and wide collar. Greta doesn't know his name. They merge into one.

Greta flicks the light on so the intruders can take in the size of the shotgun in her arms. They haven't bothered with masks. They watch her feed in the shells, one by one, then snap the barrels back into place. There's a wild half-smile on Greta's face. 'No,' says the young man in front. He throws the tool at her and she ducks.

She's right on their heels until they reach the junction with Rue de Castiglione. Close enough to grab their belts. Then she feels the strength in her legs fading and lets the shotgun bark twice. Angry, congested coughs, almost at point-blank.

The boy in the jacket arches his back and screams as the contents of the first cartridge lash his buttocks. The other one has pulled a yard or two further away from Greta. He feels the shot sting his lower back but does not cry out. The pain spurs both boys on. Greta pulls up, bends forwards at the waist and rests one hand on her thigh, chest pulsing.

'Too many cigarettes. Too much wine. I'm out of condition.'

The following evening, Jacky, perfectly barbered and wrapped elegantly in a pressed chalk-stripe suit, ushers Fabio into the restaurant, followed by a man who can only be Dodo.

Romana has warned Greta about his ugliness, but it is still a shock. Eyes from some dark corner of the deep ocean, a broken beak of a nose and an Adam's apple that threatens to burst out of his neck. He is habitually slack-jawed, his sharp, crowded teeth permanently on display. He's almost as tall as Robert but there is a weakness in him.

The men take their seats in the corner booth, laughing at everything, not too confidently. Greta brings menus and says: 'You left something here last night.'

A glance passes between them and Fabio stiffens. 'That's for Jacky. He's going to sell it for us. You guarantee our return.'

'The package has already been incinerated.' Their faces darken so quickly and dramatically that it is almost comical. 'I'm joking,' says Greta. 'I wanted to know if it was real or not. Now I know. We can't talk out here. Come into the kitchen.'

A pan of stock is bubbling on the range, but neither chef is at his station. Greta closes the door firmly behind her and leans against it. There is a moment of silence, because the eyes of Fabio and Dodo are fixed on the curious object that Greta has taken out of her pocket. It's the size of a lemon, but green in colour. A dull, dark green. The men are squinting, trying to read the yellow markings.

'It's an American fragmentation grenade,' says Greta, hooking her right forefinger into the circle of the pin. 'The fuse burns for two seconds. You won't get past me and out of the door in time if that's what you're thinking. We all go together.'

'It's not real,' says Dodo. 'They make replicas for the movies.'

'Training,' says Fabio.

'Are you ready to die?' asks Greta. 'Because I am. I'm not going to sell that shit for you and I'm not going to let your boys steal it back so you can put me in your debt. You leave my staff alone or we make a nice sauce now. A bucket of blood from each of us, mixed together. Decide.'

Romana has their coats ready for them, standing by the door. Dodo is holding the envelope containing the powder in both hands. They both eye Romana as they shuffle past but say nothing.

Greta's voice rings out as they leave. 'Tell Monsieur Paul to come himself. No more monkeys.'

A front of warm air pushes its way up from the south. Summer, and the life of the streets, suddenly begins in earnest, as if by common agreement. The garden of the Tuileries teems with girls in their light dresses. Greta is unable to enjoy any of it. She broods in her room like a child with a summer cold banished from the sunshine. The tension builds as each day passes uneventfully.

On the Friday morning, Jacky knocks for her and nods his head, answering her raised eyebrows. 'Remember what we said, Greta. You promised.'

'I am calm,' she says.

Lucien Fazi is at the best table, the one with views in four directions. The man next to him has a frog-like face, very pale. His

appearance is flawless, from the lustre of the black shoes to the slick
cap of inky hair, below which a scar is said to run from ear to ear.

The other two men at the table have their backs to Greta. They
turn as she approaches slowly over the paving stones.

Fabio is on the side closest to the road. The presence of the Fazi
men has obviously had a tonic effect on his confidence. He begins
to clap as Greta draws near, then makes a sharp hissing sound. He
drags his eyes up and down her body, nodding his head apprecia-
tively. Dodo, next to him, joins in the applause.

'Enough,' says Paul. He is eating a casserole of duck leg and
beans and his eyes remain on his plate. His voice is weaker than
she was expecting – low and cracked. It adds to his power. The
other men fall silent instantly whenever he speaks. Paul indicates
the empty chair at the head of the table and offers Greta a moist,
pale hand.

'*Laba diena*,' he says, in a wretched accent, holding her fingers
and watching her closely.

'You should say *dobry den*, monsieur.'

'I was speaking Lithuanian. That's the only thing I ever learned
how to say.'

'I am a White Russian,' says Greta.

'Sure, sure. I have a Lithuanian girl. Perhaps you met her when
you broke into my home?'

It's like a cloud obscuring the sun. Suddenly all she can see are
his pale hands on Morta's thighs, hips, waist. These clammy claws
running over that young, unblemished skin. Control yourself, she
thinks.

'I have already sent apologies for trespassing on your property,
monsieur. I'm happy to say sorry again, in person.'

'I have a lot of girls from different places,' says Paul. 'If I don't
like a girl, I can always throw her away. Do you know what I mean?'

Greta holds his gaze steadily. 'I have paid my debt for that intru-
sion. It's time to move on. Jacky and I have a business proposal
for you.'

Paul glances at Lucien, then drops Greta's hand and picks up his cutlery again. He's not being dismissive, she thinks. He is incapable of leaving food alone if it is in front of him.

'We need money,' Greta tells him. 'We know how to obtain it, but we want your blessing, Monsieur Paul. More than that – your help. We plan to cross the French border.'

'She says she wants to work for me too,' cries Fabio. 'I don't let her, until she comes on her hands and knees.' There is a squeal of delighted laughter from Dodo.

Greta ignores him. 'The job is a long way from Paris, Monsieur Fazi. Low-risk but lucrative, if done right. Naturally we would pay tribute to your family. But I want my fair share too. I'm not going to work for free any more, not for you or anyone else.'

Fabio and Dodo swear in unison at her audacity, but Paul silences them with a growl. '*Abbastanza.*' He sits back in his chair, looking at the younger men opposite with tired eyes.

The white beans appear to have defeated him. He runs his tongue over his teeth as he talks to his men. 'You're brave, isn't it? When Lulu is with you. You weren't brave when you came without him. It's the same with Momo. He's always threatening to come waddling down here and shoot this woman.' Paul shrugs. 'I keep saying, sure, this is the address: off you go. Funny thing – he hasn't made it over here yet.'

He turns to Greta. 'I've got a lot of brave boys. But they didn't grow up in the countryside, like you and me. They don't recognize an old farmer's trick when they see it.'

'Trick?' She isn't going to help him.

'Filling a shotgun cartridge with salt crystals instead of buck-shot. So that a naughty boy who comes over the fence to steal a chicken gets a nasty fright and a few red marks on his arse, instead of a ticket to the morgue.'

'We don't give our recipes away here, monsieur.'

Paul laughs. 'I say the secret ingredient was rock salt. It was well done. But if you want to work in Italy, I can't help you. I have obligations there.'

'I was talking about the Swiss border, monsieur. Jacky will give you all the details.'

Paul isn't drinking wine – it's the sweet orange soft drink they stock for children. He picks up his glass and looks at it for ten seconds.

'Monsieur Jacques can talk to Lulu about it. No promises. In the meantime, the naughty boys won't bother you any more. Do you know why?' Paul points at Jacky, who is standing three paces away, hands held in front of his body. 'I know he's an ideas man.'

'Monsieur Jacques does all the planning,' says Greta. 'I make sure everything runs on castors. We split the proceeds fairly.'

'Oh, I trust Jacky to do the right thing. He has been making your donation to the community fund every week, rain or shine, since you opened. Straight out of the till.' Greta cannot stop the distaste from showing on her face, and Paul gives a sharp laugh. 'He didn't tell you about that. There's a lot you don't know about Monsieur Jacques. Isn't it, *maricón?*'

'That's it exactly, Monsieur Paul.' Jacky inclines his head, gives a little smile. There is no hint of tension in his voice.

'There was a time when Jacky didn't obey the rules. He has it straight now. It's good when people learn a lesson. We should reward them. Also, I'm a patriot, aren't I? I'm told you have a relationship with a man who guards the safety of the Fourth Republic.'

Greta glances around at the nearest diners.

'You can't talk about it. *Bien.* If you are fighting on the side of the angels, I don't distract you. These brave boys don't disturb you any more. In fact, this is going to be the safest place in Paris from now on. You can leave your door unlocked. Unless *Monsieur le maricón* falls back into his old habits, that is.' He jabs a warning finger at Jacky. 'If this one gets himself in the soup again, madame, then you are on the hook for all the payments.'

Paul spreads himself in the chair. He has a habit of stroking his tie with his hand to make sure it's hanging straight. The men on the other side of the table mimic him unconsciously, settling back and widening their legs.

'I'm grateful, Monsieur Paul.' As Greta says it, she slides the steak knife with the serrated edge out from under the sleeve of her sweater and lays it on the table for Paul to see. His face creases into a slow smile. 'Enjoy the rest of the meal,' says Greta, rising from her seat. As she passes Fabio she says: 'You. Fucking *hiss* at me again.'

The thing she drops into his lap is the colour, size and shape of an M26 grenade with the pin removed. It has the effect of making him yelp like a puppy and jump out of the chair. The dark-green ball falls on to the ground and rolls towards Paul's feet as Fabio staggers back away from the others. Dodo tries to stand but jams his thigh painfully against the table edge.

Lucien has not moved a muscle. He watches Greta as she walks away from the men without a backward glance. Paul is laughing. It's louder than his speaking voice. He picks up the avocado pear that has come to rest against his glossy shoe and sets it on the white tablecloth in front of Fabio's seat with finger and thumb. '*Voilà!*' he says. 'Well done. Brave boys.'

Along the pavement, people have turned to see what is causing the commotion. Fabio is holding his head in his hands, staring at the bruised piece of fruit. Dodo is dabbing at himself with a white napkin. He has spilled wine all over his crotch.

21

Jacky wants Dutchman for the Geneva job. He won't tell Greta why.

She lurks in a corner of the *cercle* alone, playing twenty-one in a robotic way. Making all the mathematically correct moves she has memorized, with one eye on the front door.

Dutchman and Lucien are upstairs at a drinking table, but she's sure they haven't spotted her under the dark glasses and headscarf.

There's a six-handed poker game at the big table to Greta's right. She wonders if a team is working that night, signalling to each other about the strength of their hands.

She stiffens when she hears cursing from the entrance. Jacky Lellouche is outlined in the doorway with his arms raised. A slight man in a tight suit, walking like a dancer. Greta can hear the doorman snarling at him. She is about to stand up when Lucien runs down the steps.

The body language of the men on the door changes when Lucien reaches them. They back away from Jacky, suddenly unsure. They all know him, of course. He has been banned from every gaming circle in Metropolitan France.

Lucien smoothing things over. Smiles and handshakes all round. The ones that make a rustling noise, Greta supposes, although she is too far away to tell if banknotes are changing hands.

But the big doorman feels the need to make a performance out of patting Jacky down before he lets him through, up and down the legs. She can hear Lucien's impatient voice. 'All right, you made your point. Do you think the guy is a gunfighter?'

Greta raises a hand to stop the banker sitting opposite her from dealing the next hand. I need to powder my nose, she tells him. Lucien has his back to her as she glides towards the group of men.

The doorman is squatting next to Jacky now, groping round his ankles. 'You like what you feel down there?' asks Jacky. 'Want to go somewhere private?'

Lucien wedges himself between them and slides a proprietorial arm round Jacky. The security guard is backing off, finally, with an ill grace. Greta stops walking. She's out in the open on the thick carpet.

The men still haven't seen her. Jacky is looking back at the bouncer and blowing a kiss. 'Come and find me later, but I do it to you, okay? You don't do it to me. I'm not that kind.'

The elastic snaps. The big man grabs Jacky by the back of the neck and smashes him over the roulette table at the foot of the staircase. The players sitting round it yell as one, the piping voice of the croupier coming over the top. The shift manager is thumping down the stairs now. Jacky is making the most of it, groaning like a dying man, rolling around on the table and knocking the bets everywhere before he is released.

Greta hangs back, one hand resting inside her bag. It takes several minutes to restore order. The manager walks the bouncer back towards the front door with a hand on his elbow. Dutchman has come down and is standing next to Lucien, staring at the big man as he is led away.

Upstairs, there are drinks on the house. Dutchman kisses Greta's hand. He has heard all the stories, he says. Jacky is still straightening his collar and tie, smoothing his hair back down. Then he winks and holds up the thousand-franc chip he palmed when the bouncer threw him over the table. 'You know this place belongs to my cousin,' says Lucien. 'You are stealing from Paul Fazi.' Jacky throws back his head and laughs.

Greta can read the amusement on Dutchman's face as he watches

Jacky. Funny little fellow, the red-haired man will be thinking. The big nose and the ears that stick out from the head. What is this little leprechaun going to teach me about armed robbery?

The Swiss, says Jacky, after the waitress has left them. He shakes his head. The blockheaded, mooing Swiss, who have everything handed to them on a silver plate and never stop complaining about any of it. A nation that never spent a night out of a soft bed. And, he says, the good burghers of the canton of Vaud have just done a very foolish thing. To protect their delicate ears from the noise of traffic, they have passed a law banning heavy vehicles from using public roads at night.

So? Lucien is lifting his drink carefully with a napkin underneath it. Dutchman is glaring at Lucien. It's obvious what he's thinking. Why did you bring me here? What is this cuntery?

'When do the big banks transport large amounts of cash?' asks Jacky, and the other men say it together: 'At night.'

'The change in the law,' says Jacky, 'means a Swiss bank no longer has the option of using big, armoured trucks when driving through Vaud. From now on, across that canton, such deliveries will be carried out by the Swiss postal service. Ordinary little vans, ordinary little postmen, on deserted roads, in the middle of the night.'

Dutchman is no longer laughing at Jacky.

The same angry bouncer is working on the door as they fetch their coats on the way out. The man is calmer now. He looks Greta up and down eagerly – eating her with his eyes. He helps her into her coat. 'I hope you were lucky this evening, madame.'

'Not really. I had to look at your ugly face.' She kisses Jacky on the cheek. 'Why don't you keep your fucking hands off my friends next time?'

They use Greta as bait.

A woman on her own in the middle of the night, in front of an old heap with the bonnet up, in the headlamps of the postal van as it approaches.

She can see the driver and passenger talking animatedly. Two men with grey hair on a run they know like the bottom of their pockets: Zurich to Geneva. They react slowly, braking late and almost running into the car on the narrow road that snakes round the north shore of the lake.

Talking about their grandkids, thinks Greta, preparing her face. The man in the passenger seat is supposed to keep the rifle on him at all times. She can see it broken on his seat. He doesn't want to scare her with it. Doesn't even lock the door behind him when he gets out. He is looking at Greta with great concern when Dutchman takes him from behind in a bear hug.

The battle lasts seconds. Greta watches the road while Lucien rips a jacket and hat from the bigger of the two Swiss men. Dutchman ties the prisoners' thumbs – a commando trick he learned in the war. He orders the men to be quiet in German. There is no need to bother with gags.

When they are ready to leave, they push the decoy car out into the road behind to block both lanes, then stab out the tyres. Dutchman drives west in a uniform too tight for him. Greta and Lucien stay in the back with the postal workers, in disciplined silence. From time to time, Lucien checks the thumb-ties and blindfolds to make sure the men are comfortable. There is a gentleness about him.

Jacky is waiting at the border in a car with French plates. He doesn't even want to look at the captives they leave locked in the back of the van. He doesn't want to get involved in moving the money across either, after he finds a box of paperwork from the bank: a staff roll call, payment schedules, federal and cantonal tax statements.

Lellouche sits in the car and leafs through it while the others curse him. There is no bullion, just French currency, but money is heavy enough. It's hot work for three.

The crossing is a tiny post next to the River Rhône. There is no sign of life anywhere on the last stretch of Swiss territory. Greta starts when a French border guard runs out of the wooden hut on the other side of the line. But Lucien winds his window down and hands over an inch of banknotes with a wink. Monsieur Paul's arm is long.

Then they are passing the sign: France. The speed limits for cars and trucks. There is a collective shout of triumph, the banging of fists on windows. Even Jacky Lellouche looks up from his ledgers for a second and grins.

They all go to Heaven together. Nothing but champagne will do. Then Dutchman invites half the nightclub back to his new flat at Longchamp. The big red-haired man knows everyone in the night-time world. He works on the film sets, looking after the actors and fixing them up with whatever they need.

When Greta passes through the lounge, there are famous faces all around. One of the gypsy guitarists is playing in the corner. A massive thing like a cello. Women are dancing barefoot.

Jacky stands apart from them all. She joins him on the terrace that overlooks the racecourse, and he tells her about the stunts he pulled when he first came to Paris.

He had a team that used to go through the race-day crowds like a hot knife – watches, wallets, jewellery. Quick as cats. They would bundle it all up and throw it over the fences to people outside. No one was ever arrested.

He touches Greta on the arm while they are talking. Dutchman has come out on to the balcony, bearing a bottle. The host is doing the rounds, pouring himself into groups of actresses and dancers. Jacky is watching him all the time.

Dutchman wants to show Greta his collection of paintings. Not all of them are stolen. The furniture is modern, Danish teak. He reels off the names of manufacturers that mean nothing to her. It is a single man's apartment, designed to impress women.

He has laboratory cocaine, pure and fine, straight from Germany. The kind that gives you an intense rush of energy then wears off quickly without causing a headache or blocking the sinuses. There is no need to cut it with a razor blade. He leads her to the bathroom and scoops a little pile on to a tiny antique silver snuff spoon.

She is laughing when he takes her by the waist and begins to dance. Then she sees over his shoulder that he locked the door behind him when he followed her in. The hubbub of the party is suddenly far away.

Dutchman kisses her, sliding his hands up her back to grip her shoulders. He has the knack of making you aware of the strength in his upper frame without squeezing too hard. She tries to turn him round so she can reach the lock. He allows their bodies to pivot towards the door, then he spins her back away from it, turning the push and pull into dance steps.

This is how it is, she thinks, when you run out of road. When you're all out of tricks and clever ideas. Just a woman and a man, fifty kilos heavier. She knows she must allow him to kiss her. It's just the price, she realizes. He will do the same thing to all the girls he brings in here. This is the price of the cocaine.

After a minute she tries to squirm out of his grip but there is another squeeze, a hint of the great force he could summon from his chest and triceps if he chose to. He will not release her until he has taken as much as he wants. He is a dangerous animal. She cannot anger him. Everything is a negotiation now.

When he breaks off, she forces a smile. 'I need a drink.' She must not allow the words to sound fearful. She must keep everything light and bright. He is holding her face in his hands, stroking her, looking deep into her eyes. 'I can't stand that chemical taste in the back of my throat,' she says.

His gaze is disturbingly intense for a moment. Then he swallows a deep breath and says: '*Bien*. Let's get you some more champagne.' Her eyes close in relief when he slides the lock open and steps aside. As she walks out of the room ahead of him he links his hands round her middle, pulling her back, and presses his lips to her ear. 'I would love it if you stayed the night.' She manages an approximation of a girlish giggle.

*

'Stupid,' says Greta, as Jacky is driving them away. 'Stupid girl.'

'It wasn't your fault. I asked you to keep him busy.'

'I should have stayed on the balcony. I ought to know what men are by now. I'm not a child. There is no excuse for a woman of my age allowing herself to get trapped like that.'

'We don't become friends after one run. That's not how it works. They want to use us. They will never accept us as equals.'

Greta brings her head back up from where it was hanging, close to her knees, and opens eyes that have been screwed up tight. 'I hope it was worth it.'

'So I found his passport upstairs, a few other things. The book is in his new name, the one he was given in the Legion. I have contacts there. I can find his real identity in their records. I still have some friends left.' He cuts it off. He didn't mean to say all that out loud.

'When are you going to tell me what you are playing at?'

'Patience,' says Jacky. 'When are you going to trust me?'

'Never.'

'That is why I adore you. It works both ways, Greta. What are you going to do about the girl?'

'I already told you. The kid I knew died a long time ago. It's about money and guns now.'

'And I told you that I don't believe a word of it. The girl is the only reason Monsieur Paul is still alive. That's it, isn't it?'

'I have forgotten Morta.'

'I'm not buying it. Who are you going to kill first when she is safely out of the house? Paul or the red-haired baboon?'

Greta laughs. 'Is it that obvious?'

'No,' says Jacky, his face unexpectedly serious as he takes his eyes off the road to look at her. 'No. I would not say that your feelings are obvious at all. Your face is much harder to read these days. You are an altogether different sort of animal.'

Painkillers again. 'You might as well leave them on the bedside table,' Greta tells Robert. She is sliding back into a troubled dream when the telephone rings downstairs. 'The Corsican,' says Robert, unable to hide his disapproval. He never uses Lucien's name.

She applies lipstick and mascara carefully in front of the bathroom mirror, a knot tightening in her stomach. No youthful date with the dreamiest of boys ever inspired such lavish attention to face and nails and wardrobe.

Greta steps out of the restaurant in a full-length Chanel coat in a dogtooth pattern over a plain belted dress. A beret sits on top of her head. Lucien casts a critic's eye over it all from behind the wheel of his car, then nods stiffly. He is impeccably barbered and dressed in a grey suit, simple but good.

'I saw you talking to Dutchman at the party,' says Lucien. 'Did he say much?'

'They always do, after a sniff.'

'What did you tell him?'

'The truth – that I'm trying to find a good doctor in Paris. I asked him about the *milieu* guy, the one who checks the girls over. It turns out that I saw him that night, leaving the White House. An old man in spectacles with no rims.'

'What did Dutch think about that?'

'Told me to find someone else. Anyone. Stay away from that creep.'

'It's what they all say. Did you find out anything about the politician, Greta?'

'I couldn't think of anything clever, so I kept it close to the truth again. I said the doctor sounds like an important guy. There's a rumour that he's going to help us get to a government minister.'

'And?'

'Dutchman changed the subject quickly.'

'Scared?'

Greta frowns. 'I don't think so. He's a tough character. It's more like he was disgusted. *What horror*, he said. Screwed up his face like he felt sick. Where are you taking us, Lucien?'

'There's been a change of plan. We're going to a place I've never used before.'

'Is someone following you?'

'Perhaps. Just a feeling. Marie says I'm paranoid.'

Greta inclines her head sympathetically. 'How has it been with her?'

'Difficult, but she will hear you out. I've done my best. You get twenty minutes. I stay with you all the time.'

The girl sits at the writing desk, sideways on so she faces them as they shuffle into the hotel room. Lucien takes off his suit jacket and hangs it carefully in the wardrobe then kicks off his shoes and sprawls on the bed. Trying to keep everything relaxed.

Greta remains standing before the girl, one hand cupping the other in front of her body. Her head is bowed. She takes a deep breath and begins.

'I've made a mess of everything, ever since I left Lithuania. The way I behaved with you was my biggest mistake. You were still a small child, in my head. I understand now that you are a woman. Old enough to decide your own future. I came here to beg you to forgive me, Morta.'

'My name is Marie now.'

Greta nods. 'If you like. We earned that, your mother and me. I don't blame you for hating us. That was the bit I forgot. I lost my family in the war, and there is nothing I wouldn't give for a minute with any of them. I forgot the other part of it. We hate them sometimes, don't we? The people who abandon us.'

'I don't hate either of you, I just don't believe in you. Can you imagine how many hours I spent praying alone? When they let me out into the grounds, I picked wildflowers.'

'Flowers,' says Greta, her voice cracking.

'My mother told me it was a code they used when the Germans came. If you thought you were in danger, you put fresh flowers in the window so the partisans would see you were in trouble.'

'Yes. It was a sign we used.'

'I did what she told me to do. I kept it up for years. Any flowers I could find around the house, in a vase on the windowsill in my room, with the curtains open. All I did all day long was pray for you to come. When no one answers your prayers, you stop believing.'

Curse me, thinks Greta. And there was a time when I didn't think I could weep any more. Look at me now.

Morta sifts through the letters laid out on the desk for her while Greta is repairing her make-up in the bathroom. Lucien lounges on the bed and smokes in silence. When Greta comes out, the girl says: 'What do you want me to do?'

'Tell me which ones are real and which are forgeries. I want to understand what they did to you.'

'Then what happens? To the people involved?'

'Whatever you want, darling. Just give me their names. I swear to you that I will make them *suffer*.' Greta is becoming emotional again.

'That's exactly what I don't want. Tell her.'

Lucien glances from the girl to Greta. 'I don't know. She's some kind of pacifist.'

'Tell her properly! Like you mean it!'

He swallows and sits up on the bed. 'There are conditions. She cannot bear the thought of anyone being hurt in her name. I have made her a promise. No more violence.'

'Look at her face,' laughs Morta. 'What an idea. She won't know what to do with herself. It's your answer to everything, isn't it, Greta?'

'Sweetheart. We are talking about bad men. What exactly am I supposed to do with them?'

'Do you really think I need a lesson from you in what men are like?'

Greta sinks slowly into the second chair. The plans and calculations that have been forming in her head in recent weeks have been knocked into disarray.

The girl watches her with something like amusement. Her lips curl into a cruel smile. 'Did Lucien tell you about the time I ran away?'

'From Paul Fazi? You got away from him?'

'It's when I first understood how things worked here. I was a wreck when I first arrived at the White House. Sick from crying all the time. I lay on the bed and prayed, in the clothes I came in. Hand-me-downs from the convent. Only Paul was allowed to enter my room. He tried to feed me by hand and I bit his wrist!'

'Good for you,' Lucien grunts from the bed.

'No, it was stupid. We all need to eat.'

'How did Paul react?' asks Greta.

'He wasn't angry. He just said I would learn soon. *Life is education, isn't it?* A couple of days later, one of the other girls came to my room. It was in the early evening. I had cried myself to sleep again. She knelt by the bed and whispered. She said the police had been tipped off about a missing child. There was a car full of *gendarmes* parked on the main road. It's hard to take things in when you've just woken up. At first, I didn't realize who she was.'

'A girl working there?'

'The youngest after me. She said the men who had brought me to the house were so scared of the police that they had run off into the woods and left everything unlocked. It was now or never. That's when I realized the door of my room had been left open for the first time.'

'Go on,' says Greta.

'I put my shoes on and followed her downstairs. It was like a dream. There were no men around. I could hear the radio in Maman's kitchen, but no voices. No guards anywhere. The front door was on the latch.'

'Tell me you ran for it.'

'Straight down the middle of the drive, over the gravel. I didn't try to hide. And there they were, in the car!'

Greta looks at Lucien in disbelief and he nods. 'Police. Real police.'

'Three of them,' says Morta. 'With a spare seat for me. They were the most handsome men I had ever seen. As tall as Lithuanians. What's the matter, Lulu?'

His hand is over his face. 'I know what's coming.'

'Where did they take you?' asks Greta.

'To the *gendarmes* in the village. I met the captain himself. The man in charge of the whole district. He bowed to me. All his men saluted my courage, he said. They could not imagine the hardship I had endured. Tomorrow they would ask me to make a full statement, but tonight I must rest. There was no accommodation suitable in the police station, so a room had been prepared in the *mairie*, no less.'

'The town hall,' says Greta, in Lithuanian.

'That's when I had this sick feeling. It's like you're listening to a violin, and it starts to slide out of tune. They had laid things out for me on the bed: a robe and a nightdress. It was all wrong. All the *frou-frou*.'

'Too sexy.'

She nods. 'I didn't want to put it on. One of the tall policemen was waiting outside, shouting at me to hurry up. They suddenly stopped being friendly. He barged in and took me by the wrist when I wouldn't come out. The others were waiting for me downstairs.'

'Paul?'

'And Ange, smoking cigars. A record was playing. The doctor was with them, and the police captain was sitting opposite. He had taken his cap off and was smoothing his hair with one hand. When he saw me, he indicated Paul and said, "May I present Monsieur the Mayor." Everyone laughed.'

'Good Christ,' says Lucien quietly.

'They didn't beat me or anything. Paul just asked me if I had learned something. If I understood France now. When I said yes, he opened his arms and made me come to him. Before we left, he told me to go and kiss all the men goodnight.'

A noise from the bed. Lucien's teeth are round his knuckles.

'When we got back,' says Morta, 'Paul took everything I owned and burned it on the lawn next to the well. He said I would have to earn the right to clothes and blankets. If I learned how to behave, I could become the best-dressed girl in France. But from now on, everything I wore would be chosen and paid for by him. He was very passionate, in those days. I suppose he was really in love with me then.'

Lucien makes another choking sound.

'Paul asked me what I would do next time if someone opened a door for me. I knew what to say.'

'That's not love, for Christ's sake.'

Marie looks over at Lucien. He has taken his fist out of his mouth and is sitting on the edge of the mattress, rocking.

'Listen to him, Greta. He talks like a priest. How many people has he killed?'

'I don't know.'

'What about you? How many men have you strangled with piano wires?'

'I don't keep score.'

'But you want to lecture me like a pair of schoolteachers. You want me to give up everything for you. *Voilà*, Greta. You know the conditions now. No more fighting and killing. No one else gets hurt for my sake.'

22

There is no rest, though Greta craves it. She has accepted a commission from Monsieur Balard and the work he has for her is a slow, patient business that swallows the long days.

Balard supplies the names: the wife of the Algerian separatist leader Djamel Hannachi, his ageing parents, political contacts in Paris, old university friends. Greta stalks them as they cross the city, loiters nearby when they take their ease. She studies the Hannachi circle, learning their routines, looking for the stragglers in the herd.

Greta is rarely to be found at the restaurant in the evenings now. When she returns unexpectedly early after following the imam of a mosque to his mistress's house, she marvels at the bonds of friendship that have grown in her absence. Robert has worked up quite a double act with Jacky.

The tall Lithuanian is nuzzling Greta's neck and purring: who is this beautiful stranger?

Jacky is counting the cash in the till. 'What about me?' he shouts.

Robert blows him a kiss. 'You are also looking beautiful this evening, Monsieur Jacques.'

'Well, would it *kill* you to tell me sometimes, darling?'

She's in bed with Robert later when she asks him if he ever pictures Jacky with other men. He doesn't appear to understand the question. It's not something people talked about, she says, when they were growing up. Isn't he curious about what men do to each other? Does the thought of it disgust him?

Robert assumes a troubled look, as if he is pondering the subject for the first time. Then his laugh booms out. She really thinks he's a village boy, just arrived from the farm. He has been working in Paris for eight years now. Nothing would shock him.

Greta is surprised to learn that he has kept the lake house running as a business for months, hiring youngsters from the town to collect the money and watch over the boats. He has bought a motorcycle so that he can go to the Compiègne forest to check on things.

'I had no idea,' she says. 'And you're making money?'

'You mean you didn't think I had it in me. We're breaking even. I'll install a full-time manager one day. They can live in the flat and take a share of the profits. A better deal than I ever got.'

They ride out to the lake together when she gets a free Sunday. She agrees to sit obediently behind, gripping him round the middle, on the condition that he teaches her to operate the machine at the first opportunity.

He'll build his own place on the edge of the water one day, he says, with a Riva speedboat parked outside.

Greta insists on cooking for him at the tiny stove in the apartment above the boatshed. Everything is light and full of easy laughter, just like the first time she stayed there. It's a perfect July day, the sun glossing the lake outside.

There was a hesitancy about him in their earliest days together that used to trouble her. It was always she who initiated proceedings, cornering him, shoving him on to the bed. The nagging thought that her passion was not reciprocated in equal measure. Now there can be no doubt about the pull she exerts over him. He sulks and frets if she denies him her body even for a few hours. He is only happy when he is inside her. They stay at the boathouse for two days and nights and fuck eleven times, on the mattress, in the bathroom, against the walls.

They are packing their things on the Tuesday morning and Greta is thinking about her period, counting out the days of safety on her fingers – *seven before and seven after* – when a Simca in the famous black and red livery of the G7 taxi company drives slowly down the winding slip road that leads to the gate of the boatyard.

Another envelope, smaller this time. The shots are in colour.

'It's him,' says Greta, after ten seconds. 'He's shaved off the walrus moustache. I'll have to think of a new nickname. He's even lost a little bit of weight.'

'Is still an elephant,' says the Spanish taxi driver. Both women chuckle, breaking the tension. 'That is how we say in my language. How do you say?'

'A three-door wardrobe.'

'I like! Tell me what you are thinking.'

'That he's easy to spot, from a mile away, even without the bristles.' Greta is remembering the worthless promises Balard made her as they stood on the empty roof of the Arch. *He will be arrested immediately if he returns to France. You need have no more worries.*

The man she still thinks of as the Walrus is surely back in Paris now, from the second photograph. Haussmann blocks loom in the background, out of focus. He is in a city park, not quite identifiable, with another, younger man. They are side by side on a bench, looking down with delight at something close to their shoes.

'Does one of them have a dog?' asks Greta.

'They like to feed the birds when they talk.'

'Is that his handler?'

'I can't understand you.'

'The man who looks after him. His contact in Russian intelligence.'

'*Hostia!* What Russian intelligence? They cut him off absolutely after he makes a *cagada* with you. They don't reply to his messages. The other man in the photograph is from the Paris police.'

'The police know he has returned to France.'

'Why not? His old friends take care of him. A lot of Communists in the police syndicate. The orders come through them. He believes he is still working for Moscow.'

'And who do we believe he is working for?'

'A Monsieur *Balard* . . .'

There is more, but Greta doesn't take it in. The fat man must know where I am, she thinks. It wouldn't be hard to track her down to the restaurant. Almost the same spot where he last saw her, on her hands and knees on the pavement. Someone has told him to leave me alone, she thinks. For now.

Balard is keeping this man on a leash, like a snarling dog. Waiting to see if I screw up and become a liability. Then what? More shots in the street. Two bodies, she supposes. A Communist intrigue. Or a sordid tale of revenge in the criminal underworld.

'You accept the invitation?' the woman is saying. 'I can drive you there now?'

'What's that? No. I've got transport of my own. Tell your colleague I will meet him at two.'

Robert is wheeling the motorcycle through the gate as she says it. He looks strong, hunched over the bars to hold the heavy frame upright. It's a big Gnome-Rhône, like the ones the Germans screamed around on in the war. His eyes burn at the curly-haired driver through the glass windscreen of the cab. A glower of displeasure

'Incredible,' the Spanish woman says, in a soft voice.

'What?'

'You are a very lucky woman.'

The lobby of the Coq d'Or is full of signed photographs of people who have dined there in recent years: Chaplin, Bergman, Onassis. England's new queen with her tall husband. The General, looking uncomfortable in civilian clothes.

Greta's table is ready. The host will join her in a moment. He has hurried out on a brief errand. She pours herself a glass of champagne from the bottle that is waiting on ice, nodding with approval at the label, then gropes under the table for recording devices.

They are in an alcove in the quiet section on the far side of the bar, almost a private room. Only one other table in the grand dining hall is occupied. A quartet of Scandinavians, under-dressed, over-awed by the surroundings. Tourists, thinks Greta.

Greta knows instantly that the man who comes walking towards her, wielding a tube of tightly rolled paper like a swagger stick, is Russian. His head is shaved smooth. It reminds her of the Walrus, except this man is about thirty-five, not sixty, and he has taken a great deal of care with the razor, so there are no bumps or cuts on his skull. There is a smell of sandalwood shaving soap as he kisses her cheeks.

'I never thought the day would come,' says Greta. 'A Soviet soldier who doesn't stink.'

'Do you mind if we speak Russian? It will be . . . easier today.' He glances over at the bar and then at the far end of the room, where a young waiter is loitering, as though recalling the languages spoken by every member of staff. 'I ordered for both of us already.'

'How charming. Isn't your Spanish woman joining us?'

'Nuria gets bored in restaurants.'

'I rather like Nuria.'

'She was supposed to bring you here. Pat you down. Check your bag.'

'I'm not armed. Even if I were: you've been helping me, ever since I came to France. I'm not going to kill you before lunch.'

The Russian shoots her a reproachful look because the head waiter is approaching, pushing a trolley with a metal device on top. It looks like a silver bell in a frame, with a ship's wheel screwed into the crown of the bell. The waiter, in black tuxedo to distinguish him from his white underlings, greets the Russian man warmly then launches into an explanation of the dish.

He will bring a raw duck to the table and butcher it in front of them. A fat Rouen bird that has been strangled to retain the blood. The legs will be hacked away and taken to the kitchen for the second course. The breast will be cut into strips to be sautéed at the table when the sauce, the centrepiece of the dish, is ready.

To construct the sauce, the head waiter will place the carcass of the animal into this instrument of torture and turn the screw to crush the bones, pressing the blood out into a pan at the bottom. Claret and lemon juice and the puréed liver of the duck will be added to the pan. The mixture will be left to reduce slowly.

Greta keeps her eyes on the head waiter as he works, and the Russian keeps his eyes on her. They will eat oysters while the sauce thickens.

After the waiter has gone, the Russian says: 'I'm sorry I kept you waiting. Something tickled me. There's a caricaturist sitting outside, doing sketches of passers-by for fifty francs.' He unrolls the scroll of paper. A row of faces with exaggerated features, coloured lightly in pastel. From left to right: Mykolan, Molotov, Malenkov, Karpov, Stalin. 'What do you think?'

'That you know how to spoil a nice meal. Karpov's nose isn't right. I suppose he's the least famous, though.'

'So far.' The Russian tuts with disapproval as she reaches for the bottle. 'A Lithuanian woman can't fill her own glass.'

'We're not in Lithuania. How long were you posted to my country, comrade?'

'A year and a half. Long enough.' He shudders.

'Bad memories?'

'One stands out. A man haemorrhaging from a very precise cut to the carotid artery. Dipping my thumb into the wound. Watching a young partisan leap from a first-floor balcony.'

'How dramatic. She must have been quite the athlete.'

'I have only jumped from that height once, when I was with a . . . friend whose husband came home unexpectedly. I twisted my ankle badly. It was difficult enough and I wasn't holding a bloody razor blade in one hand.'

'You are haunted by that image, comrade?'

'I am haunted by the fact that I saved Comrade Karpov's life that day.'

'But you are his enemy now. That means you belong to Mykolan. You are one of those good Russians. Is that the story?'

The oysters arrive, closed, one more than the number they ordered. The Russian asks for another bottle of Tribaut, then fiddles uncertainly with the first shell, trying to find the hinge with the broad, flat knife.

Greta makes a gesture of impatience: give that to me. She shucks the oysters deftly, holding them wrapped in a cloth to protect her hands. They are cold and plump. When Greta and the Russian have finished and the boys in white are fussing around them, she says: 'I hope your employer is picking up the bill.'

'The Boss covers reasonable expenses. I am going to push my luck to breaking point this time.'

Greta laughs. 'Do you know what we say? You're going to shove your grandmother into the nettles.'

The phrase makes the head waiter chuckle. The French is for his benefit. He wheezes in mock horror as he looks at the detritus of the oysters Greta's companion has left on his plate. 'Monsieur has missed the best part! Where it attaches to the shell.'

'The foot,' says Greta, joining in the tutting. 'It's called the foot of the oyster.'

The head waiter stirs the bubbling blood of the duck with a silver spoon. It does not coat the back yet. Some things cannot be rushed. He will return in five minutes.

'Mykolan,' says Greta, swirling champagne thoughtfully. 'The kindly uncle all of Russia wants to replace Stalin. That amiable man, who sent his friends to the gallows in the purges and crushed the Ukrainians after the war. You are really his man?'

'I hope I'm my own man. Sometimes there are no good options. We choose between evils.'

'Indeed. How is the old Boss?'

'Dying. Still dangerous.'

'Will he appoint a successor?'

'He plays the other four off against each other. He can't imagine a world without him. I have brought a letter for you from Russia.'

She places the envelope he passes her on the far side of the table, away from the cooking gear. The blood has reduced to the consistency of thin melted chocolate, and it is time for the head waiter to fry the slices of duck breast. He removes the skin first. He deglazes the pan with cognac afterwards.

The sauce is dark and glossy, earthy and complex. The lemon juice cuts through the richness. There is rapture on the Russian man's face as he eats slowly and silently. Either fine food is always an emotional experience for him, or there is something especially poignant about this meal. Greta opens the letter. She catches her breath at the sight of the handwriting.

Salutations! The rogue who will be eyeing you, no doubt hungrily, across a café table as you read this is Vassily Andreyevich Litvinov.

A villain's life has made him lose his hair, but you may recognize him yet. When last you met, you were crossing pistols over the prone body of Maxim Karpov. Our postman here is the reason Karpov survived his encounter with you. Comrade Vassily tells me that this fact gnaws at him.

You and I have spoken about this Russian over the years. He contacted me for the first time in 1946, when he let it be known that he was seeking to reach a compromise with the main Lithuanian partisan groups and so bring about a ceasefire. He presented himself as a simple soldier weary of the business of murder and oppression. Although our efforts failed, I was never quite able to shake off the strange feeling that he may have been telling the truth.

It is right to say that those of us in prison have been made more comfortable, thanks to this curious Muscovite. I will not say who is in the net here with me now, and who got out. We are all in the same camp and the others still treat me as officer commanding. I am not sure why they have any faith left.

I was in solitary confinement at the point of death, when Vassily's people found me. A course of antibiotics saved my life. He trained as a doctor and administered the injections himself. Perhaps it was a clever trick designed to win my trust. If so, I am afraid it was somewhat successful.

Vassily Andreyevich has a proposal to put to you. I promised I would order you to listen. I keep that promise now. There is another order. Use your instincts. They are the sharpest I have ever come across. If you do not trust this man, kill him for me, will you, darling? Like a dog. Without hesitation.

Listen to what he has to say but do not on any account put yourself in danger for my sake. If my freedom is the prize, it is not worth it. I do not believe it would make any difference to anyone now if I came to the Free World myself.

It is time for the whole truth. When I sent you away, I gave you a task you could not refuse. I wanted to make sure that you would really leave the forest. It was an act of subterfuge. I do not expect you to achieve the impossible. I know, in my heart, that the reunion with the person we discussed – the thing I have longed and prayed for – will never happen now. I am resigned to my life here.

My darling girl.

I release you from all obligations to me. I sent you out of Lithuania because I wanted you to live. To really live for yourself. You have always given us everything. Now it is time for you to be happy. That is my final command.

My best. My bravest. Until we meet again, in a better place.

'You really didn't read it, did you?' says Greta.

Vassily is pursing his lips, dabbing at them with a napkin the way a woman blots her lipstick. 'I promised Laima I would not.'

'I'm afraid I know your full name now, comrade.'

'What of it? I have known yours for many years, and a good deal more besides. I know that you never wear scent, and that your handbags must have leather straps, never metal chains, so that you can always move silently when you need to. You never left the forest, did you?'

Greta cannot reply.

'You can never switch it off,' he goes on. 'You stroll along the Rue de Rivoli, admiring yourself in a shop window. All the time, you are looking at the reflection of the cars passing behind you. The doorways and balconies of the building opposite. Anywhere a hunter might be lurking.'

'And how is daily life in Moscow these days, little friend? Happy and carefree?'

He grimaces as though he has been jabbed in the belly. They both chuckle, without humour.

Marie Antoinette glasses are placed in front of them. A palate-cleanser, the head waiter announces. Apple sorbet, with a generous slug of calvados. Acid and alcohol do battle, scouring every trace of duck from their mouths. When they have finished they look at each other in silence, feeling the blood round the belly doing its slow work, the chemical changes in the brain.

Greta turns in her chair and beckons one of the junior waiters. 'What was that drink? Calvados? It's as strong as brandy? Bring the rest of the bottle,' she tells him. They will need two shot glasses. And some privacy.

She drives the pace now. 'Assuming I do this thing for you. How quickly can you get my people out afterwards?'

'It won't be a week or a month. Mykolan will see to it as soon as he can if he is left holding the reins alone. The first job will be to extricate ourselves from the bog of Korea. I can say with some confidence that there will be a general armistice for all anti-Soviet partisans within a year of the death of Stalin. That's assuming Karpov follows the Boss into hell.'

They slam the glasses on to the white tablecloth at the same time. *Na zdorovye!*

'Why England? Why me?'

'Who else but you? Your family's blood is all over Karpov's

hands. You can't reach him in Moscow, but I can finish the thing for you. We can remove the stain of Maxim Karpov together, with the right chemical.'

Vassily fills both glasses and takes a sniff at his own, his eyes rolling back as the cloud of alcohol fills his sinuses.

'The British are the great poisoners, Greta. It's the only place where they have toxins unknown to Soviet scientists. Incredibly concentrated, with no taste or odour. I have someone with access to the laboratories in *Wilt-shire*. But I don't have a courier I can trust.'

'England is difficult for me,' says Greta. 'Drink!'

'Good health! It's difficult for everyone.' Their eyes meet and do battle. 'Maxim Karpov,' says Vassily, 'has left strict instructions on the tests to be carried out in the event of his unexpected death. I may not be in a position to interfere with the autopsy. Do you see? So it cannot be something common like warfarin. It cannot be a radioactive agent.'

She needs to focus hard now to pour the shots without spilling any of the calvados on the white tablecloth. 'In Lithuanian, this time! *Į sveikatą!* To your health! I know what you are about, comrade. If the poison is discovered, the finger will point straight at London. And the trail will lead to my door soon enough. A fascist, reactionary plot, with a woman trained by the British at the heart of it. That is why you want me.'

'I need a woman's touch. It's a delicate job. If any of this stuff is spilled—'

'You need someone to take the fall if things go wrong. An old enemy of the Soviet Union. But who will stop me talking if I am caught with this terrible weapon on my person?'

'Me. That is one promise I can make. You won't live long enough to be a danger to anyone else.'

'Drink!' *Bang*. 'You'll do it quickly and cleanly? I have your word?'

'Like a *hare*.' He throws back the shot and chops the blade of his free hand on to the tablecloth next to the empty glass, harder than he meant to. The noise echoes around the dining room. His face is quivering with feeling. The alcohol is doing its work, a solvent stripping away the layers of polish. She is getting to the heart of him.

There is fear in his eyes now as he searches for the right words. 'You ask me what life is like in Moscow. It is the worst it has ever been. It is worse than thirty-seven.'

'How long does Stalin have left?'

'He had another stroke a fortnight ago. They are small but becoming more frequent. He forgets the names of Karpov and Malenkov while he is talking to them. It fills him with rage. He paces, paces, cannot be still. His arthritis torments him when he sits. The arteries harden. His body is strangling him from the inside. He cannot hold out for long. But what use is our patience if Maxim Karpov steps into those soft boots with the worn-out soles? He must not be the successor. Karpov will not close the prisons.'

Tears, at last. 'I knew it,' says Greta. 'I knew you were one of those men. Pour enough of this stuff into you, and it spills out of the eyes.'

He has spread a napkin over his face. It is hard for him to force the words out. 'They are building camps again, for the Jews.'

Greta senses that she is in better shape than the man on the other side of the table, although her vision is shifting focus queasily and there is the faint roar of the sea in her ears. The waiters have left them alone but are watching their descent with much amusement from the far side of the dining room.

When Vassily is able to take the napkin away, she sees how the drink is weighing his eyelids down. Below, the pupils dart over her face, her neckline, searching for some kind of tell.

'Look at me,' says Greta. 'Look me in the eyes, curse you. Is Laima really alive?'

'You read the letter.'

'There is no date. And I know your tricks. Is she still alive?'

'I swear it.'

'Will you release her if I don't make it back?'

He is dabbing at his forehead with a napkin. 'I have a policy. Never make promises you can't keep.'

'I want you to try. Do this for me: take a letter back with you. Laima has a daughter here. I'm going to write down everything I've found out about the girl. See that the mother gets it.'

'A daughter,' says Vassily, 'in France.' Then he tries to say *communication*. The word has six syllables in Russian and it takes him several attempts. 'Communication can be problematic.'

'I'm putting a loaded gun in my own mouth for you, Muscovite. This is the least you can do for me.'

23

Greta brings it all up, leaning against a tree in the Tuileries on the long walk back: the oysters, the duck, the burning spirits. The stairs are hard to negotiate. When she reaches Robert's room, the dark hump of his back faces her side of the bed. It takes an age to remove her stockings.

'Like a distillery,' he says gloomily, when she has settled herself.

'I'm sorry, Father. I will try to behave better in future.'

'Who was the man you met today?'

'It's better you don't know, my Giraffe.'

'Not everyone would put up with this, Greta, understand? I heard that you kissed a man at a party. Was this the same fellow?' There is an edge to his voice that cuts through the haze in her head.

'I told you when we first got together that I can't be a little wife to you. There are things I can't give you and a lot of things I can't tell you.'

'You tell me nothing. Are you seeing other men? Do you seduce them? Is that part of the great work?'

'There is a reason I don't talk about my work, darling. To keep you safe.'

'As if you give me a moment's thought,' he spits. 'Every time you walk out of here, understand, I'm afraid it's the last time I will ever see you.'

'I'm not planning on running away, Robert. It's the opposite. I'm trying to build something here.'

'For yourself. I have never been in the picture.'

'No more of this.' She sits up in the bed, laboriously. 'I can't listen. It's pathetic. I told you what the deal was a long time ago. There are things you don't get from me. Sweetness, warmth. Find a French girl for all that. I'm not going to look after you like your fucking mother. I'm a different kind of animal and I can't change now. That's the deal. Take it or leave it. It's time to decide.' She is groping around on the carpet next to the bed for the stockings she discarded. Where will she go now? Back to the streets. A bar on some corner, if they will serve her in this state.

His big palm pats her thigh, just above the knee. It takes her a moment to refocus. He has come round the bed to squat beside her. He grips her hand and kneads the knuckles between thumb and forefinger.

'I will take it,' he says. 'I decided a long time ago, *Gretute*.'

She tells him some of it. A halting monologue. Bless me, she thinks. I can't remember my last confession. A wave of drug-like relief comes over her when she has forced the words out.

Robert shakes his head. 'I can't believe you met a Russian agent today. You let him buy you lunch?'

'There is more than one Russia. There are at least four factions. Stalin is dying and the others are fighting over the crown already, like weasels in a sack.'

'Then don't jump into the sack! What if the people you are trying to make friends with here found out – the French, or the Americans? That you sat eating duck *à la Presse* with the enemy of mankind?'

'They will never find out.'

'What does the Russian arsehole want you to do for him, Greta?'

'That's enough now. I have a poison headache.'

'Whatever it is, I know it's bad. Let me help.'

'You handsome fool.'

'I'm good for fucking, is that it? But nothing serious.'

Greta is biting her lip, feeling her burden, the crushing weight of it. Perhaps that's the source of the pain behind her temples, not the alcohol. She lunges at him to keep herself from saying more. She is about to press her lips against his but remembers her wretched breath and kisses his forehead instead.

'Not this time,' she says. 'You are too pretty. I drag everyone down with me, you see. Down into death. Not you.'

Robert frowns and makes a lowing sound of annoyance as she kisses his brow, over and over. 'Speaking English again,' he complains.

The Algerian restaurant is as plain as a factory canteen, but there is a bar at the end of the room where two men sit on tall chairs.

Greta and Lucien are on Balard's business. They have been talking sparingly, for Jacky's sake. He is there to eavesdrop on the only other diners, and to translate from the Arabic.

One other table is occupied. Two women and an old man, in traditional dress, lapsed into silence now. Three children who are becoming tired.

Greta puts a hand over her glass, making a face, when Jacky tries to refill it.

'You're turning your nose up at the bounty of Africa,' he says.

'I'm not in the mood tonight.'

'It's not like you to refuse alcohol. Is it really that bad?'

'I can't tell good from bad any more.'

'So it's a little rough around the edges,' says Lucien. 'Like everything else from Algeria.'

'We are the only French people left in this place,' says Greta, noticing the looks cast at them from the bar.

'*We*,' says Jacky. 'We French?'

He takes a mouthful of the ruby wine – a Grenache from Mascara. His eyes flicker constantly from the men at the bar to the family round the table in the far corner. One of the women stands up and walks across the room to smoke away from the children. She is pale with very dark hair – almost blue-black. An almond face.

'I think it's time you packed a bag,' says Jacky. 'I have one prepared. Passports, money. You have to know when it's time, Greta.'

'She's Hannachi's only wife,' Greta says, looking over his shoulder at the woman who is smoking. 'The newspaper said he had three more in Algeria.'

'It's a lie,' says Jacky. 'They are trying to discredit him. He doesn't even go to the mosque. He's a Marxist-Leninist.'

'I told them I can't do it with plastic explosive,' breathes Greta. 'It's too hard to get the dose right. What if the Algerian is driving down a street full of people when it goes off?'

'You won't have a say in it,' says Jacky. 'I know Balard. He will simply present it to you: the time, the place, the method.' Jacky is looking closely at Greta, but she only has eyes for Djamel Hannachi's wife. The girl he met at secondary school.

'She's so beautiful,' says Greta. The Algerian woman stubs out her cigarette in an ashtray on the bar and hails one of the men perching there, resting her hand on his shoulder. She does not go with her head covered. She looks very Parisian, very modern.

The old man at the table in the bleached-white cap and long sleeveless coat is her father-in-law. He is reading to his eldest grandchild, a girl of eight. The two little ones tumble and sprawl over the bench seats in the lazy aftermath of the meal. Toys and books are scattered among the ends of flatbreads, mounds of cold semolina.

'You know Balard,' says Greta. 'From back then, the Resistance.'

'As much as anyone knows him. He was a Judas, if you like. He had a position in the Vichy government. He pretended to collaborate, but he was passing their secrets to our side all the time. It's how he built his reputation. Very dangerous work. Greta?'

She is looking at Hannachi's children. When she tears her eyes from them, Jacky is leaning in close.

'You owe Monsieur Balard nothing, Greta. You told me yourself that he has lied to you. He will drop you like an old sock. Do not do this thing for him. There is no coming back from it.'

Jacky rises, picking up their bill, smoothing the front of his suit with the other hand. He gives a little half-wave as he walks to the back of the restaurant, passing Hannachi's wife. Jacky exchanges a few words with the barman. The Arabic men sitting close by on the tall stools stop talking for a moment to eye him. They resume their conversation when they hear that he is speaking French.

Lellouche stops on his way back to Greta because the youngest child has wandered into his path, in the aisle that runs the length of the restaurant. Jacky waits for the boy indulgently.

Djamel Hannachi's firstborn son is not yet three. He has the mother's eyes. The child drifts towards Greta, looking elsewhere. His dark pupils are vast below the thick lashes, absorbing every detail of the room. He reaches out to steady himself, finding her stockinged leg with his fingers. He turns to look up at Greta, surprised by her presence.

'It's time to go,' says Jacky. He is halfway to the door when the child falls to its knees next to Greta. She stoops quickly to pluck him from the floor.

The mother smiles as Greta approaches the corner table, carrying the boy. Greta is murmuring nonsense into his ear, distracting him before he has the presence of mind to cry.

The grandfather takes him from her, chiding him, lifting him high like a trophy. Greta smiles back, extending a hand to Hannachi's wife. The false name – the one on her passport. Enchanted. Enchanted.

It's late when they get back to the restaurant, but Greta doesn't want to go up to Robert yet.

Jacky is assembling a line of bottles on a table for two in the dark dining room – wine ordered by diners but left unfinished.

'I don't want any more to drink,' says Greta.

'So spit it out.'

She picks up the first glass reluctantly. 'Monsieur Jacques? Did Fabio really break your ribs? Is he the reason you went to stay with Jeannot and Clothilde?'

'He's one of them. Smell first, then swirl it around.'

'Why do they always call you a *maricón*, Jacky?'

'Oh, my poor girl. It's like this: some men like oysters, others prefer mussels.'

'Fool. I mean why use the Spanish word?'

'A lot of the men have passed through the Legion. That is the legionnaire's word. I suppose it used to be full of Spaniards and the word stuck. Sniff again. Now take a proper mouthful with a lot of air.'

'Was it true – what Fabio said? That you just lay back and let them do it?'

'Not everyone can afford to lose their temper. Some of us must keep our heads. Stop wasting time.'

'Well, the first one's easy. Petrol. Riesling.'

'Perfect. Keep going.'

'The next one is obviously a Chardonnay. Three is a Sauvignon.'

'Not good enough,' says Jacky.

'I don't know. It tastes different.' She fills her mouth again, swallows and makes a face. 'Don't you get tired of just taking it from them and keeping quiet?'

'When you have taken a lifetime's worth of abuse you are very welcome to come back and give me a lecture about it. Now stop changing the subject. Are they good or not?'

'The Chardonnay is good.'

'How do we know?'

'From the first whiff. Like a struck match. Then the finish.'

'Long?'

'I can still taste it now,' says Greta. 'Fine. The last one is a Sancerre.' She spits in disgust. 'That's enough. It's making me feel sick.'

She is possessed by the sudden desire for something sweet and bitter at the same time. She boils espresso on the stove in the kitchen and pours it over vanilla ice cream, Italian-style.

When she takes her seat again a brick of banknotes, ringed with a rubber band, is on the table between them.

'The last one was a Pouilly-Fumé,' says Jacky. 'Not a Sancerre. You were just on the wrong side of the river. This is from the jewellery we bagged in Grenoble. That's your half.'

'You took your sweet time fencing those rings.'

'I was waiting for the right buyer. I went to the Bookseller in

Versailles in the end. He wanted forty per cent commission, but I got him down to twenty.'

'Not bad.'

'He made remarks of an anti-Semitic nature throughout the negotiation.'

'That fucking reptile. I'm surprised you went back there.'

'I wanted to see what was in that back room he goes into. He forgot himself this time. I don't think he is very afraid of me. He left the door ajar while he was rooting around.'

'And?'

'A safe the size of a bank vault. You could stand up in it. Did you think about what I said, Greta? About knowing when it's time to leave the stage?'

She can't help touching the money while she eats, riffling the edges of the brick like a pack of cards, hefting it for weight.

'It's not enough to retire on. I need another Switzerland.'

'There is always time for one more thing, Greta, until there isn't. Until you run out of time.'

'And are you going to take your own advice, monsieur?'

'I always have a bag packed upstairs. I have a plan.'

'Why don't you leave now?'

He laughs darkly, turning away. A sliver of street is visible through the gap between the blinds. He stands and goes to the window.

'What are you looking at?'

'Nothing. And no, I'm not going to listen to my own good advice. We never do. I want one more thing. I want to take that twenty per cent commission back.'

He takes his seat again, grimacing as she bolts the last of the melted ice cream, dinging the spoon against the steel bowl. 'Do you eat like this in front of Robert? I'm amazed he can bring himself to touch you.'

'We're both savages from the east. No knives or forks in Lithuania.'

'Don't talk with your mouth full. And you are supposed to be Russian now.'

'Mmm. The fool with the bookshop is Balard's man,' says Greta. 'He can't be touched.'

'I don't think he will suspect me. He doesn't think I'm brave enough. And if I'm right about what's in that back room, I will soon be far away, in a warm place where the name Balard has never been uttered. Tell me this, Greta. When you did the job in Marseille, how much C3 did you slip into your pocket? Enough for a heavy safe? Nod or shake. Don't spray.'

Greta takes her time over the last few spoons, then dabs her mouth with a napkin. 'Enough to sink a battleship.'

The shop is in that little triangle of old streets between the Swiss Lake and the front gate of the Palace of Versailles. The owner lives on the top floor of the same building, but he is a man of iron routine. Friday nights are set aside for his mistress in the city.

Greta is in ballet pumps with rubber soles and a Breton jersey that reminds her, when it is too late, of prison stripes. Jacky, exceptionally, wears cotton slacks and tennis shoes. A sweater with a shawl collar. The casual clothes make him younger and harder.

They wait for a resident to come out of the door on the street and catch it before it clicks shut, slipping into the dark courtyard behind. The back door of the shop is hidden below the staircase that leads to the apartments, and Jacky must work in near-darkness. It takes him almost ten minutes, with the suede roll resting on the box for the electricity meter, the implements as small and sharply engineered as a dentist's tools.

Inside, he walks in front, putting the toe down before the heel like a partisan, like a Forest Brother. Mamluk rugs cover most of the shop floor. The furniture is arranged in chronological order from front to back: Empire, Restoration, Second Empire. Jacky's gloved fingertips flutter over a display of silverware: model biplanes, cigarette boxes, a cocktail shaker with a slide like a trombone. Watching over them in the darkness: the stuffed head of a white tiger.

Up the steel staircase at the back and into the mezzanine office. No more finery now. Everything is plain and utilitarian in here:

bare brick and a Turkmen rug in madder red, very worn, a border of raw concrete round it. Jacky goes through the cabinets that hold the paperwork for the business while Greta works a lump of putty into the corner of the safe door.

The blast is a crack, like the report of a sniper's rifle, not the loud bang she was expecting. The tip of her finger will fit in the hole ripped in the steel, but it's not big enough for a serious prising tool.

Jacky whispers questions, as the sharp smoke curls round their heads. 'Is this the wrong kind of metal? Could the explosive have deteriorated? Is there enough left?' She can see his eyes burning.

'Shut up and let me work!' The remaining C3 comes to around two hundred grams, Greta guesses. She wedges all of it into the hole they made, then dodges out of the doorway after him.

This time the explosion makes the front windows of the shop shudder in their frames. When they take their fingers out of their ears, the office is full of smoke. A pile of paperwork Jacky left on the desk has been tossed into the air and the sheets are floating down like enormous snowflakes.

'Quickly,' says Greta. 'Half the street will have heard that.' But Jacky moves with maddening slowness, stopping to open one of the dull-brown card folders that are jammed into the safe to sort through the contents.

He actually takes the seat behind the desk while Greta is raking watches and lengths of gold chain and coins into her old satchel. 'What the hell are you doing?' she hisses. Over his shoulder she can see typed pages in French and German and a ledger full of names and addresses, handwritten in an elegant looping script. She snaps her fingers and waves a coin in front of his eyes. 'Krugerrands!' Then she hears a key turn in the front door of the shop.

The Bookseller moves quietly. Only Greta heard the first sound. There is nothing else for a full minute. She stabs a finger through the thinning smoke, silently ordering Jacky to get out of the seat and hide. He ignores her.

She flattens herself against the rough brickwork next to the office door. She is waiting for a squeak, a rustle of clothing, as the owner ascends the stairs. Not a breath of noise comes to her through the open door.

Then a voice. 'Lellouche? Is that you?' Jacky is sifting through the files spread on the desk in front of him. He doesn't look up. A snub-nosed automatic that reminds Greta of her Baby Browning is edging through the doorway. The smoke has cleared, and she can see every contour of the gun. 'You greedy little Hebrew bastard,' says the voice behind it, trembling with outrage.

He will turn and see me, thinks Greta. Any second. But Jacky is holding up a single sheet of paper, very carefully, fingertips on the corners.

The man does not turn his head. He edges closer to the desk, moving silently, eyes forwards all the time, peering intently at the document. He doesn't have his reading glasses, thinks Greta. He can't see what I can see from here. The red stamp, of unforgettable design. The imperial eagle looking over its right shoulder, the wreath in the bird's claws. The swastika filling the circle.

Adrenalin makes Greta misjudge the chop, with the grip of her own pistol, against the base of his skull. It's savagely strong. He drops to the floor, on palms and knees. His forehead sinks into the rug. He recovers with a long moan. He looks up at her, murderously, then glances around the room, taking in everything.

'I don't keep cash here,' the Bookseller says. 'There's gold. Enough for the likes of you two. Take it and leave the rest. I'll give you an hour before I telephone.'

Jacky doesn't seem to hear. His attention has returned to the papers on the desk. When he speaks, his voice is surprisingly calm and firm. 'These are Gestapo files. I'm taking everything.'

'Steal those papers,' says the Bookseller, 'and Balard will pursue you to the ends of the earth.' He looks from Jacky to Greta. 'A Jew and a Catholic. There will be nothing left of either of you to bury. I will see to it personally that your bodies are dissolved in acid.'

Greta squats next to him. 'I need to talk to Jacky in private. Lie down for me. I won't tie your hands if you put them in your pockets and promise not to move. Come over this way.' She pulls at one of his shoulders to help him shift his weight so that his face rests on the thick rug, as if to make him more comfortable. Jacky stands up behind the desk, watching. Only he sees Greta nod her head, making a decision.

The man is grunting from the unusual effort of moving himself with the strength of his abdominal muscles. He cannot see or hear Greta resting her handgun lightly on the rug. Her other hand is inside her satchel.

When she is satisfied that he has thrust his hands as deep as they will go into his trouser pockets, she cuts him with the stiletto on the left side of his neck, from just below the ear down to the collar-bone. She presses a knee into his back, drops the knife and holds his head down against the wool with both hands.

Jacky turns away but says nothing. The flapping and gasping subside as the Bookseller lapses into unconsciousness. Greta keeps her weight on him through the knee as his body empties itself of blood. The rug absorbs most of it.

She drives too fast through the narrow backstreets. There is a quiet lane on the north side of the grounds of Versailles where a single arc-lamp casts a bright pool of light.

Greta finds her Chanel coat in the boot of the car. She takes off the Breton jersey carefully. The sleeves are saturated with the Bookseller's blood. She puts on the coat, buttoning it up to the neck. Then she screws the jersey into a tight ball and lobs it over the fence that marks the edge of the palace estate.

In the car, Jacky is reading a brown folder full of papers on his lap in the light from the street lamp. He seems improbably calm, his fingers flicking backwards and forwards through the years.

'The man threw nothing away,' he says. 'His kind keep everything, for insurance purposes. But there is no insurance against you, is there?'

'You knew he would be at home tonight,' says Greta quietly. 'You wanted him dead, and you set him up for me.'

'Ridiculous woman. Did you think I wanted to see that? My hands are still shaking.'

'No, Jacky. They are completely still.' She looks at his face in the harsh light. 'Who are you? What are you looking for?'

'Evidence. But it has to be good. There is a lot of rubbish around.'

'What are you talking about?'

'Forgery, my darling. And blackmail. The great French industries.'

'Our friend did more than make passports, didn't he?'

'He amassed a fortune in the war, erasing signs of Jewishness from the documents of people who could afford his services. But the real boom years came afterwards. Half of France needed to get their records discreetly altered.'

'Collaborators?'

'Yes, of course. *Collabos*. Who else?' He is becoming impatient with the interruptions, fluttering through the papers at a furious pace.

'He falsified documents,' says Greta. 'For the traitors who worked with the Germans.'

'For anyone who paid. It was a catfight then. Everyone pointing the finger at everyone else. There were all kinds of tricks. If you wanted someone arrested, you could go to our friend and *voilà* – an old list would turn up. Payments from the Gestapo to their informants, let's say.'

'With your enemy's name on the list.'

'Yes, of course. Wait.'

A large envelope. He lapses into silence as he scans the handwritten pages inside.

'Is this your way of getting me out of France?' asks Greta, biting her knuckles, trying to force out the nagging memory of the Bookseller's face. She is icy-cold suddenly, despite the coat. 'Making me cut my ties with Balard?'

'Greta. I thought the man was with his mistress tonight. Be quiet for a moment.'

'You hate Balard. It kills you when you see me working for him.'

'My darling,' says Jacky, holding up a handwritten note. 'Is this the Lithuanian language?'

*

There are only two pages. The first is written in the Bookseller's own hand – the one she remembers from a dinner invitation left for her at a boarding house, long ago. He took care to practise the Lithuanian grammar first, adding the tricky accents after he had spelled out the words correctly. She pictures him poring over this sheet of paper in his reading glasses, consulting a dictionary.

The second page is where he begins to imitate Morta's writing. The same handful of phrases, over and over. Did they make her write these words for him to copy, or was there an earlier letter to crib from, to get the slope of the letters just right?

Did the customer supply the phrasing, pacing in front of the forger's desk in the little upstairs room, declaiming the lines like an actor? Did they revise and redraft the words together, those men, as they strove to imitate the voice of a pining teenage girl?

I long to throw my arms around you
I long to throw my arms around you, my mother
So that everything we have lived through seems like a dream.

24

Nothing happens for three days. Then Lucien calls the restaurant early. Can Greta be ready in fifteen minutes?

He drives her to the hotel where Morta once waited for them. As they are riding in the lift, he says: 'You're going to have to take your medicine now. Remember that I'm here.'

Greta doesn't fully understand until she sees the two Indochinese men standing next to the bed. Of course, she thinks. That's how they come for you. With a friendly face. The taps are running in the bathroom.

She can't think of any good reason to submit to them. When Monsieur Trinh takes her neck from behind, she snaps her head back and hears a satisfying grunt of pain. She stamps at their shoes until her high heels snap.

At the end she is on her back in the corner, kicking up at Trinh, watching the blood trickling from his nose. He has ripped her silk stockings off and he tells her, in magisterial French, that he is going to strangle her with them and leave her hanging from the doorframe like a suicide.

'Thank you.' Monsieur Balard comes in from the bathroom, wiping his hands fastidiously on a towel. 'Lucien, please,' he says. And then Greta is on her knees, hands held fast, watching the stiletto in Lucien's hand inch towards her throat.

'Where were you on Friday night, young lady?'

'With Jacky. At the restaurant.'

'Naturally. And he will tell the same story. And all your little friends will confirm the alibi, will they not, if the Paris police call?'

'Monsieur,' says Greta noncommittally, like a soldier, staring at the Moor's Head in its blindfold and the patina on the knife blade round it.

'But I am not the police.'

Balard throws the damp towel on to the bed. Lucien settles on his haunches and lets the knife hang.

'A young woman brandishing a shotgun,' says Balard. 'The silhouette appeals to a certain kind of man. I am not one of them. Did you come to France to strike poses, or are you a professional soldier?'

'What would you ask of me, monsieur?'

'Keep next Sunday, the thirteenth, free in your diary. It is not a request.'

'There's a demonstration in Paris on that day.'

'A carnival for agitators. North Africans are planning to pour into the centre from the suburbs. And from Lyon, and from their nest in Marseille. The same terrorists who have been tossing grenades at police officers. I will not allow an African army to take Paris. Do you follow? Their leader is due to address them on Sunday evening.'

'Hannachi.'

'He flies in the night before, on the Saturday. He plans to address the crowd on the theme of self-government for Algeria. He must not deliver that speech. Lucien will supply the details.'

'Is there money in it, monsieur?'

'How bold you are! Little mercenary. I am prepared to offer you much more than that: the gift of French citizenship. The real thing, not a fake passport that will land you in jail before long. Gentlemen.'

She fears that Trinh will aim a kick at her as they leave, but he is content with a stare that drills into her skull. Lucien waits for thirty seconds, then sits with legs folded under him, exhaling. He flicks the switch that retracts the blade.

'You and Balard,' says Greta.

He shrugs his shoulders.

'Your cousin doesn't know?'

'Absolutely not.'

'What if I told him?'

'You won't live long enough to get the chance. You stay with me now. We all go to Switzerland together. I babysit you until the Sunday. After that . . .'

'You drop me down a deep hole.'

'Sunday is going to be nasty. Balard doesn't want tongues flapping afterwards. You place the plastic explosive under Hannachi's car before the demonstration. I am supposed to put all the logistics in place.'

'How much C3?'

'I worry about all those details. You don't even trigger the device.'

'His family will be in the car at the time,' says Greta.

There is no reply.

'People will panic,' she tells Lucien.

'The crowd will scatter. We are expecting a hard core to remain on the streets. There's a small army gathering to deal with them.'

'What are we going to do, Lucien?'

He shrugs again. 'There's only one thing I care about now. But we both need Switzerland, whatever happens. We need money. If you're going to get out, it had better be then.'

'You and I care about the same thing,' says Greta.

When they return to his flat in the late evening, he makes her leave her handbag in the locked boot of the car. He frisks her carefully before he lets her inside the door. 'I'll take the sofa. Don't try anything. We need our beauty sleep.'

'Show me your knife.'

'Greta.'

'It's not a trick. I keep seeing that blindfolded African man everywhere. Tell me about him.'

'The Moor's Head is the symbol of Corsica.'

'Why would a man who is not Corsican have a knife with the Moor's Head engraved on it?'

'He went on holiday and bought a crappy souvenir.' Lucien is trying not to yawn.

'No. I'm talking about a very good stiletto like yours.'

'He has a close friend from the island,' says Lucien.

'How about a business partner?'

'Something like that.'

'What if the business was called Stay Behind?'

'Greta. It's time for bed.'

Jacky Lellouche fails to show in the morning at the meeting place in Gentilly. Dutchman arrives late, with a face like bad milk. Dodo is riding along with him.

They leave their cars in a clearing in the wood that straddles the border west of Satigny. The van is waiting for them in exactly the place Jacky said it would be.

Now the four of them are crammed together in the same cabin. The more nervous Dodo becomes, the more he talks. 'I'm the only one who is not scared of you, Lulu. Do you know that?'

'Only because you haven't seen Lucien in action,' says Dutchman.

'Has anyone, recently? I think he went soft.'

'Watch your mouth. Lucien racked up the numbers in Indochina. He doesn't have anything to prove to the likes of you. Nor do I. I was fighting Communists when you were clamped to your whore of a mother's breast.'

'That's *citrons*,' says Dodo. 'They don't count. How many real people, up close? Europeans?'

A stolen Frégate and a motorbike have been left in the right place too, off the lakeside road that runs through Buchillon.

Greta drives off alone in the new car, grateful for the silence. She waits outside Lausanne to pick up the Mercedes truck, then overtakes it to race ahead and give the men a three-minute warning.

The big banks are using unmarked vehicles now. They lost faith in the Swiss postal service after the first robbery. But the law is unchanged: no heavy lorries or armoured cars in the canton of Vaud.

As Greta pulls off the road, Lucien and Dutchman are wheeling the motorbike into the eastbound lane. They tip it over with a crash and Dutchman, in helmet and long leather coat, lies down on his back in the other lane, squirming among the shards of broken glass. The bike's headlamp lights him up. One of the wheels is still spinning.

It takes an eternity for the bank vehicle to trundle into view round the bend. The road is narrow here. It would be impossible for the Mercedes to pass the wreckage even if the driver became suspicious and floored the accelerator.

When the young man climbs out, they can all see that he is not the type to leave an injured motorcyclist lying motionless on a country road in the middle of the night. The driver is checking Dutchman's pulse when Greta clamps a rag soaked in halothane over his mouth.

'Gentle enough for you, Buddhist?'

Lucien doesn't answer. It will be breathless work now. The plan is simple. Get the Mercedes off the road, transfer everything to their empty van. Back to the cars. Then they split up and cross the border at three different points.

The first job is to shift the dead weight of the driver into the back of his own truck. Lucien goes through all the keys on the ring, muttering curses, before he finds the right one. Then everyone swears in unison. There is no cash. The Mercedes is groaning with gold and silver ingots, neatly stacked in metal crates like a shipment of ammunition. Transferring it to the other van will take hours.

'We adapt,' says Greta, after a long silence. 'We find a secluded spot and take our time. We work in shifts.'

'There's not time to heave all of it across,' says Lucien bitterly. 'No. We'll have to crash the border in this heap of junk. Get in.'

'*He* will need to be watched,' says Dutchman disgustedly. The prisoner has come round, and Dodo is crouching next to him in the aisle that runs down the truck between the stacks of bullion. Dodo is whispering to the young man, looking out through the open doors at the others.

'I'll watch him,' says Greta, squeezing in next to Dodo. She answers the question that flashes in Lucien's eyes with a firm nod. 'Let's get moving.'

The man from the bank curses his employer. There was supposed to be another guy with him, riding along with a rifle. They should never have let him leave the warehouse alone. It's always the same at the end of the summer holidays. No one wants to come back to work.

He is twenty-two and expecting his first child. A Catholic, a French speaker. He runs a football team for kids.

'They always do this,' says Dodo, with a scientist's curiosity. 'They always want to make friends with you.' He takes hold of the man's face and squeezes his jaw.

'Cut that out,' says Greta. 'We need him to stay quiet.'

'Make me.' Dodo begins to flick the driver's eyeballs with his fingers, through the blindfold. He holds Greta's gaze.

She has risen to her feet when Lucien brakes hard. Her shoulder hits the back door of the truck, but it stays closed. Dodo's head cracks against the side of a metal crate full of silver bars. The driver wails, joining the tyres in a chorus of despair.

Greta opens the door, then pulls it shut again instinctively. There's a noise outside that she has not heard for what seems like a lifetime. The heavy clatter of serious small arms. She braces herself and jumps out.

Greta leaves Dodo cowering in the back of the Mercedes. Dutchman is on his belly underneath it, holding a pistol in two hands. Lucien is on the other side of the road, crouching below a low farm wall. He dashes over to Greta, and the gun opens up again. Aiming high.

'They overtook us a couple of miles back and chose the best spot for an ambush,' says Lucien. 'They didn't even glance when they passed. Very calm, no uniforms. They will be the guys Jacky talked about. Ex-army. Hired by the bank. They've got Sterling guns.' A short burst, on cue, as if to emphasize his point.

'This isn't right,' says Greta. 'Jacky said they stopped using these guys.'

'Go and tell them they don't exist.' He sights along his handgun but does not fire. Dutchman is screaming at Dodo in German. 'You little bastard. Get out and be a man.'

'Fine,' says Greta. 'I want you both to shout and empty those magazines. You don't need to hit anything, Buddhist. Just make a lot of noise, then shut up and stay out of sight.'

After the shooting subsides, the armed men are not expecting to hear a woman's voice crying for help. Greta puts one hand out, then the other, then shows her face, creeping round the side of the van. A hostage, in considerable distress.

'They ran for it,' she shrieks, pointing east along the wall to the thick woodland that falls down to the lakeside. 'They let me go.'

'Advance,' says a gruff voice. 'Slowly.'

'So *scared*,' says Greta through the tears as she approaches the men. There are only two, both crouched in good firing positions on either side of the road. One rises as she staggers closer. He can see that she is unarmed.

'They went towards the woods,' Greta tells him. 'I thought they were going to . . .' She falls to her knees when she reaches the man, wrapping her arms round his legs and dissolving into sobs.

The second guard is standing too, edging forwards cautiously out of cover. Greta is babbling, her face pressed into the first man's hip. He looks down at her wild hair, the streaks of dirt and tears on her pretty features, and takes his finger out of the trigger guard of the submachine gun. He squats to drape an arm round her shaking shoulders. He carries a sidearm in a hip holster.

'It's so unbelievable to me,' says Dodo. 'Tied up? So they can identify us?'

'Handcuffed to a tree,' says Greta. 'Radio smashed. They're out of our hair.'

They are in the back of the bank vehicle again, squashed into the spaces between the crates. The driver is lying along the aisle between them.

Dodo gives a long whistle of derision. 'It's not just Lulu who's gone soft.'

The men in the cabin can hear through the gap in the screen behind their heads. Lucien tightens his grip on the steering wheel.

'What's the point in killing for no reason?' Dutchman calls out. 'Do you think that's what soldiers do, kid?'

'He is desperate to join the club,' says Greta. 'Aren't you?'

'I will step up, sure,' says Dodo. 'If no one else has the stomach for it. This bastard could have told us his friends were following behind. He needs to take some medicine.'

Every time Dodo speaks, the blindfolded man at his feet moans with terror. Dodo looks down at him with detached interest.

'I could pop his eyes out. It's not that hard. You can manage it with a spoon. I offered to do it to the girl, at the house, instead of messing around with drunken doctors and anaesthetic. It's like pulling teeth. Better to get it over with.'

'Which girl?' says Greta.

Dodo is dabbing the tip of a finger at the inside corner of the prisoner's left eye, through the cloth, making the young man moan and roll his head from side to side.

'I know what you want,' Greta tells Dodo in a low voice. 'You want to know what it feels like to kill. I'll tell you all about it. Which girl at the house?'

'What did he say about *eyes*?' Lucien is turning to shout over his shoulder.

'Slow down,' says Dutchman. 'We're getting close to the border.'

'What is he doing now, Greta?'

'Easy,' says Dutchman. 'Watch the road.'

'Fazi,' murmurs Dodo, putting his lips close to the prisoner's ear. 'Remember it.'

'No,' says Greta.

'Please,' sobs the driver, squirming on the floor. 'Don't tell me anything. I don't want to know.'

Dodo smiles. His bulging eyes are fixed on Greta the whole time. '*Lucien Fazi*. The other man is called *Van der Meulen*. The woman's real name is *Zofija*—'

A hard slap shuts him up. Dodo can't take in what has happened for a couple of breaths. Then he lunges at Greta, trying to rake her face with his fingernails, as the brakes and tyres screech again.

Lucien pulls Dodo through the back doors by the hair and stands him up against the side of the van, his right fist cocked.

Dutchman tries to prise them apart. 'Not him. Lulu. You can't. Think it through.'

'I heard nothing,' says the prisoner in the blindfold. 'Nothing.' He is shaking with tears.

'It looks like I slipped up,' says Dodo in a blank, toneless voice. 'I suppose we'll have to shoot him now. I can do it if you don't want to, Lulu? Maybe you saw too much horror in Indochina?'

Lucien tautens his abdominal muscles, ready to throw a punch. Dutchman says: 'Lulu. No.'

'I'll do it,' says Greta. 'Give him to me.'

She helps the driver down, holding his arm all the time, whispering. *I'm going to get you out of here. Just put one foot in front of the other.*

Dutchman snarls at Dodo: 'Fuck do you think you're going?'

Dodo says: 'I'm supposed to stay with her all the time.'

'You sick puppy. You want to watch her do it? She doesn't need an audience.'

'Orders,' says Dodo, under his breath. But Greta hears it. And she just catches the motion, from the corner of her eye. His tell. Dodo touches the bulge under his jacket with his fingertips, gently, unconsciously.

That's why he's here, she thinks. To make sure I return to Paris. With a sack over my head if necessary. *I babysit you, until the Sunday.* But they don't trust Lucien to do the babysitting.

She takes her Sauer out while she is turned away from the men, still holding the prisoner's arm and whispering to him. Then she spins round and points the gun at the dead centre of Dodo's shambles of a face.

'Get him out of my sight,' she tells Lucien. 'Go. All of you. Drive away.'

25

There is no sleep. Lucien returns to his flat at seven in the morning. He makes coffee, shaves, puts on a fresh shirt that Romana has ironed and left hanging for him.

He sits on the edge of the bed and drinks the hot coffee, thinking about what Dodo said in the back of the bank truck. *I offered to do it to the girl, at the house, instead of messing around with drunken doctors and anaesthetic.*

The girl at the house.

He has swirled out the dregs from the cup and is sharpening his stiletto on the coarse ring of unglazed ceramic that runs round its base when the telephone rings. 'Of course,' he replies, feeling the familiar tightening in his stomach. 'Always. I'm coming now.'

The doctor has the usual brass plate displaying his name and academic credentials next to the front door of his building. A German name, thinks Lucien. There is a smaller plate announcing the psychiatrist who has the rooms above.

Lucien sees immediately that the girl is drunk. The doctor is visible for a few seconds behind her in the doorway. A spray of unkempt silver hair. Those glasses with no rims. Greta saw him once, at the White House, finishing up with a different girl. Ancient, she said. Chinless. A chauffeur drove him away. How does an ordinary doctor afford a driver?

'Ordinary!' laughs the girl, reeling across the back seats. 'He's been with Paul since the beginning. Sits at the top table.'

'You're flying,' says Lucien. 'It's not just booze, is it? Show me your eyes.'

She throws her arms round his neck and kisses him before the door of Lucien's flat has closed behind them.

'Slow down,' he says. 'Talk to me. It's Saturday. It's not your day for the doctor.'

'A lot of big things happening this weekend. Everything is rearranged.'

'You got drunk together, in his surgery? First thing in the morning?'

'Doctor's nerves are bad today. He will perform an important operation later. His hands must not shake.'

'What kind of operation?'

'He wouldn't say.' The girl flops on to her back on the sofa with her arms above her head. 'Why won't anyone kiss me today? All he wanted to do was hold me. The poor man. Very weak nerves. Do you want to see my present?'

'I have a bad feeling about that doctor.' Lucien walks into his bedroom and shuts the door. No one answers the telephone at the restaurant. Where are Lellouche and Romana? God knows what has become of Greta. Too many moving parts coming loose, he thinks. Events are spinning out of his control.

In the living room, the girl is sitting hunched over the desk where he used to write his weekly reports to Monsieur Balard.

'We need to talk,' says Lucien. 'I want you to tell me everything the doctor said this morning. About the operation.' Then he looks over her shoulder and sees what she is doing.

The girl is crushing two white tablets on the dark wood, using the base of his coffee mug as a pestle.

'It's pure heroin,' she tells him, her tongue poking between her lips. 'He prescribes it to everyone. You can swallow it like aspirin, but it's better to snort.'

'How much have you had already?' Lucien asks. He is gripping her wrist harder than he meant to. He releases her and steps back awkwardly.

'You never thump, do you, Lulu?'

'Of course not.'

'I wouldn't blame you if you thumped me,' she says. 'I was the one who went to the girl, the next time it happened.'

'What does that mean?'

She lays her head on the table, squashing her nose into the powder, and sniffs sharply.

'Jesus,' says Lucien. 'Enough.'

'Thump me if you want to.'

He takes both her hands. 'Let's get out of here. We can run for it now. There's no need to hurt anyone. I thought that's what you wanted.'

'I don't deserve to be rescued. I didn't tell you everything.' The first waves are coming over her.

'All right. Tell me now,' says Lucien.

'A girl came to me and said the front door of the White House was unlocked, and the *gendarmes* were waiting.'

'I remember the story.'

'Well, the next time, I was the one they sent. To the new girl who arrived. It was me who told her to escape. I knew what would happen.'

'This is how they break your spirit,' he tells her. 'They make you think it's your fault. They want you to feel worthless.'

'Well, it's worked.' Then she smiles, despite herself. He knows what she is feeling. Warmth and heaviness spreading through her. She stretches herself like a cat.

'They can't see you like this,' says Lucien desperately. 'The eyes.'

'It wears off. It's nothing. Come with me.'

'For God's sake. They will kill you.'

'You worry too much. Mmm.' It is the face of someone inhaling the kind of delicious smell that transports you back to childhood. 'I'm there, Crazy. I'm there already. Come with me.'

He looks down at the smudged white powder.

*

Afterwards, they rest on the bed together for a while, dreaming but not sleeping. When they undress each other, every sensation is heightened. Every contact brings a mild shock. Her skin is cool to the touch. He kisses her neck, inhaling the scent of her hair. He feels that he is drowning in sweetness.

'Why should I run away with a thug like you?' She is astride him. The sun through the blind is a halo.

'I'm not like the others.'

'That's what all the men say, Lucien.'

'I work for Balard,' he gasps as she shifts her weight. Oh. *Oh*. God help me. 'I'm not really a brother,' says Lucien. 'I am a spy.'

When he wakes in the afternoon, the refrain is playing in his head like the nagging chorus of a summer hit. *I am a spy*. For a moment, he can't remember if he dreamed the words or really said them out loud.

Then his head rises from the mattress. He reaches out and grasps the covers alongside him, sheets that are wildly disordered and imprinted with the memory of her body. Empty.

The drug in his system slows everything, but fear overcomes it. She is not in the living room or the bathroom.

The girl has fled.

Papers are scattered across Jacques Lellouche's single bed. The wardrobe is empty. A pile of suits on hangers and the cardboard boxes that were stashed below them are spread on the floor. There is a spindly contraption made of steel in the middle of the carpet. Jacky is standing next to the machine in shirtsleeves, shuffling a deck of cards and casting a critical eye over Greta.

'I think you need another appointment at the hair salon,' he tells her.

The slap is the first real blow she has ever dealt him. His eyes water and his cheek reddens. But when he speaks, his voice is unaltered.

'An opportunity came up here. I could not let it pass.'

'I just walked back to France over the Jura fucking mountains.

You left me hanging out there. And your plans were bullshit. Everything went to hell.'

'I could not say no to this chance, Greta.'

'There was no cash, just gold and silver bars. Paul will keep all of it. What do you have to say for yourself?'

Jacky smiles and holds the fanned deck out to her. 'Pick a card.'

'You've lost your mind. What is all this fucking crap?' She kicks the steel device sitting on the floor between them.

'So I'm putting my affairs in order. Everything is falling into place. I've nearly got them where I want them.'

'Who, you madman?'

The cards fly between his fingers in a continuous blur. 'Everyone who has ever wronged me. Just imagine, Greta, being given the chance to set the past straight.'

'You're insane. Everything is collapsing. Balard is going to kill me.'

'He sent someone here, Greta. An Indochinese man kindly requested that you surrender to them by six o'clock this evening, in preparation for tomorrow. Monsieur did not spell out the consequences of refusal, but we can both guess.'

'I'm not doing Hannachi for them. They'll bury me in the woods afterwards anyway. I'm dead either way.'

'Outstanding.' He smiles, the skin round his eyes crinkling. The way he used to smile when they pulled off a job together and were counting out the proceeds. 'So it's time for you to get out of here, darling.'

'You need to disappear too.'

'Very soon. One last document is all I need. I found the owner yesterday. All that remains is to agree the price.'

'I see what this thing is now,' says Greta, stooping. She runs her fingers over the metal frame. 'It's a machine for putting corks in bottles. These are the labels. Fake labels and glue. That's it, isn't it? You fucking reptile.'

The back door slams. Romana's voice, from the bottom of the stairs. Calling Greta's name.

'It's time,' says Jacky. 'You're going to have to leave them all behind.'

'None of it was real champagne, was it? The stuff you've been selling here. It's cheaper than everywhere else because you mix it yourself. It's a blend of some other crap.'

'Only for the tourists! Americans, British. How can they tell the difference between Crémant and the real thing?'

'All those times.'

'Greta?'

'All those times you poured me a glass of champagne, at the end of a long day. None of it was real.'

His face falls. 'That is really what you think of me?'

Romana bursts into the room before she can answer. 'Greta. The girl came. An hour ago.'

'Morta was here?'

'Looking for you. I let her in. Nobody knew where you were.' Romana turns to the door and bites her lip. Her ringed hand seizes Greta's wrist. 'Something scared the shit out of her.'

There are more footsteps on the staircase. Heavier steps. Romana talks quickly, dropping her voice. 'The girl became hysterical, Greta. Said she was sorry. She was going back to the White House. She ran like the devil was after her.'

'What scared her?'

Romana bites off the reply as Robert's broad torso fills the doorway.

'Enough of this,' says Greta. 'I can't be a babysitter, on top of everything else. That girl needs her mother. It's time.'

Robert and Romana are talking loudly at the same time and Greta throws up her arms for silence.

'*Out*,' she barks. 'I would cut your balls off,' she tells Jacky, when the others have left. 'If I thought it would make any difference. You're not a man, with or without them.'

Jacky looks at her mournfully. 'Pick one,' he pleads, thrusting the deck at her.

She dashes the cards out of his hands and he dives to the floor after them. She kicks over the corking machine before she strides out. 'Serpent,' she tells Jacky.

He is on his hands and knees, plucking the fallen cards from the carpet. 'It was champagne with you,' he says. 'With you, it was always real.'

Romana has disappeared, but Robert is waiting for Greta on the landing. When she tells him where she is going, he tries to prevent her from leaving. She threatens to shoot him. They eye each other furiously. Then her face thumps against his chest as they embrace tightly.

Lucien screams around the Boulevards of the Marshals with the radio turned all the way up to drown the noise of the engine.

The news is all Djamel Hannachi and the march tomorrow. The police are urging people to stay out of Paris. Hannachi is supposed to be flying in from Algeria tonight, but there is a last-minute development: a new appointment to the cabinet of the Fourth Republic.

Lucien lets out a roar of anger and frustration when he hears the name. He slams his palms on the wheel and the car wobbles dangerously as it passes a line of ambulances. He punches the radio to silence it.

The last time he saw the man's face, he was crushing it against an iron gate outside a shuttered house in Billancourt.

The next interior minister of France. Another one of the girl's predictions that has come true.

Lucien is shuffling a list of the places she might have run to. A thought stabs at him and he turns off the boulevard, racing south. Has she gone back to the doctor for more white tablets to crush? It's worth a shot, Lucien thinks. There are hotels the girl has used before too, where they will know her face and give her a room on the account of the *milieu*. Another outside chance.

He tries to shove the most obvious, most crushing thought to the back of his mind, but the voice will not be stilled. She has gone back to the White House with your secret, it says. You cracked eventually and gave her the thing she wanted all along. You fool. Another girl has betrayed you.

Lucien is about to get out of the car when he sees them in the driver's mirror. Three people walking along the pavement on the other side, towards the doctor's surgery. A slight girl in the middle, being hustled along by the men on each side. One is Neapolitan. Lucien doesn't know the second man. As they draw level he peers over the sill at the girl, shrinking low into his seat.

A Eurasian *poule* he has seen at the White House, at the parties. One of Paul's favourites. Pretty and obedient, the eyes always downcast. She arrived like that, his cousin boasted once. Trained since childhood, in one of the best houses in Macau. She was a gift, a sweetener from the big Chinese man. From Mr Li. Her head is bowed now, lower than ever, as they reach the door. The doctor takes a long time to answer. When the callers have disappeared inside, Lucien throws the car into reverse and tears away.

The restaurant opens at six on Saturday evenings. The dining room is immaculate, with fresh flowers on every table. The special that night is one of Jacky Lellouche's favourites: veal kidneys with mustard, on a bed of spinach.

Balard's men spill out of their black Citroëns just as Jacky is throwing the doors open. He asks them if they would like a table for thirteen. Everyone else screams as the glass breaks and the tables are overturned.

On her hands and knees, Romana watches the men drag Jacky upstairs. They shove her into the wine cellar with Marcel. Crouched in the darkness, they can hear furniture breaking on the upper floor as the men tear the bedrooms apart.

All Balard's people have served in Indochina and North Africa. They use the upstairs landing for the *passage à tabac* – the gauntlet of fists and feet. They do not have a field radio to generate electricity, so they hold Jacky down in the bathtub and feed a rubber hose down his throat instead, stopping his nose with their fingers. The first time they pull the hose out, he requests that they use champagne instead of water. After that he does not make jokes.

*

Greta is hurrying out to her plane at Orly when she sees Djamel Hannachi forty yards to her right, giving an impromptu press conference to the journalists who have finagled their way past the police on to the runway.

The family Hannachi never sees are all around him in a thicket of bodies and legs. As she is queuing on the mobile staircase, Greta hears the woman in front talking to her companion. 'The government changed its mind. They were going to let him address the demonstrators tomorrow. But they are making him turn round and go back to Algeria.'

France has a new minister of the interior, the woman says. This is his first decision. A good start.

Hannachi's daughter is almost nine – too big for her father to pick up now. He has picked her up anyway. The wife with the blue-black hair and the heart-shaped face is attempting to restrain the little boys. Flashbulbs are going off and the Algerian is raising his voice over the interruptions of the reporters. Greta cannot hear what he is saying.

'Algeria is the best place for him,' says the woman in front of her. 'We don't need these parasites over here.'

As the plane climbs, Greta sees that it is following the Seine north-west. I wonder if we will fly over the White House, she thinks. From this height she will be able to see the cars parked outside, even make out individual figures. Paul's creatures. Has the girl run back there by now? What did she want with Greta today? What did she see at the restaurant that terrified her? Of course, the plane does not stay low for long. Greta begins to lose track of the silver band of the river in wisps of vapour. Soon they will be above the clouds.

Vassily's Englishman is waiting for her in the Golden Lion in St James's. He is chatting so animatedly to the barmaid that Greta assumes he knows the woman well, but then he turns and greets her as though she is an old friend too and she sees that he is simply a habitually amiable, garrulous man.

'Hello, old girl. You're looking well. How was the journey?'

She buys a large Scotch and soda for him and a lemonade for herself. She can't help noticing how his hand shakes as he pours half the soda into the tumbler.

'Windy,' he says. 'I get windy these days. But I don't funk things. Know what I mean?'

'Not really.'

'I suffer from nerves, but they don't stop me getting the job done. How are your nerves?'

'Up and down.'

He places a hip flask inside the bag which she has left open on the stool between them, using her folded sweater as a soft nest.

The flask is about four inches square, covered in black grain leather. There is a metal oval in the centre of the leather for an engraving, left blank.

'They took it out of the lab in a perfume bottle,' the Englishman says. 'Hell of a job switching it over.'

'I never wear perfume. If anyone who knows me saw it, they would become suspicious.'

'Hell of a job. The thicker the gloves, the more likely you are to fumble it. There's no smell, but I mixed it with booze. Any idea who it's for? Someone who likes brandy? No. Sorry. Stupid of me.'

'I can't . . .'

'Of course not. Play the ball. Play the ball that comes your way, don't think about the game.'

When she is getting ready to leave, he touches her hand lightly. 'Shan't be a bore on the subject, but you will be careful? Spill that on your hand and it's the end of you. Clear?'

'Crystal-clear.'

'Good old girl.' His eyes are very glassy now. He has a plump, pleasant face, like an overgrown schoolboy. He raises his glass. 'To the victory of the workers.'

'To your health,' says Greta.

It is late by the time Lucien reaches the last hotel on his list. He hammers the bell for the night manager. Yes, the man remembers

Marie. Who could forget such a girl? No, monsieur, they have not seen her for weeks.

The restaurant then, Lucien thinks. It's the thing he has been putting off, because it is the last hope. After the restaurant, there is nowhere else but the White House.

It's possible, after all, he tells himself. Perhaps Greta made it back to Paris, despite everything. The girl would have fled to her, naturally.

That she is sleeping there now, he thinks, in one of the rooms above the restaurant. That she is safe and well fed and happy and did not run back to Paul Fazi with the news that his own cousin is a poisonous traitor. That love exists.

Lucien approaches the Place de la Bastille at a crawl. He is like a man being dragged to the gallows. The final truth lies at the far end of the Rue de Rivoli. If the girl is sleeping at the restaurant, there is no need to rouse her. If she is not there, she will be with his cousin.

The cops have closed the street to cars at the eastern end. The Boulevard Beaumarchais is barricaded ahead too, and he pulls over to think about the route. He needs five minutes to reorientate himself.

The early sun wakes him, and he presses his eyes with his palms. Several hours have passed. The drug, he thinks, catching up with me. No, just honest exhaustion. I've been flogging myself for days. Christ. I'm as weak as a kitten.

He leaves the car and walks west, feeling a growing sense of despair. The hopeful fantasies of the previous evening are dispersing in the air of a cold autumn morning. The crowds are already gathering. He can see them surging along the banks of the Seine. The Île de la Cité, the place where Hannachi was due to speak, is at the centre of everything. The background noise builds as he walks the streets, like a strengthening wind.

Lucien turns right on Mont Thabor and almost barges into Ange and Dodo. He doesn't even start with surprise. Every nerve in his body feels dead.

'You look like shit,' growls Ange. 'You didn't sleep?'

'Virus.'

'We've been hunting for you everywhere. You don't answer the phone now?'

'Out,' says Lucien.

Dodo strides off ahead towards the restaurant without a word. There is an angry scowl on his face. Lucien falls in step with Ange.

'What are we doing?' he asks.

'It's the Balard thing.'

'The Balard thing.' Lucien is too tired to feign surprise. He sees Dodo shake his head contemptuously, five paces in front.

'It had to happen sooner or later,' says Ange. 'Just take it calmly, will you, Lulu? No rough stuff.'

'All right.' He walks round the corner in a waking dream. A man in civilian clothes is standing on the corner, cradling a rifle. The man nods at Ange as they pass. Lucien's knees and back are aching. There are no tables on the pavement outside Jacky Lellouche's restaurant. The blinds are closed but he can see men moving inside.

'It will be a relief for you,' Ange is saying.

'A relief. Yes. Do I go in?'

They have come to a halt, Dodo behind him now, alongside Ange, to cut off his escape route. Only two, thinks Lucien. Swing at them? Make a dash for it? What's the point, if the girl has given me up?

You poor sap, says the voice in his head. She was stringing you along all the time. And with that thought, calm and acceptance come over him. Most people go through their lives without learning anything. I discovered something worth knowing, in the end. There is no love.

'Just stroll in,' says Ange, motioning with a hand. 'You're doing well, Lulu.'

I'll walk through the door, thinks Lucien. I'll take two steps, stop and close my eyes. Perhaps it will be a wire, thrown over the head from behind. Or a gun at the nape of the neck. It might be quick. What does it matter?

If the girl was a trap, then there is no love. And if there's no love in this world, I don't want to live here.

Lucien fills his lungs with air and pushes through the door of the restaurant.

26

They have stacked the tables and pushed them to the sides of the dining room.

Monsieur Trinh is directly in front of him, sitting on an upturned crate.

An army officer in fatigues is standing at the bar, studying a map of Paris spread across the polished wood. Two plainclothes men with rifles loll in the doorway that leads to the kitchen.

Lucien hesitates, two paces inside the front door. The men around him are not exactly hostile. They have the absolute indifference of the very tough.

Monsieur Balard is sitting opposite Paul Fazi at the single table set up on the right of the bar. There are coffee cups in front of them and they are both leaning back in their chairs. Both are dressed in dark suits and ties.

Like a mirror image, thinks Lucien. Or the heads on a playing card. Two halves of the same black king.

'Come and take the weight off your feet, Crazy.'

Lucien obeys his cousin, pulling the chair back from the table and reversing it before sitting.

'You know everything?' he asks Paul. 'You two have been talking the whole time, behind my back?'

'It's a lot to take in, isn't it?'

Lucien blinks at him in bewilderment. He can find no words to offer his cousin in reply. He turns to Balard. 'I suppose you worked with Paul during the war, monsieur?'

'A long time before that. I spotted his promise early on. And I heard about you many years ago. A strong young man. A *Caïd* of the future.'

'What did I tell you?' says Paul. 'We're talent scouts, Lulu. You're the talent.'

'You will accuse me of using you,' Balard continues. 'I plead guilty to the charge. I am obliged to use all kinds of men. You are one of the good ones. A man who will only fight if he believes he is on the side of right. Do you follow me?'

'I think so, sir.'

'Other men are simpler. They are motivated by money. We will make use of that kind later.'

'You paid for all of this, Lulu,' says Paul, sweeping an arm to take in the scene around them. Two more armed men have walked into the room. Balard's Indochinese guard is forcing a crate open with a crowbar. Steel pipes are piled inside, like thick gun barrels, thirty inches long.

'I paid for it,' says Lucien, thinking about post vans and bank trucks and gold and silver and bricks of banknotes.

'You're the best earner I've ever had, Lulu. Everything has to stay off the government books. That's where we come in, isn't it? Geneva popped up just when we needed a lot of cash for Stay Behind. And for today.'

'Today cannot go ahead,' says Lucien. 'I lost the Lithuanian woman.'

'An inconvenience,' says Balard, checking his watch. 'But the plans are updated, not scrapped. Monsieur Hannachi is given a temporary reprieve. His supporters are still here, infecting the streets. I must outdo Hannachi in eloquence today. I must prepare my oration soon.'

'Don't worry about Greta,' says Paul. 'We'll have her in the bag soon. There is plenty of value to be squeezed out of that.'

'She is on our side. She hates the Reds.'

Balard and Paul smile indulgently at the same time. They were expecting it.

'Chivalry is an admirable quality,' Balard tells him. 'Sentimentality is not. The woman has disobeyed my orders.' He stands and gathers up his gloves and scarf. Paul and Lucien rise too, and the uniformed officer at the bar snaps to attention.

'We are all soldiers,' says Balard, to the whole room. 'Our cause is bigger than any individual. Fifteen minutes, please, Lucien. The team leaders will muster outside.'

When the Fazi cousins have resumed their seats, Paul says: 'What do you think of the new headquarters?'

'I'm surprised Jacky agreed to it.'

Paul laughs. 'That is one Jew whose haggling days are over. He's a tough one though. Tougher than anyone realized.'

'I don't know him well. We play cards occasionally. Aren't you angry with me at all?'

'The opposite, Lulu. We need someone who can operate the machine from both sides. Someone who will keep the wheels turning after I am gone. We need brains.' He nods ironically at the window, and Lucien turns to see a pair of eyes and the bridge of a nose that can only belong to Dodo. The tall man is glaring at them through a gap in the blinds.

'The machine is a beautiful thing to watch when all the parts are spinning,' says Paul. 'Each of us has our role. That gold you stole is on its way to Asia now, by diplomatic bag, courtesy of Monsieur Balard.'

'To your big Chinese friend?'

'Mr Li trades gold for American dollars. He exchanges the dollars for piastres in Saigon. Those pretty little Indochinese bank-notes. It shakes out at eight francs to the piastre. That's what you get on the street. Now what does he do with his big pile of piastres? Those little works of art. Think, Lulu.'

Lucien is fighting tiredness, stretching his eyes open with his fingertips. He is remembering Indochina, the old hands and their constant whispers about the traffic in currency. 'He takes them to a bank.'

'*Voilà*. He goes to the Bank of France, where the official exchange rate is fixed at seventeen francs to the piastre, and wires it back to me. We've doubled our money without lifting a finger. We're swimming in francs.'

'It's twisted. I can't get it straight in my head.'

'A real Fazi would say it was beautiful. I don't even need gold. All I need are rusty old cars.'

'Cars?'

'Anything. A ship full of junk sitting in the Port of Marseille. When it gets to Haiphong, Mr Li signs the import sale papers. But the cars he is signing for are brand-new *Traction Avants*. The invoice is four times the real value of the goods.'

'And he pays it?'

'All of it, without complaint. The point is to generate a lot of local currency cheaply. Then my agent goes to the bank near the cathedral in Saigon and wires the money back to me at seventeen francs to the piastre.'

Lucien is nodding. 'I suppose you split the extra francs with Mr Li at the end. But I don't understand why the French government lets it happen. Why do we overvalue the Indochinese currency?'

'So the poor bastards fighting out there can stretch their wages twice as far. Don't you remember how it was? Everyone lives like a king. You can import whatever you want from France. A brand-new refrigerator full of cold beer. It stops the men putting their rifles in their fucking mouths.'

'You can't create money from nowhere,' says Lucien. 'The taxpayer picks up the bill in the end.'

'Now you're thinking. It's why some politicians don't like the arrangement. Not everyone wants to inflate the piastre. So we need the right people in place in the government.'

'This new guy? The interior minister?'

'The cat you roughed up is one of ours, sure. He was Balard's choice. I made it happen.'

'Why are you grinning? What kind of filth do you have on that guy, Paul?'

'One lesson at a time.' He taps his watch. 'You're due onstage, Lulu.'

They walk out of the restaurant together. Dodo is pacing up and down the pavement, scowling and clawing at his hair.

'Unbelievable,' he snarls. 'You're just going to let Lulu walk away, after everything he's pulled?'

'I'd keep your hands off him if I were you.'

'A fucking *maricón*-lover,' sneers Dodo. 'You should have seen his face when I showed up for Geneva instead of Lellouche. He was looking forward to a suck after the run.'

Lucien is looking down at the hand gripping his upper arm.

'You're brave today,' Paul tells Dodo.

'Braver than him,' says Dodo. 'He was soft as shit in Switzerland. Didn't want to hurt a fly. And he's got something going with the Lithuanian woman. I don't trust him.'

'Trust him or don't trust him,' says Paul, 'but show him respect, boy, if that's what I tell you.'

A Berliet is parked on the next corner and Lucien can see figures climbing into the back. The army officer who was poring over the map has escorted Balard to the military vehicle and is walking back towards the restaurant. Lucien tries to push past but Dodo checks him with a growl.

'You can't be thinking about promoting Lulu above me. It's unbelievable.'

Paul looks from one young man to the other. Dodo is taller by two or three inches. A bitter anger is distorting his unlovely features. Lucien is stockier.

'Back home,' says Paul, 'we handle this how, Crazy? No, you won't remember. You were too young.'

'I remember,' says Lucien. 'We take it in turns.'

'*Voilà*. Hold his left hand, Dodo.'

'Do what?'

'Take Lucien's hand. You get to hit him first.'

'Hit Lulu?' Dodo's Adam's apple wobbles in his long neck.

'You called him a cocksucker, boy. Get it all out of your system. Do your worst.'

Dodo winds his arm up like he is trying to hit the bell with a sledgehammer at the fair. His feet leave the floor at the top of the swing. It's a cuff, not a punch, the heel of his hand rebounding from Lucien's temple. But his weight is behind the blow, and it makes Lucien stagger half a step back and close his eyes.

'Don't let go,' he tells Dodo, grimacing through the sting of pain. 'The first one to let go loses. It's all right!' He says this in a cheery voice to the army officer, who is watching the ceremony unfold with an expression of distaste. Two grown men clutching each other by the left hand and exchanging blows with the right.

'There's no problem,' Lucien calls out, smiling at the uniformed soldier. When Dodo's eyes flicker in the man's direction, Lucien punches him in the face, straight down the barrel. There is a thump as he hits the pavement. Lucien pauses to adjust his jacket and tie before stepping over the groaning body and walking past the frowning officer. You can tell what the spectator thinks about the strange ritual. Corsicans. *These fucking people.*

'Papa,' says Dodo uncertainly, from the floor.

'I'm here.' Paul bends down and pinches Dodo's face.

'I'm hurt, Papa.' The slap silences Dodo. His head sinks back on to the concrete.

'Don't call me that in public,' hisses Paul. 'I've told you how many times? We can work together, and we can drink together, but we can't be father and son.'

Twenty men sit in the back of the Berliet. Lucien recognizes four from his time in Hanoi. One is from the same regiment as him. The other three are legionnaires. They nod at each other in greeting but no one smiles or shakes hands.

Balard is the only one on his feet. He stands at the back by the tail plate with a steel pipe in his hand. He has taken off his long coat and suit jacket and it makes him younger and stronger.

'Each of you has been allocated a section of riverbank,' says Balard. 'You have forty to fifty men each. There might be as many as thirty thousand of the enemy in Paris today. With five thousand police on duty at most, plus a few reserves. And us, gentlemen. And us. That is not nothing.' A low murmur passes around the vehicle.

'Still, we are outnumbered and that means we need to work together. The national police will push the worst of the terrorists in our direction. They will all be funnelled towards the river.' He pats his gloved palm with the pipe. 'These will feel heavy very quickly. So make it count, please. When you hit something, break it.'

There is the noise again – a collective growl of approval. The men are eyeing each other eagerly.

'Most of you have been in Indochina. A few decided to come back from Algeria for this. Many of you will have found the last few years extremely difficult.'

Lucien finds that he is looking intently at Balard, emotion rising in his throat.

'Some of you have been adrift, getting into trouble with the law. Searching for meaning. I am no philosopher, but I have one unshakeable belief. All my life, politicians have told me it is necessary to make a choice. We can either go with Russia, or with America, and there is no other option. Gentlemen, I choose France. I choose France. Have a drink before you go out. It begins at midday.'

27

Greta is not used to air travel. The awful thought strikes her for the first time as she is disembarking from her return flight at Orly on Sunday afternoon: there is no escape from this place.

There is no rear door you can slip through in an airport. All the passengers are funnelled along the same long corridor and must emerge through the same exit. A sea of eyes. Taxi drivers are waiting with surnames scrawled on to pieces of card: Zagré, Marchand, Pézard. A strange moment passes when she is unable to recall her own surname – the one she was born with – and must think hard to remember it.

The taxi rank is moving fast and there are no G7 cabs waiting for her. She checks her watch and tightens her grip on the leather strap of her handbag. The hip flask from the man in London is inside, a cashmere sweater wrapped round it.

Greta frowns. This is no time for mistakes. She cannot stand around on the pavement loitering, in enemy territory. Paris is Moscow now. Then she sees a Simca parked seventy yards to her right on the other side of the road. The horn sounds.

The car is facing away from her as she approaches. The driver wears the same flat cap the Spanish woman wore the first time Greta saw her. She must have adjusted it more carefully this time, because no curls spill from the sides. The head does not turn as Greta draws near the Simca. There are four men in a Frégate parked on the far side.

They burst out as one, exactly at the moment Greta hears feet pounding along the pavement behind her, and as she realizes the registration number of the Simca is wrong.

When the head of the G7 driver revolves at last, the face is that of a man, cruel, southern Italian. I must be exhausted, thinks Greta. She instinctively scoops up the bag in both arms and holds it close. Then grasping hands are on her.

Nobody touches her on the ride to the White House. Ange is waiting on the gravel drive, beside the grand entrance. 'I have prepared madame's usual room,' he caws. They struggle to pull her from the back of the car until he takes her by the throat.

Dodo and Momo are waiting upstairs in the room with the piano. They hit Greta in turn, two holding her upright while the third man sets himself. It is all in the mid-section. They have the professional habit of not damaging the faces of women.

When she falls they stamp on her, but it is a messy, unsatisfying business. They crowd in too close and get in each other's way. They take a step back, a breath. The kicks are better aimed now – into her ribs, hips and thighs.

Dodo shouts in delight, raising his hand for a pause. 'What did I hear? Is she begging? Are you begging?'

Greta lifts her face from the carpet. 'Please,' she says. 'I'm pregnant.'

The hands of men under her armpits. Her knees drag on the corridor carpet. A door is open on the left. Ange barks a command, and they stop.

He walks into the room where the girl is waiting, arranged for Greta, on her knees in corset and stockings with a silk gown round the shoulders. Maman Fazi stands behind the kneeling girl, silent, staring at Greta through the big panes of her spectacles.

The girl's head has collapsed forwards, but the old lady works her fingers deep into the roots of her blonde hair and yanks the head upright. The room has been turned upside down. The television set is smashed, ripped from the wall.

'Do you know this woman?' Ange asks the girl. 'What did she say to you when she broke into your room that night, Marie? Wake up.' Ange slaps her face and jabs a finger at Greta. 'Have you been seeing her, Marie, in the city? What have you been doing, little *cunt*?'

'Morta,' whispers the girl. 'My name is Morta.'

They dump Greta on a pile of cushions in another room, in handcuffs. Something stirs close by, and she feels a rush of new fear. Animals moving around her in the darkness. The blindfold is raised and an Indochinese face is looking at her uncertainly. A painted finger bisecting a pretty mouth. There is a younger girl sitting in the corner of the room, head bowed, holding her knees. The Indochinese woman strokes Greta's back and tells her not to talk. Then she folds over her work, cleaning the wooden pipe with a long needle, lighting the lamp with a match.

The pipe is like a flute. A line of elephants is carved along the side, each one holding the tail of the next with its trunk. The Indochinese woman rolls Greta on to her side when the pipe is ready and puts it to her lips. As Greta gasps and coughs, the woman takes the pipe to the girl in the corner. The girl raises her head. She is Eurasian, from the features. There is a large black patch over her right eye and a white dressing below it.

The Indochinese woman's voice is light and musical. She is speaking French, coaxing them to take the pipe again in turn. Greta has the power to tune in and out of human speech now, to reduce it to a warm, pleasing babble if desired, as though she is adjusting the controls on a radio set. One word, repeated, resonates in her head: aeroplane.

In the back of an army truck parked on the Pont Saint-Michel, Marcel the sous-chef is hugging himself while his feet patter uncontrollably on the floor. Jacky Lellouche looks at him from the seat opposite, through his good eye, and says: '*Calme-toi.*'

Jacky's right eye is so swollen that it looks like two pouting red lips have grown over it. His upper and lower jaws no longer align properly, so that you can see teeth in the corner even when his mouth is closed. He has been sick down his good shirt, but it is mostly water. His lower belly is still swollen from the hosepipe.

Balard says: 'I may as well say that I despise your kind. Mincing around without a care in the world, while the rest of us have to be so careful, all our lives. You make clowns of us.'

Jacky raises his head to look at the grey-haired man. 'The boy and I are not lovers, Balard. He is young. Let him go.'

'It is too late for that, Lellouche. This is your last chance. Give back everything you have stolen. Tell me where the documents are, and we go straight to the hospital. Otherwise, it is time for the *flipper*.' Marcel looks up at him and he grins. 'Yes, young man. A game of *flipper*. You two are the balls. If you make it to the next bridge, you win. But there are plenty of things to bounce off on the way.'

His Indochinese bodyguard releases the chains that hold the tail plate up, and Marcel sees the men strung along the Quai Saint-Michel. There are seven or eight figures shifting in the darkness, spread out like a sports team. Each holds a steel pipe.

'The final chance,' Balard says.

'Don't run,' says Jacky. He is reaching for Marcel.

The boy stays on his feet when they hurl him out, but Jacky's arms and legs are too weak to break the fall and he sprawls on to the cobbles. The rear lights of the truck illuminate them, in a cloud of diesel fumes.

'We don't run,' says Jacky. He stands up slowly and his arms enfold the shaking boy. 'Criminals run. We are good people.' The truck is pulling away and the men with the pipes are closing in round them in silence.

From Pont Neuf, Lucien sees them go down, watches the pipes rise and fall. The sound of metal on flesh carries to him. Then he hears the sharp noise of the pipes hitting the cobbles. Jacky and Marcel are lying flat, and it is hard for the men standing round them to strike the bodies cleanly without catching the flagstones.

Lucien knows he will not make it over there in time. There is a knot of North African men in his way, corralled at the junction where the bridge meets the south bank of the Seine. White men circle them like pack hunters.

Lucien has not used his own pipe yet. When he walks on to the bridge he can see figures moving, down on the quayside. Teams of Balard's people are picking up bodies and heaving them into the river.

He wanders east in a daze, his ears full of the screams and the percussion of the beatings. The Île de la Cité itself is calm. The police have withdrawn and left Balard and Paul in control of the island and the south bank that faces it.

There are men he knows, from the army, from the *milieu*. The youngest of the quartet of Neapolitan thugs wanders past and Lucien grabs him, roaring questions into his face. Where is everyone else? The boy is falling-down drunk, babbling nonsense. A woman, a girl, an aeroplane. The White House.

'Greta,' shouts Lucien.

'Yes. She caught a plane at Orly. No – a small plane. How many did you get?' the boy asks Lucien, gesturing at the metal tube in his hand. His eyes are wet and shining.

Lucien runs south, away from the water, through angry streets that have not yet submitted to the rule of the steel pipes. Police cars are on fire. An Arab pushes past him near Mabillon, sees the weapon in his hand and throws a punch. Lucien takes it, absorbs the shock, does not hit back.

At last he sees what he has been looking for, by the entrance to the Métro station: a telephone box that has not been smashed. He riffles through his pockets for coins, slams them home, dials the White House. 'Why don't I have enough change?' he yells when the call is cut short.

A group of dark-haired men stalk past, their heads turning from side to side. Lucien catches someone's eye, through the glass of the phone box, as he is patting his pockets. The men stop.

When Lucien opens the door they have formed a half-circle. The ugly chef who worked in Vincent's bar in Marseille is speaking quickly in Arabic. He carries a house brick in his hand now, not a meat cleaver. The man switches language and calls out to Lucien. 'Frenchman. I know you. Come out, Frenchman.'

'What the fuck are you talking about?' spits Lucien, staring him down. The steel pipe is bobbing in his hand and the sight of it makes the men bristle nervously. 'We are all Frenchmen,' Lucien says.

He lunges to his right then dodges left like a racing winger, aiming for a gap that has opened in the wall of men. He shoulders his way through and accelerates into a desperate pelt. He hears the pipe clattering where it fell to the pavement behind him.

They are leading Greta down the steps of the main entrance of the house when Lucien pulls up, tyres carving through the deep gravel and throwing up dust.

Ange is holding her up on one side, Dutchman on the other. Dodo is pacing, scowling at the sight of Lucien's car. Behind the men, Maman Fazi has her arms folded and is observing the scene without emotion. An Indochinese woman, tiny and beautiful, wrapped in a bathrobe against the autumn night, carries Greta's coat and bag.

Lucien stands facing them all, looking slowly from one to the other. Dodo is not pleased to see him. There is a bulge under the patch pocket of Ange's sports coat.

The front door is open, and Lucien can see a man cradling a rifle at the foot of the staircase in the entrance hall. There will be many others like him on a night like this, spread over the floors between Lucien and the girl.

Dutchman is awestruck. 'You were seen, Lulu, surrounded by Algerians. How the fuck did you get out of there?'

'I smashed them all up,' Lucien says indifferently. 'How do you think?'

Dutchman releases Greta's arm and runs to him. A crushing hug.

One of them still trusts me, thinks Lucien. Only one. 'All right,' he says brightly. 'There's still work to do. Let me help with the woman. There's a light aircraft in the top field?'

Dodo and Ange exchange an uneasy glance. 'We have everything under control,' says Ange levelly. 'No need to trouble yourself.'

'I promised Paul I would put Greta on that plane myself. It's my fault she got loose after Geneva. Let me drive you up there.'

'*Bien*,' growls Ange. 'Me and Dodo go in the back.'

They both have revolvers in their waistbands. They squeeze themselves in with Greta in the middle, her head nodding. 'She's taken a beating,' Lucien observes without emotion. 'Did she smoke something too?' He slaps Greta's face to rouse, not to hurt, and she gives him a faraway look.

'Her bag,' Lucien says, as if suddenly remembering it. 'Hey!' The Indochinese girl answers his call and comes to the window. 'Is she bleeding down there?' Lucien asks.

'A little bit. It's not too bad.' The girl hands him the leather handbag through the window.

'Wait. *Putain*. What's this?' It's Ange's scraping voice.

'I don't want blood all over my seats. Neither will the pilot.'

'Let's check that again. You know what she's like.'

Lucien throws the bag to Dodo, who catches it mechanically then looks at it in disgust. 'I've already been through this once.'

'It's a good job for you,' Lucien tells him. 'Women's things.'

In the mirror, Lucien watches Dodo searching the bag. He is thinking about a story Greta once told him, in which she nearly killed a man with a can of hairspray. Dodo doesn't remove the aerosol.

Ange stares at the back of Lucien's head all the time as they drive. The handle of the revolver is visible above the waistband of his trousers. Lucien drums his fingers on the steering wheel.

I need to go back to the house, he thinks. Marie must be there. The girl who did not give me up. Surely I can talk my way past the guards.

Greta's eyes are closing, her head lolling on one side. That's a good soldier, thinks Lucien. I've done what I can for her.

When Greta opens her eyes, the pain throughout her lower body is reasserting itself. She no longer has the ability to tune out unpleasant sensations at will. The internal warmth of the opium is fading.

There are four seats in the Cessna. Ange is directly in front of her on the right, his body turned in so he can talk to the pilot. Dodo is sitting on Greta's left.

Only the pilot is strapped in. He is saying reassuring things. 'We stop for fuel once, this side of the mountains. That will get us all the way to Africa. Now look over there and you will see Orléans.'

'Not me,' says Dodo. He is gripping the edge of the seat on both sides of his legs.

Greta looks out of the window and sees a constellation of lights far below. She experiences a rush of vertigo that makes her reel in her seat and lunge for the one in front to steady herself.

'Good evening, madame.' Ange is laughing at her disorientation.

The pilot is still talking loudly over the vibrations and the engine noise. 'Only one brief stop. We can carry about forty gallons.' He glances over his shoulder when Ange speaks.

'I know you,' Greta tells the pilot. Dodo slaps her face, but she carries on talking. 'You climbed into bed with me at Jeannot and Clothilde's place. You told me you flew planes. When did you sink to this level?'

Dodo has his long fingers round her throat. Her cuffed hands strain to relieve the pressure.

'Cut that out,' says the pilot. 'You can't do that in here.'

'It's dangerous, Dodo,' complains Ange. 'Wait until we get there.'

'You're working for a gang of murderers, my friend,' says Greta, when she can speak again. 'I hope you're proud.'

The captain doesn't want to look at her. He shouts so the sound will carry to the back seats. 'I fly for whoever pays. I can't afford to have politics now.'

Dodo says: 'I'm saving it up. Every word buys you another slap when we get to Algiers. When I can take my time.'

'But not the face,' says Ange, feeling his own thoughtfully.

There is a pocket of turbulence that makes the plane dip and wobble. Dodo groans. Greta feels a spasm of pain up and down her abdomen and grimaces, despite herself.

Only Ange appears unconcerned. 'No one is going to touch your face. You call us murderers. We are patriots.' He glances at the man next to him, but the pilot is putting on a pair of headphones to listen to the radio. 'Paul is giving you to Balard for a fortnight. You are going to do in Algeria what you failed to do in Paris. You pay Hannachi a visit at his home. No wife and kids around. Very clean and simple. After that, you tell Balard the truth about whatever the fuck you've been doing for the Russians. If Balard lets you live, you go to work for Paul. Don't worry about your baby. A lot of men will pay extra for an hour with a pregnant woman. It's just their thing. We all have a thing. Yours is tall men.'

Dodo laughs. That tall guy. What was the phrase he used? She's like a jungle cat, in the bed. Dodo is almost as pale as his father now, very scared but trying to make himself brave, spitting out the cruellest words he can find.

First, he narrates the death of Jacques Lellouche, as passed on by eyewitnesses. Dodo lingers lovingly on the details.

Then he turns to Greta's immediate future. They will let her see the kid. Mothers pining for lost children are no good to anyone. They can't work, can't smile for the men. The baby will go to an Algerian woman and Greta will be allowed a visit once a week. The arrangement costs money, of course. It will be added on to her debt. He exhausts himself eventually.

The effects of the opium pipe have faded entirely now, and Greta is hurting more than she has ever hurt.

She's like a jungle cat in the bed! Greta imagines Robert saying these words in the low voice she used to find so soothing. Dodo cackling with laughter.

What other secrets could Robert have told them? This is the special torture of betrayal: the way it sets the mind spinning back over every conversation, every confidence she might have let slip in the ruin of the bedsheets.

Robert's face in the early light. So handsome, she thinks. But not a fool, after all. Beautiful Judas.

The plane lurches again and Greta's body stiffens. Another flash of pain from the mid-section. Now Laima's face, worn and lined, replaces that of Robert.

The general holding court in the forest, the young partisans gathered round her for the lecture. A difficult lesson: Capture and Interrogation.

'We all freeze,' says the general, 'when the bag goes over our head. We become limp and compliant. It is simply a survival instinct. We do not want to anger our captors. But observe: there is an iron rule. We never let them take us anywhere. The next place they take us will always be worse. There will be more of the enemy, with fewer opportunities to escape. They will be able to take their time with us, to linger over their evil work. That is why we always fight where we stand. Even if it hastens the end.'

'Give me a drink,' says Greta, looking out of the window.

'What did she say?' asks Ange. The engine is operating at a higher pitch, like a car that has changed gear.

'I need a drink. In my handbag.'

Ange raises his eyebrows. Dodo finds the hip flask, wearing the expression of someone being asked to rummage through the entrails of a dead animal, and hands it to the older man.

'That was the other thing the tall guy said,' Dodo shouts. 'She's a drunk these days. What's in there?'

Ange is unscrewing the cap, sniffing gingerly. The movement of the plane makes it hard.

'It's one of the best Armagnacs money can buy,' says Greta. 'Too expensive for pigs like you. Give it to me.'

Dodo slaps her face again, thoughtlessly, then raises a placatory hand as Ange gives him a lingering look of displeasure. 'Well, can you blame me? It's disgusting. She's carrying his child and she wants to guzzle brandy. No wonder he got rid of her. This kind of woman is so disgusting to me.'

He reaches out to accept the flask. Ange has taken a long drink and is smacking his lips.

'By God,' says Dodo, following suit. 'I believe it is Armagnac.'

He holds the flask out towards Greta then snatches it back with a sneer. 'She would, as well. If I poured it on the pavement she would get down on all fours and lick it up. Do you want to hurt your man's child? They are disgusting when they turn into drunks.'

'It's too good for you,' says Greta, and Dodo backhands her and Ange raises his voice and the pilot joins in, telling them to cut it out, name of God.

It is a clear night. They can see the lights of small villages. Spiders' webs of towns, with the lit roads stretching out from the centre. Lightning on the horizon, somewhere in the east, that makes Dodo flinch and peer out of the window anxiously.

'It's a hundred miles away,' says the pilot. 'We'll outrun it. Nothing to worry about tonight. We're going round the mountains, not over them. We're not crossing Spain.'

He talks for ten minutes, with long pauses. All pilots curse the name of Spain, it seems. A land of dark mountains and treachery. He takes the flask when it is offered.

When Toulouse appears, ahead and to the right, the captain announces it cheerfully, breaking the long silence. On their left the sun is beginning to rise.

Greta is peering at the others from where she sits, slumped into her coat in an apparent state of dejection. The pilot is wiping his brow with the sleeve of his sheepskin jacket. They have just passed the flask round again and he holds it in his left hand, the cap open.

Ange's eyes are closed, right in front of Greta, and he is licking his lips as if to moisten them. He looks exceptionally wizened. The wrinkles in his face seem deeper, as if the skin has shrunk from dehydration.

Ange's eyes open when he realizes Dodo is talking, in Corsican not French. It began as a stream of low muttering but has been rising in pitch and volume. The younger man's bulging eyes swivel from side to side.

'Poison,' exclaims Ange, and Greta stiffens. But he means that the pilot is poisoning them. He and Dodo are suddenly both shouting at the other man, talking about oxygen, fumes from the engine. Something about the atmosphere in the cabin has become unendurable. All the men are tugging at the collars of their shirts as though they're burning up.

When the captain turns round to face Dodo, Greta can see that he is already past the point where he can comprehend their questions. His eyes are pinpricks. They flick over to Greta. 'What's she saying? What's she saying?' The others look at her too. She is muttering in Lithuanian. 'You don't take me anywhere. You don't take me.'

Things happen at the same time. The plane begins to lose height. Dodo screams something about the hip flask. Ange reaches out to grab Greta's head with both hands.

Dodo leaves her alone at first. He can't remember where the flask is. He is scrabbling on the floor for it, as if finding it will somehow reverse the cascade of dreadful sensations running through his body. The pilot ignores him, his head nodding.

Greta manages to fend off Ange, even in handcuffs. He can't find a purchase on her neck from where he is sitting. He goes up on one knee so he can reach her better.

She shrinks back as Ange looms over her. She draws her knees tight against her chest, pushing her muscles to the edge of their range of motion. When the heels of her shoes are almost level with her ears she fires a short, sharp kick that catches Ange on the very point of the jaw. Sweat sprays from his face as his head snaps back.

Dodo is on her, even as the plane begins to howl like a Stuka at the top of the dive. He claws and cuffs her with manic strength. The hatred in his eyes is worse than any blow.

In front of them, Ange has fallen sideways on to the pilot and the man is trying feebly to push the dead weight off himself. Neither of his hands have touched the controls of the plane for a long time. In the dim light outside, Greta sees the earth rushing up to meet them. Horror courses through her like an electric shock.

Dodo goes for the strangle and she throws the cuffs over the back of his head and pulls him close. He is not expecting the move and thrashes blindly. He releases his grip, throws his head from side to side, then tries to rear away from her, exposing his long, scrawny neck. Her hands are by his ears, and she cannot strike the target with them. Her teeth clamp on to his throat instead.

Terrible strength, from somewhere. It is as though her body believes that clinging to Dodo is the only thing that will save her from death. Every fibre of her fights to hold on to him. Her jaws struggle towards each other, trying to force the teeth to meet.

A man is screaming, as if in competition with the tortured air-craft. Then she hears the engine rip itself apart with unmistakable finality, a noise like a shelf full of porcelain sliding on to a stone floor.

Dodo breaks too, very suddenly. Greta releases him and tries to right herself, unable to distinguish between up and down. Gasping and spitting, she blinks out at a red world, her eyes awash with blood. The tops of hills, trees, telegraph poles and wires. Everything is accelerating.

Dodo's head flops at a right angle to his neck. She tries to wedge his soaked body between her and the seats in front to cushion the impact. A green field punches them.

28

The tail of the Cessna has broken off completely. One wheel strut is snapped at the front, so the fuselage leans to the left. That means Greta is forced to clamber over Dodo, over the body that absorbed the blow, to get to the door closest to the ground.

She has an attack of delicacy, a horror of touching the body, in case he spilled some of the contents of the flask on himself while drinking. Standing in the soft mud outside, fighting to stay upright, she is struck by the absurdity of it. She can taste Dodo's blood in her mouth. If the toxin has made it into his bloodstream, she has surely poisoned herself too.

Greta wipes her lips, looking around, seeing no signs of human life. It is very early. Rich, flat farmland with ranks of hills rising to the south. The mud is thick between the rows of green crops, and the plane has carved a deep furrow in it. At least the pilot sank the wheels into it, not the nose. Still, she feels as if a tank has rolled over her and crushed every inch of her body.

Greta rifles through Dodo's jacket, finding the handcuff keys and the things he took from her bag when he first searched it: a roll of cash and a deck of playing cards, both kept in one piece by rubber bands. The bag is under the seat along with his revolver. Neither is stained with blood. She feels eyes on her as she collects everything.

The pilot is sprawled across Ange, his chin resting on the hump of the older man's back. His pupils have almost disappeared but there is a lucid expression on his face. He is trying to speak, hardly able to move the lips.

'*Nord*,' the pilot says.

'Don't try to talk.'

'I fought the Germans,' he says. 'Like Jacky. I mean, I didn't win any medals. I followed orders. I mean . . .'

'I know what you mean.'

'I wasn't always like this.'

'I know.'

'You won't leave me for the rats? I was in *Libération-Nord*.'

'Do you want me to shoot you?'

His eyes close in relief. 'I did not dare to ask. You owe me nothing. I am sorry for all of it.'

'I know. Rest now.'

'Will you burn all of this?'

'I think I have to, don't I?'

'I think so. The poison. What if a child should come?'

His breathing is easier. Greta hopes he is falling asleep. She checks the mechanism of the pistol with fingers and thumb.

But the pilot's eyes open suddenly. 'You bit his Adam's apple right out.'

'Yes.'

'I heard about someone doing that. I never believed it was possible. Do you think his blood has poisoned you too?'

'We'll find out soon enough,' says Greta.

'I hardly drank from the flask. I was pretending. Now it is splashed all over me. Don't come too close.'

'Fine. Do you know where we are? Which way is Corbières?'

'Head south. Keep Toulouse on your right. I have a map, but you must not touch me.'

'Thank you. The debt is paid. Is there anything else you want to say?'

'No. I am content. Finish it.'

But he does breathe one more word, despite himself, when he feels the gun barrel brush the side of his head. It is the word they all reach for at the end, the soldiers slumped in their wrecked machines, in the pockmarked fields.

'Mother.'

The first car Greta sees contains a family of four. She believes the father is going to stop and allow her to squeeze in with them, but his eyes expand as the car slows and he changes his mind. She realizes that the single button of her jacket has come undone. The blouse underneath is soaked in Dodo's blood.

She holds the handbag in front of her body when the next vehicle appears from the direction of Toulouse. It's a Fourgonnette in green and yellow. She pulls a wad of notes out of the bag and thrusts it in the driver's face before he can take in her wild appearance.

The family have a business, delivering canisters of gas. He is the son. An ordinary person at the start of the working week. He can't take her all the way to the farm, but she will find a taxi in Limoux. A young man who has been brought up well. He shakes Greta's hand, does not stare, does not ask questions.

She keeps the cash in a pile on the bedside table while she is talking to the doctor.

'It's not a question of money,' he is saying. 'It's a question of having the right tools, the drugs. You ought to be in a hospital.'

'If you don't want to do it, I'll find someone who does,' says Greta. 'We all know there is a woman in every town. It will be easier for her, if the thing is already dead. Do it now, or I'll find a housewife in a backstreet. Time to decide.'

The doctor addresses Greta but looks at Madame Clothilde all the time as he prepares his hands. 'You will need a lot of help afterwards,' he says. 'Above all, you will need to talk about what has happened to you. You won't feel like it, but . . .'

'Enough of this,' says Greta. She is gazing away from them, through the window at the bare fields outside. Rooks patrol the avenues between the vines. 'Just get it out of me.'

*

On the third day Clothilde sits on the end of the bed and spreads them out – the things Jacky has been sending to them over the last year. The latest parcel arrived a fortnight ago.

Greta recognizes the handwritten ledgers she helped him steal from the antiques dealer in Versailles – that beloved former colleague of Monsieur Balard. Everything is becoming clearer to her now. The files are from the Paris headquarters of the Gestapo in the last year of the German occupation, signed, addressed and dated.

Greta shuffles a pack of playing cards as Clothilde rummages through a suitcase full of older material, left by Jacky for safe keeping over many years. Photographs, love letters, suicide notes, statements from bank accounts the intelligence services use to make secret payments.

'What are these things you can't put down?' asks madame, as Greta scrambles the cards on her lap like a croupier, collects them, riffles them, shuffles them overhand, Indian-style, Faro-style.

'Jacky had this deck the last time I saw him. He kept asking me to pick a card. He was trying to tell me what he had been doing – collecting dangerous secrets. I was angry with him, and I didn't want to listen. He must have slipped the cards into my bag before I left for London. I only began to understand when I found them and looked at them properly. Some of the same names are in the German records.'

Jeannot is hovering at the doorway, reluctant to intrude. Greta beckons him in with a cry of joy and he kisses her tenderly but refuses to sit. He has his work clothes on and anyway, there is no room for him on the bed.

'I have seen those before,' he says as Greta lays the cards out face-up in rows on the bedcover between her legs, like someone setting up a game of patience. 'The Allies issued them in forty-five. The Nazi-hunters used to pay out for every man captured. Very few were issued though. I believe the French authorities raised objections.'

'One hundred thousand francs for this big bastard,' says Greta. The face on the card in her hand is handsome and broad, with a red beard.

'The knave of spades,' reads Jeannot. 'I can't pronounce it.'

'He has changed his name now and goes by Van der Meulen. *Dutchman*, to his friends. He led the Flemish Legion of the Waffen SS. There is a Gestapo file on him here, gushing with praise. He joined the French Foreign Legion after the war. Dutchman works for French intelligence now, unofficially, along with several other men whose faces appear in this deck of cards.'

'What a sack of *shit*,' says Clothilde, rising from the end of the bed. 'What are we doing in this country?' Her husband can only hiss with inarticulate fury.

Greta cannot eat yet, but she walks down to the kitchen after they have finished their supper. Clothilde makes Ceylon tea for her, not too hot, with lots of sugar and milk instead of lemon.

Afterwards, madame clears the table and spreads out Jacky's war medals and the certificates that go with them and photographs from his suitcase. Two small portraits are in the middle.

'Jacky's brother and his niece,' says Clothilde. Greta is sipping tea. Jeannot has fallen silent by the fire, passing a hand over his ruddy face. 'Jacky was in Algeria, running a business, when the Germans invaded. He could have stayed there. It was safer for Jews. But he wanted to come and get the brother and his daughter. The girl's mother had died by then. He could not persuade his brother to leave France. So he joined the Resistance here.'

And indeed, there is a photograph of Monsieur Jacques posing with a stolen German submachine gun in the doorway of a shop, somewhere in Paris in the melee of liberation. People are moving around him in blurs, too quick for the camera.

'I cannot imagine Jacky shooting anyone,' says Greta. 'Even a stinking Nazi.'

'Not at first. His imagination was his great weapon. What was that stuff called, Jeannot?'

'Carborundum.'

'Jacky's big idea. Do you know what it is? Like crushed diamonds in a paste. You feed it into a German tank. The sharp pieces work their way through the machine. They tear everything to shreds, so the engine seizes up after a few hours. The Germans never knew they'd been sabotaged. They thought, you know, old Panzers, giving up the ghost after a long war.'

'How clever. That's very subtle.'

'He did it so there would be no reprisals against civilians. Do you see? Because the Germans didn't know they had been hit by the Resistance. That was his style, at first.'

'At first?'

'He was a killer by the end. Does that surprise you? Little Monsieur Jacques. It was because of the brother.'

Jeannot rises from his chair and walks out of the room.

'He does not like to talk about those times,' says Clothilde. 'Our daughter died too, you see, fighting the Germans. Adrienne was our only child. Dead at twenty-two, before she had children of her own.'

Greta senses Clothilde's own unsteadiness and touches the photograph in the middle of the table gently to get her back on to Jacky's family. The girl in the shot is perhaps fifteen years old.

'Can you see the resemblance?' asks Clothilde. 'It was the first thing I thought, when you showed up at my gate. Something about the eyes. Jacky adored his niece.'

'I'm not sure I can see it. I feel about a hundred years old. The girl is so young in this picture.'

'Estelle was still at school. Such a clever girl. Already working with the father, typing up letters, doing his accounts. He was a successful lawyer in Paris.'

'I think Jacky told me that.'

'A good man, but very stubborn. He believed absolutely in the laws of this country. And he killed them both, because of it.'

'He killed himself? And his daughter?'

'I mean that his stubbornness condemned them both to death. His belief in the rules, if you like. Jacky said that to me once, when I was telling him off for being a bad boy. *There are no laws for me now, Clo. Not after that. No more France, no more laws.*'

'What happened to the brother and the niece, madame?'

'Jacky had kept them out of the Germans' hands for years. He spent a fortune so that they would be passed over by the French police when they were rounding up Jews. The Lord knows what Jacky did to get that money. His brother thought it was all his own cleverness, of course. It was on that night in July 1942, when they arrested so many, and packed them into the velodrome with no food and water. Jacky knew it was going to happen and tipped off his brother. What did the fool do? He went down to the police station and strode up to the desk, the girl by his side. He heard that they had been arresting women and children, and they were not supposed to do it. It was a nonsense. But there he was, arguing with the cops, waving pieces of paper. He was still arguing a point of law when they ripped Estelle away from him.'

Greta looks at the photograph as she listens. Jacques Lellouche's favourite niece has had her hair set carefully. Waves of curls flow down one side. She is made up as if trying to look older, but there is something very young in the eyes.

'I don't know if it ever really sank in for Jacky's brother,' says Clothilde. 'Perhaps he was arguing with them right up to the end, demanding to see his daughter. He must have annoyed the guards on the train because they invited him into an empty car, to listen to all his objections, they said. He launched into it. The procedure had not been carried out according to the principles agreed between the occupying forces and the French government. The train must stop and turn back. They listened for as long as it amused them, then they beat him silly. That was the end of it.'

'He died?' asks Greta.

'Not on the train. But he could not work when they arrived. It was the first thing they did. You must have heard about it. They separated the healthy people from the sick and injured. We never found out if the niece went there too.'

'Went where? We were on a train. Where are we now?'

'I'm sorry, Greta. It's my fault. I'm not telling it the right way. We are at Auschwitz now, my love. We are at Auschwitz.'

29

Greta leaves Clothilde and Jeannot on the tenth day, promising to return for Christmas. She will come bearing champagne and three *poules de Bresse*, one each. Well, she needs to outdo Jacky now.

He was planning to leave France soon. It's obvious to her in hindsight. There are property brochures among the documents he left with Jeannot and Clothilde. A leaflet advertising a new apartment complex in Acre, with views of the sea. It looks like a pleasant place from the photographs. Jews and Arabs mingle in the streets.

There is a man's name on the back with a Paris number, both written in pen and underlined. When she calls the number, a young woman tells her she has reached the Israeli embassy in the eighth *arrondissement*. Greta gives the switchboard operator the name Jacky wrote on the back of the leaflet.

He has the rank of a junior diplomat, and a Chemex coffee maker which he likes to show off to visitors. Greta slides a single fat envelope across his desk. A taster, she says. She will give him one week to make enquiries. There is a lot more material like this if he wants it. She indicates the name Balard with the tip of a painted nail and the man nods gravely. He is not really a diplomat.

Greta has kept a left luggage locker at the Gare de l'Est since the first week she arrived in Paris. She starts when she opens the metal door, then looks around instinctively, as if someone might be watching.

She curses herself. Stupid girl. Reacting the way an amateur would to something unexpected.

The gun is still inside, along with a quantity of currency. Nothing has been taken from the locker, but one item has been added. A single Russian word is written on the outside of the white envelope: *Ty*. You. A car key is inside, with a fob bearing the logo of the G7 taxi fleet. There is a blank white card with an address on one side and another Russian word on the reverse: *Tvoy*. Yours.

The Simca is four streets away. God knows how long it has been sitting there, through nights that are becoming cold. It starts at the fourth attempt. The tank is almost empty. I wonder, thinks Greta. I wonder if that Spanish woman ever looked after it.

She parks on the corner of Castiglione and Mont Thabor and slumps low in the seat, a beret covering half her face. Diners come and go. She recognizes some of the faces from the fringes of criminal society. In less than two weeks, Jacky's restaurant has come down in the world.

When the Church of Our Lady of the Assumption chimes ten times, she walks past the restaurant to the street door that leads to the alley off Mont Thabor. She picks the lock more quickly than a drunk would open his own front door with the right key. The lock on the back door of the restaurant has not been changed. Two unfamiliar faces look up at her: a pair of chefs she does not recognize, cleaning the kitchen down. They are young, with brutally short hair like new military recruits. Before the men can react Romana is running towards Greta, swearing in Italian, falling to her knees.

'*Never was it known,*' recites Romana, hugging the stockinged legs, '*that anyone who fled to your protection, or sought your intercession . . .*'

'Not now,' says Greta. 'Get up. Tell me what I've missed.'

'Nothing good. This is a *milieu* place now. What the fuck are you two looking at?' The chefs turn back to their sinks hastily. 'There's a table full of those pigs in there now. My arse is black and blue.'

'Romana. The thing I asked you to hide for me. Do you remember?'

'No. Greta. There are five of them. You're not that quick.'

'Do you have it or not?' She is holding the woman's head in both hands.

'In the wine cellar.'

'Fetch it. Fold it up, put it under a coat and take it to the kitchen for me. If anyone asks what you're doing, ignore them.'

Fabio is the first to see Greta approaching the table. He is about to light a cigarette, but it falls from his mouth. Momo, the fat man she once tried to strangle with piano wire, is next to him. There are three other faces, younger, that she half-remembers, around the mess of dead glasses, spilled food, plates they have used as ashtrays. The laughter dies.

'Smoke if you want to,' says Greta. Fabio looks at her through his brows as she draws near, as though he is afraid to move his head. There is murder in Momo's eyes. She holds his gaze insolently. 'You showed up here eventually, Babyface.'

'I showed up.'

'Only when you thought I was dead. Smoke.' She picks up the cigarette and proffers it to Fabio. He takes it between his lips. 'Perhaps I am dead. I've come back to haunt you.'

The men quiver when she reaches into the bag hanging from her shoulder. All that emerges is a silver lighter finished in black leather.

Fabio looks at the flame for a moment, mistrusting it. Then he leans forwards, his eyes turned up towards Greta. He casts them downwards as the end of the cigarette fluffs into flame and he draws life into it.

Greta takes her other hand out of the bag smoothly, not too quickly. She holds the can of hairspray behind the lighter, lining it up with the crest of Fabio's perfectly styled hair. Romana fixed his quiff that very morning in the salon, with lashings of flammable lacquer.

Greta's thumb turns the knurled ring on the lighter to boost the flame to maximum strength as she presses the nozzle on the aerosol.

The other men are shouting instructions at each other, but it's hard to hear properly over the screams. Momo whips a cloth from another table and wraps Fabio's head in it, snuffing out the human torch at last. They all watch Fabio subside on to the carpet. Greta has reached the kitchen door and Romana is holding out the shotgun.

When the youngest and boldest of the Neapolitans ventures down the passage after her, Greta kicks the door open and blasts at him with both barrels. He ducks back into the dining room, howling piteously.

'Come here.' Momo has left Fabio to roll around on the carpet. He grabs the boy and pulls him close. There are red spots all over the left cheek and the side of his neck. Momo picks at them, growling at the boy to hold still. He puts something to his tongue, licks it and begins to laugh.

'It's an old trick,' he says. 'Rock salt in the cartridges. She's pulled this one before.'

Momo picks up a metal drinks tray from the cash desk, then slides along the wall next to the entrance to the wine cellar. The corridor that leads to the kitchen is round the next corner. He shouts and sticks the tray out into space. There is an answering cry from Greta, and the shotgun roars again – one barrel this time. When Momo draws the disc back and inspects it, its surface is undamaged.

'No buckshot,' the fat man says triumphantly. 'Look – all of you. The salt doesn't even fly ten feet. It didn't reach the tray. It just makes a noise.' He adjusts his tie. 'I want her. Let me go in first. You can pile in behind, but walk, don't run. No more acting like frightened children. Just watch your eyes with this stuff.'

Greta doesn't fire when Momo strides towards the kitchen. She watches him enter from beneath the metal table. The back door of the restaurant is wide open. Romana and the chefs have fled. Momo feels the cold air on his face. His hand is raised to protect his eyes. The other men are crowding close behind him, trying to look over his shoulders. Perhaps the woman has run for it too.

Greta pops up from behind the silver work surface, snapping the shotgun closed. Momo knows, from the amusement in the corners of her mouth, that the shells in the gun are real now. There are more cartridges ready in her hand.

In the dining room, Fabio hears the shots, the pause, the second crashing volley. All he can do is whimper in anticipation from beneath the tablecloth. Then he feels Greta's shoe on his chest.

She kicks the white cotton away, exposing his livid, shining face. There is a whiff of burnt hair and skin. The shotgun barrels prod his windpipe. 'Talk to me, little friend. I've been away for a while. Tell me the news. How are things up at the White House?'

Fabio has put about a thousand miles on the Porsche in a matter of weeks. It's impossible not to picture him screaming around in it, showing off. Greta takes it to a specialist garage in the sixteenth. She instructs the manager to scrub every surface and fumigate the cabin. 'Vermin have been crawling around in here.'

She doesn't mind waiting a day for the mechanics to complete their checks. If what Fabio said is true, now is the time for patience.

The *milieu* is wobbling, he told her, between pleas for mercy. Some of Ange Suzzarini's men downed tools as soon as he disappeared. The rest melted away when a regional newspaper reported a light aircraft reduced to ashes in a field hundreds of miles from Paris. The brothers guessed Ange and Dodo were among the dead, even if the official verdict was inconclusive: the pile of human remains inside was burnt beyond all recognition.

Lucien has vanished too. He was last seen storming off after Monsieur Paul barred him from entering the White House. There was an angry exchange at the door. Rifles were raised against Lucien, but not fired. Other captains are retreating from the streets they once terrorized across Paris and Marseille, unsure of their strength.

The men who protected the brothers from on high have their own worries. Monsieur Balard himself is in trouble with the politicians, forced to give an account of his work in endless meetings and committees. Newspapers hostile to the government are still running stories about the September demonstration – the night when, as one headline put it, the Seine ran red with the blood of innocents.

The House still stands though. The engine room, the fortress.

Greta looks at it through the opera glasses Jacky once gave

her: the great façade, the broad entrance, the turrets topped with black witches' hats. It is the beginning of October and the day dawned cold and cloudless. A blue day. A sniper's day. The smell of smoke at sunrise in the high pressure. There are four sentries posted around the grounds, two men each at the front and back entrances, three more making endless circuits of the house. Firearms are kept out of sight, but she senses the threat of them. The last strength of the *milieu* has been gathered here.

Greta sleeps through the day, in the car or in a bivouac made from the tarpaulin she once used to cover it, screened by the branches of fir trees. She probes their defences at night, crawling to the edge of the woodland that surrounds the house, noting the movements of the guards.

She watches the back door of the château from the treeline, hoping for another glimpse of Paul Fazi's mother. There are no clients now, no chauffeurs. Everything is hunkered down. No girls left inside, Fabio said, except one. Except one.

When Greta returns to the hide on the second evening, she feels the sensation of being watched again, just like when she opened her locker in the Gare de l'Est. She looks around carefully. A cigarette packet has been left in the crook of two tree branches, at eye level. A flash of blue-purple in a sea of green and brown. A soft pack, full of Caporals. Lucien Fazi's brand.

Greta stands very still and says: 'Shoot me if that's why you're here. Do it if you're going to do it.'

There is no breath of wind anywhere in the trees all around her.

'I've changed,' says Greta in the same clear voice, shockingly loud in the stillness. 'Do you see? I'm patient these days. We can go in together if you like. There's a way we can do it without killing.'

There is no reply. She tucks the cigarettes inside her blouse.

Late the following morning, three cars trundle up the long drive. People are leaving the house from the front entrance, the first time she has seen it used since she arrived. She recognizes the fourth man to emerge as Paul Fazi, although he must have lost a quarter of his body weight. Greta can see the change in his face, under the chin, through the lenses. A man she does not recognize places a long coat round the *Caïd*'s shoulders.

Greta gets up on one knee and pulls the Sauer out of her bag. Is Paul taking Morta with him? If so, there is nothing for it but a straight sprint from her position to the front drive, across open grass with no cover. It's the only way to head them off.

She will intercept the convoy of cars at the gate so the men who guard it cannot come at her from behind. She will take them all on at the same time, head on, a pistol in each hand. Drop the guards and blow out the windscreens, then the men behind them. She breathes deeply, settling herself, suppressing a stab of hopelessness. It will be one against seven.

It's time, Greta says to herself. For the end of everything. If the girl comes through that door next, with a man's hand on her shoulder. If Morta comes out.

They are revving the cars. She cannot see Paul now. He is in the back of a *Traction Avant* whose windows have been sprayed dark. No one else emerges from the White House. The grand door closes behind the men.

The afternoon is warmer. The sentries dawdle and stretch. Tiredness overcomes Greta, a delayed reaction to the adrenalin of the morning, or to everything else that has happened to her. She trudges back to the hide and the tarpaulin that hangs between two birches. I need water, she thinks. I haven't been taking care of myself.

She is fast asleep when the firing starts, half a mile away. The bangs are in groups of three at first: the single probing, ranging shot, then the quick two-three afterwards. A killing finger, lingering on the trigger of an automatic weapon.

When she gets to the edge of the trees there is the thump of a grenade then a long barrage of gunfire. Torrential staccato fury, which drives out all thought. She stops running. No one can walk into that.

There are no men outside the front of the house. The ones who were guarding the gate and grounds must have dashed inside when the firing started. They didn't know that kind of storm was waiting for them. Silence falls, swift and absolute.

The front door is ajar, a man's body across the threshold. He was running away, shot in the back. Greta checks his pockets for identification, reverting to her training. Then she tells herself to wake up. It doesn't matter who he is. Even after all she has been through, it is hard to walk into that silent house, a house where death has visited.

Another body, prone at the bottom of the stairs. It could have been the fall that killed him. Then she lifts his head and sees the face. No. Not the fall.

She picks her way from room to room on the ground floor, through slicks of blood and spent shell cases, counting the dead men. The rear door is wide open, and she can see the stable block stretching away from the house on her left. The man on his back in the gravel is the last guard left in the house, by her reckoning. Then she hears the sound of woozy singing.

Maman Fazi has dragged herself by the elbows along the entire length of her cavernous kitchen to ransack a low cupboard under the sink. She is looking straight at Greta, sitting up with her back against the cupboard door. Bottles and jars are strewn around her on the flagstones. The old woman found what she was looking for eventually. She is drinking from a bottle of *aquavita*, peering at Greta through spectacles as strong as magnifying glasses.

'*Voilà*,' says Maman. 'One of them came back. One of the whores.'

'You are drunk, madame.'

'What of it? My hip is broken.'

'But you are alive.'

'She did not need to shoot me. She could see I was no use to anyone.'

'Who visited you today, madame?'

'An old gypsy woman, as I thought. I let her in myself. A crone bent double under a sack. The sack was full of cruel things.'

'You invited the woman in,' says Greta.

'I have always been kind to the gypsies. This one killed many.'
Her face is clouded with sudden pain, either from the hip or the
thought of her palace guards. 'Many, many.'

'But more are coming,' says Greta. 'You are waiting for them.'
Maman gives a sneering laugh. Greta squats next to her. 'Did she
take the last girl, your visitor? Did she take the princess?'

'That little whore went trotting out after her.'

'Which way did they go?'

Maman gives a sneering laugh. 'Why don't you go and look for
them? All the whores together.'

'Your visitor ought to have killed you too, madame. She does
not know what I know. That you stand behind all the men. You
sing the poison to them in their cribs.'

'Stupidity,' says Maman, turning her eyes away and raising the
bottle to her lips.

'Lucien sang me one of your lullabies. Very pretty. All about kidnapping children. *Don't you cry, my pretty one. Papa is out, hard
at work. Hunting for a rich man's son.*'

'It's nonsense. An old story.'

'Did they go out of the front or back door, madame?'

Maman laughs. 'Come close. I will whisper it.'

When Greta leans in, Maman lunges between her thighs and
grabs hold of her with thumb and fingers, pinching and twisting
the softest flesh. Greta cries out and smacks the hand away. Then
she slaps the old woman's face with the back of her hand, knocking off her glasses. It is a different face without them, the eyes small
and diamond-hard.

'*That* is our secret,' says Maman gleefully. 'Not gold, not silver,
not the white powder. Everything we have is built on the thing
between a girl's legs.'

'Which way? Don't make me hurt you.'

'I never beat a girl in my life. They come to us of their own free
will. Every woman wants a man to make a whore of her. You know
it's the truth.'

Greta grips Maman's powdered face with her palms and works the tips of her thumbs into the corners of the eyes. The woman is too weak, or drunk, to raise her own hands in defence.

'I swear to God,' says Greta. 'I will squeeze them right out of your head. Which way did they go?'

Greta sees things that others would miss. The impressions of footsteps are clear to her, even in grass that has been cut short. There are dark spots along the trail.

How did they climb over the fence that runs along the edge of the woods? Slowly and painfully, she concludes, finding more dark stains next to one of the metal posts. They will not have made it far inside the treeline, she thinks. Then she hears Morta's voice, calling for help.

The girl is sitting with her mother's head in her lap. Morta is crying bitterly, speaking French. 'I don't know what to do. I don't know what to do.'

Laima is stroking her arm, trying to soothe her in Lithuanian. 'No. No, my child. No, no. Do not distress yourself. It is too late for that.' She smiles when Greta looms over them and sweeps off her beret.

'My general,' says Greta. 'You killed more than the malaria today.'

'But they have riddled me with bullets. I am out of practice. I did not need to shoot my way out of prison.'

'Vassily Andreyevich released you,' says Greta.

'A door was left open. I walked through it.'

'He kept his end of the bargain, even though I let him down.'

'Vassily told me you had died in an air crash.'

'It was true. I mean, it's true that my plane went down. The Russian must have thought I was dead. He did as I asked. But where were you?'

'Igarka.'

'Jesus and Mary.'

'I did not walk all the way, fool of a girl. I hid myself on trains when I was in the east. The trains that carry timber.'

'But it's three thousand miles.'

'It seemed like the whole world. And nothing, at the same time.'

'What are you two saying?' sobs Morta.

'Translate for us,' says Laima. 'Tell her that she is the most beautiful thing I have ever seen.'

'Your mother loves you very much,' says Greta, in French. 'I knew that she would come.'

'Translate,' orders Laima.

'I am saying that I knew you would come for her. I knew it when I read your letter. You wrote that you had given up hope, that you were resigned to your fate as a prisoner. I knew those words could not be true.'

'Tell her this. Quickly. Tell her she is so beautiful, I cannot believe she came from me.'

'Wait,' Greta can hear car engines throbbing, other sounds.

'Where are you going?' says Morta.

Greta can make out the direction better from the fence. The noises are coming from the front, the far side of the house. Tyres on gravel. Car doors slam. Dogs are barking.

When she is back at Morta's side, the girl is rocking Laima's head and stroking her hair, over and over. The face is very worn, a decade older than the one Greta remembers. The skin is slick with the girl's tears. Laima's expression is peaceful.

'Come,' says Greta. She pats Laima's coat pockets for concealed weapons.

'What are you doing? We have to take her with us. I will carry her.'

'You will do no such thing. There are standing orders for times like this. We must look to ourselves now. The forest will keep her for a while.'

'I'm not just going to leave her lying here.'

'Our general wrote those orders, Morta. We are going to obey them.'

30

They hack up the slope that curves round the north of the house. They can hear men behind, the eager dogs. They have been spotted. Greta lets the pursuers come close, through the pines, holding Morta's arm tight, then empties her automatic pistol at them with a roar of defiance. She leads the girl out into the open at a dash while the heads of their pursuers are still down.

The break in the trees is the wide strip of bare ground that the Cessna pilot used as a runway. It runs north-west along the high, level ground to the north of the château.

Halfway along, a hump rises three metres from the flat grass. The hillock is so perfectly round and regular that it is surely man-made. The last time Greta saw it, she was in a light aircraft taxiing past at sixty miles per hour, silly from opium.

Morta starts to fade as they hit the steep hillside, but Greta shoves her onwards and upwards with a wild yell. 'Fight. Don't give up.'

A raised lip runs round the top of the hillock. There is a depression in the centre into which the women throw themselves and lie for a minute, exhausted from the long sprint.

When they can talk, Greta takes out the revolver and presses it into Morta's hands. 'Fight or die,' she tells the girl. 'It's time to decide.'

Greta scans the treeline with the opera glasses. Men are forming up along the edge. They can see Dutchman next to a broad oak, barking orders and gesticulating.

He is the reason they are hesitating instead of pouring across the open ground towards us, thinks Greta. He is a soldier, and he knows something of her. The little hill is too exposed. He fears some kind of deception.

The only cover is a cube of concrete about the size of a car lying directly to the south. It might be a tank-trap from the war. Three men run over to it and crouch there. Four more jog across the strip a hundred yards to the east, out of range.

'They will circle all the way round us through the trees and come from the other side too,' said Greta. 'It will take ten minutes, but it means they can rush at us from two directions.' She takes hold of the girl by the collar. 'Then we'll both have to do some shooting, Morta. No more Buddhism. Are you ready?'

'I can't shoot anyone. I just can't.'

'We fight or we die,' says Greta. 'Aim for the centre of the man. Don't try to hit the head. Take the safety catch off now, like I showed you.'

Dutchman bides his time. He was a good officer once, thinks Greta. His voice booms out from behind the concrete cub. 'Give up. There is no escape from here.' Fair enough, she thinks. It works sometimes. There's a chance he could save the lives of some of his men. You can't blame him for trying. She fires a single shot in reply.

The first attack is lacklustre: two men from each side, running bent over, looking for any scrap of cover in the terrain: a ditch or a large pothole to lie in. Greta tosses a grenade, not very accurately, but the blast is enough to send them scurrying back to their positions. It makes them think for a while.

The men get closer the second time, almost as far as the ramparts. Dutchman is among them. She rolls objects the same size and shape as grenades down the steep sides of the hillock and they turn tail. But the men on the south side don't retreat all the way back to the tank-trap. They have found a low ridge to lie behind. There are no more explosions.

Dutchman is crawling to one of the things she threw. He's within pistol range but Greta leaves him alone. She hears him chuckling. He holds it up to show his comrades and there is a chorus of laughs.

'Pinecones,' says Dutchman. Then louder: 'Good one, Greta. Does that mean you are out of toys? Are you ready to stop this nonsense now?'

A minute of silence passes. Dutchman stands up and barks an order. Morta gives a cry. 'They're coming from my side.'

There are shots now. Greta moves back from the lip and takes hold of Morta's arm, squirming close to her.

More shots, very close by. She lays her own pistol down and feels for the grenade in her bag. It is the last one. Not yet, she thinks. Not until they are on top of us. Perhaps we pretend to surrender and wait until we feel their hands on us. Then the pin comes out. There will be two bodies, at any rate. We will be together at the end, Morta. They won't take you anywhere, my girl. If I can't have you, no one else will.

Grasping fingers grip the turf in front of her. A man is trying to pull himself up over the edge of the hillock. So bold. They must think we are out of bullets or cowering in terror. The sight of the hand makes her lip curl in hatred.

No, she tells herself. Not that way. Let the girl survive if she wants. Let her decide. She takes the grenade out, primes it and rolls it gently over the edge, on to the heads of the climbing men.

The blast sparks a confusion of noise. There are shots, but not from Morta. The girl has dropped her weapon and has her hands clamped over her ears. Men are crying out all around, but these are no jeers of triumph. The attackers wail with fear and surprise.

Then Greta recognizes the sound she has been praying for. The regular, pitiless crack of a sniper's rifle.

Dutchman's body is the last one Lucien checks. His face is emotionless, but he throws the rifle on to the turf beside the red-haired corpse.

Morta is coming to him, picking a path round the dead men.

They embrace, then Lucien sinks to his knees, his arms still round her in a circle.

'Forgive me,' he says. 'I tried to keep my promise. I waited until the last second.'

She is trying to give him something. The revolver. She places it in his hand. It takes him a while to understand. He checks the cylinder carefully. The gun is empty.

'I was shooting to kill at the end,' says the girl. She finds the sharp contours of his face, then the lapels of his jacket, and pulls him upright. 'I never thought I would do it. But I wanted to live.'

They linger in the trees for two hours, close to the White House, waiting for police sirens, but no one comes.

Greta keeps the girl busy. Collecting firewood, more than they will need. Wild apples from the trees and canned food from the Porsche. By the time the women have assembled a fire, Lucien has finished digging.

He climbs down into the hole to lay Laima's body gently in the leaves and soil. He does not speak or recite prayers afterwards, as the Lithuanian women do, but he kneels by the graveside alone for a minute while Greta kindles the fire. Silence descends on the forest.

'I can't understand it,' says Lucien. 'People must have heard the noise of the explosions for a mile around.' Things become clearer when they turn on the car radio. Monsieur Balard has been arrested. The interior minister of the French Republic has resigned. The Paris police are in disarray.

'So are the local *gendarmes*, evidently,' says Greta.

'Especially them,' Lucien answers. 'Have you forgotten? They belong to the master of the house. His day is closing.'

Later they pass a wine bottle round and Greta tells Morta stories of her life in the woods. Washing with ash from the fire when there is no soap. Burning peas of plastic explosive to heat water quickly without smoke.

The partisans were sitting round a fire just like this when they heard how the atom bomb had been used against Japan in 1945. The news electrified Laima.

'She thought the Western Allies were sure to help all the people in the east of Europe. With this new weapon in their hands, the Americans would stand up to Stalin and force him to pull his armies back to the borders of Russia. It never happened. I was not with her when the news emerged of the first Soviet atomic tests. That was four years later.'

'I can imagine how she must have felt,' says Morta. 'That no one would come now. Lithuania was finished.'

'We all felt that, I think. But we never gave up.'

Greta and Lucien talk for a long time after the girl goes to lie down, filling in the gaps. It is after midnight when Lucien checks that Morta is deeply asleep and comes round the fire to sit next to Greta.

'She doesn't want to go with you,' he says.

'I know. I suppose we'll have to fight over her then. What do think? A duel in the woods?'

'No thanks.'

'Scared to take me on?'

'I'm afraid that we will both be killed, Greta. And then who does she have left?'

The flames are ebbing. Greta wraps herself in her coat. 'What did you say to your mother-in-law, Lucien? When you were kneeling by the grave.'

'I promised that I would look after her daughter until my own death.'

'That's what I thought.' She yawns extravagantly. 'Jesus and Mary, I'm tired.'

'No duel then, Greta?'

'In the morning.'

She is exhausted but can't fall asleep, swaddled tightly in the coat, facing away from the spot where the lovers are curled in each other's arms.

One woodland glade is much like another, thinks Greta. What

better place than this to bury Laima? I suppose all the forests in the world were joined up once.

The animals driven into cover by the terror of the gunfire have begun to show themselves again. A rabbit flashes its scut. Eyes gleam, further away. The sight does not disturb her. She knows it is a fallow deer cropping.

It's not a bad place, thinks Greta. Among all the free, the wild things. She hears Lucien and Morta get up in the night and creep away together. She closes her eyes and lies very still until they are gone.

31

Greta sees Lucien one more time. Just before Christmas, they find out that both Paul Fazi and Balard are in the south. The opportunity is too good to pass up.

The journalists who were once loyal to the head of the SDECE turn on him after criminal charges are announced. When he is released on bail, Balard flees Paris and the newspaper men huddled outside his front door.

He is reported to be wintering in Sainte-Maxime at the same time Paul Fazi crosses the Mediterranean from Corsica in a private plane. Lucien knows the pilot from the army.

Paul still keeps a flat in Toulon. He stays out of sight for a week, sending his men out for provisions.

At last, Paul breaks cover. He drives into the hills north of Guillaumes to check on an old heroin laboratory that has been padlocked since the death of Ange Suzzarini. He travels with the doctor and two bodyguards. Lucien stays three cars back.

Lucien does not recognize the armed men. He shoots the first from a distance and the second up close. Afterwards, the doctor vomits weakly in the shade of a wall while Paul sits on the dusty ground outside the farm building where his empire began. The doors are open. Someone has looted the place and there is no product left.

'He's a quack,' says Paul contemptuously as they listen to the doctor retching. 'I need a specialist.'

'How bad is it?'

'If the radiation doesn't work, they cut the voicebox out. It doesn't matter. We don't need to talk. I've written down everything for you. It's in the briefcase in the car. The main thing is the combination for the safe in Saigon. The paperwork for the bank accounts is in there.'

'Do you remember my girl in Hanoi?' asks Lucien. 'The one who cooked for me.'

Paul looks up at him. His eyes are slits under the winter sun. 'She was a terrorist, Lulu. We saved you from her.'

Lucien smashes his cousin on to the ground with the back of the hand. 'I knew she was *Việt Minh*. I didn't want her to die, Paul. What are you trying to say?'

'You always want to fix women. Save them. It's going to destroy you.'

'Drink something.'

Paul swigs from the bottle, gargles and spits. There is only a small improvement. The obstruction in his throat is permanent. 'I always tried to watch over you,' he says. 'Even in Hanoi. I didn't want you to make the same mistakes I made as a young man. I was soft with women too. A *poule* I used from time to time showed up on my doorstep one day, with the ugliest baby I had ever seen. Christ knows why, but I took them both in. I never believed he was mine.'

'Dodo,' says Lucien.

'I should have listened to him, of all people. He was convinced you were sleeping with the little Lithuanian tart. I thought it was jealousy. He knew I wanted to hand everything over to you.'

'Let's not call that girl names,' says Lucien.

'The big joke is that if you had asked me, I would have given Marie to you. I finished with her years ago.'

'Don't make me hit you again.' He knows that if he strikes Paul a second time, he will not be able to stop.

'You think you're so pure, isn't it? You want her, like I wanted her, when she was offered to me. I wanted to own her completely, every hair on her head. Don't pretend you're any different.'

But Lucien is walking away from Paul. He pulls the doctor to his feet. Then he makes them kneel next to each other, facing Mount Ventoux. It is a clear, cold day. The doctor has wet himself and is incapable of speech.

'I know it wasn't your idea to take that girl's eye out,' Lucien tells him. 'I just want to know what happened.'

'We needed all the ministers,' shrugs Paul, 'foreign, colonial, interior. We got someone to invite the guy to the parties. He likes to come on strong with the girls, isn't it? You know the type.'

'He reminded you of a man you knew years ago. A judge who was supposed to have knocked a woman's teeth out. Except the story wasn't quite true either.'

Paul grins. 'The old wheezes are the best ones, Lulu.'

'So our politician gives this half-Chinese girl a thump one night and she runs out of the room screaming for a doctor. The next time the minister sees her, she is wearing a patch and he is reaching for his wallet. But there was nothing wrong with her eye, was there?'

'We had to remove it, Lulu. The guy is no dummy. The suspicious type. What if he sent his people to grab her? There had to be an empty socket under the patch.'

'And then he's on the hook for ever. All three ministers in your pocket. Whatever Balard wants is signed off: Hannachi, Stay Behind, the currency scam. And the *milieu* does what it likes without interference. But tell me, doctor. What did you say to that young girl when she came to your surgery?'

The old man looks up at him. Huge, canine eyes behind the elegant glasses. 'Check-up,' he says.

'But you must have given her a general anaesthetic.'

'Said it was a little shot to relax her.'

'I see. Remind me which eye you removed. I saw the patch, but I can't remember now. Was it her left or her right eye?'

The doctor tries to respond but no sound emerges. He raises a wretched finger and lays it on his right cheek, pointing up.

Lucien takes a step back and shoots him in the spot he is indicating, through one pane of the rimless spectacles.

'*Bien*,' says Paul, nodding. 'He was a fucking quack anyway. I'm ready.'

'Not you,' says Lucien.

'What are you talking about? Everything is set up for the next *Caïd*. You can crank the machine up again.'

'No thanks. I'm not going to shoot you, Paul. Do you know why? I'm acting under orders. Someone has ordered me to keep you alive. That's right. A *woman*.'

Greta ties Paul and Balard to wicker chairs, back to back, in the storeroom above Vincent's bar in Marseille.

Bobby the barman has given Paul a bloody nose and they have ordered him to wait downstairs. 'No more of that now,' says Greta angrily. 'We don't damage their faces.'

'Where are we with the bidding?' Lucien asks her, checking the restraints.

'The Israelis take Balard back with them tonight. No legal proceedings. That's the deal I agreed with his successor at the SDECE. Nothing will come out in the newspapers. Monsieur disappears without a trace. I told the Israelis they can talk to Paul before they decide if they want to make an offer for him. What are you saying, monsieur?'

Balard is completely calm when she removes the gag. There is an almost saintly expression on his face. His voice still carries a power. 'You, young woman, will be forgotten in an instant,' he tells Greta. 'But people will remember me as a man who saved France from ruin, three times.'

'Was that all there was? Put the gag back in. I'll tell you what your legacy is. Jacky once made me watch a gang working the park by the Tower in Paris. One man was doing the card trick: find the lady. But it was just a distraction, to make it easier for the pickpockets. A policeman showed up and scattered them, but they used the confusion to steal everything in sight. I thought it was very clever at the time.'

'I know them,' says Lucien. 'Romanians.'

'Exactly. I didn't realize what Jacky was trying to show me at the time. The point was that the policeman was in on it too. His big entrance was part of the routine. He was real police, but he was working with a gang of thieves. Perhaps he was the leader. Do you see, Monsieur Balard? There is no longer any difference between the police and the criminals. That is the world you have created. No, no more. Don't try to speak.'

She adjusts the rag clamped between his teeth. 'It took Jacky a long time to figure you out. He knew France was full of collaborators trying to alter their records. He didn't think someone who had ordered the deportations of Jews would have the nerve to reinvent himself as a hero of the Resistance. The power of forgery.'

She taps Paul's cheek with her fingertips. 'The Israelis want a chat. They might make an offer for you too. If not, there are plenty of others on the table. The new prefect of the Paris police is also interested in what you got up to during the war, Paul. There are files still open from the 1930s relating to an organization called the *Cagoule*. Does it ring any bells? If all else fails, Mr Hannachi in Algeria might put a little bit of money on the table. The highest bid wins.' Greta leans in close. 'Do you understand what you have become, Paul? You are a *commodity* now. You belong to me. And when our visitors from Tel Aviv walk in, in a moment, you will perform for the men.'

There are long negotiations before Laisvūnas agrees to meet her. He has heard things, Greta thinks. Disturbing rumours about her activities have reached him, along the strands of his web.

Money tips the balance. She tells him that she has the entire sum he asked for a year ago, and that she will have his Porsche shipped back to West Germany in pristine condition on delivery of the weapons.

Greta can see Laisvūnas eyeing the bodywork as he pulls into the stopping place for lorry drivers just on the French side of the border. He is driving a 1951 Alfa Romeo two-seater. The only other vehicle in the dismal lay-by is a Citroën van with empty front seats.

He checks his hair in the driver's mirror before he gets out. He's wearing a full-length shearling coat and a forced smile.

'No hard feelings?' Greta calls.

'Time is a great healer. You have the full deposit in cash, as agreed?'

The sample is in his boot: a sniper's rifle. He draws the suede cover back to let her look. There's a coffee can which he picks up and rattles with another attempt at a smile before putting it down again. He's wearing heavy gloves despite the mild weather.

'How do you adjust the sight?' Greta asks. 'Is it that tiny little screw? Can you turn it with your fingernail? Could you show me?'

'Greta, you are the expert. I don't have your skills, alas. I don't eat my own cakes.' He really doesn't want to take those gloves off, she thinks. He wraps the gun in its cover and follows her to the Porsche. His eyes rest on the Swiss watch on her wrist as she opens the boot.

'Thank you. And the bullets?'

'In the can. Please check the calibre, Greta, while I secure this properly.' He is bent over the gun, fussing with the cloth, making a meal of the simple task.

Greta glances up and down the road, looking for traffic, then slams the sharp edge of the boot on to the crown of his head.

Laisvūnas makes a snorting sound and sinks on to his haunches, fingers spread over his skull. She puts her foot against his shoulder and sends him sprawling in the dirt.

'What are the bullets dipped in? Strychnine? A nerve agent? Something radioactive?'

'I'm bleeding, you mad bitch.' He is staring at the palm of his hand in disbelief.

'Go and get the coffee can. Take the shells out and put them in your mouth.'

'You've lost your mind.'

'Humour me. Suck those bullets like sweets. If the ammunition doesn't come from Karpov, you've got nothing to worry about.'

'You're bluffing, Greta. You're guessing.'

'The Russians were on top of me as soon as I crossed into France. You must have told them I was coming. And I know what this means now.'

She flicks open the stiletto, the one she took from his cellar, showing the Moor's Head.

'I'm Lithuanian. I collect knives. My friends give them as presents.'

'You mean your customers. You've been selling guns to the people running Stay Behind in France for years. You told me yourself: you're a trusted supplier. An honorary Corsican, almost. Paul Fazi gave you this himself. But you are not the kind to turn down the chance to collect from the other side too.'

'This is a total fantasy,' he snorts.

'Those were the hard years, weren't they, after the war? No one could afford to be choosy. You sold to anyone who would pay. You have been working for Moscow since then, Laisvūnas, passing on everything you find out. Stay Behind is no secret. Not any more.'

'Greta, you are making wild stabs in the dark.'

'You paid a man to forge a letter from Morta to Laima. You were going to lure the mother here and sell her to Moscow. You had already sold the daughter to Paul.'

'Oh God.'

'I found Morta, Leo. She told me everything.'

'No.' He is looking past Greta. Men are emerging from the back of the van, in an unhurried way. Humourless, practical men in worn suits. They might be a crew of gravediggers. Washington finds the men it needs.

'Colonel Howell is sitting in your living room now, babysitting your wife and son, while his people tear your house apart. They want to know what you have done for Maxim Karpov over the years. I suggest you tell them everything.'

Laisvūnas rolls on to his feet and throws himself towards the back of his own car in a low dive. But the nearest men are on him before he can reach inside the open boot. His gloved hand grips the edge for a moment before it is wrenched away by stronger arms.

'He was going for the coffee can,' shouts Greta. 'Don't let anyone touch it.'

32

Spring arrives early in Paris in 1953. By the beginning of March, it is warm enough to eat outside the recently renamed *Monsieur Jacques*, at the table with views in four directions. Greta has signed the place over to Romana but spends most evenings there, eating well and drinking sensibly, replenishing her strength.

When men invite her to dine with them, she turns them down with a charm and diplomacy that would surprise anyone who met her when she first arrived in the city.

One evening, as Greta rises to leave, she glances in the window of the dining room and stops. There is a strange optical illusion: her own reflection juxtaposed with the shape of the tall waiter inside the room.

It reminds Greta of an image that once lived in her imagination, briefly but vividly. A family portrait, with Greta holding a child and a very tall man standing behind them, resting his huge hand on her shoulder.

No more of that, Greta says to herself. She blinks and she is back in the present: a slight woman with green eyes, beautifully dressed, always alone.

The papers Jacky Lellouche bequeathed to Greta begin to form the basis of a new career.

Jacky always said that if you threw a rock in a Paris street, you would hit someone who had climbed into bed with the Nazis.

It turns out that there are interested parties who are willing to pay for information on the most enthusiastic collaborators.

Greta is having lunch at a bistro in Montmartre with her handler from the Israeli embassy when the death of Joseph Stalin is announced.

The waiter turns up the radio behind the bar. An old White Russian man exclaims religious oaths. The other customers tell him to be quiet so they can listen to the details in the bulletin. The Soviet leader succumbed to a stroke, says the newscaster, after years of heavy smoking.

Greta's reaction raises eyebrows around the room. She begins to giggle uncontrollably, muttering a name to herself in between the gusts of laughter. The Israeli man is at a loss. Other patrons are staring at them.

'I'm sorry, monsieur. Please ignore me.'

'You are going to have to tell me what is so funny, Greta. And who is *Vassily*?'

'A bold and cunning man. A stroke! Oh dear!' She bites her knuckles.

'Vassily is Russian?'

Greta nods.

'In Paris? Was this a man . . . in my line of work?'

'When I met him, he was in the business of waiting for Stalin to die. I believe he lost patience in the end.' Another fit of laughter. She lays her cutlery down on her plate because her hands are shaking too badly to eat.

The Israeli man chews patiently, his eyes on Greta, waiting for her to control herself.

'Vassily Andreyevich asked me to pick up a present for his boss in Moscow,' she says. 'Strong brandy.'

'I understand. They don't have the luxuries over there that we take for granted. You sent Vassily some French cognac, I suppose?'

'British. A rare vintage. To be delivered by hand.'

'He must have been grateful.'

'It got spilled in transit.' Her face creases helplessly again.

'Bad luck for Vassily. But I gather things worked out all right, Greta, or you wouldn't be laughing about it.'

'It's better for me that it got spilled. It saved my life.'

She dabs at her eyes with a napkin. There are sharp glances from diners at the tables nearby. People are straining to hear the radio bulletin.

A power struggle in the Kremlin, says the presenter. Who will emerge as the next General Secretary of the Central Committee of the Communist Party of the Soviet Union? Other Russian names reverberate around the room. Mykolan, Malenkov, Molotov. Maxim Karpov. Greta's smile fades when she hears this final name.

'There's no need to feel sorry for Vassily,' she tells her companion. 'I didn't make my delivery, but someone else did, no doubt. Another fool. I wonder what he told them? A gift for Maxim Karpov!'

'The Russian lied to you?'

'Let's say he didn't tell me whole truth. The brandy was never intended for Brother Karpov. It was for the Russian *Caïd*. The Boss of all bosses.'

Bobby the bartender is a different man. He dresses smarter and walks taller. The old *milieu* of the Fazis has almost died out in Marseille now, he says. Other thugs are trying to fill the vacuum, but small business owners like Bobby are banding together to see off men who demand protection money.

'We have learned how to stand up for ourselves at last,' he says.

Bobby credits Greta with the change, and he makes himself available to her whenever she travels to the south coast. Early one April morning he drives her to a holiday chalet on the edge of Cassis.

'Police detectives are some of my best customers now,' Bobby tells Greta. 'It's good to have them in the bar. They're rolling up the last of the *milieu*. Cops always talk, after a couple of free drinks. I'm sure it's him. Let me come with you in case he tries anything.'

'There's no need. Not with this one. Will you go and make sure the boat is ready?'

The early light is dancing on the sea. She is sure Robert will have a girl in the chalet. It's almost a disappointment when he opens the door and she looks into the bedroom behind him to see an empty mattress on the floor.

It's all about his first reaction now, she thinks. Will he weep and fall to his knees, bury his face in my stockings? What then? What do I do? If he tells me his life has been a film playing in monochrome since the day I left, and that it just burst into colour: orange and yellow.

He makes it easy for her. He's too Samogitian for dramatic displays. He tries to gape with shock and reel back away from her, but it fails to convince. He knows I came back from the dead, she thinks, and that I've been looking for him. Whatever is left of the *milieu* warned him, gave him this place to lie low.

'You're alive,' Robert gasps. 'I don't believe it.' He does his best, but this kind of role is beyond him. He is strictly a comic actor. He smiles with the mouth but not the eyes.

He tries to feign a rush of emotion when she closes the door. She allows him to pull her to him. There is no fear of his height, his strength, although the arm is tight across her back. She has an awareness of her own power now.

Greta indulges herself for a second and allows one hand to slide up over his torso, under the white vest. The oblique muscles undulate like furrows in a field. His hand is on her back, kneading the area below the bra strap. The ghost of a touch further down. His fingers are fluttering round the waistband of her skirt. Her eyes snap open and the spell is broken. He is searching for the bulge of a pistol, a knife handle.

She pushes him away and holds his face at arm's length. 'Even more beautiful than I remember.' Robert doesn't know how to react. There is an intensity in her eyes, her voice, that he shrinks from. He cannot meet her gaze.

'I dreamed of how it would be,' she tells him. 'I feel like a ghost that has been allowed to return to the living world. Can you see me? Am I flesh and blood?'

'Greta. It's going to be just like it was. Even better. You have come home to me.'

She makes Robert drive along the coast road. She has brought everything they need for a picnic, she says.

He glances over at her all the way along the Calanques.

The road curls round the headlands. He is making a bad job of it, struggling with the spindly gearstick, the long throw that foxes everyone. She cannot remember if she ever allowed him to drive the Porsche before.

'I used to hear this muttering in my head,' Greta tells him, laughing. 'Like someone else was living in there. *Stupid girl. You're no good. Everything you do will go to hell.*' She knows there is a manic edge to her own voice, but she doesn't care.

Robert is trying to smile in reply, but he is obviously scared. 'What happened to the voice, Greta? Did she disappear?'

'*He*. He just left one day.'

You cannot park next to the sea at Les Goudes. They pick their way across the moon landscape towards the water. Robert goes first, looking around all the time. It's still early and there are no other people.

The speedboat is a real Riva Tritone, as sleek as a marine predator.

'I hope it's the right kind,' she says. 'The one you said you always wanted.'

'It's perfect.'

She doesn't tell him she wants him to pilot the boat. She just climbs into the back and reclines across both seats. He takes the wheel, running his hands over the controls.

'Straight out to sea,' she tells him, pointing west.

When they pass the Île Maïre and the smaller island next to it, he turns north towards the coast. Greta corrects him with a sharp command. It's a tone she hasn't used before, and his eyes linger on her as he steers.

'I don't like the waves today,' he says.

'Keep going straight out.'

The boat rocks queasily after she tells him to cut the engine. They are in deep water, feeling the ocean currents. There are no other vessels in sight. He is pale, playing with his hair distractedly.

Greta takes a bottle of champagne out of her bag and a single glass for herself. She shows him the pistol for the first time and orders him to strip. The swell makes it hard for him to undress because he needs to steady himself with a hand on the dashboard.

'I thought about fucking you,' Greta tells him. 'One last time. I can't do it. What a sight though. Those young girls never knew what hit them, did they, when you first came to France?'

'*Gretute.*'

'You actually told me the truth when we met – or some of it. You really were penniless when you came here, living on the street. That's what Laisvūnas said. It's when he spotted you, driving around Paris in a stolen car. He didn't have a Porsche then, but he had money, didn't he? Good contacts already. Rich clients like Monsieur Paul. And a place to stay.'

'We shared a room, yes.'

'Then you went into business together. He was hopeless with girls, of course. A nervous wreck. But you! A magician. They didn't stand a chance, did they? Especially the little Lithuanian girls. Homesick and lovesick at the same time. A man who makes us laugh can do what he wants with us.'

'I don't know what Laisvūnas has said to you, but he is a bad man, understand, and a dirty liar. Why do you think I turned my back on him? I am ashamed that I ever knocked around with that guy. That's why I didn't tell you about me and him.'

'Do you know what the working girls call men like you? *Boyfriend pimps.* If they fall in love with you, you never need to hit them. You just stop calling for them at the school, at the children's home. You ignore them when you want to punish them. It's worse than a beating for a girl that age. Morta told me all about it.'

'That kid who came to the restaurant?'

'The one who screamed the place down when she saw you, that's right. The poor child had made up her mind to escape that night.

What bad luck. She was looking for me and she ran into one of the men who sold her to Monsieur Paul.'

'Mistaken identity. I could tell straight away that she had psychological problems, Greta. She's fucked in the head.'

'You made her that way. Did you split the proceeds from the sale? Or did Laisvūnas keep it all? Get in the water.'

He lowers himself in slowly, his weight propped on his elbows, then holds the side of the boat with both hands, as if afraid of getting his hair wet. She can see his tonsils as the cold shock makes him gasp.

'Was Paul your first customer? Or did you sell a hundred girls before Morta?'

Either from cold or shame, Robert cannot answer.

Greta leans closer. 'How much did Paul pay you to spy on me?'

'The restaurant. That's all I wanted. I didn't want to spend the whole of my life hanging off your skirt. I needed some security.' His eyes plead with her. 'I never thought that you would stick around, understand, with an ordinary guy like me. I thought you would disappear.'

'And abandon my family? I would have given you *everything*.'

'Greta, you know I won't make it back to the shore. You're not this cruel.'

'I would have given you both everything I had to give.'

'I can't swim that far. You're going to have to shoot me.'

'A child killer doesn't get a bullet. Let go of the side now. Push yourself away. Or I'll break your hands.'

'Jesus and Mary.'

'Shove yourself off properly.'

'You have to shoot me, Greta.'

She leans over the side. 'I *have to*? I don't think you understand. You don't get to decide, little friend. Not any more. It's me who decides now.'

Acknowledgements

Thank you: Ed Howker, Julia Kingsford, Nikita, Mum, Dad, Roy, Michèle Worrall, Matt Day, La Couronne, The London Library, Nicole Witmer and Bill Scott-Kerr.

Patrick Worrall was educated at a comprehensive school in Worcestershire and King's College, Cambridge. He has worked as a teacher in eastern Europe and Asia, a newspaper journalist, a court reporter at the Old Bailey and the head of the Channel 4 News FactCheck blog. His first novel, *The Partisan*, was inspired by a World War Two photograph of three young female freedom fighters he saw in a museum in Kaunas, Lithuania. *The Exile* is his second novel.

It is the summer of 1961 and the brutal Cold War between
East and West is becoming ever more perilous.

Two young prodigies from either side of the Iron Curtain,
Yulia and Michael, meet at a chess tournament in London.
They don't know it, but they are about to compete in the
deadliest game ever played.

Shadowing them is Greta, a ruthless resistance
fighter who grew up the hard way in the forests of
Lithuania, but who is now hunting down some of the most
dangerous men in the world.

Men who are also on the radar of Vassily, perhaps
the Soviet Union's greatest spymaster. A man of cunning
and influence, Vassily was Yulia's minder during her visit
to the West, but even he could not foresee the
consequences of her meeting Michael.

When the world is accelerating towards an inevitable
and catastrophic conflict, what can just four people
do to prevent it?